Once They Wore the Gray

"Another dramatic story by a finalist for the Spur award of Western Writers of America." —*Amarillo Globe-News*

"Well worth reading, especially as it treats . . . an aspect of the Civil War that is often slighted in the history books." —*The Shootist*

Hannah and the Horseman

"I think Johnny D. Boggs is well on his way to being a major western writer." —*The Shootist*

"This book displays an admirable sense of percolating pace and point-blank prose."
—*The Post and Courier* (Charleston, SC)

"Johnny D. Boggs moves his narrative at a lively clip, and it never turns mawkish." —*Fort Worth Star-Telegram*

This Man Colter

"Humor, action, and a wonderful character in Gwen McCarthy make this a delightful read." —*Roundup*

"If you're into the true wild west, you will enjoy this rugged tale set in west Texas." —*Rendezvous*

Foundation of the Law

"As is to be expected with a Johnny Boggs novel, *Foundation of the Law* is full of those authentic historical details that make his stories so rich and believable."
—*The Shootist*

Law of the Land

"Making bad guys into sympathetic characters is not the easiest feat but Boggs succeeds." —*Southwest BookViews*

"It is an engrossing story, and is told with Boggs' meticulous attention to authentic detail and believable characterizations. If his characters, including the Kid, don't look like, sound like, and behave like Boggs describes them, they should have." —*The Shootist*

"Boggs' unique approach to the Lincoln County War's legal skirmishing is both eye-opening and memorable."
—*True West*

The Big Fifty

"While I was reading *The Big Fifty* sometimes I would forget 'my favorite son' had written it."
—Jackie Boggs, Johnny's mother

"Johnny D. Boggs has a keen ability to interlace historically accurate information amid a cast of well-described characters and circumstances." —*Cowboy Chronicle*

"A fine novel that will leave you with the taste of grit in your mouth, and the smell of spoiled buffalo carcasses in your nose." —*Roundup*

Spark on the Prairie

"Brilliant." —*Roundup*

"Stunning." —*Persimmon Hill*

"This . . . continues a long-needed look at those who brought law and order to the frontier—not with six-guns but with law books." —*True West*

"A finely crafted historical novel with fully developed characters playing out their lives against the backdrop of early Texas settlement." —*American Cowboy*

East of the Border

"This is an amusing glimpse at a decidedly different side of some of the Old West's most famous names."
—*The Denver Post*

"We need more books like *East of the Border.*" —*Roundup*

"*East of the Border* is a fun, lighthearted look at the thespian deep within every cowboy." —*True West*

"Boggs takes the historical facts . . . and gives us a fascinating tale of West meets East." —*The Shootist*

Dark Voyage of the Mittie Stephens

"Delightful entertainment, which combines elements of the traditional western with an Orient Express–style whodunit and a *Titanic*-like romance." —*Booklist*

"Based on a real disaster aboard the *Mittie Stephens*, this novel supplies suspense, a love story, betrayal, loyalty, bravery, and deceit wrapped up in a tight plot supported by wonderful, three-dimensional characters and a sense of place that evokes the smell of burning cotton bales and the screams of terrified passengers."
—*Roundup*

Purgatoire

"Spur Award–winner Boggs takes a common western plot—old gunslinger looking for redemption—and injects it with genuine humanity. Solid fare from a reliable genre veteran."
—*Booklist*

"Boggs is unparalleled in evoking the gritty reality of the Old West, whether it's the three-dimensionality of the characters or the look, sound and smell of the muddy streets and smoke-filled saloons."
—*The Shootist*

"Johnny D. Boggs deftly charts the dual resurrection of a dying Colorado town and a perishing breed of man."
—*True West*

Northfield

"Lively and entertaining . . . a vibrant retelling of the Old West's most notorious and deadly bank robbery."
—*Publishers Weekly*

"A fast-moving and strangely poignant tale that never pauses to rest."
—*The Denver Post*

"This book stands head and shoulders above others of its kind."
—*Roundup*

"The kaleidoscopic effect pays handsome rewards, fueling the action from all vantage points in concise, frenetic bursts that might even leave you feeling a mite poorly for those doomed outlaws."
—*Booklist*

Camp Ford

"Boggs' carefully researched novel boasts meticulously drawn characters and captures in a striking way the amazing changes America underwent during the span of one man's life. An unusual, very rich western that should attract not only genre readers but also baseball fans and Civil War buffs."
—*Booklist*

"As baseball stories go, *Camp Ford* by Johnny D. Boggs is a home run . . . Think *The Longest Yard* . . . about baseball and without the glamour . . . Timeless."
—*USA Today Sports Weekly*

Killstraight

"It takes a skilled author like Johnny D. Boggs to drive the genre into new literary railheads, as he does in his novel *Killstraight*."
—*Tucson Weekly*

Doubtful Cañon

"Boggs's quirky western doesn't take itself too seriously, making this a fanciful and fun ride into some dangerous business."
—*Publishers Weekly*

"Boggs delivers a colorful, clever and arresting tale."
—*Santa Fe New Mexican*

"Uses its non-serious side to appeal to younger readers . . . well-flavored tale."
—*The Tombstone Epitaph*

Walk Proud, Stand Tall

"The author's deft hand at characterization and the subtle way he fills in the blanks as the story progresses makes *Walk Proud, Stand Tall* a tender story hard to resist."
—*The Denver Post*

"Boggs deftly balances the bitter and the sweet, the harsh landscapes and the humanity. That he manages it entertainingly is our reward."
—*Santa Fe New Mexican*

The Hart Brand

"Though an ocean away, *Kidnapped* and *Treasure Island* come to mind when reading this Western; Boggs' tale nearly matches the quality of those written by Stevenson."
—*True West*

"Some consider William Dale Jennings' *The Cowboys* the best Western coming-of-age novel. Others would argue it's *All the Pretty Horses* by Cormac McCarthy or *When the Legends Die* by Hal Borland. With *The Hart Brand*, Boggs stakes his own firm claim."
—*Santa Fe New Mexican*

"Boggs, who writes with a finely honed sense of character and a keen eye for detail, combines historical fact with fiction to create a Revolutionary adventure from the vantage point of an average participant." —*Booklist*

"Johnny Boggs has produced another instant page-turner . . . don't put down the book until you finish it." —Tony Hillerman

"The relationships and setting shine: Daniel—striving at once to solve the case and reconnect with Comanche ways—is a complex, winning protagonist." —*Publishers Weekly*

"A rousing story with an emotional and philosophical depth that will surprise readers who don't expect complexity from a Western. . . . Explores the clash between white and native cultures . . . fundamentally different and strikingly similar." —*Booklist*

Soldier's Farewell

"This is not a simple Western . . . Boggs' familiarity with the landscape . . . puts the reader right into New Mexico and particularly through the rugged landscape along the Río Chama. And while this may seem to be a fairly traditional Western, the conclusion is anything but. Another good read."—*The Roundup*

"Boggs . . . showcases his talent for period detail, atmosphere, complex characters, and the ability to evoke a stark landscape." —*Booklist*

"Ultimately, *Soldier's Farewell* is a tale of two brothers falling far short of what their father expects of them, and what they expect of each other. This is another fine novel by one of today's better writers of Westerns." —*Tucson Weekly*

RETURN TO RED RIVER

JOHNNY D. BOGGS

PINNACLE BOOKS
Kensington Publishing Corp.
www.kensingtonbooks.com

PINNACLE BOOKS are published by

Kensington Publishing Corp.
119 West 40th Street
New York, NY 10018

All Kensington titles, imprints, and distributed lines are available at special quantity discounts for bulk purchases for sales promotions, premiums, fund-raising, educational, or institutional use.
Special book excerpts or customized printings can also be created to fit specific needs. For details, write or phone the office of the Kensington sales manager: Kensington Publishing Corp., 119 West 40th Street, New York, NY 10018, attn: Sales Department; phone 1-800-221-2647.

PINNACLE BOOKS and the Pinnacle logo are Reg. U.S. Pat. & TM Off.

ISBN-13: 978-0-7860-3734-6
ISBN-10: 0-7860-3734-2

First printing: May 2016

10 9 8 7 6 5 4 3 2 1

Printed in the United States of America
First electronic edition: May 2016

ISBN-13: 978-0-7860-3735-3
ISBN-10: 0-7860-3735-0

BOOK I

CHAPTER ONE

Janeen Yankowski had named Mathew Garth's zebra dun. At least, when naming the horse, Mathew had used the word the cook and servant frequently said. *Debil*. It meant "idiot," only a lot more bad mannered—if you understood Polish.

"*Debil*," Mathew whispered as he swung off the gelding. He meant himself, however, and not the dun.

Spurs, boots, and half of his leather chaps disappeared into the snow, and Mathew trudged through the freezing whiteness until he could wrap stiff reins around the top string of barbed wire.

Debil. Idiot. Crazy cattleman. Damned fool. He had never cared a whit for the devil's rope. By thunder, Mathew had always despised barbed wire. He had cursed Joseph F. Glidden when that DeKalb, Illinois, inventor had gotten his first patent for the latest in modern-day improvements: sharp-barbed steel fencing wire. Mathew had spoken out against the use of such wire to anyone who would listen in saloons in southwest Texas, to other cattlemen in San Antonio, to shipping-yard owners in Fort Worth, even to state legislators in Austin. Fencing in the Texas ranges would ruin the cattle industry, he had argued. Yet here he stood in front of an endless stretch of a barbed-wire drift fence. On his range.

And Mathew Garth had let it happen.

Moving down the line of drift fence, plowing through snow up to his thighs exhausted him, and Mathew, though now in middle age, remained lean, leathery, and tougher than mesquite. Each breath burned his lungs. He figured the temperature to be in the teens—warmer than last week.

Most folks thought it never got cold in this part of Texas, that it never snowed down here. He recalled something Groot, the mustached, old cook Mathew had known almost as far back as he could remember, had told him in January, when the winter storms had first hit.

"Well, Mathew, it's finally happened. Hell done frozed over."

With a grunt, Mathew leaned against the icy drift and began scraping away at the frozen snow, glad to be wearing gloves. Even with the lined deerskin, the ice felt like razors on his fingers and palms. He pushed away the ice till he saw the stiff brindle hide, then carved a path down. It took him several minutes before he found the brand. After scraping away more ice, he leaned closer for a better look.

Mathew bit his chapped lips and swore.

The brand was the Rafter I, more commonly known as the Turkey Track.

Climbing over the dead steer, Mathew began removing more snow. The Turkey Track ranch lay way up in the Texas Panhandle, almost to the no-man's-land, far north of the empire that Thomas Dunson had chiseled into this raw country and that Mathew Garth had kept alive. These cattle had drifted in the blizzards for five hundred miles.

The next brand troubled Mathew even more. It was the Circle 43. Mathew had never heard of it. Another carcass also held the Circle 43. The last steer Mathew uncovered had been marked with another brand he didn't know. Not that Mathew knew every brand in the state of Texas, but he forged those into his memory. When he got back to the ranch, he would look in the latest *Brand Book of Texas*.

With another curse, he straightened and stared at the big emptiness that stretched on forever. Gray clouds dimmed the day. Mathew couldn't remember the last time he had even seen the sun, but at least it wasn't snowing. Just overcast, with a biting wind tearing through his coat and the muffler wrapped over his slouch hat. Dark as it was, he could still make out more mounds that lined the drift fence. Some of those appeared higher than where he stood now, and under those snowbanks, Mathew knew, lay dead cattle. Some of them his. Most from ranches north, maybe into Kansas, perhaps even Nebraska.

They had drifted in the blizzards, moving with the wind, until they reached this drift fence. Here they had stopped, unable to move through the barbed wire, and had frozen to death.

Hundreds of them.

He trudged again through the snow, following the ditch he had blazed, until he reached the zebra dun. The leather reins seemed frozen harder, so brittle that he would not have been surprised had the ends broken off when he unwrapped them from the top strand. Mathew had to use a gloved hand to pull up his stiff leg and slip the toe of his boot into the stirrup before he managed to climb into the saddle with a grunt. His butt felt cold. But at least he still had feeling in his feet, his toes.

"Come on, Debil." He neck-reined the gelding and turned back north, toward the ranch, riding into the mocking, brutal wind. Both horse and rider kept their heads down.

For years, ranchers had cursed barbed wire. Such contraptions had been invented for farmers—to keep longhorns from trampling over their crops—and Mathew Garth, like most of his ranching neighbors, loathed the damned thing. Barbs and thin, steel wire had lamed many a good horse, torn flesh off plenty of Texas beef, even crippled or at least scarred up drovers by the score.

Then came the winter of 1880–81, a harsh one, not in Texas, but way north on the High Plains. Cattle drifted in the wind, kept drifting, and come spring, "floaters"—crews of cowboys from ranches as far north as Wyoming—drifted into South Texas. They came to gather their beeves and herd them back to the range, hundreds and hundreds of miles to the north. Which they did, after a long while. After they left, the Texas ranges had been pretty much picked clean.

When the Southwestern Texas Livestock Association held a membership meeting after the spring gather—or what passed as a roundup that year— Mathew had spoken out against stringing up wire. But the T Anchor had already enclosed more than two hundred thousand acres. Old Charlie Goodnight announced that he would fence in his ranches. Mathew held out, and he stopped a few other ranchers from putting up those fences. The Garth name carried a lot of weight in Texas, much as had the name of Thomas Dunson, Matt's surrogate father, decades before.

A year later, ranches up in the Panhandle began putting up fences to keep cattle from drifting down and eating grass meant for Texas longhorns. After the winter of 1884–85, those fences stopped plenty of cattle from Kansas, Nebraska, and the Indian Territory. And when the ranchers met that summer in San Antonio, Mathew relented.

He brought in freighters. They came with tons of barbed wire. Quite a few of Mathew's hired hands balked at stringing up fences, which Mathew understood and even appreciated. Cowboys were, well, kind of uppity. They'd do practically anything—as long as they were horseback. But put a hammer and wire stretcher in their hands, or—even worse—a post-hole digger, and they'd moan and curse, or up and quit. More than a few had drawn their time and tried to find someplace in the West where you couldn't find barbed wire.

Those places, Mathew had learned, kept growing scarcer.

Back in January, Mathew and his wife, Tess Millay, had been in Galveston when the first blizzard struck. Eleven degrees on the Gulf of Mexico that night. Matt and Tess had stepped out of their hotel the following morning—had to go to a mercantile to buy winter duds—and stared in amazement at the beautiful bay . . . covered with a layer of ice. By the time they had left, the bay was frozen three or four inches deep, and six inches of snow covered the city's streets.

He kept riding, deciding that Debil had a better sense of direction than he did. All this snow made it hard to find landmarks he had been relying on since Dunson had claimed this land as his own. Mathew could have simply followed the trail the gelding had made when they had left the ranch headquarters that afternoon, but his range covered a lot of sections, and he wanted to see more, no matter how bad he would find everything.

And Mathew Garth knew things were bad. There weren't that many drift fences this far south, and he had to figure that the Panhandle and North Texas ranges had fared a whole lot worse than down here. The dead cattle here had eluded drift fences far to the north. No telling how many cattle had died on the West's vast ranches.

Thousands, he figured. The blizzard, the fences, would take a hefty toll on ranches across Texas, across the entire West.

He had seen enough.

Carcasses filled streambeds where longhorns, Herefords, and other breeds had crashed through the ice. Others had walked off bluffs, crashing to their deaths. Some had been mired in bogs, or ditches, to starve and freeze, or, if lucky, be trampled by the hundreds of cattle drifting with them.

Reining in Debil, Mathew found something he had missed on the ride to the death fence. The ice and snow in an arroyo had been dyed crimson, and as he dismounted and moved toward the carnage, he let out another harsh, wintry sigh. Two cows and a calf had been caught in a quagmire, it appeared, only none had been fortunate. He read the signs quickly, shook his head, mounted the skittish gelding, and rode on.

Wolves had always been pests down here. Those Mexican lobos had feasted on the longhorns, and Mathew's cowhands most likely had branded those cattle—although he would never know for sure, not after the job those gray brutes had done.

He had to think, however, that he had fared better than most. Most of his cattle, though certainly not all, grazed south of the drift fence. They would have drifted, of course—that's what longhorns do—but they would find shelter in the arroyos and draws and thickets all the way until they reached the Rio Grande.

A mile or two later, he reined in the dun. Ahead of him and off to his left stood the Mexican wolves. Six, by his count, snarling, watching, likely still hungry. He had left his gun rig back home. Years had passed since he had ever needed the Colts, Remingtons, Smith & Wessons, and Merwin Hulberts that lined the gun cases in his office. Oh, he would strap on a gun belt during the gathers, or when he rode off to San Antonio, San Angelo, or Brownsville. This day, he just didn't feel like carrying extra weight, knowing that Debil would have enough trouble plowing through snowbanks.

His right hand reached down and, without taking his eyes off the wolf pack, he found the comforting hardness of the stock of a Winchester rifle. The heavy rifle had been a Christmas gift from his sons—too much rifle, Mathew had figured—in .45-60 caliber, though most models he had seen had been chambered for .45-75. This one had a half-round, half-octagon barrel. It was a nice present, though Mathew preferred his old Yellow Boy.

He drew the rifle from the scabbard and braced the stock on his thigh.

Those lobos weren't stupid. They had experienced rifles before, and the sight of the Centennial silenced them and sent them running off toward the high country. Mathew brought the rifle up, aimed, but never jacked a round into the chamber. Slowly, as the wolves vanished in the white landscape, he slid the heavy rifle back into the scabbard. Wolves had to eat, too, he told himself, but that wasn't his reason for not shooting those pests. He just didn't have much use for guns, though he owned far too many.

Except when hunting, Mathew Garth hadn't used rifles, shotguns, and especially revolvers in years. He had not pulled down on a man since . . . a lifetime ago. Twenty years now.

The wolves were gone. Mathew spit into the snow and spurred the dun into a trot. He could make out the ranch now, and he wanted to get home, warm up, check those brands he remembered.

"Debil." Again, he spoke of himself and not to the zebra dun. He glanced at the trail the wolves had left.

What was the bounty being paid on wolf pelts these days? If this winter turned out to be as bad as things looked, he might have need of that extra cash.

CHAPTER TWO

Sight of the ranch warmed him. The scent of cedar burning in the fireplaces relaxed him. Beyond the clump of trees he saw the . . . the "empire." At least, that's what Thomas Dunson had called it. Dunson had founded the empire. Mathew had kept it. He rode past the graveyard, a testament to what it took to keep an empire.

The ranch house Dunson had built had been made of timber and stone, flat roofed, far from fancy, first one room, then two, later four, and six by the time Dunson had died. Years later, Tess had insisted on something bigger, better, fancier, so they had paid a small fortune to haul in wood, hired carpenters, and put up a frame addition, complete with a covered front porch. Two parlors, one formal, one familiar. A library where Matt would do that awful paperwork that came with ranching, but with a rounded, large window where he could stare out at his demesne. Bedrooms for Tess and Matt and the two boys.

The original stone house now held the winter kitchen, a guest room, storeroom, even a bathhouse, and the living quarters for Janeen Yankowski. They had offered Groot Nadine a room, but he had sworn, spit, and complained that his place belonged in the bunkhouse with the boys. Recently, Tess had resumed talk about putting in an indoor privy. Matt kept resisting such a foolish notion.

Behind the house stood a stone corral, eighteen by fifty-six feet, because back when Dunson and Mathew had been fighting to keep this place, horses needed to be handy. Beyond the corral stood a single-story tack room, originally adobe, now with board and batten siding and a side-gabled roof.

Another shed, and the privies for the hired men, rose off to the north, and, shaded by the cedars, set the bunkhouse and a well.

To the west lay the foundations for the homes Tess expected to build for their two sons, Tom and Lightning. A well divided the two layouts, with a privy and yet another corral behind the stones.

South of the house stood the barns, the first one, two stories of sixteen-inch adobe blocks, twenty-four feet tall at the gable peak facing the west. Beyond that lay another barn, also built by Dunson, along with a workshop and feed barn Mathew had overseen, a well, a lean-to, a round pen, and two outhouses. Just beyond that, where the timbers grew, flowed the Rio Grande, lined with several more corrals.

After reining in, Mathew swung out of the saddle and led the horse into the barn. He saw no one—even a ranch the size of this one ran a skeleton crew during the winter—but smelled Groot's coffee. Once Debil had been unsaddled, rubbed down, and put in a stall with a good dose of water, oats, and hay, Matt grabbed the Winchester Centennial and stepped out

into the cold. Groot made better coffee than Janeen
Yankowski, and Matt was tempted to head to the
bunkhouse, tell the old belly-cheater what he had
found. But those brands remained fresh in his mind,
and he wanted to check the *Brand Book*. Pulling up
his collar, he moved through the freshly shoveled
path of snow to the frame entrance of his home.

Janeen Yankowski gave Mathew an earful, mostly
in Polish, some in English that Mathew had trouble
recognizing, but he got the gist of everything.

A small woman with steel gray hair and brilliant
eyes, she could have been anywhere between forty
and four hundred years old. Feisty as a young colt,
with temper and tongue, she could cook, curse, and
comfort. This evening, she was in a comforting mood.

"Boots. Off!" she directed. Frowning after Mathew
had followed orders, she snapped at him to remove
his socks, which took some doing. Mathew hadn't realized how wet those woolen rags were till he tried to
peel them off his feet. "Frostbite!" Janeen yelled.
"Want no toes? Hop on crutches?" She disappeared
for a couple of minutes, came back with some kind of
liniment and a towel, and proceeded to drag the
barefooted Mathew to the fireplace.

When it was all over, Mathew Garth sat in his
leather chair, his feet rubbed down and wiped off,
and now propped up on a pillow on the hearth
before a roaring fire.

He asked for brandy. Janeen said she might bring
him some coffee. At least he would have a few minutes of peace and quiet. He had to admit to himself—
never to the cook—that he felt better and probably

owed her. He very well could have lost some toes to frostbite, maybe both feet.

Janeen came to the ranch fifteen years back. Tess had found her in Fredericksburg, a city of mostly Germans in the Hill Country northwest of San Antonio. Janeen Yankowski cooked better than Groot, too. But Mathew doubted if she could make ten sacks of flour last all the way from the Rio Grande to the Kansas railheads. Or make burned grain taste something like coffee.

He opened the *Brand Book*. He was still flipping through pages when Janeen Yankowski brought him the coffee and stopped to stoke the fire. He had not moved from the comfortable, toasty spot when the cook returned with a pot and refreshed his cup. The book was halfway open when she finally came in and sweetened what remained of his coffee with two fingers of brandy.

You never realized how many cattle outfits spread across Texas until you opened a registry of brands. These days, there were even brands for sheep and goats, but Mathew kept going through the cattle and horse brands, listed alphabetically by the rancher's name.

He did find a Circle 43, but it was from a small outfit up in Nacogdoches and that brand was registered on the shoulder. The brands he had seen had been burned into the steers' hips. The J Lazy J he did not find.

The door opened, but Mathew kept leafing through the final pages. Nothing. The dead cattle he had seen at the drift fence did not come from Texas.

As he closed the book, Mathew drained the china cup and cursed.

"That bad?"

He looked up into those green eyes of Tess Millay. Oh, most everybody in Texas called her Mrs. Garth— so had the preacher who had married them—and Janeen Yankowski and maybe two other ladies in town used her given name, Therissa, but to Mathew, Groot, and to Tess, she would always be Tess Millay.

Tess of the River. He had met her on his way back from the war, in Memphis, Tennessee. The River had been the Mississippi back then, where she had worked in dance halls and on steamboats, charming and cooling men in Natchez and New Orleans, Cairo and Saint Louis. White skin, golden hair, eyes hard and dark as jade. Twenty-some years underneath the harsh sun and dry winds of southwestern Texas had darkened and hardened that skin, and the hair now had begun to turn gray, but those eyes had not changed at all.

She could be a cold woman, relentless, brutal, but she always warmed Mathew Garth. Today, even with the brandy and coffee in his stomach and the fire restoring life to his feet, he could use some warmth.

"It ain't good," he said, pulled his feet off the hearth, and set the cup and *Brand Book* on the floor.

Tess came over and kissed him, straightened, and waited.

"Worse than '72," he said. "I counted fifty dead. Then I stopped counting. And uncovered one snow-bank. Just one. Must have been a dozen or more beeves under all that snow."

She sucked in a breath, held it, and went to the de-canter. After all those years, Tess Millay could read Mathew's mind. She filled two glasses and brought them over, handing her husband one.

"We'll get through it," she said.

Their glasses clinked. They sipped.

Mathew wasn't so certain about that bit of optimism. He had invested in a railroad, at his wife's suggestion, that had failed to get one rail laid out. A bank in San Antonio had a loan with a payment due in November. Another note would be due in Fort Worth next year.

"We might be skinning dead carcasses for hides to sell," he said.

She finished her drink without comment.

"Where are the boys?" he asked.

Boys? Tom and Lightning were men. Wet behind their ears, certainly, but grown men.

"In town," she said.

Matt had brought the brandy to his lips, but he lowered the glass.

"Together?" he asked.

With a smile and a shrug, Tess took his glass, killed the liquor, and returned to the decanter. "Cabin fever," she said. "Lightning said he wanted to go. Tom said he'd tag along." She turned toward him. "Lightning didn't object or argue. Even said he'd welcome the company."

He watched her bring the glass to him.

"Been a long winter, I guess," he said.

Tess shrugged. "You should get out of those clothes. Wash up."

He came out of the chair, moved it back to where it belonged, and walked to the curved window. The sun had set, but he could still see the vast whiteness that went on to the north, perhaps as far away as Canada. Covering how many dead cattle?

The brandy warmed—but did not relax—him.

"The boys have sense enough not to ride back tonight, I hope," he said.

"I think you know them."

He cut off his laugh. Oh, he knew those two well enough. They wouldn't ride home tonight. Maybe not even tomorrow. His head shook, and he killed the shot. That might add up to more debts, he thought, once he had to pay for damages.

He let out a sigh and watched the darkness outside deepen. Tess came to him and put her arms around his waist. She squeezed hard. She had always been a slim woman, but solid, hard. Some say her heart was just as hard.

"It's the end of February, Mathew," she told him.

"Yeah."

"Winter's almost over," she whispered.

He turned to face her. "Yeah," he said. "But spring's gonna be a hell of a lot worse."

CHAPTER THREE

The words read DUNSON CITY, but the fading sign would have been more accurate had it said: Dunson Town, or Dunson Village, or Dunson Dot on the Map, or Dunson Switching Point on the Del Rio Spur of the Southern Pacific Railroad. Two saloons, one for the cowboys and another for the railroaders because cowboys and railroaders went together like nitro-glycerin and a handler with dt's. One hotel, which did most of its business when the trestle that crossed the canyon west of town got washed out in a flash flood. One brothel, because the soiled doves didn't care if they had to smile for a cowboy or a railroad man as long as he had just gotten paid. A handful of houses, mostly adobe or stone. A bank, which would have gone insolvent years ago if not for Mathew Garth's ranch and the two upstairs offices it rented out to a doctor/dentist/veterinarian/undertaker and his brother, a cobbler/carpenter/mason/postmaster who also swamped out the two saloons. Two cafés, one Mexican, the other Mexican. A livery. A depot.

A mercantile, which housed the post office where Fionntán Hanrahan spent time sorting mail when not making adobe bricks, swinging a hammer, or repairing cowboy boots. A Catholic church (other denominations met once every other month in the mercantile). Two cemeteries. There was no constable or marshal. The nearest peace officers worked out of Fort Stockton, the county seat, better than one hundred miles northwest, and the county hadn't been formed until it had been carved out of Presidio County back in 1875.

Although the town lay closer to the Rio Grande than the Pecos, several inches of snow and ice covered the usually dusty streets, the surrounding hills, and mesas, the branches of the junipers, oaks, and mesquites, and filled much of the washes that had been cut into the limestone-hard country. Smoke wafted from the chimneys and the stack of the rotary snowplow that had pulled into the depot that afternoon. The Southern Pacific's ticket agent could have made a fortune had he charged admission. Snowplows—even the wedge plows more common across the West—were a rarity this far south.

Tom and Lightning Garth had arrived in Dunson City just after the snowplow. They had studied the ice-crusted, yellow-painted fan blades, the red engine, its snow-covered roof, but, unlike most of the town's residents, had been quickly bored by the novelty and found the livery first, the Rio (where cowboys drank) next, and finally Gloria's Palace. Now they sat inside José's Place (not María Luisa's Café), washing down enchiladas and refried beans with black coffee.

José's lovely young daughter, Araceli, came by and topped off both cups of coffee.

"*Gracias,*" Tom told her with a smile.

Lightning said nothing. Just slopped up the grease with a piece of tortilla and stuffed it in his mouth.

The teenage girl disappeared to the table where the Hanrahan brothers, Doc Aonghus and hammer-swinger Fionntán, sat with bowler hats still topping their heads and their coats still buttoned.

Tom picked up his cup and sipped the coffee.

He was two years younger than Lightning. Slimmer. Quieter. Looked more like his dad, though he certainly had his mother's eyes. He wore woolen trousers, thinly striped blue and green, tucked in tall black boots, a black bib-front shirt, and gray woolen muffler. His battered black hat with a dented crown, the right side higher than the left, rested, crown-down, beside his empty plate. He had shed his gloves, now tucked in a pocket on his leather-lined, red and black plaid mackinaw that hung on the back of his chair. A .38 caliber Colt Lightning, nickel plated with ivory grips, rested in a holster on his right hip.

Lightning still wore his tan canvas coat and his high-crowned black hat with the telescope crown. He had removed his gloves and his Smith & Wesson Russian, keeping the .44 top-break revolver near his plate of supper. His pants were black woolen, his shirt a heavy woolen red and green plaid, and his bandanna yellow silk.

Both men wore spurs.

They looked nothing alike. Lightning was taller, heavier, with pale blue eyes and dark hair that reached his shoulders, his skin so dark he could have passed for Mexican or Indian—though no one would mention that to Lightning's face. Without looking up, he swallowed the last bite of tortilla and chased it down with the coffee. After a moment, he rocked back on the legs of his chair, burped, and grinned across the table at his brother.

"Getting late," Tom Garth suggested.

The grin never faded as Lightning reached inside his coat, found the Aurora watch in his shirt pocket, and brought it out.

"For you, maybe," he said, and slid the handsome watch with the blue-spade hands back into the shirt pocket.

A few tables closer to the potbellied stove, Aonghus and Fionntán Hanrahan rose, dropped a few coins beside their empty plates, pulled up their collars, and headed for the door.

"See you, boys," the doctor called out.

Tom nodded at the brothers. "Stay warm."

"Aye . . . maybe in July," Fionntán said with a chuckle.

The door opened. The bell rang. Cold wind filled the café before the door closed.

"It's my birthday," Lightning said.

"Not till August," Tom told him.

"It's your birthday," Lightning said.

"On the twenty-sixth of May."

"Close enough."

Tom found a Morgan dollar in his pocket and laid it on the table. "We ought to check into the hotel," he suggested.

"We could've stayed at Gloria's," Lightning said.

"Hotel's a lot cheaper."

"But not as much fun."

Tom shook his head. "What's fun in Dunson City? We've seen our very first rotary snowplow. We've had four draught beers and two rye whiskeys at the saloon. We visited Gloria's. We've had supper. I think that's all Dunson City has to offer, especially on a night like this. Less you want to rob the bank."

Lightning rubbed his chin as if considering that option. "We'd be stealing our own money," he said, and shook his head. "Pa is on the board of directors."

Tom stared out the window, but saw mostly just frosted glass.

"Nightcap?" Lightning said.

"I guess." Tom knew he had never won a debate, or even reasoned with Lightning.

They bundled up, nodded at José and his daughter, and stepped onto what passed for a boardwalk in Dunson City. Tom led the way, on purpose, and turned into the hotel. Behind him, Lightning swore.

"Best get a room first," Tom said, and he pushed open the door.

"Why?"

"Because we have money right now."

Even Lightning had to laugh at that as he followed his kid brother into the lobby.

The rooms might have been Spartan, and the Dunson House had no restaurant—guests were sent to one of the two Mexican eateries—but the lobby would have been opulent outside of San Antonio, Austin, Galveston, or Houston. A fire blazed in the stone fireplace, and the Garth boys walked across the hardwood floor, stepped onto the giant Persian rug, and looked at the portrait that hung over the mantel.

The gold plate screwed into the bottom center of the frame read:

THOMAS DUNSON, *Empire Builder, Texas Giant*

Their grandfather. More or less. Everyone in Texas, and all the way up to Kansas, had heard about Dunson. He came to Texas from England, but no one ever mentioned a British accent. On the other side of the Mersey, across from Liverpool, he had been born in Birkenhead. But he was Texan, through and through. Dunson had come across half the continent on a wagon train, then left for Texas. Lucky. Indians had attacked the train, wiped out practically everyone, and Dunson had found young Mathew Garth, herding a cow, dazed, in shock.

So the hard man had adopted the green kid. That proved Dunson had a heart, romantics would argue. Not true, the skeptics knew. Mathew had a cow. Dunson had a bull. The hard rock from England wanted a ranch. He needed the cow more than he needed the boy. Or so he had first thought.

But it had worked. They drove across the Red River and all the other rivers—the Brazos, Colorado, Llano, Concho, Pecos, and many others—till they reached the Rio Grande. They had outlasted and outfought Don Diego Agura y Baca, who had once claimed all this land.

Dunson had built that empire, kept it with his own iron will, unbending principle, and bullets from his—and later Mathew's—guns. When the war broke out between the states, he had stayed behind, increased his empire, and found himself "cow poor," as the saying went. So he had driven a herd north, bound for Missouri, before Mathew had taken it from him and turned west for Kansas.

The newspapers, the history books, and even that play that Lightning and Tom had seen in Fort Worth three years back, all claimed that Thomas Dunson had saved Texas with that first cattle drive to Kansas. Groot, Laredo, and a few of the other old-timers who had known Dunson and Mathew during those years, said otherwise. Mathew Garth? He never said one word.

Neither of the brothers had ever known their grandfather. Lightning had been a suckling newborn when Dunson had died; Tom hadn't even been born. Once Mathew had taken the herd away from Dunson, the iron-willed man had found his own gunman and gone after his adopted son. To hang him. But, if the stories were true—and how many Texas tales were really true?—a gunman named Cherry Valance had shot Dunson before being killed himself, and when Dunson met Mathew on the streets of Abilene, the empire builder had collapsed. Tess and Mathew had taken Dunson by buckboard, all that way south, across the Indian Nations, through swollen streams and the baking sun. Dunson had sworn he would live to see Texas, and he had.

Mathew and Tess buried him on the south side of the Red River.

The two brothers hadn't even seen their grandfather's grave.

"Ol' Groot says he didn't really look like that," Lightning said.

"Painter never met him," Tom said.

The portrait hadn't been finished until a few years

back, when the railroad tracks reached this far west, the hotel went up, and Dunson City had been christened.

"But Ma says he sure got the eyes right," Tom said.

Cold. Hard. Gray like lead. Just as deadly, uncompromising, like the bullets chambered in the brothers' revolvers.

"Neither one of us got his eyes," Lightning said.

"Because he ain't really kin to us," Tom said. "Pa said Dunson found him, half-starved, plumb out of his head—"

"Yeah, yeah, yeah. I've heard the story a million times. But I'm kin to him. I feel that blood runnin' through my veins. Me and him?" He jutted his jaw at the portrait—and Tom had to notice that there was some resemblance between Lightning and the old man. But, well, maybe that French-named artist had studied Lightning and not Tom or Mathew when he had created this illusion.

"We gonna check in or just gape at a dead man?" Lightning said.

Shaking his head, Tom walked to the mahogany registration desk. The bald man with the black string tie and black Prince Albert had been waiting patiently.

"Evening, gentlemen," he said.

"One room," Tom said. "One night."

"Of course." He found a key and turned the registry where Tom could sign. "How's your mother, your father?"

"Cold," Lightning said.

The clerk grinned. "Who isn't?"

Tom fished greenbacks from a pocket in the mackinaw, counted out a few ones, and left them on the counter. When he turned, he saw the door closing. Dropping the key inside his coat pocket, he pulled on his hat and hurried to catch up with Lightning.

His brother had covered half the town. Tom swore, his breath frosty, and stopped as Lightning pushed back his coat to reveal the butt of his Smith & Wesson and pushed open the closed doors of the saloon.

Where the railroaders drank. Not the cowboys.

CHAPTER FOUR

Because Dunson City was such a small burg, and what with the freezing temperatures outside and the lateness of the hour, only nine railroaders were in the Knuckle Coupler. Five sat at a table in the corner near the stove, playing stud poker. Three stood at the bar, talking in thick Irish brogues with Sean Dublin, the beer-jerker with a brown patch over his left eye who had called himself John Smith back when he had worked at the Rio, the saloon where the cowboys drank. The last railroader, a brakeman, lay passed out on the floor. One of his colleagues, or perhaps Sean Dublin, had at least rolled him over so he didn't choke to death on his own vomit, which now served as his pillow.

Lightning Garth made a beeline for the bar, slamming the doors shut to make sure everyone knew he was here, but carefully stepping over the brakeman, and not even nicking the drunk with the rowels of his spurs—though the thought crossed his mind.

He arrived at the far corner of the bar, away from the poker players and the beer drinkers, and kicked over the spittoon on purpose. He stuck a foot on the brass rail that ran along the bottom of the bar that had been hauled in from San Felipe del Rio when the Southern Pacific's tracks were being laid. San Felipe del Rio, which had been shortened a while back to Del Rio, wasn't much of a town. Neither was Dunson City, and most people expected the Knuckle Coupler to move west down the line to Sanderson or maybe even a place with a future.

Lightning Garth had decided it was his mission in life to run the railroad saloon out of town.

"How about a whiskey, Smithy!" he called out.

Behind him, the door opened. Lightning glanced at the mirror and smiled at his brother. "Make it two whiskeys, Smithy. Rye is our pleasure tonight."

The barkeep moved down the bar, grabbing a half-empty bottle off the back bar. He placed the rye in front of Lightning.

"The name, Lightning, is Sean Dublin."

"Well, you'll always be John Smith to me." He tapped the bar.

Sean Dublin, or John Smith, or whatever his real name was, fetched two shot glasses and slid both in front of Lightning. The bartender hooked a thumb at the mirror, which showed a reflection of Tom Garth as he moved around the unconscious brakeman and joined his brother at the end of the bar.

"This is a new mirror, Lightning," Sean Dublin said. "The owner would like to keep it longer than the last one."

Dublin filled the glasses with the amber whiskey, and Lightning picked his up, killed the rye quickly, and threw the glass as hard as he could, past Sean Dublin's ear, and smashed the mirror.

Tom Garth swore.

The railroaders cursed.

Sean Dublin hurriedly began collecting whiskey bottles and putting them on the floor, hiding himself while shouting, "No guns! No guns! No shooting! For the love of God!"

Grinning, Lightning was already removing his coat and gun belt. The canvas coat, he set on the bar beside the rye bottle Sean Dublin had left behind. The Smith & Wesson and the leather rig, he tossed to the back bar, knocking over a few bottles the beer-jerker hadn't bothered to collect and sending spider-web cracks from the bottom of the mirror to the far left corners.

"Are you crazy?" An icy edge accented Tom's voice as he pulled off his mackinaw, hat, and gun rig. "There are eight of them." He laid everything neatly on the bar.

"Nine." Lightning's jaw shot out toward the brakeman. "But I don't think he'll need watching."

Tom spread out.

"Ma and Pa'll kill us," Tom said.

Lightning laughed. "Not if these boys do it first."

The dealer at the card table came up, overturning the table as he picked up a whiskey bottle and shattered the bottom against the rolling edge of the table. The other players charged. So did the boys at the end of the bar, cursing in their Irish brogues. Some shed their coats. One slipped on a pair of brass knuckles. Another had a Chicago nightstick.

Snatching the rye bottle off the bar, Lightning

threw it end over end at the charging beer drinkers.
It shattered against the first man's face and down he
went, clutching his bleeding face. Tom grabbed the
nearest chair, pitching it at the feet of the poker
players, watching three of them crash to the floor.

Tom turned over the table. That slowed down the
one with the busted whiskey bottle, which he wielded
like a knife, and the man with the brass knuckles.
Quickly, Tom grabbed another chair. He wondered if
he looked like that gent with the white cape with the
red lining, that guy with the slick mustache from the
circus Tom and Lightning had seen in El Paso that
time. The one with a whip and a chair, barking fiercely
at a lion that, unless Tom's vision had been playing
tricks on him, had no teeth.

The three men who had spilled to the floor came
up, but at least one of them limped now and the
second had a busted nose.

To his right, Tom heard curses, grunts, the breaking of glass, the busting of heads. Yet he knew better
than to check on his older brother. Take his eyes off
the five men before him, and he would be dead, or at
least beaten into obliviousness.

He feinted with the chair, watched the railroaders
jump back. Stepped back. They began to circle him,
but Tom swung the chair around quickly, keeping
them from enveloping him completely. He wet his lips.

"Listen, boys . . ." he began, like he was about to
plead for mercy.

Then he slammed the chair across the head of the
man with the brass knuckles—that one appeared to
be the most dangerous—and what was left of the

chair, he brought down hard against the wrist that held the busted whiskey bottle.

The momentum carried him through the horde of railroaders, and he stumbled against another table, overturning it, but not before he snatched the heavy ashtray off the top. Spinning, ducking, he brought his arm back at full cock, and sent the ashtray spiraling into the forehead of the poker player with the glass eye and crooked nose. The man dropped hard and lay faceup, arms outstretched, on the floor, sawdust soaking up the blood that poured from his forehead and down the sides of his head. Tom was glad to see the man was still breathing.

"Criminy!" one of the men said. That one had picked up the leg of the chair by the body of the man with the brass knuckles. Which, Tom figured, was better than having him pick up those heavy knuckles.

The one with the busted whiskey bottle was on his hands and knees, spilling blood from his mouth and nose, and he waddled around like a castrated steer, bawling just as loud, too.

Three of the five out. Tom kept backing away from the two remaining ones. Now he had a clear view of Lightning.

One Southern Pacific worker lay on the floor—the one Lightning had smashed in the face with the bottle of rye—but the others had Lightning. The burly one with the striped britches and soot-blackened face had grabbed Lightning from behind, pinning his arms back, letting the rawboned redhead with the handle-bar mustache punch Lightning in the gut.

Lightning bent down, almost taking the burly gent with him, but when the railroad man jerked him back up, Lightning brought his legs up, knees bent, then kicked out, and the boots and spurs slammed into the redhead's face. He turned and fell against the bar, knocking over the glass of rye that Tom had not gotten a chance to taste. The redhead rolled over and slid down the bar onto the spittoon that Lightning had kicked over.

The big man roared, started to push Lightning toward the bar, but Lightning brought his right leg in and the rowel of the spur sliced through the striped britches. Down went Tom's brother and the railroad man. Tom didn't have a chance to see how that fight played out.

Because the two men after him charged.

Tom ducked underneath the leg of a broken chair—or was it the nightstick?—and felt his hat sail off his head. He came up fast, grabbed the shoulders of the other one's coat, and pulled him forward while bringing his own head down. The man's nose and mouth slammed against Tom's skull. Teeth bit. He saw orange dots from the collision. Felt blood soaking in his sweaty hair. He pushed the man against the potbelly stove and heard him scream as the palms of his hands burned and blistered.

Breath rushed out of his lungs, and Tom fell against the wall of the saloon. Somehow he managed to keep his feet, and turned, ducking as the nightstick—it wasn't a chair leg—crashed against the wall and sent a two-year-old calendar falling to the sawdust. The last of the men had managed to slam that stick into the small of Tom's back.

Railroaders! He didn't care much for those men. Tom and Lightning had shucked their guns, to make this a fair fight. The workers on the S.P. had no such convictions.

The club came after him again, and Tom ducked, punched, and came away, ducking out of the railroader's grasp. His vision blurred. Just breathing ached, but Tom didn't think the nightstick had busted or even cracked any ribs. He tasted blood and realized his lips were bleeding. Didn't remember how that had happened, though.

He saw the club come up, start down. He stepped inside, taking most of the blow on his left shoulder. Tom tried to punch, couldn't, so he grabbed the railroader's ear, and twisted.

"That . . . ain't . . . right . . . you damned brush-pop—"

Pulling and twisting, Tom heard the nightstick fall to the floor. The railroader fell in the opposite direction as Tom released the ear. The man bounced across the floor, spit out venomous curses and froth like some rabid dog. As the railroader tried to climb back to his feet, Tom kicked him in the jaw with his boot.

The jaw, Tom knew, was broken. The man went down, spitting out blood and teeth, and crawling in a blind rage.

The door opened. Tom glanced up, saw the one with the burned hands, crying as he tumbled out into the snow to cool off his hands. Breathing hard, Tom picked up the nightstick and tapped the back of the head of the man with the broken jaw, who dropped onto the calendar and just slept, and bled.

Tom had to blink several times before he could see clearly, but as he walked around the floor, carefully stepping over busted furniture and broken railroaders, he saw Lightning lifting himself off the floor. His brother weaved to the bar and leaned against it for support.

Tom joined him there.

Lightning grinned. Tom just bled.

Then the gunshot deafened both brothers.

CHAPTER FIVE

Tom Garth reached for his double-action Colt, still holstered and lying atop the neatly folded mackinaw on the bar top. Lightning grabbed a shot glass in his right hand and started to turn to throw it at the open door. That's where the shot had come from. But both men froze, staring at John Smith, alias Sean Dublin, who was standing next to the shattered mirror of the back bar, holding a bleeding left arm. A sawed-off shotgun bounced off his shoes.

The two brothers glanced at the man standing in the doorway, and their eyes hardened as they looked back at the bleeding beer-jerker. Lightning threw the shot glass at Dublin, who ducked as the glass bounced off his shoulder and crashed against a bottle of wine.

"You'd shoot us in the back?" Lightning said. He pointed at the ten-gauge. "With that scattergun?"

"I . . . uh . . ."

Lightning moved around the bar and started to jerk his Smith & Wesson from the holster, but cut the palm of his right hand on shattered whiskey bottles. He cursed, bringing his hand to his mouth to suck the blood and cool the pain, and shook his hand before reaching, slower this time, for the .44.

"Leave it," Tom told his brother. To his amazement, Lightning listened, though he took his gun rig, shaking the shards of glass as he stepped around the bar.

"Back away, Sean," Tom said. The barkeep also did as he was told.

Lightning fished a handkerchief from a trousers pocket. Tom studied the man holding the smoking Winchester rifle.

"Boys," the man said in a friendly greeting. Lowering the barrel, he stepped over the still-unconscious brakeman and weaved through the wreckage of bodies now beginning to stir and furniture that had been reduced to kindling.

"Reckon we owe you our thanks, Mr. . . . ?" Tom waited. You didn't ask a man his name out in these parts unless you were a gossip or just plain rude. Tom was, well, merely . . . curious.

"Teveler," the man said. He laid the Winchester on the bar, the barrel pointed in the general direction of Sean Dublin. "Barkeep," he said in a Texas drawl, "three whiskeys." It wasn't a request, but a demand.

That got a smile from the Garth boys, watching the bartender, arm profusely leaking blood, fumble with glasses and a bottle. His shoes crunched the glass on the floor as he stumbled, wiped the mess off the bar top with a wet rag, and set three tumblers in front of the men.

"I'll take mine neat," Teveler said. "No blood."

"Likewise," Lightning said.

Dublin managed to pour bourbon—about the only bottle remaining intact—into the glasses.

"And one for yourself, mister," Teveler said as he raised his glass. "To show no hard feelin's."

Dublin drank straight from the bottle.

"Leave the bottle, Smithy," Lightning said. "And go bleed somewhere else."

After a sip of the bourbon, Teveler turned around, hooking a heel on the rail and scanning the saloon— or, rather, the remnants of a saloon.

"Must've been some fight," Teveler said. "Wish I could have joined in earlier."

"You came at the right time," Tom said.

The brothers shot a glance and studied the stranger.

He appeared an old man, somewhere between fifty and sixty, with more miles than years. His boots were scuffed and worn, and the spurs he wore seemed to be old military issue, maybe from the Confederacy. The chaps had more scars than his pockmarked face, his patched coat seemed real thin for this winter, and his hat had been battered into a wreck. The steel gray mustache drooped, and the stubble on his tired face appeared uneven because of the scars. A thin man, he likely needed the gun belt to keep his duck trousers from falling down, but his eyes, a cold pale blue, held a deadly spark.

"Well, Mr. Teveler . . ." Tom began.

"Call me Jess," he said. "Had a ranch over Duval way."

Duval lay west of Corpus Christi, not far from one of the few ranches—the great King Ranch—that would have made Mathew Garth's holdings look like a sorry homesteader's claim.

"Thanks, Jess," Lightning said as he buckled on his rig.

Jess Teveler turned. "So this is Dunson City."

"That's right." Tom sipped his bourbon.

"Iron Tom Dunson would be sorely disappointed."

The railroaders began dragging themselves and their unconscious pards out the front door. Sean Dublin sat on one of the few upright chairs, plugging the bullet hole in his arm.

"You knew Dunson?" Tom Garth stared. This old saddle tramp, this Jess Teveler, seemed old enough to have known his grandfather.

"Nah." Teveler killed the bourbon, turned around, and leaned against the bar. "Nobody *knew* Dunson. Nobody ever knew that hard rock."

Lightning stepped around, suddenly suspicious. Panhandlers came to Dunson City fairly often, some on the rails, some riding the grub line from ranch to ranch. This Jess Teveler certainly looked like a tramp, but few of those sorry souls ever claimed to have known Thomas Dunson.

"How are things in Duval?" Lightning asked.

The saddle tramp snorted. "Son, I ain't been in Duval since right after the war."

"You said you have a ranch—"

Tom interrupted his brother. "He said he *had* a ranch . . ."

A mirthless laugh rolled out of Jess Teveler's mouth as the last of the railroaders dragged the passed-out brakeman into the night. "Carpetbaggers," he said. "You boys are too young to recollect them hard times."

"Reckon we are," Tom said.

"What brings you this far to Dunson City?" Lightning asked, still suspicious.

"Lookin' for a place somethin' cooler than the one I just left."

Tom chuckled. Lightning kept his hand on his holstered pistol. "If it's topped twenty degrees outside," Tom said, "I'd be surprised."

"Well, it was hot when I left San Angelo a few days back. Mighty hot. For me. How far to the border?"

"You can spit across it," Lightning said.

"Good enough. Thanks for the whiskey, and the excitement. Glad I could do you boys a service. But I ain't sure even this cold spell will stop a Texas Ranger. I'd best ride."

He held out his calloused hand, still cold because the saddle tramp likely owned no gloves. *And he had ridden all the way from San Angelo . . . in this weather?*

Tom shook it. The man's grip felt like a vise. "Pleasure to meet you, Jess. I'm Tom. Tom Garth." He tilted his head toward Lightning. "This is my—"

"Garth?" Jess Teveler said in astonishment.

"That's right." Tom backed up toward Lightning, who spread out a few steps. Now Tom's hand found the butt of his revolver.

"Kin to Mathew Garth?" Teveler's eyes narrowed.

"He's my father."

Those deadly blue eyes seemed to bore through Tom's very soul. After the longest while, Teveler's head bobbed. "Yeah," he said. "Reckon I see the resemblance. Then your mama would be . . . ?"

"Therissa," Tom said warily.

The stranger chuckled. "Yeah. Makes sense. Tess of the River. You got her eyes."

"I'm Lightning Garth," Lightning shot out, tired of being left out of the conversation, being ignored. "Tom's older brother."

Teveler studied Lightning, but not as long, not as hard, not as serious as he had examined Tom.

"Lightnin', huh?" He picked up the tumbler, found it still empty, and reached across the shards of glass for the bottle of bourbon Sean Dublin had left behind. He filled the glass with only two fingers of liquor and sipped it rather than gulping it. "Lightnin'," he said, as if trying to resurrect some dormant memory. "Lightnin'."

As he drank, he examined Lightning a little longer, wetting his chapped lips with his tongue and with the bourbon. "Yeah," he said after a while. He took another sip of whiskey. "Lightnin'. Yeah. Yeah. I recollect now. Yes, sir, you would be Lightnin'."

"I would be," Lightning said, "because I am. Lightning. Lightning Garth."

"They kept that handle on you, eh?"

"It's my name. Ma even wrote it down in the Bible."

"Your . . . ma?"

"We're brothers." Lightning hooked his thumb at Tom. "I'm the oldest. Fastest." He grinned. "Meanest. And best-looking."

Jess Teveler killed the whiskey and tossed the empty tumbler aside. He grabbed his Winchester, jacked a fresh round into the chamber. That caused the brothers to grip their pistols a little tighter. They held their breaths until the saddle tramp lowered the hammer and dropped the barrel toward the floor.

"Been an interestin' evenin', boys. Glad to've met you. But like I said, Mexico's waitin'." He shifted the rifle to his left hand and held out his right.

Tom shook first. Lightning next.

"You did know our grandfather, didn't you, Jess?" Tom said.

"Water under the bridge, son. Water under the bridge. And like I said. Nobody ever knowed Dunson.

That was a long, long time ago. You can tell your pa you saw me, that I say howdy. Your ma won't likely recollect me much." He looked at Lightning. "And your . . . well . . . don't mind me. Gettin' to be a dotterin' ol' fool."

"You need a job?" Tom asked.

Lightning shot his brother a look of pure fury.

"No, Tom. 'Preciate the offer, but right now, what I need is Mexican dirt under my ol' hoss's hooves." He pulled his hat down, his collar up, and strode across the floor to the poker table, still overturned, where the railroaders had been playing. They had left a few coins and greenbacks on the floor, which Teveler picked up and stuffed inside his trousers. That caused Lightning to grin at Tom. Afterward, the saddle tramp nodded again at the brothers, even Sean Dublin, and went through the open door. Darkness swallowed him.

"You boys gotta pay damages," Sean Dublin said after the stranger had gone.

"Not after you tried to back-shoot us, Smithy," Lightning said. He took the bottle from his brother's hand and pushed his way onto the boardwalk.

When they got into their room in the hotel, shed their gun belts, hats, and coats, Lightning took a slug from the bottle and sat on the edge of the bed.

On the settee, Tom struggled to pull off his boots. His muscles had begun to stiffen, and he realized how scratched his knuckles were. His shoulder ached.

"You ever heard Ma or Pa mention Jess Teveler?" Lightning asked.

"They don't mention hardly anyone." The right boot came off. Tom tossed it toward the door.

"That man's a gunhand," Lightning said.

"Be glad of that."

Lightning shrugged. "Oh, Smithy wasn't gonna shoot us in the back. You know that as well as I do. Ain't got the guts. Just tried to scare us. I was just keeping that beer-jerker in his place."

"Pa will make us pay for the damages, though. No matter what you told Dublin." The second boot didn't want to come off, and, fancy as the hotel was by Dunson City standards, the guest rooms came without bootjacks. Inside the boot, his foot screamed in agony.

"Well, it was an interesting night, for certain." He crossed the room and offered the bottle to Tom.

Tom's head shook. That hurt, too.

He let go of the boot still stuck on his foot. Lightning made no offer to help.

"Why did you go into the Knuckle Coupler anyway?"

"To start a fight," Lightning said. "What the hell is a Knuckle Coupler? I never understood why stupid railroaders would give that stupid bucket of blood a stupid name like that stupid Knuckle Coupler."

"It has something to do with railroads," Tom said. He pulled at the boot.

"No fooling."

Lightning hopped onto the bed, boots and spurs still on. With a heavy sigh, Tom shook his head. One bed. He would have to share with his brother, and if Lightning didn't kick off his boots soon, they would be paying extra for the ripped blanket and sheets.

Finally, his boot came off.

Tom realized his big toe was bleeding. Some rail-roader must have stomped his foot during the scuffle. The sock was already stained, the blood dried, and it would hurt like hell when he pulled off the sock.

CHAPTER SIX

In the old days, Groot Nadine had worn his hair long. Now his head resembled a cue ball, but his gray mustache drooped long and unkempt—to make up for what he had lost atop his skull.

Beard stubble dotted the rest of his face, and he rubbed his hands on the apron stained with bacon grease and filth as he limped around the stove. "Don't tell me you want breakfast, too," he snapped.

Mathew Garth stood in the doorway to the bunkhouse, letting two of the hired men escape before he stepped inside, closing the door behind him.

"Coffee's all," Mathew said. "I ate breakfast back at the house."

"Yeah." Groot went to the coffeepot. "What did that Prussian *puta* fix for you this morn?"

"Polish," Mathew said as he shed his coat and hung it on a rack on the wall. "Not Prussian. And she's no *puta*." His tone let the stoved-up cook know that any other reference, in jest or otherwise, would not be tolerated.

"Damned foreigner," Groot muttered, spilling coffee as he filled a tin cup.

"We're all foreigners," Mathew said.

"Well." Groot limped over and handed the cup to Mathew, who had wisely kept his gloves on. "What did you et for breakfast? Taters? That's about all she knows how to cook."

Off on the top bunk in a corner, a Texas drawl sang out: "Them was good taters you fried me and the boys this morn, Groot. Mighty tasty."

Groot spit against the stove. It sizzled. "Shut up, Laredo. You gonna lay in bed all morn?"

Laredo rose. He was fully dressed, even in boots and spurs. "Ain't much to do, is there? They don't pay me to shovel snow."

Old Laredo, who had ridden with Dunson, had been among the hired men at the ranch to refuse to string up any drift fence. He had not quit, though, not like some of the cowhands. Laredo Downs was loyal, but some things he would not do. Matt respected him for it. Hell, now Laredo had been proved right. Men like Laredo Downs were hard to find these days. He would give you more than an honest day's work. Rode for the brand. Well, maybe he rode for Mathew Garth. After all, during that cattle drive to Abilene all those years ago, Mathew had pulled Laredo out of a flooding stream. Mathew never spoke of it. Neither did Laredo. But Laredo certainly remembered it.

Mathew sipped the coffee and hooked a thumb toward the window. "Sun's out."

"The sun!" Laredo dropped out of the bunk, almost tumbled to the floor, then hurried—the jingle bobs on his spurs singing a tune—to the door. Even limping, Groot made it first. The door jerked open. The cold wind blasted them, but both men stepped out into the frosty morning.

"Glory!" Groot said.

"Son of a gun," Laredo echoed.

"Man, that's hot." Laredo stepped into the snow, swept off his hat that rarely left his head, and leaned back to soak in the rays of warmth. Warmth being relative. It wasn't thirty degrees outside.

Groot and Laredo quickly turned. "You rode out yesterday," Groot said. Both men asked the question at the same time. The words were different, but not the query.

"Dead cattle everywhere," Matt said grimly.

Groot cursed. Laredo returned the battered black hat back over his white hair. "Drift fence?" he asked.

Matt tossed the coffee onto the pile of snow. "Like you figured, Laredo."

Both men cursed again. Groot kicked the wooden column. Laredo spat. Mathew walked back inside the bunkhouse, and the two men followed. They filled their cups with Groot's coffee and sat at the table where the hired men took their meals. Matt picked up a biscuit, broke off a piece, stuck it in his mouth—not that he was hungry. It just gave him something to do.

"Well . . ." Groot started, but couldn't think of anything else to say. So he just shook his head.

After Mathew washed down the biscuit with some of Groot's bitter brew, he asked: "Ever heard of the J Lazy J brand?"

Groot shot a glance across the table at Laredo, who

rubbed the beard stubble on his chin momentarily. Laredo Downs shook his head. So did Groot.

"Me, either," Mathew said. "Not in the *Brand Book*. That was one of the brands I found on dead beef piled up along the drift fence."

Again, Laredo cursed.

"Other was the Circle 43. That—"

"What about our beeves?" Groot asked.

Mathew's head shook. "Not good. But maybe not as bad as places up north." Again, he drank some coffee, broke off another bite of biscuit, but left it on the napkin near the plate. The biscuits must have been from last night and had already hardened.

"There's a Circle 43 brand up in Nacogdoches," Mathew said. "But I don't think it's the same one I found on the carcass by the drift fence."

Laredo Downs drank and leaned back in his chair. "No. Wouldn't be from Nacogdoches. Winds came in from the northwest. That's too far north and east of here for any beeves to drift that way."

Groot snorted. "You figure 'em beeves come from Colorado maybe?"

The laugh that rushed out of Mathew's mouth held bitterness. "Maybe Canada."

He finished the coffee and rose. "Ask some of the hands if they've heard of those brands," Mathew said. "Long shot, I know, and likely doesn't matter one way or the other where those beeves came from."

They stood and walked to the door.

"What you reckon it'll mean?" Laredo asked as he opened the door.

"We'll find out come spring," Mathew said. "But you best sharpen your skinning knife."

He pulled up his collar, and all three men watched the two riders easing their horses toward the big barn near the house.

Laredo Downs whistled. "Those boys rode out together?"

"Rode back home together, too," Mathew said, his mood lightening. "That's a good sign."

"Probably snow-blind," Groot muttered. "Don't see one another."

Mathew was already walking through the snow, heading to the barn to greet Lightning and Tom.

Inside the barn, he frowned. Sun shot through the open doorways enough that he could see the bruises on the faces of the two brothers. Where Tom's lips weren't split, they were swollen. A dark bruise had already formed beneath Lightning's right eye, and his shirt was ripped. Tom had already lost the nail to his thumb.

"You fight each other?" Mathew asked. Which would not have been the first time—this year, in fact.

"Nah." Lightning hung his saddle on a peg and dropped the blanket in the sun to dry out.

Considering Lightning's answer, Mathew pursed his lips for a moment and turned to Tom, who was leading his horse into a stall. "How much money do I owe?"

Tom shrugged, grabbed a handful of hay, and began rubbing down his sorrel.

"Not a damn thing, Pa," Lightning sang out. "Fool beer-jerker in that bucket of blood pulled a Greener on us. Was gonna shoot us in the back." Tom kept working on his horse.

"By 'bucket of blood' . . ." Mathew measured his words carefully. "You mean . . . ?"

"Knuckle Coupler," Tom said without looking away from his sorrel's withers.

"We might have run them railroaders out of the country after all." Lightning grinned, but just briefly. Smiling hurt.

"I've told you boys to stay out of that grog shop," Mathew said. "We wanted that spur. Lobbied two years to get it."

"Yeah, yeah." Lightning tossed oats into the stall that held his chestnut. "We got a spur. That connects Dunson City to the Southern Pacific in Del Rio. It don't do us no good."

"It will," Mathew said. His voice stopped both brothers. Tom dropped the hay and moved out of the stall. Lightning held the empty coffee can he had used to feed his horse its oats.

"You have breakfast?" Mathew asked.

"No, sir," Tom answered. "Rode out right before sunrise."

Lightning shuffled his feet.

"All right. Janeen probably has some bacon and potatoes still on the stove. Go in through the old house first. Wash up. Change your clothes. Make yourself something that might pass as presentable."

"Pa . . ." Lightning shook his head. "There ain't no need in getting a burr under your saddle."

Mathew had already turned around. They could make out only his silhouette as he walked out of the barn. "Not me, boys. But your mother's gonna be mad as a March hare when she sees you two."

* * *

Tess Millay's jade eyes glared so hard that even Janeen Yankowski made no comment, simply raked the potatoes and bacon onto the plates, along with the eggs she had just fried, and scurried out of the dining room.

Lightning attacked his food. Tom lost his appetite.

"Really," Tess said. "Really?"

Looking up, Lightning swallowed and laid his fork on the table. "The railroaders started it, Ma."

"Like hell." Tom pushed his chair back from the table, wadded up the napkin he had placed on his lap, and tossed it onto the table near his plate.

"They're nothing but railroaders, Ma," Lightning tried again. "We ain't got no use—"

Her small fist rocked the table. "No use. Why do you think your father and I got that spur run from Del Rio? So we could catch a freight to Austin or El Paso? Your father invested in a railroad that never even saw a crosstie or spike. We need that railroad. For cattle."

"Pa says it's too expensive to ship—"

"For the time being, yes. But five years from now? Ten? Twenty? When the two of you are running this spread? That's why we did this. For you. For the future of the empire Thomas Dunson, your grandfather, carved." She pointed out the window.

"Have you looked outside? When's the last time you two even saw snow this far south? Tell me something." She walked to Tom, who likely thought he was out of her line of fire, and pointed. "What did you see when you rode into Dunson City?"

He blinked. "What? Well . . . um . . ."

"Snow." Lightning laughed, but Tess whirled and

slapped him. His mouth fell open. Tom scooted back in his chair.

He wet his lips, took a breath, and tried again. "Snow drifts. Mostly. Coyote tracks. Rabbit tracks. To be honest, Ma, we didn't pay much attention."

"That's right. You didn't pay any attention. You didn't ride out to the drift fence, like your father did. There are cattle frozen to death all across Texas. Likely all across the West. This winter has been a disaster, boys. It could ruin the whole beef industry. It could ruin us. Destroy us. Crumble this empire like Rome."

"We're sorry, Ma." Lightning uttered the apology first. Tom just nodded his affirmation.

Tess's face had flushed. She sat down at the end of the table, shook her head, and lifted the cup of coffee Janeen had poured for her.

"What do we need to do?" Tom asked.

It took a while before Tess could regain her composure. "We . . ." She paused. Set the cup in its saucer. "There's nothing to do . . . till spring. Then we see how bad things really are." The cup came up to her thin lips, and she drank, then lowered the cup and rose.

"Eat your breakfast." Tess was heading out the door when Lightning called her. She turned and heard him ask the question.

CHAPTER SEVEN

"He said, 'Who's Jess Teveler?'"

Mathew Garth looked up at his wife, pursed his lips, and closed the ledger on his desk.

"Teveler," he whispered as he pushed his chair back. His lips flattened. He glanced at the glass of Scotch near him, but did not reach for it.

Tess Millay looked back in the foyer and, satisfied, closed the door to the library. She crossed the old rug until she stood in front of the desk. She saw the glass of Scotch, too, but she picked it up and drank.

"Last I heard of Jess Teveler," Mathew said, "he was in Huntsville."

"He's out of prison now." Tess held the glass to Mathew, who took it, but instead of killing off the finger of single malt, he placed it back on the desktop.

She condensed what Tom and Lightning had told her. The boys had been, typically, brawling in town, at the Knuckle Coupler. The bartender had a shotgun after the fight, was aiming at one of their sons, and Teveler had stepped in and winged the bartender.

Teveler, Tom, and Lightning had shared a drink or two before the old gunman rode out for Mexico.

"He had gotten into some sort of a scrape up in San Angelo," Tess concluded. "Texas Rangers, he told the boys, were after him."

"Figures." Now Mathew finished the Scotch. He wet his lips.

"Teveler told them to tell you howdy."

Mathew nodded. "Not you?"

"He told them that I wouldn't remember him."

Mathew let out a soft chuckle. "He was wrong about that."

"Oh, I remember him all right. He was a skunk. A killer."

Mathew shook his head. "Driven to it. Had a place well east of here. Carpetbaggers came in, grabbed it, like they were taking everything. He did what he had to do."

"He hired his gun out to Dunson." Those green eyes of hers glared with hatred.

As Mathew rubbed his chin, Tess said, "Tom offered Teveler a job."

Mathew's head bobbed. "I would've done the same, had a stranger saved my bacon. But with Rangers on his trail, I don't think you have to worry about Jess Teveler."

"For now." She went to the bar to fetch more Glenlivet. She left her husband thinking back more than twenty years.

"I'm going to kill you," Thomas Dunson said, and his hand shot down for the Colt on his hip.

That was the mutiny. They were in the Indian Nations, and by now everyone on the drive had learned that there had to be—had to be—a railroad in Abilene, Kansas, but Dunson, always that thickheaded fool, insisted on driving the herd to Sedalia, Missouri. And everyone—maybe even Dunson himself—knew that the border gangs running roughshod in Missouri would kill them all and take that herd.

So Mathew had said the herd was going to Kansas. He, Dunson's son if not by blood then by bond, was taking the herd. Stealing it. Not for himself, but for every rancher in Texas. He was doing this for Texas and, maybe, even Dunson.

The Colt shot out of the holster, and Mathew jerked his own. But he couldn't fire. Not against that stubborn cattleman. Cherry Valance, however, swept his revolver up and put a bullet in Dunson's shoulder.

So Mathew was able to take the herd, point it to Abilene. They left Thomas Dunson behind, wounded, defeated, full of hate. Dunson had told him that he would find him and then hang him, and every one of his men, from the nearest tree.

Later, in the chuck wagon, Groot had grumbled: "Good luck, Mr. Dunson, findin' a damned tree in this God-awful country."

"He'll use the wagon tongue," Cherry Valance had joked.

Jokes. But no humor. Everyone felt the edge, the damned fear. Even Mathew spent most of his time looking over his shoulder, half expecting to find Thomas Dunson standing right there, gun or rope in his hand, hatred in those cold gray eyes.

Three men—Old Leather Monte, Brick Keever and Jargens, all dead now—had remained loyal to Dunson, but Dunson freed them from the commitment, told them to ride with the herd. So Mathew had left Dunson and crossed the Nations. They had found the wagon train bound for Virginia City, Nevada, and Mathew had once again met Tess Millay. The cowhands had helped those with the train run by The Donegal, an Irish cheat, sharper, pimp, and thief. They had survived an Indian attack, a pure frog-strangler of a thunderstorm, and a stampede. And the birth of a baby.

The mother's name was Edna, one of The Donegal's girls. Dark skinned, sad eyes. So tiny, so quiet. She had been married back in Memphis, but her husband joined the Confederacy and fell at Shiloh. And Memphis had far too many widows to feed, so Edna had done . . . what she had to do. To survive.

Few memories about that time from the Red River to Abilene ever led Mathew to smile, but he did now as he thought about that time, pouring rain, lightning flashing, cattle stampeding, guns blasting, Edna screaming, Tess yelling, and Mathew sitting white-faced in the back of a wagon. Tess had handed him the newborn.

He had stammered something idiotic about breaking the baby. Said a few other things. Tess had scolded him, told him to calm down, and Mathew had finally gotten the kid to someone who knew how to handle kids, and he had hurried off to find Groot to help set another one of The Donegal's girls' broken arms.

Groot had studied Mathew closely, then commented on how funny Mathew looked.

He had said that Edna had just given birth to a baby. And Groot had shot back, "You're drunk."

Blinking, Mathew saw the glass of Scotch his wife was offering him. He took it, thanked her, and sipped before passing the glass back to her.

"You were smiling," she said.

"Yeah."

"Poor Edna." Tess drank. Then a memory caused her to grin. "Remember that night? I said we should name the boy Mathew Garth."

He nodded. "Groot said 'Stampede.'"

"Lightning," Tess said softly.

The smiles had faded. The glass went from Tess to Mathew and back again.

"Maybe we should have told him," Tess said. "When he turned eighteen."

Mathew shrugged. "We talked about it. Talked about it when he was ten . . . when he was thirteen . . . when he was . . ."

Tess killed the Scotch. "He's just so wild. So unpredictable."

"Like lightning," Mathew said. "You picked the right name for him."

She set the glass on the desk.

"How many men know?"

Mathew shrugged, but he had been doing some thinking himself.

Groot and Laredo were all that were left on the ranch who had been with the drive to Abilene. Most of the other trail hands—men like Kavanaugh, Andres, and Dale—had drifted on. Teeler Lacey had bought a place up north along the Brazos. Others were dead now. Old Leather Monte—a grizzled old-timer whom Mathew had thought would live forever, and even was fond of saying, "I have lived forever"—had broken his neck in a horse wreck in '68. Jargens had drowned crossing the swollen Canadian on a drive to Ellsworth in '73. Some sawbones said Keever's appendix had ruptured, and he had died in agony in Laredo a few years back. Joe Nambel drifted in every now and then, but Nambel was like Groot and Laredo. He knew to keep his mouth closed on certain subjects.

But Dunson had come after Mathew, and he had hired ten men to back his play—if needed.

Most of those, Mathew had never even learned their names, and he had not paid enough attention to their faces to remember them. His eyes had been focused on Thomas Dunson as the bear of a man walked through cattle standing in the streets of Abilene, determined to live up to his word and kill Mathew Garth.

Nelse Burdette had been one of the gunmen Dunson had hired, but Burdette was dead later that year, shot down in Waco in an argument over a faro game. His body had been shipped all the way down to his home in Goliad, where he had been buried in the family plot. Joe Thompson of Lampasas, who had turned from cattle ranching to killing for hire after the War between the States, had not lasted much longer. Hired guns usually didn't live too long, and Thompson had been ambushed by a bunch of angry citizens up in San Saba on July 4, 1876. Folks said San Saba had not celebrated Independence Day since the outbreak of the War between the States until that evening. Mathew had read in a newspaper that the death of Joe Thompson did more to reconcile North and South, at least in San Saba, than anything else.

There were others . . . and there was Jess Teveler.

Dunson's men had stopped with The Donegal, too. Tess had tried to talk Dunson out of revenge. Cherry Valance, who had stayed behind when Mathew had pulled out for Abilene, had tried to kill

Dunson only to die himself. But Dunson and his men—and Tess Millay and a suddenly feverish Edna and her new son—had kept north. Found Abilene. Found Mathew Garth.

After they had buried Dunson in Texas, Mathew had ridden south, back to the ranch with the money from the profits of selling the herd. Tess had gone back to Abilene.

She had returned with a baby. A wild-eyed, dark-skinned boy named Lightning.

"What the hell is this?" Mathew had snapped when he saw the kid, swaddled up.

"It's Lightning," Tess had said.

Mathew had looked around. "Where's Edna?"

"She's dead." Tears had welled in Tess's eyes, and Tess Millay had not cried in years. "I didn't know what else to do, Mathew. I didn't . . . I couldn't . . . I . . . I . . . I . . ."

He was standing now, at the big window, staring into the emptiness, the black sky, the white ground. Behind him came the sound of Scotch filling the glass Tess had taken off the desk.

"You want to tell him?" Mathew asked.

"No."

He had expected that answer. It had not changed in more than twenty years. Lightning had not been her child, but Tess had delivered him. She had been holding him in that miserable sod house in Abilene when Edna had slipped into a coma and slowly died. She had taken the baby and somehow managed to get him all the way from Kansas to southern Texas. Lightning wasn't her child, yet he was.

Tom was hers and Mathew's. Thomas Dunson Garth. But Tom was more like Mathew. In temperament. In looks, though he had Tess's green eyes. Tom was dependable. Solid. Knew what was expected of him and would do more.

Oh, Tess loved both of her sons, but she had always favored Lightning. Mathew? Well . . . maybe he favored Tom a little.

He heard her feet as she crossed the room and felt her standing beside him. She drank a healthy portion of the Scotch and lowered the glass to her side.

"You think I'm wrong?" she asked.

"No." His answer came immediately, without a second thought, and he knew—Tess knew this as well—that he wasn't lying.

"You know him better than I do," Mathew said. "I've tried . . . but . . ."

"Well . . ." Tess's free hand took his into her own. She squeezed it with affection, and plenty of people in the county would say that Tess Millay rarely showed any affection.

Mathew Garth thought about his sons. His wife. He thought about Jess Teveler. He thought about Thomas Dunson. And he remembered something he had overheard Groot telling Dunson back when Mathew had been barely in his teens.

"You knows that boy as well as anybody, Mr. Dunson, but you don't know 'm a-tall."

BOOK II

CHAPTER EIGHT

They had a saying in South Texas:

"There are only two seasons down here, late spring and Hell."

That year of 1886 skipped late spring and went straight to Hell.

Tom Garth stood up, leaving the knife on the bloated carcass and putting both hands against his back. He leaned back, trying to ease the pain in his muscles, keep that back from stiffening, and looked away from the dead steer. Blood and gore covered the fingers of his gloves, but he did not remove them as he lifted the soaked end of the bandanna covering his mouth. He spit into the mud, spit again, and looked at the endless expanse of Texas.

"I'm a rancher," a voice sounded behind him. "Not a cowhand."

"Shut up, Lightnin'!" Laredo Downs snapped. "You don't own your pa's spread yet."

"And if we don't get these cattle skint," Joe Nambel said, "even your pa might not be a rancher no more."

Nambel had returned from working in a mine all winter down in Zacatecas. Tom Garth wondered if the old man wished he had remained in Mexico. It had to be better than skinning dead cattle. Anything had to be better than—Tom looked up, wiping sweat from his brow—than . . . this.

The snow was gone, replaced by mud and blood and bones. Twenty yards to Tom's right, a fire blazed, and the stench of the burning remnants of cattle soured in Tom's belly. The whole country smelled like rotting flesh, and flies buzzed all around him. He had even swallowed at least a half dozen this day alone. But he figured he had to be getting used to this.

On this day, he had thrown up just once. Yesterday it had been at least a half-dozen times. The week before, he couldn't even recall. In the beginning, Laredo Downs had ordered the crew to skin only the hides wearing one of Mathew Garth's brands. But when Mathew rode up after a day, he countermanded Laredo's orders.

"Skin them all," Tom's father had said.

Laredo had given Mathew Garth a strange look, and Groot had chuckled, "Like olden times."

"Skin them all, Laredo," Mathew had said. "Unless you want to live with this stink for the rest of the year."

"You gonna explain that to 'em floaters when they come driftin' here?" Laredo and Groot were probably the only men alive who could challenge Mathew's authority, or question his judgment, and not rue the day. Had Tom or Lightning tried that, their ears would get boxed.

Mathew nodded. "We're not waiting on any crew from . . . hell . . . Canada . . . to come here to claim their hides, Laredo. The way things are, I hear, it might take floaters ten months to work their way down from the Red River. Skin them. Every damned one of them."

"You're right, Mathew," Laredo had conceded, and he yelled down the drift fence. "Don't worry about the brands, boys. Just skin anything in sight."

Ten months, Tom thought, to skin dead cattle from the Red River to the Rio Grande. Why . . . in ten months, the crew from the Garth Ranch might be only halfway finished skinning dead beeves here.

Tom spit again. This time, he didn't bother trying to lift his bandanna. After stretching his back muscles one more time, he dropped to the dead steer again and reached for the knife. Flies covered the blade, and Tom's streak ended. He jerked the bandanna down, leaned over the remnants of the dead animal's skull, and vomited.

For the first day, Groot had joked about things. When he rang the cast-iron triangle, he had shouted, "Come and get it, boys. It ain't sowbelly. It's *cow* belly." One Mexican vaquero named Antonio had vomited. Another called Manuelito had pulled a dagger, held the narrow blade under the stove-up cook's nose, and said calmly, "This is no opera house, señor, and you are not so damned funny."

Groot had made no jokes after that. It wasn't funny.

Flies came in swarms. Buzzards and other carrion outnumbered the crews sent out to skin the dead cattle. After the first mile of drift fence had been cleared of dead cattle, Lightning had suggested that the cowboys tear down the drift fence.

"What would your pa say to that?" Laredo had asked.

A lariat looped over a fence post, and Laredo, Lightning, and everyone else looked at Mathew Garth, sitting on a chestnut mare, dallying the end of his lariat and spurring the horse, pulling on the reins, backing the animal up until the post bent, then left the muddy ground with an ugly sucking sound.

"Tear the damned fence down!" Mathew yelled.

That, at least, had been fun.

When the hide had been peeled off, Tom dragged it to two Indian women from the other side of the river. They scraped off the remnants of flesh, rubbed beef brains against the underside of the hide, and, eventually, pegged the hide to the ground to dry in the sun.

Tom didn't know how much his father was paying those two women, but he figured they earned every cent.

He knew what he was being paid. The same as the vaqueros and other hired hands. One dollar a day. Plus food and a place to sleep. Laredo Downs would draw seventy-five a month as foreman, and Groot fifty as the cook. When Nambel drifted back into Texas and hired on with Mathew Garth, the old cowhand had said, "A dollar a day. That's what I got paid twenty years ago."

To which Groot had said, "And you wasn't worth it back then, neither."

Not that Tom or Lightning would see any of that money real soon. Their father and mother had made sure both boys understood that. Times were hard, and about to get tougher. It would be a lean year, maybe a rough two or three years.

Their mother had then said, her green eyes hard, in no mood for resistance, "And neither of you will be riding into Dunson City. Not to the Knuckle Coupler. Not to the Rio. And not to Gloria's Palace."

The best part of the day came when they returned to the ranch. All of them. By the time they had their horses watered, grained, and cleaned, Janeen Yankowski had tubs filled with hot water, and everyone stripped and bathed—even Groot—while the Polish servant tried to get the blood and gore off the clothes.

Lye soap almost tore away Tom's skin, but he never complained. It felt good. He felt clean, even if he knew he would be just as sick, and his clothes and skin just as sickening, come the next evening.

Above the buzzing of flies around his head and the calls of hungry ravens on the ground nearby, irritated that their feast had been interrupted by skinners, the sound of loping hooves reached his ears. Tom stepped back and turned to the sound. He saw his father riding a black mare.

It was an excuse to lower his knife and step away from the drift fence and the dead cattle. Groot, Laredo, Nambel, and—of course—Lightning also stopped the ugly chore and waited for Mathew Garth, who reined in near Groot's old Studebaker that had been converted into a chuck wagon.

After pulling down the polka-dot bandanna that had covered his nose and mouth, Mathew swung his left leg out of the stirrup and hooked it over the saddle horn. He fished the makings from his vest pocket and began rolling a cigarette.

"What's it look like?" Laredo Downs asked.

Mathew had ridden in from the southwest.

The lean man did not answer until he had the smoke between his lips and had struck a lucifer on his thumbnail to light it. He drew in deeply, held the smoke for a moment, and exhaled.

Mathew's head shook. "By my count, two hundred head of dead beeves per mile."

Everyone swore.

"How many miles?" Laredo asked.

He took another drag and removed the cigarette. "I rode five miles. Then got tired of riding." He looked at Laredo. "You went south this morning?"

The foreman nodded. "To the Rio Grande. Good news . . . if you can call it good news . . . is that after a wet winter, the grass is greenin' up. Most of our herd, south of that damned fence, weathered the winter all right. But not all. Found some bones in a few arroyos and canyons. And saw some turkey buzzards flyin' over some country I couldn't ride into. Others got caught in some canyons, covered with snow. Froze to death."

"Your guess," Mathew said, "as to our losses."

Laredo spit and wiped his mouth with gut- and bloodstained gloves. "Six percent. Maybe seven."

Now Mathew swore, flicked the cigarette away, and pushed back the brim of his brown hat. Tom knew his father was running numbers through his head. Eventually, a smile formed, but those eyes revealed no good feelings. "Well, we're lucky . . . or luckier than most."

"Maybe." Laredo stared down the fence. Dead cattle stretched down the fence forever.

"You want some coffee, Mathew?" Groot asked.

Mathew shook his head. "You boys want some help?" Without waiting for an answer, he dropped out of the saddle and led the black to the remuda. When he returned, he had shed his vest and rolled up the sleeves of his boiled shirt, holding a well-honed skinning knife that he had fetched from his saddlebags.

"You ain't gotta do this, Mathew," Laredo said.

"The hell I don't. If we ever want to be finished with this sorry job."

CHAPTER NINE

The dumpy man in the ill-fitting plaid sack suit smoothed his graying mustache before gesturing at the empty chair in front of his desk. He did not offer a hand to shake as Mathew Garth sank into the rickety chair.

"Good morning, Chico," Mathew said.

Chico Miller grunted, shoved a few papers aside, opened a drawer, and dumped some others there. "That's your opinion." He picked up a soggy, well-chewed cigar and stuck it between his yellow teeth.

A big man with pasty skin, a fat cucumber of a nose, and thinning hair, Chico Miller slammed the drawer shut and leaned forward, putting elbows on the desk and resting his double chin in the palms of two meaty, sweaty hands.

"Get on with it," he said.

Mathew pointed at the two massive dogs lying at the side of the banker's desk, one brown, the other reminding Mathew of a blue roan horse. Both of the animals seemed big enough to ride.

"Those are new," Mathew said.

Which got a grin from Chico Miller. He pointed at them with his chewed-up cigar.

"Cost me a fortune, too. These aren't American bulldogs, Matt. Got them shipped in all the way from England. Olde English Bulldogges." He spelled the words, just in case Mathew didn't understand how important, how prestigious, bulldogs like these two were.

And they were impressive. Large heads, muscles just about everywhere you looked, and they probably weighed eighty to a hundred pounds.

"Used them for bull baiting back in the old country," Miller said, and Mathew stared at him.

"Don't worry," the banker said. "I won't bait any of your bulls for these two boys."

Again, Mathew studied the animals, and when one of the big dogs, the brown one, rolled over, Mathew leaned closer. Pointing at the bulldogs, he asked, "What happened to them?"

Scars covered their hides, and some of the wounds on the brown dog seemed fresh.

"Damned coyotes," Miller said with a growl. "They lure these two beasts into that arroyo behind my house, then ambush them. But you're not here to talk about my dogs. And I don't think you're here as a member of this bank's board of directors. You want money."

His real name, if you believed the rumors, was Charles. Somehow, when he had been banking on the Hudson River back East, he had picked up the nickname Chic. Some said that came from his fondness with the ladies. Others said he earned it because before he had found a job banking, he had sold chickens. It didn't really matter to Mathew Garth, or Charles Miller. In South Texas, the locals quickly corrupted Chic to Chico. Mathew glanced again at the dogs, grinning at the thought that Chico Miller had spent a fortune on bulldogges—two *g*'s and an *e*— that couldn't outfox South Texas coyot's.

"I'm waiting," Chico Miller said, and shifted the cigar to the other side of his fat jowls.

"How's my credit?" Mathew asked.

"Piss poor," Miller snapped. "Or should I say, *cow* poor—like everybody else in this miserable hell some folks think is habitable for humanity."

Mathew had heard the other rumors about the lone banker in Dunson City. Back in 1873, shortly after Jay Cooke & Company had failed in September, setting off what became known as the Panic of '73, Miller had absconded with funds from that bank in New York City. He had fled to Charleston, South Carolina, worked as confidence man to charm Southern women out of their virginity, good china, and parasols—until the good men of Charleston met him with hot tar and feathers. Which was another rumor about how he had earned the nickname Chic. Chicken feathers. From Charleston, Miller had drifted to Birmingham, Alabama . . . Memphis, Tennessee . . . New Orleans . . . Indianola . . . and now, Dunson City, Texas. Mathew really didn't care what Chico Miller had done in the past. What mattered to Mathew was that the banker, for all his many faults, remained about as savvy a businessman as you'd find anywhere in Texas.

"You got any advice?" Mathew asked.

The cigar came out of the banker's mouth. "Yeah. Don't invest in railroads." The cigar returned.

That hit home. The Panic of '73 had put a dent in Mathew's fortunes when he had invested in that railroad that had failed.

The cigar came out. "Or cattle." Miller spit out the remnants of the cigar.

"Too late for that," Mathew said.

The bell over the front door to the bank chimed. Miller looked over Mathew's shoulder, removed the cigar, and yelled, "Get the hell out of here, you damned panhandler!"

The door quickly closed.

Mathew did not turn around, but Chico Miller turned toward his teller, cashier, and clerk. "And, you three. Mind your own damned business and stop craning your necks to hear what Garth and me are discussing. It's none of your damned business."

One did not have to crane a neck to hear anything Chico Miller said. Another drawer jerked open, and the banker pulled out a bottle of bourbon. He found a dirty glass and set it on a paper. And began to pour.

"It's early for me, Chico," Mathew said.

"I didn't hear me offer you a drink." Miller slugged down the bourbon, slammed the glass on the papers, but did not recork the bottle.

After wiping his mouth and mustache with the back of his hand, Miller stared across the desk. "How much you owe in San Antonio?"

Mathew answered.

"When's it due?"

"November."

Miller considered that, scratched the shadow that

had already formed on his chin and cheeks, and it was not yet ten in the morning. "And the Cattlemen's Trust in Fort Worth?"

"Three thousand."

"When's it due?"

"Next March."

"That it?" Miller refilled the shot glass, but did not pick it up. "Other than what you owe me?"

"That's it."

The banker slid the shot glass in front of Mathew, who stared at the bourbon. Chico Miller did not offer drinks or advice or cigars or anything . . . without charging interest.

"How did you weather the blizzards?" Miller asked.

Mathew shrugged. "We survived."

Seeing that Mathew was not going to take advantage of the free liquor, Miller reached across the desk and slid the glass back in front of him. "So far," he said, not to be petty or vindictive, but merely to state the facts of the matter. He hooked a fat thumb toward the window that faced west.

One of the bulldogs farted.

"Those black clouds aren't clouds, you know. Not rain. Not tornadoes. Not clouds. Flies. By the damned thousands. Flies. Like the Fifth Ward in August. And it's not August."

"I know that."

"You ride five miles out of town and the stink knocks you out of the saddle." Mathew thought about asking the banker when was the last time he had ridden anywhere or showed his face out of Dunson City. But he was smart enough to refrain. "Stinks worse than that privy behind the Knuckle Coupler after payday in the summer. And it's not summer." He stopped, picked up the glass, started to drink the bourbon, but stopped, pointing a finger in Mathew's general direction.

"And that's another thing. Your boys busted up the Knuckle Coupler pretty fair. When was that? A month ago? No. Two months. I remember now. Remember it well. How much did that set you back?"

Mathew did not answer. A man like Chico Miller already knew.

"The reason I remember that your sons tore hell out of the saloon was because the very next day Meeker came in here."

"Meeker?" Mathew asked.

"Yeah. Meeker. He wanted a loan, too, like I'd give that worthless bum a nickel. He was faster asking to go on tick than you, Mathew. But that wouldn't surprise you. Certainly, it did not surprise me."

Mathew nodded. He hadn't seen John Meeker Jr. in better than a year. His father, Big John Meeker, had been the bull of the woods in these parts back when Mathew was a boy and then a young man. Thomas Dunson, however, had dethroned Meeker, much as he had bested Don Diego Agura y Baca. The War between the States then had crippled and busted Meeker. Mathew thought back to that day . . . when he and Dunson had first laid eyes on Cherry Valance.

They had been road-branding the cattle for the trail north to Sedalia, Missouri, when Meeker rode up with only one man. From the looks of that man, though, Meeker must have figured one man was all he would need.

Meeker had been sixty years old then, or so Dunson had told Mathew, and wore his hair and his mustache, both

*white, long. Dunson had just ordered Teeler Lacey to brand
a Meeker steer with Dunson's road brand, and Mathew had
told Lacey to brand everything. Mathew had argued,
Dunson had said he'd take it up with Meeker, and Mathew
had smiled—because here came John Meeker.*

*He remembered Meeker challenging Dunson, saying the
Englishman could do anything he wanted with his longhorns, but not Meeker's. He was going to look over the herd,
and Dunson had objected.*

*Cherry Valance, with the dark eyes of a killer and the well-
oiled revolver of a professional gunman, had asked Dunson
if he planned on trying to stop them.*

*Mathew had answered with words—"I would"—and
with his revolver, which he had drawn cleanly from its holster and pointed it at the gunman from Valverde who was
now riding for John Meeker.*

*In the end, Dunson had explained his reasoning, his im-
patience, and his determination to get that herd to Missouri.
He didn't care how many good cattlemen and cowboys had
been cut down by the road agents. He said he would pay
Meeker two dollars a head when he got back from Sedalia.
Meeker had agreed, and Cherry Valance had stayed—over
Mathew's objections. Dunson had hired the gunman, and
even then Mathew had figured that eventually he would
have to face down Cherry Valance. That didn't happen.
Dunson had faced Valance, and killed him—with some as-
sistance from Tess Millay—but the bullet Valance had put
in Dunson eventually sent Dunson under.*

Thomas Dunson—and, yes, Mathew Garth—had
resurrected Meeker's cattle kingdom with that legendary drive to Abilene all those years ago. In fact,

Mathew and Big John had combined trail herds to Kansas for two or three years after that first one. Later, in 1871, they had each sent two herds to Abilene.

But Meeker was an old man. He looked ancient even before Mathew had donned the gray and joined up with Nathan Bedford Forrest to fight Yankees in Tennessee, Mississippi, Alabama, and Kentucky. In 1874, Meeker turned the ranch over to his son, John Meeker Jr. A year later, and Mathew was serving as one of the pallbearers at Big John's funeral. Within five years, the Meeker Ranch had collapsed. John junior had seen to that. Wild, restless, with no sense for money or ranching.

"The punk needed a mother," Miller said. Now he drank the bourbon.

"I never had a mother, either," Mathew pointed out. "At least, not after I was twelve."

"I did." Miller dropped the glass in the drawer and corked the bottle and made it disappear, too. "Hated the old crone."

Mathew let the comment pass with a poker face. He thought about John Meeker Jr. Of the twenty-three sections he had inherited, he now had 160 acres—a quarter section—and that was only because Big John had been granted that for his service with Sam Houston during Texas's fight for independence. And nobody in Dunson City—even the railroaders— would let John junior use the deed to cover a bet at a poker table or faro layout. Instead of Dunson City, Mathew sometimes thought, the town should have been named Meeker.

"What are your boys doing?" Miller asked.

"Skinning dead beeves," Mathew said.

"How much will that bring you?"

Miller knew the answer already, but Mathew answered, "A dollar a hide."

"And the meat?"

"Spoiled. We've been burying or burning what we can. Leave the rest for the coyot's, wolves, ravens . . ."

"And how many can a man skin in a day?"

Mathew shrugged. "Depends on the man."

Miller stared. His dark eyes did not blink. The banker would have made a pretty good poker player, Mathew figured. He cleared his throat and told the banker what Miller wanted to know.

"The hands working for me now can skin enough so that I can pay them their dollar a day and found, ship the hides to the tannery in Goliad, and have enough left over to buy grub for next month and keep everyone at the ranch fed and . . ." He almost said "happy." Which would have been a bald-faced lie.

"And how much longer will that last?"

Mathew gave the banker a humorless grin. "Well, if you could loan me enough money for a few more whetstones, so my boys can sharpen their knives, we probably can go on for another year or two."

The banker frowned. "I see no profit in that loan for me, Mathew."

"I don't, either. And I'm not doing it. Groot, Laredo, those boys . . . they won't do it much longer, either. Besides, floaters are already drifting into the country. Cowboy crews from as far north as Nebraska. We'll leave the skinning to them, and we'll go back to cowboying. Putting a herd together."

"A herd?" Miller could not hide the skepticism in his voice.

"That's what we do in this country, Chico," Mathew said.

"Not anymore, Garth." Chico Miller opened another drawer and pulled out a pad that was full of numbers and chicken scratches. He found his spectacles, put them on the bridge of his nose, and said, "The Diamond C is practically wiped out. I don't think Henry Cressell's spread will survive this year. The LX boys are doing what your men are doing, skinning carcasses, and they will be doing that till November. The XIT is looking at a loss of fifteen percent. Up in Donley County, one ranch lost fifty percent. The Texan who owed that spread decided he would eat a bullet for his breakfast."

The eyeglasses came off, and Miller stared hard across the desk.

Mathew's voice stayed calm. "Those ranches are all far north of here. Winter was harder there."

"It was damned hard here." He dropped the pad into the desk drawer and returned with a copy of the *Drovers Journal*, jabbed a finger at a paragraph, and said, "More than two hundred thousand. That's what this reporter says. More than two hundred thousand dead cattle. This winter has wiped out the market, maybe the entire industry, and not just in Texas. Across the whole West."

Mathew nodded. "Since when did you believe in newspapers, Chico?"

The banker cursed, pushed the *Journal* aside, and frowned. He opened a box on the desk and pulled out a cigar, bit off the end, stuck the cigar in his mouth, and, as an afterthought, turned the box toward Mathew.

Mathew shook his head.

Miller grinned. "Love these things. Don't know how they do it, but I'm addicted to these things. Imported from Havana. Cost me seven bucks to get a box here. In New York, they went for four bucks." He did not light the cigar. Mathew had never seen Chico Miller smoke. He just chewed the cigars until they were soggy shreds. The banker's expression quickly hardened. "Only a damned fool would attempt a drive after a winter like this one."

"They said the same thing about Thomas Dunson twenty years back," Mathew said.

"And they would have been right, too. Dunson should have wound up dead and forgotten like that man . . ." He snapped his fingers trying to recall the name. "Cummerbund."

"Cummerlan," Mathew corrected.

"Like I said," Miller said, "forgotten."

Mathew cleared his throat. Leaning forward, he said, "Our losses will probably reach seven percent. No more—"

The banker shot out a thick finger. "You don't run as many cattle as the XIT."

"So I don't have as many dead beef to skin. I'm not talking about the XIT, and you don't care about the XIT. The XIT doesn't give you any business, Chico, because it's way up in the Panhandle. I'm here. I've made you a lot of money."

"And I don't plan on losing a penny of it."

Mathew nodded. He let the silence fill the room and wondered if the clerk and those other banker types were eavesdropping, waiting, wondering what the New Yorker would say.

"Laredo your trail boss?" Chico Miller asked at last.

Mathew nodded. "He has been doing it since '82."

"And you figure a loan would get you a crew hired, say a thousand—"

Mathew shot out. "Say . . . twenty-five hundred or three thousand."

"That's a lot of beef."

"Not every steer, bull, or heifer died this winter, Chico."

Chico Miller dribbled his fingers on the desk. He glanced at the first drawer he had closed, as if considering another drink, but the Seth Thomas clock began to chime, reminding the banker of just how early it was for a banker to be getting roostered.

"Fifteen hundred longhorns in two herds?" Miller asked.

"One herd," Mathew corrected.

"Denison?"

Mathew's head shook. "It's too expensive to ship cattle from Texas. Right now." He tilted his head toward the door. "That's why all that railroad spur brings us is railroaders and trouble . . . for now."

"Then . . . Caldwell."

Again, Mathew shook his head. "Dodge City."

"Caldwell's closer," Miller said.

Mathew nodded. "Caldwell pretty much closed the cattle market after last season." Caldwell lay in Kansas just across the border from the Indian Territory. Mathew had trailed herds there back in 1879 and 1880, but that wild burg made Abilene or Ellsworth look like a Quaker prayer meeting camp. Not too long back, the city marshal of Caldwell had been killed—lynched, in fact, after getting caught trying to rob a bank in Medicine Lodge.

"Well, I could . . ." Miller stopped, shook his head, and waved at Mathew. "Go on. I'm listening."

"Dodge City," Mathew said, "gets more quality buyers from Chicago and Kansas City. Men with thicker checkbooks."

"From what I've heard, Dodge City is not exactly tame," Miller said.

"No cow town is."

Miller had picked up a pencil, began writing some numbers on a past-due notice, spent a minute doing multiplication and long division, then turned the sheet over and did some more ciphering. He studied what he had written, flipped the paper over, checked his work, then wadded the paper into a ball and tossed it toward the wastebasket, but missed. It landed on a mountain of other wadded-up papers.

One of the dogs rose to his feet, stretched, and ambled to a bowl, where it began slopping up water.

"Too much of a risk, Mathew," the banker said at last. "Not enough profit for my bank. Not enough money for *me*. If I were you, I'd sell the ranch while you can. Go back to Memphis. Isn't that where you first met your charming wife? Good city, Memphis. You can eat a lot of catfish."

"I don't like catfish." Mathew stood. Again, Chico Miller did not offer a hand to shake, but went back to his work while Mathew Garth walked out of the bank.

CHAPTER TEN

Janeen Yankowski tapped on the door as Tess Millay was climbing out of the bathtub and toweling herself dry.

"Yes," Tess said.

The stout Polish woman stepped into the room and tilted her head back toward the new part of the house. "Man to see you, ma'am," she said.

Tess rubbed the towel over her hair, lowered it, and said, "A man."

Yankowski shrugged. "Tramp."

"And he wants to see me?" She tossed the towel aside and reached for her undergarments.

"By name."

Men had asked for her by name back in Memphis, sometimes to their eternal regret.

"Where is he?" Tess asked.

"In Mr. Garth's library."

Mathew, Tom, and Lightning—and the entire crew—would be out on the ranges now, skinning dead cattle to salvage their hides along that drift

fence, or maybe beginning the gather. Tess was alone
with only Janeen Yankowski, but she had been alone
many times. In fact, twelve years earlier, she and two
servants had fought off a gang of bandits who had
ridden across the river in some idiotic attempt to
relive those raids old Cheno Cortina, the Red Robber
of the Rio Grande, had tried back in the late 1840s
and during the War Between the States. She wasn't
afraid. She had never been afraid.

"All right, Janeen," Tess said. "Tell him I'll be in
directly. Ask him if he wants a drink of whiskey."

"No need." The servant had already turned and
was closing the door behind her. "Already he helped
himself."

He turned away from the window when Tess
pushed through the door into Mathew's library, and
lifted the glass of whiskey to his leathery face covered
with gray stubble. To call him lean would have been
an understatement. The hat he held in the hand that
did not hold the tumbler of good Scotch was ripped
where the front brim met the already well-ventilated
crown. Patches covered his duck trousers, the suspenders were caked with filth, and a piece of rawhide
was wrapped around the foot of his left boot. He wore
no vest, just a cotton shirt so thin you could practically see through it, and a frayed bandanna of what
once might have passed for yellow silk.

Both the Remington revolver and russet shell belt
strapped around his waist, however, remained clean.

Tess could smell him from here.

Yet she smiled, and pulled the door closed behind her.

"Teeler Lacey," she said warmly.

He seemed shocked, but he returned her smile, revealing only a few black teeth remaining in his gums. Quickly, he finished the whiskey and said, "You remember me." He couldn't quite believe it.

"How long has it been, Teeler?" She showed him the Remington over-and-under derringer she had been hiding in the folds of her dress and dropped it on Mathew's desk as she went to the bottle of Scotch.

"Fifteen, by my recollections," Lacey said. Tess held out the bottle for him, but he shook his head, wiped his mouth, and set the empty glass on the windowsill.

She had seen Teeler Lacey before she had seen Mathew Garth or Cherry Valance or Thomas Dunson. He had come across Clark Donegal's wagon train in the Indian Territory while scouting the best route for Mathew's herd of longhorns—it was Mathew's herd by then, with Dunson coming up from the south with his hired gunmen. Tess and the girls had fed the old trail hand sowbelly, biscuits, beans, and vinegar pie— and he had worked his horse into a lather on the way back to Mathew and the boys to tell them what he had discovered. Mathew and Cherry had called him crazy.

"Mathew and I were on our way to Dallas," she said. She lifted the Scotch, tasted it, and leaned against the desk. To keep that derringer close, just in case. Tess had always been careful, especially when it came to men. "We stopped in Waco, rented a rig, rode out to your place along the Brazos."

"That's right."

"You were married. How is she?"

He frowned hard. "Left me," he said. "Nine years back."

"I'm sorry."

He limped over to the desk, only to remember that he had left the glass on the sill. He looked back for it—it must have seemed like it lay ten miles away—and when he turned back to Tess, she handed him her glass. He took it and gulped it down.

"Lost the place two years later," he said. "Been driftin' ever since."

"I'm sorry, Teeler," she said. "We had not heard."

"Yes'm. Don't matter none." He studied the empty glass, glanced at the bottle near Tess and her derringer. She made no offer. He did not beg. He put the glass on the edge of the desk and cleared his throat.

"How'd y'all fare this winter?"

Tess shrugged. "That remains to be seen."

He nodded and absently slapped his worn-out hat against his worn-out trousers. "Lots of folks in that same per . . . pre . . . per . . ."

"Predicament," Tess said.

"Yes'm."

"Mathew's not here, Teeler," she said to fill the uneasy silence.

"Yes'm. Figured that much. Rode up to the bunkhouse first. Groot wasn't there."

"They're all on the range. West section, I think." She didn't think. She knew exactly where the crews were working that day, at least, where they were supposed to be.

She could see the sudden thought in the man's

pale eyes. He straightened, looked at the closed door, then out the window, then back at Tess Millay.

"How's 'em boys?" he asked suddenly, with excitement.

"Tom?" she asked, but she knew whom Lacey meant.

"Naw. I don't reckon I ever met him. You talked 'bout him, though, when you come to visit me and . . . Helen . . . that time near China Springs. The other one. The one I held for a jiffy."

"He's fine." Tess did not use Lightning's name. "Full grown," she said. "He and Tom both."

"Stampede." Teeler Lacey nodded. "That's what we named him. Stampede. On account it was—"

"Lightning," Tess said stiffly. Yet suddenly she smiled. "I don't know why we didn't change that silly name."

He snorted. "Ain't no sillier than Teeler, ma'am."

She smiled warmly at that and thought about asking Lacey if he would want another drink. But she did not.

"I hear that Mathew might be hirin'," Teeler Lacey said at last.

"Where were you when you heard that?" Tess asked. She wondered how far the news might have spread across the state that Mathew Garth was considering a trail drive to Kansas.

"Sanderson." He waved his old hat in the general direction.

That wasn't too far.

"Sheriff tol' me as he was openin' the door to my cell." He nodded an apology. "Been some lean times of late, ma'am."

"For us all," she said.

"Yes'm. You reckon Mr. Garth . . . that he . . . might

be . . . I'm still a good cowhand, ma'am." He patted his leg. "Yank saber give me a limp when I walk, but no one can ride . . ." He stopped, lowered his head. "Well, ma'am, I'm sorry. Don't mean to brag or nothin'."

"Wait in the bunkhouse, Teeler," she said. "You'll have to ask Mathew or Laredo—Laredo Downs is the foreman here. You remember Laredo, I'm sure."

"Yes'm."

"Mathew leaves the hiring and firing to Laredo these days. Wait in the bunkhouse. It's getting late, and they should be along directly. But I'll have Janeen—that's my house servant—I'll have her fix you up something to eat. Does that suit you, Teeler?"

"To the ground, ma'am." His head bobbed, and he slapped on his hat, which sent dust drifting across Mathew's desk. "Yes'm. But I don't want to put y'all out none. I'll just heat up some coffee whilst I waits . . . iffen that's all right with you."

She said, "Nonsense. Janeen will bring over a plate of food. We don't hire everyone who comes here, Teeler, but no one ever leaves our ranch hungry. You go on now. It's good to see you, Teeler. It's real good to see you."

He limped. The saber had slashed his hip to the bone, if Tess remembered right. When she heard the front door close, she refilled the glass with two fingers of Scotch and sent it down straight—not even caring that Teeler Lacey's filthy hands and mouth had touched that glass just moments earlier. Scotch purified, she told herself, and then she found the cook, gave her orders to warm up the beefsteak, potatoes, biscuit, and coffee and bring a plate to the saddle tramp waiting in the bunkhouse.

* * *

"Will you hire him?" Tess asked.

"It'd be hard not to," Mathew said. He sat behind the desk, going over a ledger book, frowning. "That's up to Laredo, though."

"Laredo's more sentimental than you are," Tess said.

Mathew looked up. "Teeler was good with a gun twenty years ago. Good with a horse. Good with cattle. And he knows the country better than anyone."

Tess shook her head. "Lightning will be on this drive, too."

"So will Tom," Mathew said. "And Groot. Joe Nambel. And anyone else we can hire on."

"You know what I mean, Mathew."

He slammed the cover of the ledger. "We could end that right now, Tess. Tell Lightning that you're not his mother and that I'm not his father. Hell, we raised him. We're the only parents he has ever known. He's not the first kid to be adopted. Hell, Dunson adopted me."

She picked up the derringer she had left on his desk. "You know Tom better than you know Lightning." She looked at the gun. "I know Lightning." Her head shook. "I should have shot Teeler Lacey when I had the chance."

CHAPTER ELEVEN

"What's the pay?" the dark-mustached cowhand asked.

"Thirty a month and found," Mathew answered. He sat at a table on the boardwalk, or what passed for a boardwalk in Dunson City, in front of the Rio Saloon. He drank tea, but he had a bottle of Old Overholt to offer anyone who signed on or made his mark. "Twenty-dollar bonus if the herd brings in better than thirty a head at market."

The bottle of rye whiskey remained full.

"But you don't pay till Dodge City?"

Mathew shrugged. "That's the way things are."

That's the way things had been back when Dunson made that first drive, and he had been pushing five thousand head—*in one herd.* Such a number in 1886 seemed unfathomable. Even the three thousand head Mathew hoped to gather would be larger than most herds being driven north. Two thousand seemed to be the average size of a trail herd these days. But then there was the matter of money. Dunson, of course, had spent the last of his silver just to pay for the roundup. This year, Mathew didn't even have enough cash money to pay the hands doing that.

"And if Indians take the herd," the cowhand said, "or we lose 'em to bushwhackers, or if the country goes broke like it did back in '73 . . . ?"

"Then you lose three months' wages," Mathew said. "And I lose everything."

The man pushed up the brim of his hat. "Garth, my mommy didn't raise no fool." He pushed through the batwing doors, leaving Mathew alone with his un-signed book, a cup of tea that had more dust than liquid, and a full bottle of rye whiskey.

He had expected this to be hard, but maybe not this tough. Mathew had friends, or so he thought, and cowboys usually didn't mind not seeing their pay till the end of trail. There weren't many places to spend it on the trail. He figured he would need to leave three or four, maybe five, men at the ranch to look after things. He had some steady hands, but not enough to get a herd to Kansas.

"So you're hiring?"

Mathew looked up. So lost in thought, he hadn't heard the man approach him. He looked the man over in a quick glance.

Rawhide thin and juniper tough. High-topped stovepipe boots, spurs, chaps, a bib-front shirt of black and red checks, yellow bandanna, gauntlets, and a dun-colored Boss of the Plains Stetson. A Schofield revolver in a cross-belly holster.

The man grinned. "You don't remember me, do you?"

Mathew scratched his nose, then shook his head. "Can't say I do."

"You remember this name? Bradley Rush?"

Again, Mathew had to shake his head.

"I rode with Dunson," he said. "After you."

Mathew looked harder into the man's face. The blue eyes seemed cold, and the man's face had been bronzed by wind and sun, but his hair showed no gray, not even flakes in the mustache.

"Figured you ought to know that," Rush said. "Never been one for secrets."

"That was twenty years ago," Mathew said. "You interested in a job?"

The man smiled, and those blue eyes showed life, not death. "Grew up in Houston," he said. "Killed ten men. Fair fights. But I haven't done anything along those lines since '72." He tugged off one gauntlet and held up his hand for Mathew's inspection.

What Mathew saw was a hand full of calluses and the top two joints of the pinky finger missing. The hand of a working cowhand, not a professional gunman—no matter how Bradley Rush wore his Schofield.

"Rode for the Diamond 10 till the owner sold out in March. Just south of Pleasanton. Been riding the grub line since. Thought I'd see what was going on in New Mexico, maybe Arizona, but then I heard that you were planning to go to Dodge City. That's fine with me."

"What might not be fine is that you won't see a dime till we get to Dodge," Mathew told him, "and if we lose the herd, you're broke as me. It's a gamble."

Bradley Rush reached down and took the pen by the ledger. "Life's a gamble, Garth," he said as he signed his name neatly.

"Can I offer you a drink?" Mathew said, and reached for the bottle.

"No, thanks. I don't drink."

Bandannas pulled over their mouths and noses could not stop their eyes from watering as Mathew and Lightning carried the greasy, stinking skinned carcass of a dead calf to the raging fire. The smell made both men think how they might never look at a fried steak again without vomiting.

Mathew nodded and they swung the dead calf back and forth, picking up momentum, three times, and then released the remains of what might have grown up to be a fine, profitable steer. Orange flames and wretched smoke swallowed the animal as it crashed into the pit, sending sparks showering like Roman candles on the Fourth of July.

He could have been gathering longhorns for the cattle drive, riding with Laredo Downs to the south, or Bradley Rush off to the northeast. That hiring job in town the previous week had netted him three men, Rush, an old Seminole-Negro scout named Blasingame, and one of the vaqueros working with him now. The way Matt figured things, he needed two more men to make the drive. No, three—and even that would leave him a hand or two short, but manageable. Yet if he kept this crew skinning and burning dead cattle, he would lose some of his recent hires. Even Lightning and Tom seemed to be on the verge of telling Mathew to go to hell, that they were riding off to find a decent way to make a living. This, Mathew decided at that moment, would be the last day they would do this miserable chore. Let those "floaters" drifting in from the ranges to the north take over. Better than half of the dead cattle were theirs, anyhow.

Silently, he and Lightning walked back to the drift fence where Tom, Joe Nambel, and four vaqueros worked at skinning more hides. Mathew stopped, staring at the rising dust and hearing the hoofs of a galloping horse. He pulled down the bandanna and spit.

Noon. Sun burning like the hinges of hell. Too hot to be riding a horse that way, and Mathew recognized the rider as Laredo Downs, a man who knew how to treat a good horse in hot weather.

Beside Mathew, Lightning pulled down his bandanna. Tom and Joe Nambel stopped skinning what once had been a fat brindle heifer. Even the four vaqueros stopped to look and stare.

The lathered bay gelding slid to a stop as Laredo pulled hard on the reins. He whipped off his hat, pointed it south, and began talking, out of breath.

"Teeler and me was . . . roundin' up . . . down near the river. Had herded . . . what we'd found . . . into . . . Arroyo Lindo. Come back . . . with ten more head. But what we'd . . . already gathered . . . wasn't there . . . no more."

Beside Mathew, Lightning swore. Mathew said nothing, waited for Laredo to finish.

"Six horses . . . trailed them to the crossin'."

"Rustlers!" Lightning snapped, and started for his horse.

"Hold it," Mathew barked. He looked at Laredo. "Shod or unshod horses."

"What difference does that make?" Lightning said.

"Plenty," Mathew said. Back in the day, even

Thomas Dunson wouldn't begrudge a few cattle to Kickapoos or Lipans. Most of the Indians were gone now, but every now and then some braves would cross the Rio Grande if their wives and children and old men were really hungry.

"Shod," Laredo answered.

Which, Mathew thought, might be different. Shod ponies could mean bandits, white or Mexican or Indian or a mix. But in this day and age, even Kickapoos and Lipans were likely to be riding shod ponies.

"How many cattle?"

"Thirty head."

Mathew spit again. Indians had never stolen that many beeves. And even if they had, thirty head were too much to write off to hungry Indians. He did quick math in his head. Even if cattle would bring only $25 a head in Dodge City, that was a loss of $750. He couldn't afford that, not with debts and bills and loans due in months.

"Where's Teeler?" Mathew asked.

"Crossed the river. Trailin' 'em."

Mathew frowned.

"I told him not to start the ball without us," Laredo said.

With a curt nod, Mathew turned to Joe Nambel and Tom. He glanced at the vaqueros.

"Well," Lightning said behind him. "What the devil are we waiting for?"

Mathew's first inclination was to leave Lightning behind. Let him skin the cattle with Tom and one or two vaqueros, but he knew what would happen if he had ordered that. Lightning, and most likely Tom, too, would leave the two hired hands and follow the posse Mathew would organize. Better, he thought, to keep both of his sons where he could see them.

He spoke to the vaqueros in border Spanish. The oldest of the crew, Juan Quinta, nodded and answered in English. Three would finish skinning the animals while he, Juan Quinta, would ride to tell *la patróna*—what they called Tess—what had happened and then proceed to Dunson City and send a telegraph to the county sheriff.

Not that he could do anything. The rustlers had crossed into Mexico. They were out of the law's hands.

But, Mathew thought, *not mine.*

Riding with purpose, they forded the Rio Grande, flowing high from all the snowmelt but still nothing like the rivers to the north, the Red, the Canadian, the Arkansas. Laredo Downs, having swapped his winded bay for one of the vaquero's blacks, led the way. Teeler Lacey would have no trouble following the trail. A blind man could follow it.

Cattle rustlers couldn't hide their trails, especially not trying to maintain thirty rambunctious, half-wild longhorn steers.

"White men," Laredo Downs said. "Not Mexicans." He was leaning low in the saddle, studying the trail.

"How can you tell?" Tom asked. His voice betrayed him. Mathew smiled. The kid was nervous.

"Don't know the country. Movin' the herd too fast."

A voice running through his head sent a chill up Mathew's spine.

"They know me. Know I'm after them."

Looking up, Mathew saw the eyes of his sons and

his friends, heads turned to look back, staring at him. He sucked in a breath and realized he had spoken those words. Tom and Lightning blinked in surprise. Laredo Downs merely smiled.

Swallowing, Mathew pointed up the creosote- and cactus-lined trail. "How much of a head start now?"

With a shrug, Laredo turned back and stared ahead. "Two, maybe three hours. Teeler and me must've come back to Arroyo Lindo right after they'd lit a shuck." He pointed at the haze in the distance. "My bet, Teeler's already found 'em, just a-waitin' for us."

They kept riding, but smart enough to save their mounts. It was still hot, and Mexicans did not like gringos in their country. They rode at a steady, but not rushed, pace, trying to keep the dust to a minimum.

And while they rode, Mathew did some remembering . . .

"They know me," Dunson said. "Know that it's me who's after 'em."

He reined up his black gelding, removed the dust-coated black hat with his left hand, and wiped the sweat off his forehead. "Damn that Don Diego. Damn Juan Cortina."

Damn, *Mathew Garth thought with a smile,* the whole damn human race.

"Damn," Dunson said, "the whole damn human race."

Over the past seventeen years, Mathew Garth had done a lot of growing up. You grew up quickly in this country. Or they buried you. He had survived, though, and he had to thank Dunson for that.

During those first years back in the 1840s, Don Diego

Agura y Baca and Thomas Dunson had bickered and had fought like two bulls fighting for control of the herd. Sometimes it had almost seemed like a game. Don Diego's men would cross the border, steal horses or cattle, and head back to the sprawling hacienda in Mexico. Dunson would soon return the favor, taking Mathew along with him, teaching him the art of retaliation.

By the time Mathew had turned twenty, most of those raids had ceased as Don Diego conceded his holdings north of the river to Dunson. The two would even meet every now and then for a game of dominoes. Now that Mathew was pushing thirty years old, raiding had returned. Dunson was right, too. This wasn't Don Diego's fault, even if his vaqueros and gunmen and sons were stealing Dunson's cattle. Mathew, like everyone else in Texas, blamed Cheno Cortina, that old Red Robber of the Rio Grande.

His real name was Juan Nepomuceno Cortina Goseacochea, who wasn't old at all, only five or six years older than Mathew.

Since the Mexican War had ended, more white settlers were coming to the Rio Grande Valley. Even when Dunson and Don Diego were challenging each other for authority in the 1840s, Texas, then its own independent nation, and Mexico had disputed the border. Texas, and then the United States after it had annexed the republic, had set the border as the Rio Grande. Mexico claimed the Nueces. The Treaty of Guadalupe had supposedly settled that dispute, making everything official. The border was the Rio Grande.

Cortina objected . . . with guns.

If you listened to Dunson, Cortina was just another Mexican bandito, a cattle rustler, a horse thief, a murdering little punk who deserved nothing more than a rope around his neck. In 1859, he had shot the town marshal in Brownsville, had raided the town, held it for a couple of days before fording the river and returning to Matamoros. But the Cortina War wasn't over, not even after some of John "Rip" Ford's Rangers and U.S. Army troops had routed those Cortinistas on the Rio Grande a few days after Christmas. When Ford's Texans crossed the river in March at a place called La Mesa down in Tamaulipas and drove off what was left of Cortina's men, that had ended the Cortina War.

In Brownsville. In points east. Out here where the Rio Grande began to bend south, things were different. There was no army nearby to help protect anyone who dared to settle in this country, and few Rangers ever made their way this far west of Brownsville.

"I'll horsewhip him first," Dunson said. "Then I'll hang him."

"Cortina has his reasons," Mathew said.

He rode alongside Dunson, as he had been doing for ten years. In those first years, of course, Dunson had kept Mathew behind him, protecting the boy with that barrel chest and thick skull of his.

Dunson turned sharply at the young man riding alongside him. Mathew grinned, but kept his eyes on the trail ahead. It was the first time he had summoned up the nerve to challenge his foster father's iron will.

"That Brownsville marshal deserved a horsewhip and rope himself," Mathew said, still not looking to his left at the big man from England. "He ran roughshod over Cortina's men, beat up one of his riders. Cortina," Mathew repeated, "had his reasons."

"I'm not talking about Cortina," Dunson said, even though he had been. "I'm taking about those damned vermin who stole our cattle."

"They might not be Don Diego's men, either," Laredo Downs called out.

Mathew and Dunson looked ahead. Downs, who had

stopped his horse, pointed south. "Don Diego's spread lies down that way." He kicked his mount back into a walk and rode into an arroyo. "These boys is ridin' east."

"East." Dunson nodded. "Laredo."

Laredo, Texas, and Nuevo Laredo, Tamaulipas, Mexico. One of the oldest crossing points on the Rio Grande. The original village, Villa de San Agustin de Laredo, had to be a hundred years old by then. Of course, it didn't matter what side of the river you were on. Laredo or Nuevo Laredo remained tough, hard, lawless. A man could sell stolen livestock on either side of the border.

Dunson shook his head. "They won't make it to Laredo. They'll just make it to hell."

Thomas Dunson had been right, Mathew remembered as he spurred ahead to take the point with Laredo Downs and Joe Nambel. Back then, Mathew had believed that Thomas Dunson could never be wrong. At least, he had told himself that, much as he had been telling himself that since he had watched Dunson shoot down the first Don Diego vaquero who had challenged him.

Joe Nambel had loped off ahead as Mathew slowed his horse to a trot alongside Laredo.

"What is it?" Mathew asked.

"Joe got to suspicionin'," Laredo answered.

Mathew waited.

"Don't make much sense, do it?" Laredo said. "You cross the border. You steal thirty beeves. And then you drive 'em east. Laredo? Wouldn't you go south? More places to hide. More towns to sell that beef.

More chance of runnin' into some Rurales to back your play."

Mathew shrugged. "Could be they're not interested in beef."

Laredo turned sharply in his saddle. "Then why in hell would they steal thirty head?"

Ten miles from that arroyo south of the border, Dunson, Mathew, Laredo, and the other four men riding with them that time had caught up with the rustlers.

Neither Cortinistas nor riders for Don Diego Agura y Baca. Just bandits, men wearing dusty beards and white cotton, with sugarloaf sombreros, Mexican-made imitations of Colt revolvers, shotguns, and muskets. Five of them and a barefoot, sixteen-year-old boy. Seeing their pursuers, the bandits had left the kid with the cattle and ridden back to meet the challenge.

"Damned fools," Dunson had said, and drawn his Colt.

The fight hadn't amounted to much, Mathew remembered. Laredo Downs had shot the first man out of the saddle, Dunson had taken two. Mathew shot a horse out from underneath one rider, winged another in the shoulder. The cattle had bolted, leaving the barefooted kid gaping as two men covered him while others went to catch up the rustled stock.

Mathew shook off the memory, knew he needed to focus on the present. Thinking, Dunson had often told him, gets a man killed in this country. "Don't think," Dunson would say. "React."

"What you thinkin', Mathew?" Laredo Downs asked

as they came out of the arroyo, following the same path the rustlers and the cattle had taken.

"Not thinking," Mathew answered with a smile at Laredo's timing. "Just trying to forget."

But some things stayed with a man. Forever. The man whose horse had been killed was brought before Dunson with the one Mathew had shot and the kid who didn't even have sandals.

"There's no tree here suitable to hang you from," Dunson said. "So a horsewhipping it will be." He had uncoiled the blacksnake whip.

The one with the dead horse jerked a stiletto from his boot. Mathew couldn't remember who had shot him. Not Dunson, whose hands had been filled with the whip. Not Laredo, either. Certainly not Mathew, who had kept his eyes on the kid. It didn't matter.

The wounded man turned to run. He caught his bullet in the back.

Only the kid remained.

"He was the only man amongst the whole damned bunch," Dunson had said later, back at the ranch near what eventually, after Dunson's death, would become Dunson City.

Mathew would never forget that barefooted kid, how he had looked at the dead men, then back at Dunson, then slowly pulled off his shirt, turned his back to Dunson, and wrapped his hands around the thorny branches of a mesquite. He had taken his thirty lashes less one without one word.

Dunson had left him his horse. Hell, Dunson had even left him two of the beeves that had been rustled.

CHAPTER TWELVE

"Six of 'em," Teeler Lacey said, and pointed.

"That's what we figured," Mathew said.

"Yeah," Laredo said, "but we didn't figure on this."

Mathew nodded. "I know."

From the grove of mesquite and clumps of catclaw, they stared down into the arroyo where the rustlers had stopped the cattle, letting the beeves mill, graze, and drink from a spring that pooled water underneath a shelf of limestone.

"Hell," Lightning said, "most of 'em's sleepin'." He let out a short chuckle. "Musta worn 'em out chasin' 'em so hard."

Which is certainly how things appeared. Two men, a white-haired man with a dirty goatee in dingy cotton and a young boy barely in his teens remained mounted, circling the herd of cattle easily. One of them sang a soft tune. To Mathew's surprise, it was the old man doing the singing. The boy cradled an old fowling piece across the saddle and kept wetting his lips with his tongue. Yet he never looked back at the mesquite and catclaw where Mathew and the others stared down.

Near the spring-fed pool, in the shade, four men lay asleep in their soogans, sombreros covering their heads. A bottle of clear liquid—presumably mescal or tequila—sat on a rock between two of the sleeping figures. The sleeping figures did not stir.

"Somethin's movin' across one of 'em." Joe Nambel pointed at a black speck crawling over the tan duck cotton covering one of the men.

"Tarantula," Teeler Lacey said, and sniggered. "Idiots."

Lightning shot Tom a quick look, but his brother didn't notice. He just stood in his stirrups, rubbing his chin, staring at the scene below. Uncomprehending.

"Well, I'll fix their flints." Lacey began to pull his revolver, but Mathew stopped him.

"No." He sucked in a deep breath, shook his head, and drew the Yellow Boy Winchester from the scabbard. "Let's give them what they want."

"That's a fool's play, Mathew," Laredo said.

"Maybe." Mathew's head bobbed. "But we have to flush out those other four." He tilted his head behind him. "They could be behind us."

"You mean—" Lightning stopped in midsentence. Tom sank back into the saddle and drew his revolver. Lightning looked at his younger brother. "Those aren't men in them bedrolls," he said.

"You just figured that out," Tom said.

Mathew grinned. He doubted if even Tom had realized that until hearing the conversation between Mathew, Lacey, Nambel, and Laredo.

"Teeler," Mathew said. "You and the boys stay here. Laredo, let's pay those boys a visit."

The two Mexicans spread out as Laredo and Mathew descended into the arroyo and rode into the camp. Mathew kept his rifle butted against his thigh, the barrel pointed skyward. Laredo had drawn his revolver and thumbed back the hammer, but kept the barrel aimed at the ground. They reined up. No one spoke.

Mathew had to give the group credit. This part of the country lay miles from nowhere, and if Rurales or Indians or anyone might be in the vicinity, the walls of the arroyo would keep the sound of gunfire from traveling too far. Mathew saw the mesquite thicket lining the top of the arroyo, to his left, but he pretended to pay no attention to that spot. He nodded at the white-haired man.

"¿Habla usted inglés?" Mathew asked.

The old man shrugged and smiled a toothless grin. "Lo dudo," he said, "pero nunca se sabe."

That wasn't the answer Mathew had anticipated. "I doubt it. But you'll never know." It made no sense. Nor did Mathew expect the old man to whip an old Manhattan Colt revolver from behind his back. Yet Mathew was dropping out of the saddle as the old man fired. His knees bent, and he stayed down as the horse bolted down the arroyo, past the kid, past the bedrolls that did not stir. Mathew did not even consider the kid who was drawing a revolver or the old man who had shot at him. Mathew aimed the Winchester at the mesquite at the top of the wall.

Gunfire erupted beside Mathew, and on the other side of the arroyo. Mathew waited, but not for long.

A big man in a black, gold-trimmed sombrero appeared with a shotgun. *"¡Come mierda y muerte!"* he cursed, and died. Mathew put a bullet through the bandit's left cheek. One load of buckshot from the double-barrel blew his foot off as he fell backward. The second round shredded the mesquite branches above him.

Another bandit appeared far to the right of the one Mathew had just killed. Mathew swung the barrel, but was too late. The man, holding a lever-action rifle, spun to his side, dropping the rifle over the arroyo's edge, then falling after it. Joe Nambel had shot that one before Mathew could draw a bead. The tall man somersaulted and landed hard on his back across the Winchester. He did not move.

Mathew's ears rang, and the arroyo smelled of burned gunpowder and dust. Gunfire sounded around him, and he quickly scanned the arroyo and the top banks. The old man was on his knees, clutching his stomach, blood spilling from his lips as he prayed in Spanish. The kid, hand clutching a smoking Remington .44, lay spread-eagled, a small splotch of crimson on his breast, another hole in his forehead. Laredo Downs had dropped to one knee. His revolver smoked in his right hand, while his left hand held the reins to his horse, for Laredo Downs was not about to risk being set afoot anywhere, anytime, and his horse was so well trained that it did not buck or resist, but stood there, ears alert, eyes wide, nostrils flaring, but no threat to run until it felt Laredo's spurs across its flanks.

Six men, Mathew thought. The two left in the arroyo were dead or dying. Mathew had gunned down the one with the shotgun. Joe Nambel had taken care of the one on the other side. He heard more gunfire, and a scream off maybe twenty yards from where Laredo and he had climbed down into the arroyo.

"Got him!" came a voice. Sounded like Lightning, but it could have been anyone, the way Mathew's ears rang. But the voice had not been Mexican. Mathew didn't look that way. That bandit was no longer a threat. Which made five. Only one remained.

He thought: *Unless they lured us here where more outlaws waited.*

No. He jacked another round into the Winchester and saw the unfired cartridge arcing up and over and landing on the ground in the sand. He was getting rusty. He had already levered a fresh round into the chamber. Thirty-plus years ago, Thomas Dunson would have raised hell at him for such a mistake.

"You might need that bullet, Mathew! One bullet can mean the difference between living and dying in this country."

He bent, keeping the rifle level, and instinctively picked up the unfired shell and slipped it into his vest pocket. He could hear the cattle running down the arroyo, frightened into a stampede by the gun blasts. But they would not run too far, and as long as they stayed in the arroyo, they'd be easy to round up.

After they had found the sixth man.

"One more's left!" Laredo Downs yelled. He called up toward those lining the top of the arroyo. "Y'all seen anyone?"

"Maybe he runned off?" Joe Nambel called back.

"Cattle's stampeding, Pa!" Tom yelled.

"Let them run." Mathew's voice sounded odd. He looked up, then heard a short gasp. His eyes landed on the old man.

"¡Qué putada!" The old man straightened, staring skyward, and shook his head. Then he looked at Mathew as the light faded from his eyes, and he sank onto his side, still staring, just not seeing.

A shadow crossed the dead man's face, and Lightning bent over, withdrew a machete from a sheath on the man's side, and tossed the big blade into the sand—just to be careful. As Lightning examined the old man, he suddenly broke out laughing, and pointed to the sandals on the man's feet.

"First he stepped in some doo-doo, then he dies. What a shame."

"Jiminy, Lightning," Tom sang out, "have some respect for the dead."

"Why?" Lightning rose. "He didn't respect none of the living."

Mathew was studying the dead man when something caught his eye. At first he thought it was the tarantula crawling across one of the bedrolls, but then he realized that the tarantula had stopped moving during the gunfire. What had moved wasn't on the first bedroll, where the tarantula remained, but the third, and what he had seen was not a hairy spider but the case-hardened iron of a Colt revolver.

Mathew came up and put a bullet near the bedroll, showering the duck cloth and the battered green sombrero with sand.

"You can die in your sleep," Mathew said. "Or you

can sit up real slow." He switched to Spanish. *"Se llama a la melodía."*

The long-barreled Colt came up slowly, elbow on the sand, then the dark-skinned hand flipped the revolver. It sailed to the next bedroll. Slowly the rest of the figure sat up, the duck cloth and sombrero falling away. The black-bearded man in a fancy blue shirt with a silver crucifix dangling from his neck raised both hands. He shrugged.

Laredo Downs kept his revolver on the man, who seemed to be a few years younger than Mathew. As the man rose and stepped away from the bedrolls, and his revolver, Downs shoved his pistol in the holster and turned to Mathew.

"Well, I'm just a suck-egg mule," he said. "That rapscallion could've gotten us all."

"I doubt that," Mathew said, keeping his rifle trained on the smiling bandit. "But he damned sure could have gotten me."

"What do we do with him, Mathew?" Joe Nambel called out.

"Nothing," Mathew said. "For now. But you, Lightning, and Tom need to catch up to that herd." He called out to his sons, relieved to hear their voices.

"I got one of 'em, Pa!" Lightning shouted. "Shot him deader than he'll ever be."

"You all right?"

"Yeah!" That was Tom. "And you?"

"I'm fine." He could hear now. He could breathe. "Get the cattle. Drive them back here. We need to get across the river and back into Texas as quick as we can."

"What about him?" Laredo lifted his jaw at the one surviving bandit.

Mathew approached him. He never lowered the barrel. "I know you speak English," he said, "and don't tell me otherwise.

The man lowered his hands without asking. "And some French," he said.

Mathew nodded. "So tell me this. Why shouldn't I hang you?"

CHAPTER THIRTEEN

"Horsewhip him," Mathew said.

He had tossed his Winchester to Lightning, picked up the long-barreled Colt the lone surviving rustler had dropped, and shoved that into his waistband.

Teeler Lacey immediately went to the Mexican, but Joe Nambel and Laredo Downs stared at Mathew, who could also feel the eyes of his sons boring into his back.

"You heard me." Mathew's jaw tilted toward Lacey and the Mexican bandit. While Nambel and Laredo moved to help Lacey lash the young rustler to the nearest mesquite, Mathew turned to pick up the blacksnake whip lying on the ground near the empty bedrolls. The whip had given Mathew the idea. He picked it up, loosened it, and walked back to the center of the camp, stopping in front of Tom and Lightning.

"Pa . . ." Tom said.

Mathew turned sharply. "I told you to get the cattle. Before somebody else does. Now get moving."

Neither Tom nor Lightning moved toward their horses, and Mathew didn't push them.

"He would have killed us without hesitation," Mathew tried to explain. "His friends tried to kill us. He stole our cattle. Ask me, a whipping isn't extreme punishment at all."

The bandit let out a Spanish curse, probably from cutting himself on one of the mesquite's thorns as his wrists were lashed to the branches.

"You don't have to watch," Mathew said, his voice becoming more and more hollow. "A horsewhipping is an ugly thing."

Lightning managed a false grin. Tom wet his lips, but said in a detached voice. "We'll watch, Pa."

Mathew turned back to face the Mexican. He took in a deep breath. He remembered . . .

Bunk Kennelly's eyes. Mixed with fear and anger. And the eyes of Thomas Dunson, who held the whip, facing the wrangler whose bad luck had caused a stampede. Three men had died under the hooves that night. They had lost three hundred steers.

Dunson blamed Bunk Kennelly. After all, the weary wrangler had been climbing into his saddle when the rigging on his scabbard broke. The Sharps rifle fell to the ground, discharged, and sent the frightened cattle into a stampede. This was early in the drive. They had yet to reach the Lampasas River. So Dunson said he'd give Kennelly twelve lashes.

When Kennelly refused to turn around, to brace himself against Groot's wagon wheel, Dunson had seemed to brighten at what was about to happen. He lifted the whip.

Kennelly palmed his revolver. So did Dunson. But it was

Mathew who fired first, the ball breaking the wrangler's right shoulder.

Maybe that was Mathew's first rebellion against the old man. He had done it to save Kennelly's life, and Mathew's intervention had certainly angered Thomas Dunson.

The old man had holstered his revolver, handed Groot his whip, and told Kennelly to pack his gear, mount his horse, and ride off. Mathew had never seen Bunk Kennelly again. Sometimes he wondered if the wrangler had made it back to the Rio Grande, or the wound had mortified and killed him. Maybe it would have been quicker had he let Dunson drill the wrangler with a bullet between the eyes.

And later, Cherry Valance had grinned at Mathew, saying he was fast . . . but soft.

"Not that soft, Cherry," Mathew heard himself whisper.

Laredo and Nambel had backed off to the bandit's sides. Teeler Lacey ripped off the back of the young bandit's cotton shirt.

"Oh . . . my . . ."

Mathew heard Tom's voice, and he could see the pained expression on Laredo's face. He let the black-snake fall to the dust, and slowly Mathew walked to the mesquite, past Teeler Lacey, and studied the scars on the rustler's back.

"He's probably just one of 'em Penitentes, Matt," Lacey said.

Mathew felt the bile rising in his throat. No, those scars had not been inflicted in the name of Jesus Christ. This wasn't flagellation.

He recalled the kid that Dunson had lashed

twenty-nine times all those years back. Could this bandit be . . . ?

No, Mathew determined. The teen Dunson had whipped would be in his forties by now. This bandit couldn't be out of his twenties.

"What's your name?" Mathew asked.

"No sabe," the bandit answered.

"All right, No Sabe. I'm giving you a choice. Work for me. Or thirty lashes less one."

"Mathew!" Lacey objected, but Laredo Downs told him to shut the hell up, and Teeler Lacey complied.

Sweat streaked down the young man's forehead as he turned, lifting his chin to avoid one of the mesquite thorns. He couldn't turn that far, but he could see Mathew's face.

"Work for you?" he said in English.

Mathew nodded.

"Doing what?"

Mathew pointed down the arroyo where the cattle had stampeded. "Those beeves are bound for Dodge City. That's in Kansas."

"I know where it is."

"Good. And I figure you also know your way around cattle."

The man's thin lips turned up in a smile. He shrugged as best as he could do, lashed to a mesquite.

"You work for me. You help us drive our cattle to Dodge City."

The bandit's head nodded, and Mathew pulled his barlow knife from his pants pocket, unfolded the blade, and cut the lashings loose. The bandit turned, sucked the blood from a cut just below his left wrist, and straightened.

"Gather your horse, No Sabe," Mathew said. "You'll help my boys bring back the cattle you stole."

No Sabe massaged his wrists. He wet his lips. He asked, "*Dígame.* How much *dinero* is it that you will pay me as one of your vaqueros?"

Mathew snorted. "Pay you?" His head shook. "Money?" A smile stretched across his tired face. "No, No Sabe. You don't get any *dinero.* But you get to live, No Sabe. That's your payment."

As No Sabe and the others found their horses, Mathew slowly returned to the whip and, as he began recoiling it, he said to himself, "Soft, Cherry? I don't think so."

When the rustled livestock had been gathered, they dropped the dead bandits into one hastily dug grave. Dunson would have read over the bodies, but Mathew wanted to get across the river before he had to explain their presence to Rurales. They found the closest ford and crossed back into Texas. It was easiest to find the wagon road and herd the cattle—and the horses the dead no longer needed—toward Dunson City.

When they reached town in the gloaming, Mathew turned his horse back and trotted to Lightning and Tom, riding drag. He hooked a thumb in the general direction of the Rio Saloon and said, "You two thirsty?"

Lightning jerked the dust-coated bandanna from his face. "You serious?"

"No. I'm thirsty." Turning in the saddle, he called out Laredo's name. Riding point, the old cowhand looked back as Mathew waved his hat toward the cattle pens by the railroad tracks—the pens rarely used—then gestured toward the cowboy saloon. Laredo immediately understood and began turning the herd back. Joe Nambel also needed no further instructions. He loped to the pens to open the gate to the nearest shipping pen.

It had been a quiet night at the Rio, the bartender said as he drew foamy, lukewarm beers for the cowhands, sliding them expertly down the bar to the paying customers.

"He gets one, too, Jim," Mathew said, nodding at No Sabe.

"Course he does," the beer-jerker said. "He rides for you."

"You lettin' greasers ride for you, Garth?" a voice called from the batwing doors.

Turning, Mathew lowered the mug he was holding back atop the wet bar and wiped the suds off his face with the dirty sleeve of his shirt. His right hand hung just above the butt of the revolver still tucked inside his waistband. Now it gripped the walnut handle as the man with the drooping mustache and beard stubble, all the color of gunmetal, pushed through the doors. He held a Winchester rifle in his gloved hands.

Mathew thought back to the winter, when he had spoken finally to his sons about the stranger who had intervened in the fracas at the Knuckle Coupler. Months ago, the man on the dodge had worn rags for clothes. His luck, and his wardrobe, had changed down in Mexico.

"You're looking fit, Jess," Mathew told Teveler, but he did not release his grip on the Colt.

The hat, straight out of the Sears, Roebuck and Co. catalog, was black. The band, fancy, hand beaded, and colorful, probably bought—or stolen—from some artisan in Mexico. He wore new boots, silver spurs, gray-striped britches, and a blue silk shirt. A calico bandanna fell loosely across the shirt. His gun rig held what looked like a Colt Lightning—but maybe a Thunderer—butt-forward on his left hip. He was smoking an expensive cigar.

Teveler grinned. "Tequila. Mexican women. Enchiladas. Does a man well in the winter. I hear you might be hirin'."

Mathew pointed toward No Sabe, who stood, slowly drinking his beer, a boot hooked on the brass rail.

"I hire," Mathew said. "Men I trust."

"That don't include me, Garth?" Teveler tossed the cigar into a spittoon.

Mathew's head shook.

"Pa!" Lightning said. "This fella's—"

"I know who he is, Lightning," Mathew said.

"Because I rode with Dunson," Teveler said. "You begrudge me what happened in Abilene after twenty years?"

Mathew smiled. With his left hand, he scratched his nose. "Not for that. Dunson paid you for a job. You didn't quit him." Mathew wasn't about to tell him that he had hired Bradley Rush.

The man's eyes beamed. His head nodded just a little, and he let out a chuckle. "I see. It's them, ahem, other things. Since then. That it?"

"That's it." There might have been a little more, Mathew thought, which Tess would probably remind him of back at the ranch. But the more he thought of it, the more he realized that he wasn't lying to the gunman.

"It's seven hundred, eight hundred miles to get that herd to Dodge, Teveler," Mathew said. "Across Texas, the Nations, and Kansas. I can't risk having Rangers, marshals, or county sheriffs stopping me. And, for you, they would. They most certainly would."

"Maybe you ought to drive your herd to Mexico City," Teveler said.

"Maybe I will," Mathew said. "Next time. If I do, I'll send word to you that I'm hiring."

"Well." Teveler brought up the Winchester, but not in any threatening move. He rested the barrel on his left shoulder and kept his finger out of the trigger guard. "I reckon I don't blame you, Garth. And I don't particularly like the smell of greasers anyhow. That's why I had to come up from Mexico. I'd wish you luck, but that would be insincere. See you around, Garth." He spotted Tom and Lightning. "Take care, you two. Don't ride no white horses in thunderstorms."

With that, Jess Teveler was gone, into the darkness, and as Tom and Lightning stared at Mathew, he looked at the gun—the one taken off No Sabe—that his right hand still gripped.

CHAPTER FOURTEEN

"Go ahead and say it, Laredo," Mathew said as he sipped his second tumbler of rye whiskey. "Groot would."

Fifteen minutes had passed since Jess Teveler had ridden away, and the saloon remained quiet. Cowboys usually did not stay quiet in saloons, especially after their third round of drinks. Mathew had felt Laredo's stares since right after the ambush. Now he turned and gave his foreman a hard look.

Laredo Downs looked at Mathew for a moment, then quickly gulped down what remained of his whiskey and set the shot glass down. When the barkeep moved to refill the glass, Laredo put his gloved hand over the top. "Treat the other guys, Billy," Laredo said, and waited until the bartender reached the end of the bar and began to serve Tom, Lightning, Joe Nambel, and No Sabe.

Tilting his head toward those men, Laredo said, "You really ain't gonna pay that Mexican?"

"Pay him with what?" Mathew said. "I'm broke.

Cash money is hard to come by. And if we don't get that herd to Dodge, nobody's going to get paid."

"This ain't like you."

"I think it is."

Laredo's head shook. "Even Dunson didn't cotton to slavery, Mathew. That's what this is. Dunson wouldn't use that Mex the way you plan to."

Mathew grinned. "Because Dunson would have killed him in that arroyo."

He finished his drink, set the glass down, and turned. "Finish those drinks, boys," he said. "Moon's rising, so we can get those cattle to the ranch and grab some supper."

As he crossed the sawdust-coated floor, a figure appeared in front of the batwing doors. Mathew stopped and waited as the man tentatively pushed his way into the Rio. The doors slapped his buttocks, but the man didn't appear to notice. Even though Mathew stood five yards away from the newcomer, he could smell the whiskey on his breath.

"I hear," the man said, "you're hirin'."

He was younger than Mathew Garth by a few years, but nobody would have guessed it. More gray than brown flecked the week's growth of stubble on his face, his eyes appeared rheumy, most of his teeth—what few he had left—were black with rot, and red marks lined his eyes. He seemed to have trouble breathing. He could barely stand.

"John," Mathew said, nodding.

"I wants . . . to . . ." The man paused, took another tentative step, and wiped his mouth with the back of a trembling hand. His clothes were trail worn, dirty, the boots scuffed, no spurs, no gun. Remembering his hat, he quickly swept it off his head, although few men would remove a hat in a saloon. Few men, Mathew thought, would even be caught dead with a hat like that. If you could call it a hat. Maybe it had been, ten years ago.

Life had not been kind to John Meeker Jr.

"I gots," Meeker said, "to go on that drive. You gots to hire me, Garth."

This wasn't what Mathew had expected. He inhaled sharply, held the breath, and turned, nodding an unspoken order to Laredo Downs as he released the air from his lungs.

"Come on, boys," Laredo said. "You, too, No Sabe. Let's get 'em steers out of the pen and on the trail home."

He waited until the batwing doors stopped banging and looked back at the bar, where the bartender was taking the glasses from the bar to the washbasin. Looking back at Meeker, Mathew hooked his thumb toward the bar.

"You want a drink, John?"

Meeker's tongue wet his cracked lips. He kept breathing hard, and all he was doing was just standing there. "I . . ."

Mathew waited.

"I'd . . . be lyin' if I said I didn't. But . . ."

"It's all right, John. We'll make it a beer. One beer. Just one." Mathew led the way, not sure if John Meeker Jr. could even make it to the bar. As he walked, he held up two fingers and nodded at the tapped keg. Reaching the bar, he hooked his right boot on the rail, took off his hat, and tried to think about how he should handle this.

A long minute passed before Meeker found a spot at the end of the bar, a few feet from Mathew. The beers arrived, and Mathew dropped two nickels on the bar. He drank, wiped his mouth, and waited.

Meeker just stared at the beer. He stood, still shaking, now wringing his hands.

"'Bout that job, Garth," he said.

"John." The beer was warm, too bitter. He set the mug over the two nickels. "This drive might bust me before I even get out of this county. Cash is tight." The laugh that escaped surprised him. That it held no joy, on the other hand, did not. "Been accused of turning to slave labor, and"—he picked up the mug and drank half of the beer—"there's truth to that."

Meeker had found the beer in front of him. He tentatively took a sip, more suds than beer, and almost dropped the mug back onto the bar.

"This drive—if we can gather enough cattle to make a drive—is going to be like Dunson's first drive after the war. Pay comes at trail's end. We don't make it, nobody gets paid. All the cash I have is likely to go to supplies. We lose those supplies in a river crossing, a stampede . . ."

"I know . . . how it . . . is."

Mathew finished his beer. He glanced at the bartender, who, being a smart bartender, stayed at the far end of the bar, burying his nose in one of Beadle and Adams's dime novels, a cigarette smoking between his fingers.

"When's the last time you've been on a horse?" he asked, looking back at the drunk.

"Had to ride here and—"

"I don't mean riding from the quarter section you still have. I mean ride. Twelve, fourteen, sixteen hours in the saddle. In the rain. In the blistering sun. Swimming a horse across a flooding river with cattle milling all around you. For eight hundred miles. When, John? How long ago?"

"I . . . well . . . I . . . never." His willpower dissolved, and he grabbed the mug and killed all of the beer, slamming the glass down so hard Mathew—and the bartender—thought it might break.

"You gots . . ." Meeker found another idea. "You gots a wagon, right?"

"Chuck wagon? Sure. That's Groot's job. You remember Groot."

The haggard face tightened. The head nodded. "Groot. Sure. Good man."

Mathew finished his beer and started to turn.

"But you gots a hoodlum wagon, ain't you?"

The hoodlum wagon. Mathew leaned back against the bar. Hoodlum wagons had come about for longer drives, later during the trail-driving era. They were for bigger herds, to store bedrolls, firewood, and extra supplies. Larger, profitable ranches might run a hoodlum wagon. Mathew had to wonder how many ranches would be able to afford a hoodlum wagon this time.

Mathew hadn't even considered a hoodlum wagon . . . until John Meeker Jr. had brought it up. Pushing a herd of fifteen hundred or even two thousand head of cattle was one thing. You could get by, usually, with just the chuck wagon. But Mathew was hoping for three thousand head. And seven to eight hundred miles . . . He would need a hoodlum wagon.

"You need me, Garth. I can drive that wagon for you."

Meeker was right. Hell's fire, Mathew couldn't afford a hoodlum wagon. But he would need one.

He pointed at the empty mug in front of Meeker. "You want another beer, John?"

"No, sir. What I wants . . . is that job."

Mathew let out a little laugh. Shaking his head, he said to himself, "Fast—and just a little soft. Still the same, right, Cherry?"

"What's that, Garth?" Meeker said.

Shaking his head, Mathew stepped away from the bar. "The job's yours, John. Fetch your possibles. Be at the ranch first thing tomorrow morn."

He had the men. Enough, barely, to get three thousand cantankerous longhorns to Dodge City.

Laredo Downs would be trail boss, even if Mathew would be riding with him. Joe Nambel and Teeler Lacey on the point, but Mathew or Laredo could fill in for Lacey when they wanted him to scout ahead. Teeler Lacey knew that country better than the settlers and Indians that lived there. No Sabe and Bradley Rush on the swing, where the herd would begin to swell. The two vaqueros who had been working with him for the past six years, Alvaro Cuevas and Yago Noguerra, would ride the flank. At drag, swallowing all that dust, Mathew had decided to put Lightning, Tom, and John Meeker Jr. Lightning and Tom would argue, but only briefly, because nobody wanted to ride drag. He had considered putting Meeker on the hoodlum wagon, as the drunkard had suggested, but promoted old Negro-Seminole scout, Milt Blasingame, there. Blasingame could also do some scouting in a pinch, and he knew sign language better than even Teeler Lacey, so if they had to barter with Indians in the Nations, that would be a plus. Drag riders were less likely to get killed in a stampede—another reason Mathew's sons were there—and he decided Blasingame could handle a team of mules better than Meeker. Another black man, barely out of his teens, would serve as wrangler, because Joey Corinth knew horses better than most men in this part of the country. Corinth had ridden up to the ranch house two days ago, and Tess had hired him on the spot.

He saw Blasingame and Groot riding into the yard in their wagons, so he set the coffee cup on the barrel by the bunkhouse door and walked out to greet them. Groot wasn't smiling. Nor was the old scout.

Mathew stopped walking, pursed his lips, and waited for the bad news.

"That old skinflint at the mercantile wouldn't give you no credit," Groot said after he had set the chuck wagon's brake. A glance at the back of the hoodlum wagon confirmed that.

"Says he's had to put so many folks on tick, it just ain't worth the risk to him. We got what we could with what money you give us, and Milt and me even put up what little we had. Sorry, Matt. I'm just plumb sorry."

"Not your fault."

He owned, or claimed, more land than most. He had a fine house, good horses, and hardly any hard cash money. And Chico Miller had already turned down his request for a loan. Hiring hands, he had known, would prove difficult—and it had. Back when Dunson had been trying to make that first drive, the war was just over, everyone was broke and willing to gamble. Ten dollars a month, tripled if the herd brought better than fifteen (which it had).

"If we lose the herd," Dunson had said, *"you lose your wages."* And men wanted to go.

Now, in 1886, people wanted money. Not risks.

"Progress," Chico Miller called it.

"We'll empty out the root cellars," Mathew said. "The pie safe. We'll leave just enough grub for Janeen to get by—if I don't have to hire her to ride drag." He smiled to let the two men know he was joking.

Or am I? he thought.

"And Tess," he said.

Groot reached into his back pocket. "But I got us somethin'," he said, smiling. "Drummer sold it to me. I figured it might just help us out on the way north. Here."

The old cook's eyes beamed, and, from the smell on Groot's breath, Mathew knew that this pamphlet wasn't the only thing the drummer had sold to Groot.

Tess brought him coffee that morning as he sat at his desk, poring over the books. He didn't even realize she was in the library until she cleared her throat.

"That's not Shakespeare," she said as he looked up.

He smiled, but it seemed weary, as he held up the pamphlet:

THE GREAT TEXAS CATTLE TRAIL
With MAPS *and* LOCATIONS
*of River Crossings
and Water Holes*
and How to Avoid SAVAGE INDIANS

Written by MAJOR C.J.X. CARTER
——————
*Who rode with Jesse Chisum
and made his fortune "on the hoof,"
at Abilene, Ellsworth, Newton,
Caldwell, Denver, and Dodge City.*

Maps and pamphlets were common. Mathew had seen one about the Oregon Trail, and if he looked in his library, he could probably dig up the *Guide Map of the Great Texas Cattle Trail, from Red River Crossing to the Old Reliable Kansas Pacific Railway*, which he had bought back in 1875. The railroad had published that one, to drum up business, and it was pretty reliable as those things went. But the one Groot had brought from Dunson City . . .

"Shakespeare knew more about the trails than this clown." He tossed the pamphlet into the wastebasket.

"The spelling of Jesse Chisholm's name should have been a clue," Tess said.

"Not to mention that, last time I was in Kansas, Denver wasn't part of the state."

"Coffee?" Tess held the cup toward Mathew, who took it.

"Why did you buy it?"

Mathew laughed. "I didn't. Groot did."

"Groot doesn't read."

"That's right. But this drummer he met at the mercantile said it was gospel, and it only cost him two bits." He sipped the coffee. Janeen Yankowski had made it strong, and, for the Polish servant, pretty damned good. No, Mathew was just tired.

"What time is it?" he asked absently.

Tess started to answer, but then took the ladies' watch that hung from her neck. "Nine fifteen," she said.

"Hell's fire." Mathew finished the coffee, put it on his ledger, not caring if the coffee that spilled would stain some of the figures, and fetched his hat. "Too much work to be done. Didn't mean to spend so much time doing the books and such."

Tess smiled. "I'm sure Colonel C. J. X. Carter told some interesting tales."

He kissed her. "He was only a major."

"That might explain the errors."

Smiling, he walked out of the library.

Days turned into weeks, and those days became hotter while the nights didn't exactly cool down. Mathew Garth wore out one saddle, and one pair of boots, the leather on the tops of the left sides—which rubbed against the saddle—rubbed raw till the uppers split at the seams. Janeen Yankowski stitched them up, a passable job, but she was no cobbler. Mathew couldn't afford a cobbler. He began switching his boots to save wear and tear, the repaired boots one day, his Sunday-go-to-meetings—which had cost him forty-five dollars back when he had money to spare— the next. After two weeks, you could barely tell the difference between those boots.

They road-branded all strays. Like Thomas Dunson twenty years earlier, Mathew told the men that he did not care whose brand the cattle wore, they would all be road-branded with Garth's iron. If someone protested, Mathew would sort things out later. Sorting steers by brands took time, and time was one thing Mathew didn't have.

Yet when Joe Nambel and No Sabe rode up in the twilight as Mathew and the boys were kicking out the cook fire and saddling their horses to return to the ranch, Nambel grinned, "Boys, we've done it."

Every muscle ached, but Mathew showed no pain. "How many?"

"Three thousand, three hundred twenty-nine," Nambel said. He jerked his thumb at the Mexican behind him. "That's his count. Me? I never could count past twenty-one."

"Criminy," Groot said, "I didn't think there was that much beef left in the country."

"Well," No Sabe said, "maybe some came from Mexico. *¿Quién sabe?*"

Most of the men laughed, but not Mathew. He let out a welcome sigh. "All right," he said as he walked toward his horse. "Let's not lose them tonight."

He rode hard back to the ranch, slowing as he saw the rig parked in front of the main house. It was a Columbus phaeton, painted green with a gold stripe, a canopy top with red curtains, and headlamps on both sides. Only one man in the county had a rig like that. Besides, even if he didn't recognize the buggy, he knew who had come calling. The two Olde English Bulldogges lying in the front, whimpering at the sound of coyotes yipping off in the distance, were a dead giveaway.

CHAPTER FIFTEEN

Hanging his hat on the corner rack in his library, Mathew hooked a thumb toward the door. "Your dogs are outside."

"Don't worry, Garth," Chico Miller said. He sat behind Mathew's desk, his Congress gaiters propped up on the desktop, puffing one of his imported cigars while holding a snifter of brandy in his right hand. "I didn't bring them curs to bait your bulls."

"But coyot's outside are scaring them. The coyot's this far from town, they might give them more than just scars." Mathew remembered the scars on the dogs' hides, how Miller had explained that coyotes would lure those big bulldogs into an arroyo and ambush them.

"The dogs go everywhere with me, Garth," Miller said. "And after four set-tos with coyotes, they won't be running off anywhere. They'll just sit in my rig till I come outside and take them home."

Tess, sitting in a corner, rose. She held a snifter, too, but hers had been barely touched.

"The boys?" she asked.

"They'll be along directly."

Miller pointed his cigar at Mathew. Ash fell onto the floor. "Where are your boots?"

Mathew stood in his stocking feet. "Your dogs didn't just sit in your fancy buggy. They laid a trap for me."

The banker laughed. Slowly, he dragged his feet off the desk, put the cigar in an ashtray, and stood. "Before you ask me to clean the dung off your boots and kick me out of your house, you might want to offer me another drink." He fished a cigar from his coat pocket. "And I'll offer you a fine cigar. And a deal."

They had moved to the dining room, allowed Janeen Yankowski to retire for the evening after pouring the last of the coffee. Outside, Mathew heard the riders coming in—their laughter, their curses carrying in the night air—and knew, with relief, that Tom and Lightning would take their supper in the bunkhouse with the rest of the boys.

Mathew had washed up, changed his trail duds for canvas britches, a calico shirt, new socks, and his pair of boots that did not have dog manure on the bottoms. Now he sat next to Chico Miller, with Tess on the other side of the table.

"I was a bit hasty," the banker said, "in my evaluation of the cattle market. The sorry food and lousy whiskey in this godforsaken country must be destroying my mind. And the heat. And the cold."

Mathew waited.

"Supply and demand, Mathew. It's all about supply and demand."

Mathew looked across the table at Tess, then faced Miller again.

"This country still needs beef, Garth. You've got beef. Most outfits don't. They lost it all, or too much of it, in the blizzards." The banker had hoisted his valise onto the tabletop. Now he reached in it and pulled out a newspaper. He slapped it, unfolded, on the table.

"The *Kansas City Times*." He expounded no further. Another paper came out. *"Ford County Globe."* Another paper. *"Chicago Inter Ocean."* And one more. "The *New York Herald-Examiner.*" His hand reached back into the grip and came out with several thin yellow slips of papers. Telegraphs.

These he held up for Mathew to glance at but did not drop them on the table. "And I've been burning the telegraph wires with some men I know on the stock exchange. Cattle prices dropped last year to three-sixteen a hundredweight. That's a loss of fifty-plus percent from what it was back in '84. But people still eat. And they want beef. Not pig meat. Not mutton." He dropped the telegraphs back inside the valise. "At your lovely Dodge City two weeks ago"— Miller pointed a beefy finger at the *Ford County Globe*, a daily paper published in the Kansas cow town— "thirty head sold for thirty-one dollars a head. It hasn't hit that mark in years."

Miller fetched another Havana from his coat pocket.

"How much cash do you need to make your drive?"

Mathew felt that tightness in his chest ease, and the shoulders relax. He started to answer, but thought better of it.

"Dunson didn't have any money when we rode

north after the war. Maybe I was the hasty one." He caught Tess's grin, but Miller didn't. He glowered.

"Times have changed since then. This state isn't even under Reconstruction anymore." He waved a meaty palm to silence Mathew. "You have thirteen dollars and sixty-two cents left in your account in my bank. I know the amount of money you owe the mercantile, and even the tab at the Rio Saloon. You have notes due. And I'm guessing that what cash money you have on you, won't get you to San Antonio, let alone Dodge City. This isn't 1866, Garth. You need money. I'm here to offer you a loan of two thousand dollars."

Mathew blinked. It was Tess who asked the next question.

"And what do you want, Chico?"

"Collateral," he answered.

After wetting his lips, Mathew took a sip of the coffee, now cold, and tilted his head toward the front of the house. "We have three thousand, three hundred and twenty-nine longhorns. At even thirty bucks a head, that's . . ."

"A risk," Miller said. He reached for the *Kansas City Times* and tapped on the small print. "Raiders took a herd on its way to Garden City. Only one hundred head. Killed two drovers, wounded three others. Just like what happened to Cummerbund all those years ago."

"Cummerlan," Mathew corrected.

The banker shrugged. "Even if outlaws weren't still riding this country, there are Indians, greedy as a New York banker, and tornados, stampedes, river crossings. I eat steaks, Garth. That's as close as I come to investing in cattle."

"Then what?" Tess asked.

With that grin, Miller again found what he needed in his valise. He slid it across the table toward Matt, then leaned back in his chair, rocking it on the legs, and found a match in another pocket to light his cigar.

As Mathew picked up the document, Tess rose, moved around the table, and put her hands on the edges as she read over Mathew's shoulder. She read only a few lines before her head rose, and those green eyes hardened like diamonds.

"The ranch?" she said.

CHAPTER SIXTEEN

With a wry grin, Chico Miller struck a match on his thumb, and lighted his Havana. He offered one to Mathew, who shook his head, and then held the rejected cigar out to Tess, who simply glared. So the banker stuck that cigar into his coat pocket and puffed a bit on the one in his mouth. Finally, he withdrew the cigar.

"Not all of the ranch, of course. Just this place. The home. The buildings. And the six hundred forty acres specified there."

"Which is worth a damned sight more than two thousand dollars," Tess snapped.

"In good years, maybe." The cigar returned to Miller's mouth.

Mathew said, "I've never seen you smoke a cigar."

The banker laughed. Now the cigar went into an ashtray. Pressing the tips of his fingers together, he began to explain. "It's this way, friends. A bank has investors. You know that, Garth. You're on the board. I'd love to just buy an interest in your herd, give you the two thousand in cash, but, alas, that's not how I can work things. This isn't my money. It belongs to José Jiminez and Dooley McDermott. It belongs to Mayor Boone and even the Widow Morgan. That's how banks operate. I barely have enough money to pay for the room I rent in the hotel. But it's a good offer. Two thousand dollars. Cash on the barrelhead. And you've made that drive . . . how many times, Mathew?"

Mathew shrugged.

"Did you ever not make money on a drive?"

"I was never short on cash to begin a drive," he answered.

"That's not my fault. Or the bank's."

Mathew shot a glance at Tess, whose eyes continued to burn. Again, he scratched his nose and said, "I couldn't get credit at Hansen's mercantile."

"That's not my fault, either," the banker said as he reached for his cigar.

"I wonder," Mathew said.

The banker's hand froze over the end of his Havana. Looking up, he said, "What do you mean by that?"

But Mathew did not answer. He was looking at Tess, only now his wife was staring at him. They did not speak. After two decades as man and wife, they knew each other well enough that, sometimes, words were not required.

It was Tess, still holding the agreement, who grinned as she returned to document to Chico Miller. He frowned as he took the papers, leaving his cigar in the ashtray, his smug countenance suddenly replaced by one of rejection, disappointment.

Yet as soon as Tess laid the document on the desk,

she reached over and withdrew the nib pen from its holder. Smiling, Tess handed the pen to Mathew, who took it in his right hand and walked around the desk. He picked up the contract, read it, then placed it on the desktop and dipped the pen in the inkwell. His signature was florid, almost ladylike, and after dating the document, he returned the pen to the holder and lifted the paper, blowing on the ink to dry.

"All right, Chico," he said, handing the papers to the banker. "I've made deals with the devil before. Here's your agreement. Now let's see that cash."

What was it Dunson had told the men before they signed on? *"Signing on means you agree to finish. Nobody quits. Understand that. No one. Not me. Not Mathew. Not any of you. We see this thing through . . . to the finish. I never have tolerated a quitter. I certainly won't now."*

Something like that, anyhow. Too many years had passed for Mathew to remember the words as Thomas Dunson had spoken them then in this very bunkhouse.

Mathew told himself that he was not Tom Dunson. Then he spoke to the men gathered in the bunkhouse.

"Get killed on this drive, your kin will be paid in full. If you have any kin. But quit . . . quit at any time between once you've signed your name or made your mark and when we reach Dodge City . . . Quit?" He shook his pay. "You lose all your pay. And as I've told all of you, if we lose the herd, you lose your pay. I want to make that clear."

Sitting with his boots on the table, and those spurs digging into the wood, Groot chuckled. "So what you're tellin' us is that it could be more profitable for us iffen we get kilt."

Everyone laughed, and even Mathew smiled.

The banter continued.

"Is that why we got the hoodlum wagon?" Joe Nambel asked. "To haul caskets."

Groot fired back. "Nah, each man carries his own casket. It's what we call your soogans, and it's tied right behind your cantle."

"For sleeping at night," Nambel sang, "or sleeping forever."

"Sounds fine to me," Milt Blasingame said. "Just bury me where I fall, boys. It don't even have to be six feet deep."

"You sound like a preacher, Milt," Joey Corinth, the young wrangler, said.

With a snigger, the old army scout turned to verse, which, to Mathew's surprise, he recognized.

> *"He prayeth best, who loveth best*
> *All things both great and small;*
> *For the dear God who loveth us,*
> *He made and loveth all."*

"Coleridge," Mathew said, but no one heard. Not that anyone would have understood. Except Milt Blasingame. Or Bradley Rush.

"All right, boys. Sign on and draw your pay." He dipped the pen in the inkwell and stepped back from the register. No Sabe was the first to sign his name. When he did, Mathew held out a double eagle.

"What is this?" the Mexican said.

"What I owe you," Mathew said.

"But you said . . ." He stared at the gold coin as if he had never seen one before. Maybe he hadn't.

"Forget what I said. You draw wages. They ended slavery in this country twenty-one years ago." A thought ran through his head: *Was I fighting for slavery while I was riding with Nathan Bedford Forrest?* He looked over at Milt Blasingame, who would be driving the hoodlum wagon, and Joey Corinth, the young wrangler. No Sabe stepped away from the table, still staring at the coin he held in his hand. Mathew looked at the register and smiled.

He would continue to call him No Sabe, but at least now he knew the man's name. The men would be able to get a handle on No Sabe a lot better than Maaravi Abioye Babatunde y Kaden. "You're being paid," Mathew told them, "what I owe you. So you're not obligated to make this drive. Walk out now, there will still be work for you when we get back." The last sentence was something he recalled Dunson telling the men, and those words he had not forgotten or misremembered.

Groot—who had signed on first all those years ago—kept his feet propped on the table, watching the others. They came by, one after the other, making their *X* or a thumbprint or whatever they could, or signing, cursive or crude block letters, their names. One by one. No one walked out of the door, which had not been the case two decades earlier.

Fourteen men, plus Mathew, but Mathew wouldn't be drawing wages. He had decided, however, to go ahead and pay Tom and Lightning. Groot got fifty a month, and Laredo, as foreman, seventy-five. Thirty bucks for each man on the drive. For the roughly three weeks they had been working. Plus the salaries for the four men staying behind at the ranch, and Janeen Yankowski . . . he had already done the math. Leaving Tess with enough money to pay the salaries of the hired help for the three months he expected to be gone, and what he was now paying the trail crew, and just a little bit of cash for Tess, he had already spent one thousand dollars.

Maybe he should have dickered with Chico Miller or held out for five hundred, maybe a thousand more dollars.

He shook away those thoughts—math and budgets and books had always been a nightmare to most ranchers; even Dunson had hated it—and smiled as he shook Bradley Rush's hand and gave him his twenty-dollar gold piece.

One by one, they signed the register and took their cash, even the men staying behind.

This time, Groot was the last one to take his pay, which he immediately handed over to Teeler Lacey, Alvaro Cuevas, and Bradley Rush. At least Cuevas handed the old cook some crumpled greenbacks and a Morgan dollar in change.

Groot shrugged. "Poker," he said. "Don't know why I even play."

"You don't play," Lacey said. "You just lose."

Which got more laughter.

Matt closed the book, took a breath, exhaled, and said, "You're free to go to town tonight. It'll be the last town you'll see for a while."

"If," Joe Nambel said, "you call Dunson City a town."

More laughter.

"But," Mathew put a little edge into his voice, "we finish culling the herd tomorrow. Do your drinking at the Rio. Stay out of the Knuckle Coupler. Because day after tomorrow, come first light, we take those longhorns to Dodge City."

CHAPTER SEVENTEEN

Lightning Garth could make no sense of things. Here they were, last night in Dunson City, and no one could agree on what they ought to be doing, how to be spending that twenty dollars in their britches.

Laredo and Groot hadn't even come to town, but that made sense. Laredo was trail boss, and Lightning knew that he would be going over plans for the drive with Mathew. Groot? Well, that crotchety old belly-cheater would likely be getting in his two cents' worth, too, and, besides, Groot didn't have any money to spend in town. But the new hire, Bradley Rush, he hadn't come to town, either, and Lightning figured Rush would be a man to get to know, to drink with, or head over to Gloria's Palace to have a fine time with her petticoats.

"And here I am," Lightning said as he took a swallow of beer. "With you?"

"You say something?" Tom asked from across the table.

Lightning just shook his head and let out a little chuckle. His brother had barely touched his beer.

Joe Nambel and Teeler Lacey stood at the bar, drinking, laughing, and swapping lies and jokes with the bartender. They might be better company than Tom, Lightning thought, if they weren't so dad-blasted old. But that was it. His only choice. Stay with his brother, or join a couple of old-timers.

The Mexicans in the bunch, No Sabe and Alvaro Cuevas and Yago Noguerra, all going on the trail drive, had hurried off to Mass or to make their confessions or say Hail Marys or whatever they were supposed to be doing before entering the three months of purgatory known as a cattle drive. Two of the vaqueros who were sticking around at the ranch while the real men would be on the drive had joined the other Mexicans at the church. The others staying behind, along with Meeker and a black hired hand called Morrison, had agreed to ride night-herd on the bawling, brawling three thousand longhorns bound for Dodge City, and then some meat-packing plant in Chicago or Kansas City.

The last he had seen that half Negro, half Indian named Blasingame, he was bound for José's Place for some grub. Joey Corinth, the mulatto little wrangler, said he was going to get his hair cut and get a fresh shave, then ride back to the ranch. Like that little runt had any hair on his chin for a razor. Come to think on it, the kid didn't have enough kinky hair on his knob worth cutting, either.

Lightning killed his beer and was standing up, oblivious to Tom's questioning look. "I'm going to Gloria's," he said, but when he turned toward the door, he stopped.

Jess Teveler was walking through the batwing doors.

* * *

"Matt," Laredo Downs was saying, "I don't mean to question you or be contrary or nothin' like that, but"—he tapped a finger on the map Mathew had spread out across the bunkhouse table—"but, as my ma was often sayin', 'You're goin' round your elbow to get to your thumb.'"

Mathew leaned back in the chair, rocking it on the back legs. He studied the old cowhand without comment, waiting.

"Trail them to Fort Concho," Laredo said. "Up to Fort Griffin, pick up the Western Trail, and run 'em all the way to Dodge. That's shorter. Lot shorter. Hardly a body follows the old Chisholm Trail no more, lessen he's headin' to Caldwell or is from the northeastern part of Texas."

Sipping coffee next to Mathew, Groot nodded. "Way we've been doin' it for a spell now."

As if he had to remind Mathew or explain things, Groot kept on talking. That was, Matt thought with a grin, the Groot way.

"Last time you trailed a herd with us was . . . when . . . '78? And that was Ellsworth. Trail's shifted west."

"It was 1880," Mathew said, "and it was Caldwell."

"Sure," Laredo said. "I remember that. But Groot's right. It was a different trail back then. The tick line. That changed ever'thing."

Mathew didn't need anyone to explain the tick line to him. That was one reason—or what bush-whackers used as a reason—for a lot of their activity in Missouri just after the war. Tick fever. Spanish fever. Whatever one called it, the cattle of sodbusters in Missouri and Kansas started dying, seemed like, just after a herd of Texas longhorns passed through. So they put up a quarantine line, saying no Texas herds could come east of that line.

So Sedalia, Missouri, lost the Texas business to Baxter Springs, Kansas. Then Baxter Springs lost it to Abilene. Newton replaced Abilene. Ellsworth took over for Abilene. Newton replaced Ellsworth, and then lost out to Wichita. Caldwell took over from Wichita, and though you might still be able to sell a few head in other Kansas towns, the bulk of the business for the past several years had belonged to Dodge City. Queen of the Cow Towns. Hell on Earth. The Sodom of the West.

"I've been to Dodge City, boys," Mathew had to remind them.

"Yeah," Laredo said, "by train. Lot different in a saddle. You'd be regrettin' 'em extry days and nights." The cowhand drew his finger from Fort Griffin straight north to Dodge City.

Mathew put his pointer finger on the map and began making his own route. "Fort Concho. Fort Belknap. Spanish Fort and Red River Station. Follow the Chisholm Trail up Indian Territory, then take the Cut-Off and drive them straight to Dodge City."

Laredo frowned. Groot spit tobacco juice into an empty coffee cup. Lying on his bunk, Bradley Rush simply buried his nose in a copy of *The Three Musketeers*.

"But why in hell would you want to go that far out of your way?" Laredo asked.

Mathew smiled as he began to roll a cigarette. "That country," he said, "was hit the hardest by the blizzards. The old Chisholm Trail won't get as much cattle. And it hasn't gotten much for four or five years now. More grass. Less competition to see who crosses a river first. The Western Trail runs through Kiowa, Comanche, and Cheyenne country. I'd rather deal with the so-called Civilized Tribes when it comes to bartering."

Laredo glanced at Groot, who shifted his tobacco to the other cheek.

"People expect us to be taking the Western Trail," Mathew added. "That's another reason to use the old Chisholm."

As Laredo pushed up the brim of his hat, he shot Groot a suspicious look, then turned back to Mathew. "You think . . . ?"

Mathew's right hand went up. "I'm not thinking. I'm just playing things safe. We have a lot riding on getting this herd to market. More than ever. More than at any time since Dunson. I'd feel safer if we did the unexpected."

Tobacco juice pinged in Groot's cup. "Followin' three thousand stupid cows ain't the hardest thing in the world to do."

"No," Mathew agreed, "but if anyone has started planning something to happen . . . say . . . here." He tapped the spot between Fort Griffin and Doan's Store on the Western Trail. "Or . . . here . . ." His finger pointed to the western edge of the Indian Territory. "It would take them a spell to catch up with us to the east."

Laredo drew the old .44 from his waist. He laid the old pistol on the table. "Maybe I should clean this . . . before tomorrow."

With a nod, Mathew stood and started to roll up the map. Groot stopped him.

"Somethin' else just occurred to me." He tapped

over Red River Station. "I recollect a grave right around these parts."

"Dunson?" Laredo Downs was incredulous.

Mathew waited for Groot to remove his hand, then he finished rolling up the map, which he tucked underneath his arm, and walked toward the door.

Yes, he thought, *that was another reason.*

"You reckon you're safe here, Jess?" Lightning asked as he poured rye whiskey into the tumbler the bartender had brought over. "Rangers and all?"

They had switched from beer to whiskey. Well, Lightning had. Tom had declined the offer of hard liquor and bought himself another beer.

"Oh, I don't think the Rangers are lookin' for me now." Jess Teveler held up the glass in a toast or salute, then took a sip and wiped his lips with his tongue. "I'm just a workin' cowhand who ran afoul with some rich bloke in San Angelo."

"Well," Lightning said, "I'm plumb sorry Pa wouldn't hire you. He can be a hard rock—"

Teveler's empty hand went up. He kept the rye, however, near his lips.

"Your pa had his reasons. Can't say I blame him. There's a lot at stake here." He shook his head. "And I really wouldn't look forward to swallowing dust all the way up the Western Trail."

"Not the Western—"

This time, Tom cut his brother off. "Lightning." Tom's head shook. Jess Teveler finished his whiskey in two quick swallows. Setting the glass on the table, he reached for the bottle to replenish his rye.

"I'll take one more, boys, and then I'm off. When do you boys ride for Kansas?"

Lightning started to speak, but shrugged, although the act made him uncomfortable.

"Soon," Tom answered. "Still got some road-branding to do."

The whiskey vanished quickly, but this time Jess Teveler didn't refill his glass. Instead, spurs chiming, he pushed back his chair and slowly rose.

"Well, I'm off to take in some horizontal refreshments at Gloria's Palace. Wish you boys luck. Maybe I'll run into you when you get back from Kansas."

As soon as he was gone, Joe Nambel and Teeler Lacey came over, pulling up chairs, eyes on the banging doors and following Teveler's boot-steps outside. Lacey found the rye, refilled his own glass, and held it up toward Lightning.

Joe Nambel merely raised his glass of bourbon to his lips and said tightly, "You boys would do well by staying away from that gent."

"He saved our hide, Joe."

That surprised Lightning. It was Tom Garth who had spoken.

"He's a killer. Rode with Tom Dunson all them years ago."

"So did Bradley Rush," Lightning said. "You want to explain that to us, boys? You two bein' older, wiser, and with college degrees and all from twenty fancy universities back East."

Tom shook his head. If either one of those men had seen the inside of a one-room schoolhouse, he would be surprised.

"Bradley," Lacey said, "killed his men while they was lookin' at him."

"And he ain't had no trouble with nobody since . . . hell . . . I can't remember how far back," Nambel added.

"Reads books, too," Lacey said.

Lightning rose. "You two ain't my keepers. Man done right by me. That's all I know. He done right by me. Else I might be six foot under. I'll see you around."

As he walked toward the exit, Tom rose.

"Where you going, Lightning?" he asked.

Without turning around, Lightning waved a dismissive hand. "Gloria's. We won't see no females till Dodge City."

"Lightning!" Tom called out.

"Yes, Mommie. I hear you." He stopped at the batwing doors. Now, he did look back at his brother and the two cowboys. Just when he had started to feel some kinship with Tom, just moments after that goody-goody kid brother had even defended their friendship—hell, Lightning wasn't even sure he would have called it friendship—with Jess Teveler, now he was all worried and cautious and acting like a nanny or some grandpa.

"Don't worry. I ain't tellin' nobody nothin'."

And he was gone.

BOOK III

CHAPTER EIGHTEEN

"Take them to Kansas, sons."

That's what Mathew said, even if Lightning and Tom were at the back of the herd and had already pulled down the brims of their hats and pulled up their bandannas over their mouths and noses.

"Take them to Kansas."

He knew what he said. But what he heard was, *"Take them to Missouri, Mathew."* Thomas Dunson's voice.

Whipping off their hats and slapping them against their chaps, Lightning, Tom, and Meeker began yipping like coyotes, riding back and forth, getting the longhorns to start moving. Ahead of him, the other cowhands did the same. A cacophony of voices, shouts, curses, most of which proved incomprehensible.

Longhorns. Some of these, no, probably almost every last one of them, a descendant of the first cattle brought to Mexico by Gregorio de Villalobos back in 1591, after Christopher Columbus had deposited some in Santo Domingo back in 1494. Around 1690, a herd numbering roughly two hundred had been trailed to a Texas mission near the Sabine River. Now Mathew Garth had to get these cattle to Dodge City, Kansas.

All steers, all colors—red, yellow, brown, black, orange, white, gray . . . lineback, roan, brindle, mulberry, grulla, and plenty of speckled patterns—all malcontented, stubborn beasts that would hook you with their horns. Those horns, with the curved tips, could span between three and ten feet, tip to tip. Weighing between a thousand and twenty-five hundred pounds. A leathery ton of lean beef, and one piss-poor attitude, on four legs.

His horse circled around, and Mathew raked the sides with his spurs as he raced over toward the three drag riders. Already, the dust seemed blinding, and he had to shout over his sons and the loud bawling of the herd.

"Push them hard!" he yelled, and saw Tom's grim nod that he heard, understood. "Wear them out." His horse stumbled, but righted itself easily, and Mathew shifted his weight in the saddle. "Tired beef are less likely to stampede."

This time, Lightning and Meeker acknowledged him with a nod. Mathew put the spurs to the bay he rode, and loped off to the herd's left. It was a fairly long run, but he knew that the herd would thin out as the day, and then the weeks, slowly rolled by.

Clouds of dust drifted over him, so he pulled up his own bandanna as he rode. Over the clopping of hooves and cries of the longhorns, Mathew could make out a few indistinct voices.

"Ho, cattle. Ho. Ho. Ho.!"

"Get movin', you damned ol' critters. Move, damn you, move."

"Yip, longhorns. Yip. Yip. Yip."

He gave a quick wave as he rode past Joey Corinth, but the black wrangler didn't notice. The kid had his hands full with the remuda. Sixty spare horses, most of those still half-green, and six mules. Each rider had about six horses in his string, and he would use, at least, two a day—on good days. The mules would be for the hoodlum and chuck wagons in case one went lame or got snakebit. That might be unlikely, but Mathew had decided to add them to the remuda, just to play things safe. He had to make this drive. Glancing back as he loped past the remuda, Mathew felt satisfied. Joey Corinth could handle those horses.

Ahead, pulling in front of the lead steers and Laredo Downs, were the two wagons, Blasingame in the hoodlum and Groot in the chuck wagon. They would make it to the first camp well ahead of the herd.

Eight miles a day. That would be good. Mathew wanted to make ten today, just to wear out the longhorns. Twelve would be even better.

As he reached the flank, he slowed his horse to a walk and caught up with Yago Noguerra, who barked out Spanish curses and slapped his sombrero against his leg. The young vaquero, not yet twenty-five, had been riding for Mathew since 1880. The kid's first drive, while he was still in his teens, had been Mathew's last one—till now.

"How are they looking?" Mathew called out over the din.

Noguerra turned in his saddle, and wiped his face—already covered with dust and grime—with the sleeve of his yellow shirt. *"¿Quién sabe, patrón?"* He grinned and looked back at the herd.

"We'll move them fast today, probably tomorrow," Mathew said.

The vaquero answered, *"Sí."*

That was the way people communicated on the Texas-Mexico border. Anglos spoke in English. Mexicans answered in Spanish. Those who had lived in the country long enough—and Matt had for some forty years now—could understand enough of the languages to carry on a conversation.

He patted Noguerra's shoulder. "Bet you'll have to buy another shirt when we reach Dodge City. This one will be black by then."

"Es verdad." Noguerra showed his, still white, and Mathew left the vaquero to his business. Yago Noguerra knew it better than many cowhands in Texas.

"How they looking?" he called out to Bradley Rush.

The former gunman looked across the wide sea of longhorns toward No Sabe, his counterpart on the swing position, then up and down the thick line of hide and horns.

"They'll string out," he said through his already filthy bandanna.

Mathew merely nodded at Teeler Lacey when he reached the point, pleased to see the lavender-colored steer Thunderhead pointing the way. That old mossyhorn had to be twelve years old by now and had guided many a herd to the railheads in Kansas. He had been on Mathew's last drive to Caldwell. Some steers proved keepers, and Thunderhead was one. They always brought him back. Two other steers, a brindle and a black, seemed to be learning quickly.

He was glad to be out of the dust, and kicked the

bay into a gallop until he caught up with Laredo Downs, sitting on a knoll, one leg crooked over the horn of his saddle as he fired up a freshly rolled cigarette.

"Want to turn back?" Laredo grinned and drew deep on the smoke.

"Not if you want to get paid," Mathew said as he reined in the bay.

Laredo exhaled and gestured vaguely to the north with his smoking cigarette. "We get close enough, I'll send Lacey up to check things out round Horsehead Crossin'."

Horsehead Crossing was the one place you wanted to ford the Pecos River, whether on horseback, wagon, or pushing three thousand head of cattle to Kansas.

Although he nodded in agreement, Mathew's voice expressed caution. "We're a long way from the Pecos River, Laredo."

"Don't I know it." Laredo took another drag on his smoke, exhaled, and tilted his head more to the west. "But that black sky don't look promisin'. Even if she dumps a turd float in the Guadalupe Mountains, she could make things mighty damp at the crossin'."

At best, it would take them more than a week to reach Horsehead Crossing.

"We Texans never begrudge a little moisture," Mathew said, but he didn't care much for those darkening skies, either.

"We trail bosses sure do," Laredo said, and smoked some more.

"Twelve miles," Mathew said. "Early start tomorrow. Camp them at Dunson's Corner. I'll meet you there tonight."

The old foreman answered with a nod, and Mathew

loped the bay well to the left of the approaching herd. The last thing he wanted to do was scare the long-horns into running when they hadn't gone a mile.

Turkey buzzards still glided across the blue skies, reminding Mathew of how many cattle still rotted on this country. But sight of the ranch lifted his spirits. He felt it would take him a week just to scrub his body clean of dirt, and he hadn't been riding long. As he trotted the bay into the main yard, another sight made him smile.

"You're not stepping inside this house, Mathew Garth," Tess told him. "Not till you bathe like . . . forever."

He slid from the lathered bay and handed the reins to Miguel Martinez, telling the vaquero, "Saddle up the dun for me, Miguel. Cool this one off before she gets any water."

"*Sí, patrón.*"

Sweeping off his hat, he wiped the sweat and dirt from his forehead. His hair was already plastered. It had to be eighty degrees already, and the sun showed a long way from noon.

"You have everything you need?" he asked.

"Nothing has changed since the last time you asked me that, Mathew." Tess gave him a radiant smile. "Which was three hours ago."

Still, she stepped off the porch and came into his arms, not caring how dirty he was, or that she had just bathed, and kissed him hard. He pulled her closer. Finally, they released, and she stepped back.

"I don't like good-byes," she said, "but I like this."

"Me, too." He nodded at the bunkhouse.

"Juan Quinta knows what to do," he said, and Tess gave him a bemused look. "He's been doing this since Dunson bossed this spread. He can handle anything that comes up." He grinned at her. "So can you. I figure we're in good hands."

She bowed in jest. "Thank you, kind sir."

He pointed west. "John Bellamy is half a day's ride away. I told him I'd pay him seven dollars a head for any of his cattle that I accidentally slapped a road brand on. He's a good man. Can help out, too."

Tess's green eyes darkened, and her eyebrows lowered.

"By God," she said. "You're worried."

Matt's head bobbed. "That I am."

"Three thousand head of cattle. What's that you read to me in that five-penny dreadful you found years ago? 'A trail drive is nothing but two thousand ways to die.' You're the one who should be worried."

Mathew remembered that yellow-backed half-dime novel. Two thousand ways to die? No, there were countless more than that. Each steer had four hoofs, and either one of those could kill a man. So could its horn. Three thousand times five? What was that? It didn't matter, and that was just the start.

Forget Indians. They might steal a few head, charge a toll, maybe even stampede a herd, but since that first drive with Thomas Dunson all those years ago, Mathew had never lost a man, or even had one injured, because of Indians.

But he had buried many, or heard, seen, or read about other casualties on the cattle drives.

Yeah, bushwhackers and trail thieves had killed some. And drunken brawls and/or bad whiskey in trail towns had caused a few other deaths. But the trail drive itself had its own dangers.

Half-broke horses? Mathew had read the Lord's word over hired hands kicked to death, crushed to death when a horse rolled, or bucked off to have their brains bashed in or their necks broken. Lightning. Bad water holes. Or no water holes. Snakebite. You could drown crossing a river. How many cowhands had Mathew buried on some bank? The sun could kill you. Or you might even freeze to death.

He recalled Frank McCoy, twenty-one years old, with a carrot-top head and peach fuzz mustache. A hailstone had killed him back in '73 . . . on the last night before they had arrived in Ellsworth. Those stones, some the size of a big man's balled-up fist, had also killed sixteen horses and a dozen longhorns.

"I am worried," he told her, "about that, too."

She read his mind. "But . . ." She smiled again. "Those rustlers. The ones who stole the steers that you tracked down. The men that No Sabe rode with." Her head shook. "It has been a long time since Don Diego's men or Cortina's boys troubled us from across the border. I think that was just a little fluke."

"I don't," Mathew said.

Tess grew serious.

"And I'm not thinking about south of the border."

She wrapped her arms around him and pulled him close, kissed him hard, and, reluctantly, pulled back. "I have Janeen and Juan and other good men. John Bellamy. Even a few good men in Dunson City. This ranch will take care of itself, Mathew. You take care of yourself."

He pulled on his hat. Miguel Martinez was bringing the dun around.

"Do what you think's best," he told her after he climbed into the saddle. "You're usually right."

"That I am," she said, and they both laughed. Although her laughter died in her throat, and the tears formed in her eyes, as she watched her husband ride through the gate.

CHAPTER NINETEEN

He felt pretty good, not what anyone would consider relaxed, but the tightness in his chest and the straining of his shoulders had lessened. Mathew kept the dun at a trot, one that many riders would consider backbreaking, but he always felt good bouncing in the saddle. And plenty of horsemen considered the trot the easiest for a horse. He covered the ground quickly, crossed the creek, and in good time picked up the trail of cattle—his cattle, and those of neighbors, and strays that had drifted in the winter storms and somehow survived. He, like Thomas Dunson twenty years earlier, had turned a blind eye to the brands those cattle wore, and had slapped his road brand on them all.

He followed the trail north.

A trail marked by Texas longhorns. Three thousand strong. Churning up the ground like some sodbuster's plow. What was it Groot had said?

"Followin' three thousand stupid cows ain't the hardest thing in the world to do."

Certainly not here. It was something to marvel. Maybe a mile wide, although once the herd strung out, that would decrease substantially until it averaged two hundred yards across, sometimes four hundred. As Mathew trotted along, he couldn't see that the trail was narrowing, but he had been in the business long enough to know that it would.

This, of course, was not the Great Texas Cattle, which was now becoming commonly referred to as the Chisholm Trail, although the Indian trader had never carved any trail in Texas—just in Indian Territory and Kansas—and, as far as Mathew knew, had never even owned a longhorn steer. Nor was it the Western Trail, the relatively new route that took cattle into Dodge City and points northward like Ogallala, Nebraska.

Ranches spread all across Texas, so "feeder" trails could be found across southwestern Texas to the country above Houston or even as far east as Nacogdoches. Eventually, though, those trails would converge with the main trail. If you could call it a main trail. Mathew remembered heading up the trail in the 1870s. Cattle, even wiry longhorns, needed grass to eat, so the trail could shift, or widen, depending on the weather. Droughts and floods might shift the trail west or east. Yet by late spring, after a few herds had started north, and easily by summer, the trail was unmistakable.

Hooves and wagon tracks would beat the grass to fine dirt, a chalky or deep brown or red strip surrounded by a sea of grass. Wind and rain would strip away some of that dirt until the trail was something of a valley, marked by the banks of sand left there by the wind, and by white-bleached bones of the animals that had died on the trail. Men, at least, were buried. Usually.

Twelve miles to Dunson's Corner, just a speck on a map with some shade and good water. That was supposed to be their first camp, a long, hard, dusty drive, but manageable, especially seeing how early they had gotten the longhorns moving. Which is why when Mathew reached El Huerto del Borracho, he reined in sharply and cursed. Raking his spurs across the dun's belly, he raced down the ridge.

He could see the herd, a mass of various colors grazing on the open prairie. El Huerto del Borracho was properly named. The Orchard of the Drunkard. Not a damned tree within ten miles of here. Four or more riders appeared to be circling the herd, but Mathew could tell by the tracks that there had been no stampede. He glanced at the sky. Two o'clock maybe. The dun raised dust as Mathew galloped toward the camp. A fire. He saw Groot, apron on, hovering over a coffeepot. Too late for their noon break. The men would have changed horses from the remuda by now, and Groot, Blasingame, and Joey Corinth would be well on their way toward Dunson's Corner—eight miles north of here.

Instead, the way Mathew read things, they were pitching camp . . . here . . . at El Huerto del Borracho.

The dun slid, and Mathew leaped from the saddle before his horse had even stopped completely. He let go of the reins and stormed toward the coffeepot, where the cowboys had gathered. Groot straightened. Laredo, frowning, started toward Mathew, but stopped.

When he got riled, Mathew's face had stopped many a man.

"Four miles!" Mathew whipped off his hat and tossed it at his feet. "Four damned miles. I told you to make for—"

He stopped. He saw the hoodlum wagon off twenty or thirty yards north. And he saw a sight he had seen too many times on a cattle drive. A bedroll covering what appeared to be a man.

"Blasingame?" Mathew asked, his voice tight, all anger in his body released.

Tom picked up the hat, slapped the dust off on his chaps, and offered it to his father, and Laredo Downs nodded.

"Was lightin' out after the noon break," Laredo said. "Axles broke. Both of 'em."

Mathew stared harder at the hoodlum wagon. He could see the axles now, digging into the dirt. Both axles. He wet his lips. Lightning brought him a cup of black coffee. Mathew took the hat, pulled it on his sweaty head, and accepted the cup, blistering hot even through the leather fingers of Mathew's gloves. Joey Corinth gathered the reins to Mathew's dun and led it to the remuda.

"A freak thing," Joe Nambel said.

"Freak my arse," Groot snapped, and sent a river of tobacco juice sizzling in the fire's coals.

As they walked to the hoodlum wagon, Groot—the only one who had actually witnessed the accident—explained what he had seen. The last of the boys had filled their bellies with coffee and biscuits, saddled fresh horses, and ridden back to the herd. Corinth and Blasingame had helped Groot break camp, and then the kid was back leading the remuda out, the mules were hitched to both chuck wagon and hoodlum wagon, and both men set out north.

"I seen it. Back axle just broke off clean in two. That stopped the wagon, and then the front axle musta broke. Wagon lurched over to one side, comin' down the hill and all, mules brayin', and Milt, he lets loose with a curse and a scream, and pitches over the side." He let out with a string of blasphemy.

"Wagon turned over," Laredo said. "We righted it once Teeler, Joe, and me seen it happen. But it had rolled right atop that ol' boy. Neck broke. Skull caved in."

Joe Nambel's voice was scarcely a whisper. "Probably never felt a thing."

"Which is a blessin', I reckon," Laredo said.

They were at the wagon. What supplies and gear had spilled out in the wreck had been haphazardly tossed into the rear of the wagon. Mathew found a whip that must have been overlooked. He picked it up, coiled it, and set it in the driver's box.

"Mules were all right," Laredo said. "Traces broke. We got 'em in the remuda now. But this wagon ain't goin' nowhere."

Mathew could see that for himself. When the wagon overturned, two wheels had been busted, and the side panel splintered. He remembered something else that marked the great cattle trails: the broken-down wagons, some stripped for firewood, or left to rot, the wheels and axles usually taken for spare parts.

Not the axles on Milt Blasingame's Studebaker, though.

"Look at that, Mathew." Groot had dropped to his knees and pointed a crooked finger at the front axle. The finger moved to the rear axle.

"I've had axles break on me afore," Groot said. He

lifted his right hand toward Joe Nambel, the closest one to him, who took the hint and helped pull the old-timer to his feet, knees popping as Groot rose. "Never two at one time, though. And never broke like that."

"Groot's right," Laredo said. "Looks like both were sawed."

Mathew could only nod.

"Not all the way through, of course," said Teeler Lacey, who had just ridden up. "Just enough so the wear and tear would break one of 'em after a spell. Only it broke both. Same time. Fluke thing."

"My arse," Groot repeated. "I don't think murder's ever no fluke thing, Teeler."

"Listen, you ol' biscuit-roller, I didn't—"

Mathew silenced Lacey with a wave of his hand. Groot, who had started to meet Teeler Lacey's challenge, worked instead on his tobacco, and spit on a beetle, which raised its hindquarters, then scurried off into drier country.

"Didn't lose much in the way of supplies," Laredo said. "Some sacks ripped. Think we salvaged most of it, though. But this wagon." He patted the remnants of one of the wheels.

"Did Milt have any kin?" Mathew asked.

The cowboys gathered stared at one another, then at their dusty boots.

"Never mentioned nothin', no one," Groot said after a pause.

"Joey . . . that wrangler . . . he might know," Tom suggested.

Mathew nodded. "Ride out to the remuda, Tom. Ask him. Then I want you to . . . no. Is Yago with the herd?"

"Yeah," Laredo answered.

Mathew told his son: "Spell Yago for me. Send him in."

Yago Noguerra was one of the best riders in the crew. He could ride to the ranch and back and not wear out the horse carrying him both ways.

"All right, Pa." He was hurrying to the picket line of horses.

"Lightning," Mathew said, "get me Milt's bedroll and war bag. I'll see if there's anything about next of kin there."

"That's Milt's soogan over him, Mathew," Laredo said. "There wasn't nothin' wrapped up inside. Not even long johns, slicker, or an extry shirt."

"What are we gonna do 'bout the wagon, boss?" Teeler Lacey asked. "Not meanin' to be disrespectful or nothin'. But . . ."

"That's why I need Yago," Mathew said as he walked to the wagon's tailgate. Lightning was already in the back, sorting through the rolls of soogans and the mostly flour sacks that had been converted into war bags, which cowboys would generally carry from one job to the next, filled with smaller items and sundries that they needed. Razors, socks, spare shirt, soap—as if a cowboy ever needed that—maybe even a toothbrush or tobacco twists or plugs. And keepsakes.

"Do we need an extry wagon?" Lacey asked.

Mathew turned toward Groot for a reply.

"You recollect how things went with Dunson on that drive all 'em years ago? You tell me."

Mathew looked back at Teeler Lacey with an expression that said, *Anything else?*

Lacey had been on that drive. He remembered. Watered-down coffee, or grain burned in a skillet and then used as coffee grounds. Ten sacks of flour. Lacey

had commented that he had been fed better at that
Yankee camp in Rock Island, on the Illinois-Iowa
border, during the six months he had been impris-
oned there in the war.

"All right," Lacey conceded, "I reckon a hoodlum
wagon's a good idea."

"Honorably discharged, but with regret, at Fort
Clark," Mathew said. He squatted by the fire, his back
against the front wheel of the chuck wagon, as he
went through the personal items of Milt Blasingame.
"Tenth of August, 1879." With reverence, Mathew
folded the paper and slipped it into the sack.

"Where's Fort Clark?" Lightning asked.

"Brackettville," Mathew answered, and gave a wave
toward the east.

"Anything else?" Laredo asked.

Mathew's head shook. No letters, no tintypes, no
lockets. Just two packs of Starr Navy chewing tobacco,
shaving needs, a pair of woolen socks, and one scalp.
Mathew had not touched the scalp. He tightened the
drawstring on the war bag and set it beside the wagon
wheel.

"Yago," he told the vaquero as he rose. "I want you
to ride back to *la patróna*. You understand."

"*Sí.*"

"Tell her and Juan Quinta what happened. Tell
them that Milt is dead, that the hoodlum wagon we
have is worthless. We need a new wagon. The Abingdon will have to do." Abingdon, Illinois, made might
good wagons. Besides, the one Mathew referred to
back at the ranch came with tubular steel axles. Let
some sneaking, yellow-backed son of a bitch try to saw

into those. "Have Miguel Martinez drive the wagon. That means he's coming with us, all the way to Dodge City. And I need the two of you back here sometime tonight. We move out at first light."

"*Sí.*" That was another thing Mathew liked about Yago Noguerra. The vaquero wasted no time. He was already hurrying to his blood bay gelding.

As soon as the dust had cleared, Mathew looked at Tom and Lightning, who were digging the grave beside Blasingame's body.

"Fetch me the book," he said. "I'll read over Milt."

CHAPTER TWENTY

A boy, thirteen years old, stands on this burned-over patch of land called Texas. From where he is, the Rio Grande flows, a dust devil twists and turns in the sand only to die almost as quickly as it has materialized. And a rider, wearing a fine jacket and a big sombrero, trots his horse up from the river-bank to the camp the boy shares with a hard man.

The rider is Mexican. The hard man is white, an Englishman. The boy is Mathew Garth. For weeks, he has been traveling south and west with the hard man, leaving behind those horrible memories of his mother, his father, the wagon train, the Indians. Now, almost all he remembers is this hard man, Thomas Dunson.

The boy cannot quite understand the words between the Mexican and the Englishman. Civil, even polite, the words, but the tone is unambiguous, foreboding. Without taking his eyes off the Mexican, Dunson waves his right hand, urging the boy, Mathew Garth, to move away.

Mathew's legs will not work. Utterly fascinated, he stays where he is, watching, listening, waiting, anticipating.

Yet he is unprepared for the speed, the noise, the shock on the Mexican's face and the crimson splotch on his yellow shirt. Mathew has seen death before, but never this close. When the Indians attacked the wagon train, when his parents were butchered, he had been off chasing down a cow. A cow that now Dunson claimed as his own, much as he had claimed this land that they stood on at this moment.

The rights of ownership of this land have led to the drawing of pistols.

The Mexican is dead. Yet Dunson does not holster the massive Colt until he is absolutely certain.

As an eternity of the echoes of that lone gunshot ring about in the boy's ears, he hears Dunson mentioning something about a grave. The Mexican, whose speed has amazed Mathew, had not even gotten off a shot.

Dunson turns, looks down at the boy.

He can catch only snippets.

". . . a Bible . . . wagon . . . near . . . water buckets. I'll . . . read . . . over him."

It was Dunson's Bible that Mathew held now as he stood in front of the cowboys, hats in hands, somber countenances, hardly moving, waiting for Mathew to read from the Good Book, Dunson's book.

He wondered if he could count the times Dunson had brought out that Bible, to read over the men he had killed. Probably not. It wasn't like Dunson was some crazed gunman, like John Wesley Hardin, now rotting behind the brick walls of the Huntsville penitentiary, or Bill Longley, who had been hanged, legally, over in Giddings, Texas, in 1878. No, Dunson always thought he was in the right. Maybe, for much of the time, he had been. Mathew wouldn't judge him, not now.

For the first time, Mathew really looked at the Bible.

THE HOLY BIBLE
Containing the OLD *and* NEW TESTAMENTS:

*Translated out of the original tongues; and with
the former translations diligently compared and revised.*

By HIS MAJESTY'S *Special Command.*

Appointed to be Read in Churches.

Turning the cover, he saw that it had been published by Cambridge University in 1844, a year before Fate had turned Mathew over to Thomas Dunson. "Printed," Mathew read silently, "at the Pitt Press by John W. Parker, Printer to the University."

Bound in red morocco, tooled with beveled, gilted, and gauffered edges, with marbled endpapers. Mathew seemed to remember a blue silk page marker that had a gilt tassel, but that was long gone after more than forty years. He looked for some family history, a personal note, but he had looked many times since he had first fetched that Bible for Thomas Dunson to open after he had killed someone. He had never found anything to tell him anything about the man who had brought him up.

No past. Just a few vague stories about Birkenhead and Liverpool and Mersey . . . and black porter for beer. No family.

"Dunson," Groot had told Mathew more than once, "was not born of woman."

And he remembered another time Dunson had read from his Bible.

A score of years after the first rider for Don Diego Agura y Baca had been buried in the graveyard on what was now Mathew's main ranch. It was on Dunson's legendary drive to Kansas. Mathew had not known any of those men for long, but he remembered their names and, often enough, their faces. José Fernandez came from Matagorda. The one called Walker—"Just Walker," he had told Dunson when he signed on—hung his hat in Lavaca, or so Groot told Mathew later. Joe Sudden. Mathew always wondered if that was the cowhand's real name. Kelsey. If he had a first name, Mathew had long forgotten it. And Maler Rand of Guadalupe. Rand, tall, thin, never smiling. Carpetbaggers had taken his ranch up around Guadalupe after Rand had spent three years in a Yankee prison camp.

They had been the first to rebel against Dunson, challenging the big bear's authority just a few weeks on the trail. They had been the first to die.

Dunson had killed three. Mathew had sent Kelsey and Sudden to their Maker.

When it was over, Dunson had thanked Mathew for joining the fight—although Dunson had called out for Mathew's help. He had told Mathew to have the dead men buried, and the next morning, Dunson had read over the men he had killed—good men, who probably had good sense, who wanted to try for Kansas instead of Missouri.

This Bible. This very same Bible, only now it was in Mathew's hands. And Mathew had not killed Milt Blasingame.

Sighing, Mathew turned to read from the eighth chapter of Romans. And when he had finished, after he had passed the Bible to Groot, to return the Good

Book to its canvas sack and rest in the chuck wagon, Mathew thought of something else.

He spoke, softly:

> *"Oh sleep! it is a gentle thing,*
> *Beloved from pole to pole!*
> *To Mary Queen the praise be given!*
> *She sent the gentle sleep from Heaven,*
> *That slid into my soul."*

Never had he considered himself a man of letters. He could probably count on one hand the number of letters he had actually written. Books to him were ledgers or tally books. Yet once, while Tess was away shopping in San Antonio, and the boys, not even eight years old back then, lay asleep, he had gone to the library and actually pulled a leather-bound book from the shelves. Dickens and Dumas and Lord Byron. Twain and Longfellow and Shakespeare. He called his office a library. It held fifteen books, none of which he had ever cracked a spine. But on that night, he had slid out something by Samuel Taylor Coleridge, sank into his chair with his glass of Scotch. He had read. And he had remembered.

Battered hats returned atop heads damp with sweat, but the faces remained stoic.

Mathew picked up the spade. "Go on," he said, his voice as if coated with sand. "I'll do this . . . alone."

Slowly, the men returned toward the coffee and the wagon and their bedrolls. All but one. Mathew looked up and started to tell Joey Corinth to go on with the others, but the words stopped in his throat. With the death of Milt Blasingame, Joey Corinth was now the only black cowhand left on this drive. Usually, men of color would make up a third of the trail hands. Ex-slaves, hard workers, Mathew had found those men among the best he had ever trailed with. The Mexican vaqueros were more than adept, too. It was the white men, the ex-Confederates—men like Mathew himself—that caused most of the trouble on a drive.

His head tilted to another shovel lying in the mound of dug-up earth.

"Go ahead, Joey," he said. "But I'd put on gloves first. The handle of a shovel is a lot harder than the leather on a rein."

"You checked the axles?" Tom asked. He offered his father a cup of steaming, black coffee—made from Arbuckle's, not burned grain or charred acorns.

Mathew peeled off his gloves, stuck them in the pocket of his chaps, and held the cup carefully. "Yeah."

"And?"

He sipped the coffee. He stared at Bradley Rush, who sat on his soogans, hat pushed back, coffee cup within easy reach, reading from a volume of Shakespeare—or so he had heard Rush tell Joe Nambel. The book was too far away for Mathew to confirm.

"And?" Tom repeated.

His eyes locked on to his son. "You think Groot lied. Or that Laredo imagined things?"

"No, sir. I—"

"They were cut." Again, he studied Bradley Rush, who had ridden with Dunson. He shook off that thought, that nagging suspicion. Hell, Mathew had hired Rush because he . . . well . . . trusted the man. He had told Jess Teveler to keep riding, because he had never, and would never, trust a man like Jess Teveler. This was Texas. This was the West. Men came, and they left their pasts behind them. They could reinvent themselves. By thunder, Mathew had known cowhands who change their names each spring, more than they might change their shirts. Bradley Rush had done nothing to harm Mathew. He had left his gunslinging past back in Houston and turned into a literate, soft-spoken, hardworking cowboy.

So if Bradley Rush had not sawed those axles . . . ?

On the other hand, Bradley Rush had not ridden into Dunson City on that night.

"Ah," Mathew said, and sipped more coffee.

"What?" Tom asked.

"Nothing." He moved toward the chuck wagon, where Groot was setting batter for tomorrow's breakfast.

Some of these men Mathew knew. Some he didn't. Who else? Chico Miller? Mathew sniggered at the thought. Not that he trusted the banker more than he could throw him, but he could not picture that fat, miserable crook crawling on the dirt with a handsaw and sweating for the minutes it would take him to saw two axles not quite in half.

"Well . . ." Tom began.

"Tom," Mathew said. "Those axles could have been sawed a long time ago. Could have been an accident. Could have been a mistake. Axles could have been bound for firewood but got sold instead. We might never know. We lost a good man today. That's something you might want to remember. This isn't some storybook. It's real life. But in one way, we're lucky.

We are. Not Milt Blasingame. You think. You think how things might be if those axles didn't break until a week from now. Or two weeks. Maybe even three. We'd be in a lot worse shape then, with no way to get a spare wagon unless we were near a big enough town. And no Miguel Martinez to take over as a driver."

"I reckon so, Pa," Tom said. "But I also reckon that Milt Blasingame would be in a lot better shape."

CHAPTER TWENTY-ONE

When the moon, maybe at three-quarters full, rose, Mathew roped his night horse from the remuda, saddled it, and rode out to the herd. The day had been hot, yet the night cooled off considerably, and he realized just how pretty this country could be. He had been having some doubts. This close to town—not that Dunson City was much of a town, or that near, actually—he had wondered if maybe he should have hauled Milt Blasingame's body into town. To be buried in the church cemetery, if Milt was Catholic, or in the town boneyard.

No, he decided. He had done right.

Milt Blasingame had said, more or less, that a bed-roll instead of a casket, and the prairie instead of a cemetery was good enough for him. And with the moon shining, the sky clear, El Huerto del Borracho seemed peaceful, pleasant, even beautiful.

The cattle turned restful, far from worn out after only four miles walking today. The breeze came out of the north and west, but Mathew felt no scent of rain, no threat, and the skies remained clear for now, so those thunderheads seen earlier in the day remained distant. Threats, yes. But distant threats.

Even the coyotes did not howl. Respect for the late Milt Blasingame? Mathew wondered. Or perhaps they were back in Dunson City, tormenting those Olde English Bulldogges of Chico Miller's.

Alvaro Cuevas, singing a soft Mexican ballad in his native tongue, rode up toward Mathew, who reined in the liver chestnut gelding he had named Dollar.

"Buenas noches, patrón," Cuevas said.

Mathew nodded. "And to you, Alvaro."

He gestured toward the cattle. "Seem all right tonight."

"Sí. Eso me agrada."

Mathew had to grin at that. "It pleases me as well," he said.

Both men detected the noise at the same time. Faint. Jingling. Maybe the rubbing of leather. And hooves on the ground. Mathew stood in his stirrups for a better look, while young Cuevas turned, stretching his thin neck like a turkey. Alvaro Cuevas had been blessed with good eyesight, and he had to be thirty years Mathew's junior, so he pointed first.

Mathew saw it then. He felt easier now. Glancing at the moon, he figured it to be nine or ten o'clock. A wagon, driven by four mules, had appeared on the rise. A man on a dun horse rode alongside it.

"That would be Miguel Martinez and Yago Noguerra," Mathew said. He could not stop the sigh of relief that exploded from his lungs.

"Bueno," Cuevas said.

"It is good." Mathew sank back into the saddle and nodded at the night herder. "Someone will spell you around midnight. Be careful. Keep singing that pretty song."

He did not spur Dollar, though he wanted to, but knew better than to risk spooking a calm herd of three thousand longhorns. Mathew eased his way from the cattle, rode back to the remuda, and unsaddled the liver chestnut. He placed his saddle among the line of others, the saddle blanket atop it to dry in the night air, and walked back to the glow of the campfire as the horseman and the Abingdon farm wagon pulled up into the camp, the traces of the wagon jingling.

"By . . . golly . . ." Mathew heard Groot's voice as he walked from the horses. "I'll be gol durned."

When he rounded the wagon, Mathew stopped—almost in midstride. He expected to see Miguel Martinez and Yago Noguerra. Turned out, he was only half-right.

"You could say, 'I'm glad to see you, Tess.'" After setting the brake, Tess Millay stepped down from the big wagon. It was a bit of a fall, but she landed on her feet, knees bent, and came up without any loss of balance or dignity.

Mathew Garth said something else.

"Or you could take the Lord's name in vain, I suppose," Tess chided.

"What are you doing here?" Mathew said.

"You needed a hoodlum wagon. There it is. You needed a driver. Here I am."

"I asked for Miguel. Miguel's a boy," Mathew snapped.

"I'm a woman. If you haven't noticed."

"I . . ." He stopped. The men in the camp stared, eyes wide, mouths open. He turned his rage onto Yago.

"I told you . . ." But that was as far as he got.

"And here are a few words you told me, Mathew Garth," Tess said. "You said that I have Janeen and Juan. John Bellamy. You even said, 'This ranch will take care of itself.' And you said, 'Do what you think's best. You're usually right.'"

Mathew stifled the curse. He steadied himself. Drew a breath, held it, exhaled.

"You think this is right?"

"I figured it saves you wages, and that's a good thing. I think Juan Quinta can handle things for three months. And certainly no one would dare to cross Janeen Yankowski. I know how to drive a team. And I want to be close to my sons. You're stuck with me, Mathew."

"Like hell. This is eight hundred miles. Three months. I want you to go home."

"I once left Memphis for Nevada with a man called The Donegal. Remember? That would have been longer than a trail drive to Dodge City."

"And you never made it to Nevada," Mathew pointed out.

"Do you wish I had?"

He stopped, shook his head.

Tess took advantage of his silence. "You know I can handle a team. I drove the Conestoga from Abilene all the way to Red River Station," she said. "I rode with Dunson from the Nations into Kansas."

"I . . ." He found no words. Oh, he had plenty of reasons. He could point to a fresh grave, adorned with a few wildflowers Joey Corinth had found, and a crude cross made from the spokes of one of the busted wagon wheels. Plenty of reasons, solid reasons, irrefutable. Yet no words. And despite every argument that came to mind, he could not deny that he loved to see her.

The moonlight seemed to find her face, accenting it. Her tan skirt was long and full, beneath which he saw just the hint of her white petticoat with the floral designs on the edges. Her blouse was garnet, full sleeved, with black and tan lapels. The three-buttoned jacket she wore was plaid tattersall, with a V-neck, deep French cuffs, and narrow tan band. He could see that she wore gloves, a gray color, or maybe navy, and her hat was straw, shallow brimmed, trimmed with a red ostrich plume and green ribbon bow. She even carried a riding crop.

"This isn't a Sunday picnic, Tess," he said. "You got a trunk in the back for the rest of your wardrobe for the next three months?"

"The wagon bed is empty, Mathew," she said, and those eyes turned harder. "Till we fill it up with what had been in Milt's wagon. Are we going to stand here all night arguing?"

He was about to try that, but then came a shout.

"Ma!" Tom yelled.

"Ma!" Lightning echoed.

The boys, soon to be eighteen and twenty, acted as if they were ten years old again. They raced out of the darkness—they'd probably been answering nature's call—and swept their arms around their mother.

Groot snorted.

Laredo Downs went back to drawing a map in the sand for Teeler Lacey to study.

Bradley Rush broke out his harmonica and began playing "Grandfather's Clock."

"Put your horse in the remuda, Yago," Mathew said. "Joe, I'll help you with the team of mules."

The harmonica wailed. Someone began singing. A few others joined the chorus.

> *"Ninety years without slumbering.*
> *Tick, tock, tick, tock.*
> *His life seconds numbering.*
> *Tick, tock, tick, tock.*
> *It stopped short—never to go again—*
> *When the old man died."*

"Any reason you don't want me to go on this drive?" Tess asked.

Most of the men had gone to sleep, except those night-herding, and Groot, who rarely slept. Mathew sat at the dying fire, Tess across from him.

"Well, I'm past fifty years old," he said. "That means you are . . ."

"I think," she said, "that you know better than going there, Mathew Garth."

He grinned.

After taking the last pull on his cigarette, Mathew flicked the butt into the fire. "Well, then. I can name a few other reasons that won't injure your pride. The Pecos River, for one. The Colorado. The Brazos. The Red. The Canadian. The Arkansas." He pronounced the latter, Ar-KAN-sas, like the Kansans. "Then I can get to hailstorms. Stampedes. Lightning strikes. Lead. Sunstroke. This isn't Memphis, Tess. It'll make the streets of Memphis look like a church social."

"I didn't know Milt Blasingame well." She lifted

her cup of coffee, shook her head, and dumped the
dregs at the edge of the fire ring. "Who am I kidding?
I didn't know him at all. But I think I can cook better
than he can. So I can help Groot."

He could not remember the last time she had
actually cooked anything, but he played things safe.
"Picking up dried dung, cattle now . . . used to be
buffalo—or what else you can find that'll burn when
there's no wood around. Can you handle a spade?"

"A what?"

"Shovel. Most ranches hire a cook who can drive
team. You can. I'll give you that. But how are you
when it comes to handling a shovel?"

She shrugged.

"We made four miles today, Tess," Mathew said
grimly. "We've already had to bury one man."

"You want me to go home?"

"Yes," he said. Then. "No."

Her dark eyes lightened.

"Leaving the ranch with Juan and Janeen worries
me," he said honestly.

"I think they'll be fine. They bark loud." She drew
in a breath, let it go, and said, "We have to make this
drive. You've been nickel and diming things since the
winter, Mathew. I know how tight things are. So when
Yago rode in, told us what had happened, how you
needed him, well, I looked at Miguel, and I saw a
frightened boy. And I saw thirty dollars a month for
three months going to him."

"He'd earn that working at the ranch, too,"
Mathew pointed out.

"But no bonus."

Mathew shrugged. "Fifteen. Thirty. Fifty dollars.
You think that matters?"

"Does the six hundred and forty acres and the buildings you built, Dunson built, we built, matter? Let's put it this way. What if you came up thirty dollars short? You think Chico Miller would give you credit, extend your loan?" She spit. "Not by a damned sight. He wants our home. He's not getting it. I'm staying."

She rose, dropped her empty cup in the wreck pan by Groot's Studebaker, and stretched. He wondered if she planned on sleeping in that outfit, which had to be twenty years old now, but still in pretty good condition.

"I'm also good luck for men I like," she said.

Like Cherry Valance, he almost said, but held that thought. Had he said it, he would have regretted it. And Tess would have never let him forget it.

Besides, now that he sat there, watching her walk across the camp of snoring cowhands, he had to smile. She knelt over Lightning, pulled up his bedroll a bit, leaned over, kissed his forehead. Next she walked on her knees the few feet to Tom. She pushed a bang out of his eyes, patted his shoulder, and gave him a soft peck on his cheek. She rose, stretched, yawned, and walked toward the hoodlum wagon, where her soogans had been rolled out underneath the Abingdon.

He stared at his sleeping sons, then glanced over at his wife. Finally, Mathew Garth stretched out in his own bedroll and looked at the stars, the moon, the endless Texas sky. But what he really saw was just a memory. A mother kissing her sons good night. It lifted his heart.

At last, he fell into a peaceful sleep.

CHAPTER TWENTY-TWO

The Pecos River.

Everyone seemed to talk about the Mississippi, the Missouri, the Colorado far to the west, but few—outside of Texas and New Mexico Territory—mentioned the Pecos.

Really, it wasn't much to look at out in Texas, except around Seminole Canyon, a few miles from where it converged with the Rio Grande. For nine hundred miles, it flowed, usually sixty-five to no more than a hundred feet wide. Except during wet years, it wouldn't be more than seven or ten feet deep. Usually, no one wanted to drink the water. It might taste like pure brine in one spot, and a few miles downstream, turn to iron. Or you'd likely have to sift the sand out before you drank. Maybe you wouldn't get sick. Probably, you would.

If the river didn't kill you.

For it often proved deadly, to cattle, to horses, to men. Even at Horsehead Crossing.

The banks flattened here, and while sandy on both sides—where you wouldn't get ripped by the thorns on the mesquites—at least the bottom here was hard. Try to cross the Pecos anyplace else within a hundred miles, and you risked quicksand.

Wind, cold, brutal, biting, slapped Mathew's face as he rode the black gelding with the two white forefeet up and down the riverbank. He had to shout so that Teeler Lacey and Laredo Downs could hear him. Thunder rolled, rolled, and another streak of lightning lit up the western skies. Four o'clock in the afternoon, but it looked like midnight.

Dropping his reins over the black's neck, Mathew cupped his hands over his mouth and yelled again.

"How . . . is . . . it?"

Laredo heard him this time, although Teeler Lacey did not. Laredo, on a sorrel, jammed a stick into the stream, already swollen from the rains upcountry. "Quicksand!" he shouted. "Here."

"Solid!" Teeler Lacey yelled. He must have heard Laredo's yell. Lacey's steeldust splashed water while making its way back to the western bank.

Horsehead Crossing had been around forever, but crossings changed with the seasons and the flow of the river. It might move upstream or downstream, so you had to play things safe—if you wanted to reach the other side alive.

"Flowin' faster than usual, Mathew," Teeler Lacey said.

And the Pecos always had a savage, swift current.

"Can we get them across?" Mathew asked.

Lacey started to speak, but saw Laredo Downs crossing the river, so he held his tongue. He trotted his horse, reined in, and spit with the wind.

"We best get that herd movin', Mathew," Laredo said. "Pronto. River ain't risin' right now, but there's another turd float comin', and if we ain't got 'em beeves across soon, we'll be waitin' here a spell."

Mathew nodded. "Move 'em out," he said, and spurred his horse to the two wagons.

Groot, Tess, and Joey Corinth had lashed make-shift pontoons—nothing more than juniper logs—there were no cottonwoods or pines in this country—to the sides of the hoodlum and chuck wagon. The wrangler had returned to his horses, leaving Groot and Tess to await orders.

"All right." Mathew paused, wiped his face. It was wet, and not from the Pecos. A fine mist had started to fall. Lightning flashed again. Mathew waited until he heard the thunder, did some quick division in his head, and said, "Sixteen miles away. Moving fast. You're going first, Tess."

She wet her lips. Her nod could barely be seen.

"I can drive if you want me to," Mathew told her.

"You didn't hire me on so you could drive this wagon." Her smile was forced, but she unloosened the brake and snapped the lines to the mules.

"Hi-ya! Hi-ya! C'mon, you damned mules!"

The wagon lurched over mesquite saplings and cheap grass, and Mathew rode alongside, close to Tess. He pointed to the stick that could barely be seen in the darkness and the roiling water.

"That's quicksand over yonder," he yelled. "That's downstream, so the wagon's gonna drift that way. Enter about there." He pointed to a spot about ten yards past a small island in the center of the river, barren except for a few splotches of grass.

"See you on the other side!" she said as the lead mules stepped into the river.

The pontoons helped, and the mules showed strength and determination.

Water filled the inside of his boots, and Mathew reached over to rest his left hand on the pontoon, but only for a minute. Then he felt his horse swimming, and he concentrated on staying in the saddle. Get caught in the river on a day like this, when the river ran wild, and he would find himself with a bedroll for his casket and a stick stuck at the head of the grave serving as his tombstone.

Seventy-five feet. That was the distance here, bank to bank. It felt farther. The current did sweep the wagon toward the quicksand, but fifteen yards before, the mules had found their footing. Moments later, the wheels were on the hard bottom, and the wagon was climbing out of the river. Mathew looked back. Lightning came straight from the blackness toward the ground. One. Two. Three. In less than two seconds. *Sharp lightning,* he had heard Texans call it. The kind that would kill a man.

"You all right?" Mathew yelled over the wind as he circled his horse around toward Tess.

"I'm wet," she said.

The rain had moved from mist to drizzle. Soon it would be a hard, pounding torrent.

"You bring a slicker?"

She gestured toward her grip, a small bag that served as her war bag.

"Best put it on."

Turning in the saddle, he looked across the Pecos and waved his hat, but quickly understood that Groot was already moving the chuck wagon toward the bank. Mathew again looked at Tess and pointed off to the north and east. "Two hundred, maybe three hundred yards, you'll find a clearing. Head there, unhitch the teams. Picket them good till Joey gets across with the remuda. That's where we'll set up camp for tonight. Cold camp. Most likely."

"Lightning and Tom?" she cried out.

"I'll look after them."

Tess swallowed and reached for the brake.

"Wait a minute," he said. He hooked his leg over the horn, reached down, jerked on the leather strap. Carefully, he removed the spur and tossed it into the back of the wagon, then did the same with his other spur. After that, he fetched out his pocketknife and dropped it into the Abingdon's bed. Followed by his gun belt and revolver. Even his Winchester came from the scabbard.

Tess stared. "Superstitious?"

"Careful," Mathew corrected. "Storm's getting closer."

Her head shook. "Not that. I mean the black horse you're riding."

Smiling, Mathew turned back. Groot was already across the Pecos, coming up toward the hoodlum wagon. "That's not superstition, Tess. That's fact. Everybody knows that a pale horse in a thunderstorm draws lightning. See you soon."

He kicked his horse and hurried the black across the Pecos again.

He had crossed rivers in bad weather, but never like this. The river churned as the cattle swam across, pushed hard by drovers cursing, trying to stay in their saddles while the wind roared, lightning flashed, and thunder boomed. Soon, the rain came, icy, cold, each drop feeling like rock salt fired from some jealous husband's double-barreled shotgun. Afternoon, yet you could barely see, except when lightning lit up the sky.

The key, Mathew understood, to any river crossing was to keep the cattle from milling. Longhorns were good on dry land, but in a river, they panicked. They herded close together, swinging their heads, slashing their horns. One tip would tear into a hide, the injured steer would scream and swing its own head. You had to break them up, just ride right into them, and get the dumb critters moving again. Otherwise, they might drown.

Mathew positioned himself and the black near the quicksand. The long stick Laredo had plunged into the bottoms had been swept away. Rain and wind had pasted his clothes to his skin, and he felt freezing. Or maybe he felt like a damned fool, because he had asked Tess if she had a slicker, yet Mathew had not donned his. It remained strapped behind the cantle.

But for a good reason.

He remembered Harker Lockhart, a good-natured cowboy with a melodic voice. That had been in the Nations, back in '70 on the trail to Abilene. They had been crossing the Cimarron during a storm, not as bad as this one, but the Cimarron was wider and deeper that year. Harker Lockhart's horse had lost its footing, and Lockhart had kicked free of the stirrups. He had always bragged that he was the best swimmer in Texas—most cowhands would sink like a horseshoe—and maybe he was. But the water filled his tall stovepipe boots, and the slicker weighted him down.

They had searched two days for his body, but never

found it. Groot had fashioned a tombstone from a sideboard on the wagon.

"Lightnin'! Stop 'em from millin'!"

The shout snapped Mathew from his memories. He turned the black gelding, stood in the stirrups, and strained to see across the herd. A figure on a dun horse—Lightning. Mathew could recognize the horse. Although he had warned the boy about riding a light-colored horse in an electrical storm, Lightning had gone ahead and settled the dun anyway, saying, "What's next, Pa? Hobgoblins and haints?"

Another rider splashed through the churning water. Lightning brightened the sky, burning Mathew's eyes. He had to squeeze them shut as thunder spoke. His horse did a little buck in the river, but Mathew kept his seat, pulled on the reins hard to the left, and the black settled down. When his eyes opened, and his vision adjusted again to the darkness, he found another figure had joined Lightning as they rode their horses into the river, now as black as death.

The new rider wore a tan hat. Mathew could just make it out. He held his breath. Tom.

Thirty yards of cattle separated Mathew from his sons, one by birth, one by, more or less, adoption. If something happened to one, or both, of those boys, he would be powerless to do anything about it. He felt like a liar. Hadn't he assured Tess that he would look after those two?

Rain poured off his hat brim. Another succession of lightning shot across the sky, allowing Mathew brief glimpses. Lightning rode his dun horse straight into the milling herd. Tom put his horse dangerously close to the thrashing longhorns, slapping his hat, leaning in the saddle. One slip and . . .

Yet he didn't slip. Another figure—No Sabe, Mathew thought—joined them. The lightning ceased. Mathew had to wait until he could make out the figures again in the darkness. They were moving away. The cattle had stopped milling, and they reached the shallow part of the Pecos.

The boys had done their job. Which made Mathew realize that he wasn't doing his. He pushed a speckled steer back into line, and let the black swim across the deep part of the river, making sure he stayed away from the quicksand. Again, the black found its footing, and they climbed out of the river. Mathew saw the line of soggy beef heading toward camp, heard the splashing, the bawling, the thunder, the curses of cowboys. A long line of cattle still needed to cross. On the other side of the herd, Lightning and Tom were swimming their horses back across to help move more longhorns to the eastern bank.

He wiped the rain from his face and kicked his horse again into the river.

It would be a long, wet, miserable night.

CHAPTER TWENTY-THREE

No one brought tents on a cattle drive. Where would you store a tent? In the chuck wagon? Hoodlum wagon? No, there just was no room for such a luxury. If it rained, you got wet.

Tess Millay was wet.

She had rolled out her soogans underneath the hoodlum wagon and now lay atop them on her stomach, head propped up in her hands, her elbows in the mud just off the bedroll. At least she was on higher ground. By the chuck wagon, men came inside the makeshift shelter Groot had put up so he could at least get a fire going. They loaded up on coffee and beans and then stepped back into the pouring rain. It wasn't coming down as hard as it had been, but it remained steady, and cold. The lightning flashes had moved far off to the southwest, and the thunder sounded like an ancient rumble.

A pair of boots stopped beside the wheel next to her, and the man wearing those boots squatted, and gloved hands put two coffee cups just out of the rain. The black liquid inside the blue-specked enamel steamed. The man swore softly and then dragged himself underneath the wagon with her. Mathew Garth did not attempt to get onto her soogans. As soaking wet and as muddy as he looked, he likely figured she would have raised hell with him had he tried. Actually, she would have welcomed him, and the heat his body might provide. He picked up one cup and handed it to Tess. The second, he took for himself, and sipped without even blowing on the steaming brew first.

"Now you wish you were back home?" Mathew asked.

Her head shook.

They watched Lightning and Tom, last in the line, get their supper and walk, miserably, into the rain to find some semblance of shelter, somewhere they could eat and drink. Darkness swallowed them.

"They did well," Mathew said. "Both of them."

"I would not have expected otherwise." Tess found the coffee, blew on the lip of the cup, but did not drink. She enjoyed the warmth in her hands too much to move. "Would you?"

"It was no easy chore," he said.

"Did we lose any cattle?"

He shrugged. "Too dark to do a head count. We'll try that in the morning before we move off. But Laredo and Joe Nambel said that if we lost any, it would be probably no more than a few. And no men. No horses, either, according to Joey."

"Well, that's good."

He sniffed, drank. "It's just one river, Tess."

Finally, she lifted the cup and let the warmth flow down her throat, into her stomach. Mathew always bragged about Groot Nadine's coffee. She preferred Janeen's but this was, well, hot.

"Does this remind you of anything?" She turned to see him smile.

"No stampede," he said.

"No. No stampede . . . this time."

"A hoodlum wagon instead of a Conestoga."

She felt warmer now, not just from the coffee. "And we were inside the back of the wagon."

"With a woman having a baby."

She remembered Mathew's voice, screaming at them to get out of the wagon, which had split a wheel and lay crippled with five thousand frightened long-horns running all around it. And then her telling him that they couldn't go anywhere, that he needed to get inside the wagon. He had climbed in over the tailgate.

"Remember what you said when I told you Edna was about to have a baby?"

His shaking head sent raindrops onto her face, but Tess did not mind. "It probably wasn't very polite," he said, and reached down to wipe away the water with the ends of his drenched bandanna. That didn't help much.

"You said something like 'Sweet Jesus,' or 'Great God.' And I said, 'I pray that He is sweet, or that He . . .' No. 'Good God.' That's what you said. And I said, 'I sure hope He's good,' or 'He better be good.'" Another sip of coffee. "Sweet Edna."

Edna hadn't been like most of The Donegal's girls. Quiet and reserved. Ashamed of what she had to do for a living. Never really hung out with most of the women, back in Memphis or on that train to Nevada. Bettymay—now Tess could not remember that girl's last name—had been helping Tess with Edna until the wheel broke, the prairie schooner lurched, and Bettymay broke her arm.

She turned again and stared at her husband, grayer now, though not much heavier. Harder, perhaps. He had been devilishly handsome in those days—still was, at least in Tess's eyes—but on that night, in the rain, in the stampede, twenty years ago, he had been so much like a little boy. Pale. Mouth open. And when Edna had bent down and grabbed his hair with one hand, and dug her nails into the back of his neck with another, he had wailed out questions like a kid, begging to know what he was supposed to do, what he needed to do, what should he do. Then there was the baby, and Tess had wrapped him in some blanket or petticoat or maybe it had been the silk cloth of a dance-hall dress. She couldn't remember. But she had put the baby in Mathew's arms so she could finish, cutting the cord with a pocketknife, cleaning everything up, listening outside to the shots, the curses, the hooves.

And the rain.

"You did good that night, Mathew," she told him.

He set his empty cup in the mud. "You did good," he said, and turned toward her. "The past twenty years, you've done well. Real well."

She let him lean over and kiss her. She pulled him closer and kissed back. Not long. Not long enough, for her, but she was the one who pulled away.

Her emerald eyes sparkled.

"Now do you wish Miguel Martinez was driving your damned hoodlum wagon?" she asked.

He laughed, patted her hand, and crawled from beneath the wagon. The rain had begun to slacken.

* * *

The water was good for the next two days. Then, Texas looked like it hadn't seen moisture since Noah had loaded his ark. This was the country between the Concho rivers and Comanche Springs at Fort Stockton. Barren. Waterless. What the sun did not blister, the wind did. For two days, they saw no water except what was in the barrels on the two wagons and in their own canteens.

Tess had to pull on the lines to stop the mules. Quickly, she set the brake, before digging in her pockets for a handkerchief. As she wiped her eyes, she heard the hooves of a horse that reined up beside her.

"Here."

Blinking, she saw Mathew, his gloved right hand extended toward her. "Salt," he said. "You need it."

She took what she could and put it in her mouth. Her lips mouthed her thanks.

He licked the remnants from his filthy gloves.

"You need a bandanna," he said, his voice raspy. "Should have realized that before." When he began to unloosen his own, she tried to stop him, but he shook her off. "I've a spare or two," he told her, "in my war bag."

She tied the piece of silk around her neck.

"Want some water?" he asked.

Her head shook. A lie, of course. She could have swallowed a quart in one gulp.

His grin must have hurt his chapped lips, but he did not show any discomfort. "Better take a swallow." Now he held out his canteen.

She took a small sip. The warm water and the

salt burned her tongue and throat, but revived her spirits.

"More." His voice came out harder now. "We have water. Drink it."

Well, he was the boss of the herd, so she obeyed him. This time. After stoppering the canteen, she returned it to him. He surprised her by taking a drink himself, and she had to wonder if he did that only for her sake. As he returned the strap of the canteen to his horn, he looked back at the herd. Tess just stared into the endless, flat hell that was known as West Texas. The mountains lay behind them now, and the mesas. Twin Buttes should be ahead of them somewhere, but she saw only sand, cactus, twisted mesquite.

"Is it . . . ?" Just speaking hurt. "Always . . . like this?"

"Yeah." He wiped his mouth. "Here anyway." He made a vague gesture.

"Water up ahead, though," he said. "At Big Lake."

The name alone gave her even more strength. "Big . . . Lake," she said dreamily.

His laugh was cracked. "Don't set your hopes too high, Tess. It ain't that big. And many times, it ain't a lake. But it will be this time. After that big deluge we had back at the Pecos."

He dismounted, held his reins toward her, and when Tess took them, he climbed into the back of the hoodlum wagon, moving over tarps that covered the war bags. He found his own and withdrew a calico cotton bandanna, blue, red, and yellow, and tied it around his own neck. Again, she had to wonder if he did that for her, to make her feel better. Then she decided that she really didn't care. She had water. And salt. And felt a damned sight better.

When he was back in the saddle, he smiled at her and kicked the horse into a trot, heading back to the herd.

Mathew had not lied about Big Lake.

Oh, the lake was big. It covered two sections, probably more, but most of the depression held only cracked earth, scorpions, and bleached bones of horses, cattle, and men.

No river. No ditch. No underground spring. No outlet at all. Big Lake was a playa, holding water, if only briefly, by collecting runoff from a giant rainstorm. In the rainy season, travelers would regularly find water, but during other times, they might find mud, if they were lucky.

Two miles before the giant playa, the longhorns caught the scent of the water. So did the horses in the remuda. Certainly, Tess believed, the mules pulling the hoodlum wagon could smell the water. Riding well ahead of the cattle, Tess had a hard time keeping the mules under control. For a while, it felt as if she and Groot were racing their wagons across the flat, sunbaked land.

Then she saw it, not understanding what it was at first. Shimmering in the distance, reflecting the pale blue sky overhead. And in an instant, she could smell the water herself.

Groot pulled the chuck wagon ahead, parking it briefly at the edge of the playa, where he began to fill the water barrels. "Quick!" he told her when she set the brake. "We needs to get the barrels filled up afore the herd muddies ever'thin' to hell an' gone."

She understood, and used her hat as a ladle, dumping water—rainwater held in this lake that could not have been more than two or three feet deep. When the barrels and extra canteens could hold no more, Groot pointed.

"We'll make camp for the boys at the far end over yonder. Longhorns will muddy this all up before long. Up there, it'll stay clear, plateable."

Plateable? Her mind finally grasped Groot's language. *Palatable.* They took the wagons to the northeasternmost point. No shade. But water, and beyond the water, acres and acres of scorched earth. Tess went about unhitching the mules, letting them cool off before they drank. Then she picketed them with the mules Groot had already picketed from the chuck wagon. She looked well past the playa, back toward the west and south, where Mathew, Lightning, and Tom would be moving the herd. She couldn't see the cattle, the horses, or men. Only the dust that told her that they would be here shortly.

Something shot past her. Tess blinked, not sure. White legs. Sunburned face. She had to blink two or three times before she understood what she had just seen.

It was Groot Nadine, stripped down to his blackened socks and well-ventilated long johns. He was running from the chuck wagon to the water.

He yelled something over his shoulder as he leaped, and laughed, landing with a hard splash in shallow rainwater.

"C'mon!" he bellowed. "Water's damned near perfect!"

CHAPTER TWENTY-FOUR

Texas longhorns, more than three thousand strong, in a shallow playa that stretched across maybe four hundred acres. Sometimes, during the really rainy seasons, that lake would fill the entire two sections— 1,280 acres. Having slaked their thirst, some cattle had moved out of the water to graze, or find what passed for shade in this vast emptiness. Others just stood in the water.

The horses and mules had been watered, too, and two cowhands—Alvaro Cuevas and John Meeker Jr.— remained in the saddle to keep the herd from muddying up all of the lake. Every water barrel, every canteen, had already been filled, and every one would be refilled at dawn the next morning before men and animals pushed on north.

Unless they stayed an extra day.

Tom Garth soaked his bandanna in the coffee cup he had filled with water from Big Lake, and kept dabbing the cotton against his cracked lips. He sat with his back against the rear wheel of the chuck wagon, staring back at the playa. It had to rank among the most amazing sights he had ever seen.

All those cattle . . . the wide lake . . . the endless sky without one cloud . . . the reflection of the longhorns in the blue water, making the herd seem even more enormous than it was . . . and the sinking of the orange globe off in the distant horizon.

An itinerant photographer had brought his wagon, big camera, and those heavy glass plates to Dunson City a year or two back. Tom and Lightning had each paid a dollar to get four tintypes. Lightning had not been impressed with his photograph.

"I ain't left-handed," he had told the photographer.

"The image is always reversed," the photographer, a young man with a pockmarked face and bowler hat, had tried to explain. "But it is a good likeness of you."

"I like the one of my grandpa better," Lightning had said, and gestured toward the portrait hanging in the hotel lobby, where the photographer had set up his temporary studio.

"That is a portrait, sir," said the photographer—he hailed all the way from Baton Rouge, Louisiana, and was making his way to Mesilla, New Mexico Territory—"and merely how the painter imagined your grandfather, sir."

"It looks more like him than this does of me," Lightning had shot back.

"But that is you."

Lightning had rebutted. "A left-handed me."

Tom, on the other hand, had not even noticed the reversed image—but, then, he had not buckled on his gun belt for his portrait. And he had seen the landscapes and buildings and photographs of cowboys and horses and even locomotives that the photographer had tacked up on a board to advertise his abilities. It was too windy to photograph anyone outside, the young man had explained.

Now as Tom watched the cattle as the sun slowly began to set, he felt not one wisp of wind. That Baton Rouge gent would have captured an amazing picture had he been here today.

"We could let the herd and horses water up another day."

Laredo Downs's voice snapped Tom from his daydreaming. He lifted his head and lowered his wet bandanna to see his father, Downs, and Joe Nambel around the fire, sipping hot coffee instead of lukewarm water. Lightning walked up to join the three men, without an invitation, but no one objected.

"We move on tomorrow," Mathew said.

Anyone could see that neither Laredo nor Nambel liked Mathew's answer.

"Those were some hard days on the trail, Mathew," Laredo said. "A rest might do us all some good."

Joe Nambel's head bobbed in agreement. "Sore-footed beeves and horses don't move so good."

"Neither do soggy beef."

No one argued further on that point.

"What about letting the boys take a bath?" Nambel asked.

Mathew sipped coffee, considering the idea for what seemed an hour or more, but probably took only a couple of seconds. His head shook. "Water's for drinking."

"Groot took a bath," Lightning sang out in objection.

Maybe the three older men had not even noticed

that Lightning had joined them, for now they studied Lightning in fierce silence.

At last, Mathew grinned. "Groot needed a bath."

Which brought smiles to the faces of Laredo and Nambel.

"And Ma?"

Now all eyes turned to Tom, who hadn't realized he had spoken loud enough for anyone to hear.

"Well . . ." Tom tried to find his voice. "I'm not saying that Ma needs a bath . . . but . . . well . . . there's water. And . . . well . . . there's water . . ."

"Yeah," Lightning chimed in. "At least Ma should get a bath."

"And . . ." Tom suddenly fell quiet. He knew his mother, even as old as she was, remained strikingly beautiful. And Tom was old enough, experienced enough from his trips to Gloria's Palace, to know that putting one woman with a dozen or so men . . . "Maybe it ain't such a good idea," he said. He tried to think of a lie. "I mean, if you let Ma take a bath, then we'd all have to take a bath. Muddy up the water."

He dabbed his lips with his bandanna.

"Ain't deep water, neither," he added.

"Well," Lightning said. "We'll be in San Angelo directly. Reckon we can all take a bath when we ride into town."

"You won't be riding into town." Mathew spoke sharply. "You'll be staying with the herd."

"But . . . Pa," Lightning whined.

"No buts."

"Boys could use a whiskey," Nambel said.

"I'll buy them all the whiskey they can handle," Mathew said. "In Dodge City. And not before." He emptied the dregs of the coffee by the coals, then sent the tin cup sailing into the wreck pan, which startled Groot as he cut out biscuit dough.

"Criminy, we haven't even reached the Concho River and you boys want baths, whiskeys, and vacation. You hired on to do a job. I'm seeing you to it. The job is to get this herd to Dodge City. Not San Angelo."

"I'm just sayin' . . ." Joe Nambel started, but Mathew cut him off.

"You know San Angelo. Need I say more?"

Lightning shook his head, but had enough sense to keep his trap shut. But Tom figured that he understood. Although he had heard that some priests tried to set up a mission there hundreds of years ago, the town hadn't really been settled until right after the War Between the States, when the Yankee army set up Fort Concho—named after the three rivers— the North, South, and Middle Concho—that made this patch of Texas inhabitable. First, it had been called Saint Angela, or Santa Angela, until that got shortened to San Angela. That stuck for a while until someone pointed out that, in Spanish, San Angela was grammatically incorrect, so the town's name became San Angelo. No matter what it was called, another name seemed more fitting because "saints" had little to do with San Angelo.

Hell Town.

Soldiers fought townsmen, cowboys, and each other on the streets. Cowboys fought each other and sheepherders. Sheepherders fought. Townsmen fought. Gamblers fought each other. Whores fought each other. In a couple of years, the railroad was expected to reach San Angelo, so railroaders could join the fight. Hardly a week passed without a knifing or a shooting. Hardly a night went by without some sort of row in a saloon or out on the streets. Tom could see why his father found it necessary to keep the trail crew out of town. He didn't want to have to post anyone's bail . . . or pay for a funeral.

"What about supplies?" Laredo asked.

Mathew must have been anticipating the question because he answered immediately.

"If we need supplies, Groot will go to town. And only Groot." He paused, reflectively, and changed his mind. "No, your mother will go. With Groot. And me."

Tom figured it out. His mother would get her bath in the privacy of a bathhouse in San Angelo. His father and Groot would be there for protection.

"And when we leave San Angelo," Laredo said, "which direction will we go?"

"Same as I told you before, Laredo. Northeast."

"North is quicker," Nambel said. "The Western Trail, Doan's Store on the Red, and—"

"Northeast," Mathew said. "Jesse Chisholm's trail and Red River Station."

"Hell." Laredo Downs sent his own coffee cup ringing in the wreck pan.

"Hey!" Groot raised his rolling pin. "I can recollect a dropped cup causin' a stampede, Laredo. Quit actin' like some tenderfeet. And you bend one of my cups, and I'll be bendin' your ears back, boy."

If Laredo heard the old cook, he didn't appear to notice. "Why not just take the herd all the way to Missouri, *Mister Dunson*."

"If not for the quarantine, we might just do that."

"Hell's fire, Mathew. You're the hardest rock I know."

"You want out, Laredo, saddle up and ride on."

Laredo stared at the mud on his boots.

"I ain't no quitter, Mathew," he said softly. His head lifted, and he found Groot. "Didn't mean to lose my temper, Groot. C'mon, Joe. Let's spell Meeker and Cuevas. Get a little fresh air."

Usually, Tom Garth found the jingling of spurs musical, relaxing, but not on this evening. It had to be his imagination, but the tune sounded more like a dirge as Joe Nambel and Laredo Downs walked toward the picketed horses.

"Anything you want to say, Lightning?" his father was asking his brother.

"I ain't said nothing, Pa. Just about Ma getting a bath and all."

Mathew did not seem to hear.

"I've said why we're going on the old Chisholm Trail . . . at least till we reach the Cut-Off in the Nations. There won't be as many herds, the grass will be better, and if anyone's following us, they won't be expecting us to take the long way. You savvy that?"

"Why would anyone be following us, Pa?" Lightning asked.

"To kill us, Lightning. To steal the herd."

Tom cleared his throat. His father and brother whirled, eyes boring through his body.

"Well . . . ?" Mathew barked.

Tom had never seen his father like that. Those eyes seemed . . . wild. Like the mad dog they had had to kill a couple of falls back. Or . . .

He felt as if he were back in Dunson City, standing in the lobby of the Dunson City Hotel, looking up at that wonderful portrait of "Thomas Dunson, Empire Builder, Texas Giant."

That man who stood there . . . his father . . . was a stranger.

"I'm going to talk to your mother," Mathew said. "After supper, you two spell Laredo and Joe."

CHAPTER TWENTY-FIVE

Beneath a blazing sun they moved. Slowly, ten miles a day. A muddy stream. A dry arroyo. Nothing to hear but the bawling of steers, the clopping of hooves, the moan of the wind. No one spoke, at least not often. To open your mouth meant to coat your tongue with dirt, even with a bandanna pulled over your nose and mouth.

It was rolling prairie, and the grass, after the rainstorms, meant good grazing for cattle, horses, and mules.

They saw herds of sheep, but Mathew kept the cattle away from those woolies. Every now and then, they even spied a windmill. Once, they even spotted a rough-hewn picket house, a fence, a milch cow, and the beginnings of wheat sprouting from tilled earth. Mathew kept the herd away from the farm and the angry but fearful farmer, who watched from behind the milch cow.

Years back, a wayfarer would have seen nothing but mesquite.

The land grew harder. More clay now, and sandy

loam, with juniper replacing the mesquite, and cactus dotting the grasses. Cedar Hill was barely noticeable, but the Lopez Peaks, jutting out at a half mile in elevation, gave them their bearings.

Finally, after six or seven days—nobody seemed certain—Twin Buttes rose, some two hundred feet above the rolling plains. The cattle could smell the water from the river, and early that afternoon, they had forded the Middle Concho, drank their fill, and bedded down for the night.

San Angelo lay across the North Concho River. Mathew had figured that by keeping the herd along the Middle Concho, the town and its demons would be less likely to lure his men from the herd. But it was close enough to take two wagons in for supplies—and a bath for Tess.

"What do we need?" he asked Groot.

"'Bout ever'thing." Groot wiped dirty hands on his apron. "Don't give me that look. We got what we could in Dunson City—or your own bins and cellars and smokehouse. But you knows how much things costs in Dunson City. I figured we could get supplies cheaper here. Cheaper, yeah, I reckon further north, but we might run out of grub iffen we waited that long."

"All right."

Groot dropped the apron. "No argument?"

"None."

"Huh?"

"That was smart thinking, Groot. Real smart."

Groot's mustache turned as he stretched his crooked lips into a grin.

"Well, yeah, I reckon it was. I mean—"

"Don't let it go to your head. Get some grub fixed

fast for the boys. Let Joey Corinth take over. We'll take . . ." He paused, rethinking. "We'll take just the hoodlum wagon in."

Chuck wagons meant trail drives. If Mathew could luck out, maybe nobody would realize a herd had trailed south of town and kept going east instead of due north. A wagon, a stoved-up cowboy turned cook, and a woman. They could be homesteaders or beginning ranchers—plenty of folks were moving west, taking advantage of the Concho rivers—and Mathew had not been to San Angelo in years. Now, this would not fool anyone who was following the trail. But as Mathew stepped away from Groot and his cook fire, he knew he would learn a bit of news—good or bad—in a jiffy.

"Tell Tess . . . will you?" he said, and stared at the dust to the southwest. Just enough dust for one horse.

By the time the blood bay loped into camp, Mathew had a cup of Groot's hot coffee in his hand for the rider.

Teeler Lacey swung out of the saddle and handed the reins to Joey Corinth, thanking the wrangler as the boy led the lathered gelding away. He took the coffee Mathew offered him and sipped some while removing his hat with his free hand and shaking off the dust.

"Well?" Mathew said.

The battered hat returned to the top of Lacey's head. Then the head shook. "I backtracked seven or eight miles, Mathew. Ain't nobody followin' us. Not even a dust devil popped up. Nothin'. Just a whole lot of empty out there."

Mathew nodded. "That's good. Thanks, Teeler. Grub will be ready directly."

Lacey lowered the cup. "What makes you think we's bein' trailed? You seen somethin'?"

"No." He shrugged. "More of a feeling."

Lacey stared for a moment before sipping more coffee. "Fella might think that's a bit . . . what's that word?"

"Paranoid." That came from Tess.

Mathew turned to find his wife standing by the chuck wagon.

Another voice called out from the wagon's tongue. "Man ain't paranoid . . . if someone's out to plug him."

Bradley Rush dropped his coffee cup in the wreck pan. Tess laughed, and even Mathew smiled. Bradley Rush was likely the only hired hand who could come up with such a witty response.

"You think someone's trailin' us, Rush?" Lacey asked.

"I ain't paid to think. Paid to punch cattle."

Quickly, Mathew changed the subject. "All right. Thanks again, Teeler. Groot, Tess, and I are taking the hoodlum wagon into town for supplies. That's just Groot, Tess, and me. Everybody else stays in camp. We'll be back sometime tonight. First light, we pull out. Skirt around to the south, give the town a lot of breathing room, and then turn north. Toward Comanche. Then up toward Belknap. Pick up the main train and move toward the Red."

No one argued. No one spoke. Mathew spun, and taking Tess by the arm as if he were leading her to the dance floor, he moved toward the hoodlum wagon. Groot shunned his apron, barked a few orders to

Joey Corinth, who had just returned from the horse herd, and hurried to catch up with Mathew and Tess.

Raw, mean, ugly. That was San Angelo.

As luck would have it, Tess, Groot, and Mathew had arrived on a Saturday night, and not just any Saturday night. The bluecoats at Fort Concho had just gotten their monthly pay. Five-string banjos were being clawed. So were men's faces in fights in the streets. Out-of-tune pianos were hammered. So were men holding glasses full of rotgut whiskey. Prostitutes called out from their cribs, or the upstairs rooms. A few made obscene gestures.

Roulette wheels spun. Dice rolled. Pasteboard cards slipped out of faro boxes, or onto poker tables, or out of a cardsharp's sleeve. An organ grinder choked out some dirge. A barker from the back of a gaudily painted wagon sang out the miracles of "Dr. Jehovah's Wizard Oil and Miracle Elixir, Cures Liver Complaint, Constipation, Digestive Disorders, Rheumatism, Asthma, Head Colds, Gunshots, Knife Cuts, Gout, Sprains, Ulcers, Warts & Hangovers." And a frail old man with eyes sunk well into his head, more cadaver than human, danced on the boardwalk as proof of the wonders of the snake oil Doctor Jehovah was selling.

It struck her as funny, how a town like this, seven hundred or more miles from Memphis, Tennessee, could bring back so many memories.

The River Palace *had once been a queen on the Mississippi River, but by 1865, her engines had rusted out, and had she left the banks of Memphis she would have sunk to the bottom in minutes. She smelled of human rot. But she was far from dead.*

Reconstruction had arrived in Memphis, but civilization and the law seemed a long way from the Chickasaw Bluffs.

Therissa Millay stepped onto the barroom stage aboard the reliable old stern-wheeler that had become a gambling house. She sang. Back then, her voice came out sweet, lovely. Too many years had passed since that night that she had forgotten exactly what songs she had chosen. Probably one, if not both, had been in French. She had been singing, probably one of those ballads with the double entendre. "Au Clair de la Lune"? No, it was something less childish, a French love song that spoke to those who did not speak the language. It didn't matter. And as her eyes had swept across the audience, the Yankees in charge of the town, the businessmen, the merchants, the whores, the riverboat men, even the black waiters and waitresses, once slaves, now free, she stopped.

The first time she ever saw Mathew Garth.

Even back then, she would have been hard-pressed to explain what had held her gaze. He was just a worn-out lad, an ex-Confederate soldier heading home . . . if he had a home.

The applause after the French ballad roared. Coins flew onto the stage. So did flowers. Yet she ignored them, and the demands that she sing again, as she made her way off the stage, into the audience, past the chairs being pushed out from tables for her to sit, past men she knew and men she didn't. She stopped at the table where the ex-rebel sat. The man who would introduce himself as Mathew Garth.

It had ended badly that night. Like most nights on that retired riverboat. Frenchy DeLonge and The Donegal had gotten into a row, and the Irish lout had wound up breaking poor Frenchy's back. She had dreamed of getting to know

*that silent young rebel, but The Donegal had stopped that
with death.*

*Yet she had held out her hand to Mathew Garth and said
that they would meet again. Mathew had said something
about Texas, that he doubted their paths would ever cross.
And Tess had squeezed his hand tightly but secretly—so The
Donegal would not notice and get his dander up again—
and told him that he was wrong, that they would meet
again.*

*She didn't know if she loved him right then. No. More
likely, she had simply been intrigued by him. Love came
later, when Mathew Garth and his cowboys had ridden to
their rescue while she was on her way to Nevada with The
Donegal and his den of thieves and prostitutes and card-
sharps. Maybe she was certain she loved him when she had
helped Edna deliver her baby, and she had placed Lightning
in the stunned cowboy's arms.*

Tess grinned as Mathew stopped the wagon in front
of a mercantile. You couldn't find room to tether another horse in front of any of the saloons, dance halls,
or gambling houses—not to mention the brothels—
but Jernigan's Mercantile had no customers.

After helping Tess down, Mathew nodded at another empty business two doors down. "Bath, if you
want one," he said.

"Are you saying I stink?"

He did not answer. "You think you'll be all right?"

She laughed. "Compared to Memphis, Mathew, this
is the Vatican."

"Vatican . . . ain't that in Californy?" Groot asked.

She rolled her eyes, stepped onto the boardwalk,
and made the bathhouse owner's night.

* * *

The Milky Way in all its luster led them back to the Middle Concho River. Tess felt clean after the bath, but she knew it would not last, not even an entire day. Tomorrow she would be just as dirty, just as tired, and wondering if she had been a fool. She could have been back at the ranch with her perfumes and dresses and high-button shoes. But then she would have been miles from Mathew and her sons.

Groot kept bragging about his purchase at Jernigan's store, that the boys would love him even more when he showed them the airtights of tomatoes and of peaches that he had bought. Mathew said nothing, just flicked the lines and kept the mules going. Suddenly he reminded Tess of the hollow-faced, gaunt man in the gray shell jacket—or what once had been gray—with the gold and yellow trim. How silent he had been. Yet that had to be better than who her husband had reminded her of at other times on this drive.

Thomas Dunson.

She felt a chill crawl up her spine.

Yet she relaxed as Mathew pulled the wagon into camp. He set the brake, yelled at the men gathered around the campfire to come help unload some of the grub into Groot's wagon.

Mathew helped Tess down, and he turned, started toward the fire.

Then, seeing a stranger standing on the other side of the fire ring, Mathew froze.

CHAPTER TWENTY-SIX

Jess Teveler wore a long, linen duster to protect his clothes from the trail, but Mathew could see the gun belt buckled across the gunman's waist. The black hat, which had appeared so new a few weeks ago, had been coated with dust and bent some from the wind and rain. The boots carried the scratches of mesquite, cactus, and the rough terrain. He wore chaps, too. Teveler had been talking to Lightning when the wagon had arrived. Now Lightning refilled the visitor's cup with fresh coffee.

"Hey, Pa," Lightning said as he returned the pot to the hook that hung from a cast-iron tripod set over the fire. "Look who come a-visiting."

"Teveler." Mathew rested his hand on the butt of the Colt revolver.

"Garth." The gunman was smart enough not to push back the tails of his duster for quicker access to that Thunderer he wore on his left hip.

He sipped coffee and gestured toward the Abingdon wagon, where Meeker, Nambel, Lacey, Laredo, Bradley Rush, and Yago Noguerra busied themselves moving the supplies from San Angelo out of the wagon. Groot told them what needed to go into his Studebaker.

"Need a hand?"

Ignoring the question, Mathew eyed Lightning. "Aren't you supposed to be nighthawking with your brother?"

Lightning's head shook. "No Sabe rode out when Jess arrived. Said he'd spell me so I could visit with Jess." He grinned widely and hooked a thumb toward the visitor. "Jess's been telling us all some big windies about Grandpa."

"That so?" Mathew looked back at Teveler. So it was Jess now. First-name basis. Not just once, but three times.

"Well, I imagine you could tell the boy some stories, Matt. More 'n me. I just knowed the man a short while." More coffee went down his throat. He licked his lips. "But you can learn some mighty interestin' things in a week or so oftentimes." Again, the mug pointed at the workers by the two wagons. "You sure you don't need a hand?"

"Lightning will help them. Enjoy your coffee."

Lightning did not argue. He hurried around the fire, glanced a confused look at his mother, and took an airtight of tomatoes from Groot.

"Fine coffee," Teveler said.

"You could get better in town, I warrant," Mathew said.

Teveler grinned. "No, I reckon not. Not in San Angelo."

"You're pretty close to a rope here, aren't you?"

The grin widened. "I figured the law might not look for me this close to that there town."

"There was a likeness to you that I saw on a wanted dodger while we were buying supplies."

"Was I handsome?"

"No illustration. Just a description."

"Must've been some other fella. Blessed with my good looks."

"And your name."

He finished the coffee. "You gonna try to collect that reward?" Still, Teveler made no move toward his revolver.

"I'm no lawman. And I never begrudge a man a cup of coffee, or even a hot meal, in my camp."

"You're a good man, Matt Garth."

"You were a good man, too, Teveler . . . once. Or so I hear."

Teveler moved, crossed toward the chuck wagon, and dropped the cup in the wreck pan.

"I'd like to repay my debt, Garth."

Mathew's head shook. "Coffee's always on the house, Teveler. Like I said."

"But I figured you might be hirin' now. Permanent-like. Least till Dodge City."

"How so?" Mathew asked.

Another grin stretched across the gunman's face. Mathew guessed that he had not shaved in a couple of weeks. "Heard you lost a man," Teveler said.

"Where'd you hear that?" Mathew asked.

"A little grave told me," Teveler replied. "At Dunson's Corner."

"We're full up. Commissary man from Fort Concho ran into me in town, by the way. Wanted to look at some of our beeves. I thought that selling some steers here might be a good idea since the army pays better prices often enough, and since I told him we'd be moving on at first light, I'm sure he'll have a few troopers with him. To drive any beeves he buys back to the fort. Likely bring more men than he needs, too, since soldiers aren't real good with cattle."

Teveler adjusted his hat. "I see. Then I reckon I'd better ride on, eh, Garth? Bound for the Nations, I think. Lawless country up there, but a man can lose himself. I'll be seein' you, Garth. You take care."

Mathew was aware that work had stopped behind him. As Teveler disappeared into the shadows, Mathew did not look back at the wagons. He made for the coffee and filled a cup—he did not care whose—and squatted by the fire.

"Wait a minute, Jess," Lightning called out. "I'll help you with your horse."

Mathew frowned and his stomach twisted into knots, but he said nothing. Tess, Laredo Downs, Joe Nambel, and Teeler Lacey gathered around the fire, while Groot kept instructing the others as to the proper placement of the merchandise. When they had finished, they wandered off to their bedrolls, and Groot joined the others by the fire.

"I swear, Mathew." Teeler Lacey was the first to speak. "If he was followin' us, I never saw no dust. No nothin'."

"He wasn't following us. Not since Big Lake, at least. Probably not since Dunson's Corner. He probably rode this way, figuring he'd meet up with us here."

"Why would he do that?" Joe Nambel came to a realization. "You think him . . . Jess Teveler . . . you think he's after our herd?"

Mathew shrugged. "He gave us fair warning. Said

he was off for the Nations. If he wants the herd, that's where he'll try to take it."

"But why on earth . . . ?" Nambel did not finish.

Laredo looked off toward the remuda. "Lightnin's takin' a likin' to that no-account."

"Yeah." Mathew tested the coffee. It didn't taste so good now.

"Is there really some bluebelly from Concho comin' out to buy some beeves?" Groot asked.

"No," Mathew said.

"Damnation, Mathew Garth," Groot said. "You never told no lie before. Not even to some rapscallion on the owlhoot like Teveler."

"He didn't lie." Tess waited until everyone looked at her. "The commissary officer at Concho did happen by the store where we were loading the wagon. He recognized Mathew. Asked if he were trailing a herd. Mathew told him yes. The officer said he might be interested in buying some cattle, said he would be willing to bring some men out tonight, and he could pay in a government voucher or scrip." She waited. "And Mathew told him . . ."

Mathew shrugged. "That my beeves are going to Dodge City."

"Might've been a good idea, though," Groot said. "Sell a few cattle. Army can pay top dollar. Give us some more money iffen we come 'cross some hard times. And the fewer mossyhorns we got, the less trouble we got. That's how I think." He punctuated his statement with a sharp nod.

"Those Yanks at Concho got paid today," Mathew said. "You think I'd let a bunch of drunken soldiers come into my camp? Hell, they'd stampede the whole herd halfway to Mexico."

* * *

By morning they were moving, east and then north, and then in a gradual northeasterly course, slowly at first, taking advantage of the water, the green grass. Springtime brought color to this country, with the hardwoods on the mesas, the cottonwoods by the rivers, and the wildflowers. Bluebonnets, Indian paintbrushes, Mexican hats, black-eyed Susans. Longhorns are not particular. They ate those, too.

Texas's Hill Country lay east and south, but this land was hilly enough. Across the Colorado River and on toward the town of Comanche. The trail was easy to follow. Other herds had followed the route, too. Other trail bosses must have decided to try the Chisholm Trail instead of the Western Trail to Dodge, or maybe they would find the railroad at Denison and ship out their cattle there. Mathew had considered Denison, but the price the railroad charged made it more profitable, more sensible, to keep on north for Kansas and its cheaper rates and better cattle prices.

Every now and then, they would find reminders of the previous winters. White skeletons of cattle, even some horses, in sinkholes or creek bottoms or cane-brakes or just alone in some rolling country, already scattered by buzzards, coyotes, wolves.

Misting rains began west of Comanche and lasted four days. Barely hard enough for a rancher to even think of it as moisture, but it certainly soaked a man's—or woman's—clothing, and wet saddles could rub a cowpuncher's backside raw. Yet it was more of the skies that fouled men's moods, not the wet. Not cold. Not hot. Not even humid. But foggy and dank and dark.

Mathew and Teeler Lacey rode alone into Comanche, the former to check for any telegraphs that might have been sent, for he had left word with Juan Quinta and Chico Miller that here he would be able to get any news or messages. Teeler Lacey rode a bay but led his black, his favorite horse, which had thrown a shoe. Comanche offered many things, including a good farrier.

"Mathew Garth," said Paul Ransom as Mathew and Lacey rode into the livery. "As I live and breathe."

"Brought you some business, Mr. Ransom." Mathew dismounted, shook the gray-headed giant's crushing hand, and nodded toward Lacey and the black.

"You might as well get a whiskey, Teeler," Mathew said after Ransom started work on shoeing the black.

"You is human after all, ain't you, Garth?" Lacey grinned.

"Don't get drunk."

Lacey laughed. "Spoke too soon. You ain't human."

Although the town had not been incorporated until 1873, it had been around for many years. For a few short years right before the war broke out, Thomas Dunson would come all this way for supplies, for Ransom's work with anvil, heat, and iron. Hell, he didn't just shoe horses. He was practically the closest thing to a horse doctor in Texas.

"I was thinking about Dunson just the other day," Ransom said.

"Oh." Mathew rolled a smoke.

The liveryman began telling the story of when Dunson had first brought Mathew to see Ransom.

This was even before Comanche had been established back in '58, back when Ransom ran a little horse ranch on Indian Creek and did a little side business with other ranchers in the area.

"You asked Dunson—and I don't reckon you was barely twenty then—why he come all this way . . . three hundred miles . . . to get a hoss shod.

"And Dunson tells you that a hoss can mean life or death in this country, and that he planned on livin' forever."

Mathew fired up the cigarette and flicked the match into the flames.

"He did, you know?" Ransom said.

Mathew cut short his drag, and smiled at the smithy. "I know that. I even remember it . . . I was there . . . and you've sure told that story enough."

"Ain't what I meant, son. Meant that Dunson lived forever. He's still around. I can see him in you. Specially now. You drivin' a herd?"

Mathew nodded.

"Ain't takin' that new trail?"

"And miss your company?"

That made the old man give a wide smile. The hammer pounded the iron before the shoe returned to the flames.

"What made you think of that story, Mr. Ransom?"

"Oh . . . nothin'." The smile was gone. Then so was the iron shoe, disappearing into a bucket with a loud hiss and a cloud of steam.

"Had us a little ruction a few days ago. Deputy got hisself kilt."

Which wasn't that uncommon in Comanche. John

Wesley Hardin had killed a lawman here. That's what had gotten the man-killer sent to Huntsville.

Mathew sailed the cigarette, barely touched, into the fire. He guessed what the farrier would say even before the old-timer had turned around from the blazing fire.

"I reckon you still remember a gunman named Jess Teveler."

CHAPTER TWENTY-SEVEN

The sheriff, Clarke Stamford, and his posse stopped in at camp that evening. Looking like the politician type, the lawman reminded Mathew—not in looks, but rather how he carried himself—of Chico Miller. Rumpled sack suit, bowler hat, not outfitted for a posse. As far as Mathew could tell, the sheriff didn't even carry a short gun, just a single-shot rifle in the scabbard of his saddle. The posse didn't look that much better. A few cowboys, maybe two or three town merchants, and one ex-Yankee sergeant, a big black man still wearing his army blouse, but duck trousers and a straw hat.

Their clothes remained wet from the light rain that had finally stopped earlier that afternoon. Apparently, they had taken off after Teveler without thinking about rain slickers or india-rubber ponchos.

"We're lookin' for a murderin' scoundrel named Jess Teveler," Sheriff Clarke Stamford said as he looked over the men lining up to be dished out supper by Groot and Joey Corinth. "Killed one of my deputies the other day. Killed a gambler in San Angelo, too, last winter."

The details of the killing in Comanche had been given to Mathew by the farrier, Paul Ransom. According to witnesses, including Ransom, Jess Teveler had been sitting alone at a table in Galloway's Grog Shop, sipping a porter and taking advantage of the free sandwiches and pickles that the saloon offered during the dinner hour. Nobody had really paid much attention to the stranger until Jace Karnes came in, ordered a beer, fixed himself a ham sandwich, and turned around.

"You're that Teveler fellow!"

Karnes dropped the knife he was using to spread mustard over a healthy slice of rye bread and drew his Remington .44. "Killed a gambler in San Angelo."

Everyone in the saloon looked at the stranger. A few decided to leave at that moment, and others distanced themselves from Karnes and the stranger with the black hat and dark beer.

"This ain't San Angelo, is it?" Teveler sipped his beer, but only a few men noticed that he was drinking with his left hand, and that his right had disappeared underneath the table.

Jace Karnes was thirty years old and had been begging for a deputy's job for the past ten years. He had only gotten it after Clarke Stamford had been elected sheriff of Comanche County. Karnes had always bragged that if he had been a deputy back in 1877, the town of Comanche would be known for where John Wesley Hardin had been killed by Jace Karnes, and Deputy Charles Webb would still be breathing.

"I reckon it'll be me, Jace Karnes, that collects the reward they've posted on you in San Angelo," Karnes said.

Some folks said Teveler sang out, "It'll be somethin' else you collect, bud!" But Ransom had told Mathew that Teveler said nothing.

His right hand came up, and the double-action revolver he held barked. Gun smoke filled the saloon. The doors to Galloway's Grog Shop pounded, and Jess Teveler was galloping out of town before most people understood what had happened.

The deputy had his pistol out, but not cocked. He bled out with three bullets in his stomach before his wife could reach the saloon, where Ransom and others had put him on a table and sent for the doctor.

"Ain't the reputation a town like Comanche would care to have," Ransom had told Mathew. "Place where outlaws gun down sheriff's deputies."

"You expect him to light a shuck with a trail herd?" Mathew told Sheriff Clarke Stamford. Mathew felt thankful that Tom and Lightning were riding around the herd.

"Well . . ." Paying little attention to Mathew, the sheriff carefully studied the men in line for supper.

"Maybe not . . ." It was the old army sergeant who spoke now. "But he might've stopped in for some grub or a whiskey."

Mathew reexamined the black man. He had shaved his head, but wore a gray-flecked mustache and goatee. He set deep in the saddle, relaxed, his one hand on the reins, the other not too far from the holstered gun in a green sash that also held a sheathed

D ring bowie knife. This man, Mathew determined, was the real leader of the posse. He was better than the rest of the lot combined. Hell, he even had a slicker strapped to the back of his saddle along with his bedroll.

"Grub maybe," Mathew said. "Coffee for sure. But no whiskey. Whiskey on a trail drive is a bad investment."

"Bad investment most times, ain't it?" The old soldier showed straight but yellow teeth as he smiled.

"I never turn a man away from coffee or food," Mathew said. "You're welcome to some."

The sheriff turned in the saddle. "This all the men you got?"

"Three men are circling the herd," Mathew said. "Two of them are my sons. The other's Joe Nambel, and I've known him since I was a kid. They aren't the man you're looking for."

"I'll be the judge of that. Let's go check those—"

"One of you may go." Mathew shifted the cup to his left hand, while his right gripped the Colt's butt. "Only one." He felt every man in his crew moving closer to the weapons they carried.

The sheriff swallowed as his face paled.

"Those beeves are wet, irritated, and just a little spooked from the rain and fog and gloom. I'm not risking you stampeding them eight ways from Sunday. If you don't take my word that the man you're looking for isn't riding herd on those cattle, that's fine. But all of you aren't going out there. Not this evening."

"That killer . . ." the sheriff began. "You sure he ain't been here?"

Mathew took his hand off the Colt and smiled,

shaking his head, returning the coffee cup to his right hand, and took a sip. "Sheriff, you haven't even told me what this gent looked like."

"Tall, lean. Older. Maybe my age or so. Black hat. Fine spurs. Put three slugs in Jace Karnes's belly from his .41 caliber Thunderer. Jace was a good man. Didn't have no call to shoot him a-tall, exceptin' that Jace recognized him from that poster the marshal at San Angelo sent out. That's how we know his name is Jess Teveler. Maybe you've heard of him."

"I've heard the name," Mathew said.

"Well . . . ?" The sheriff swallowed.

Mathew shrugged. "Black hat. Older man. I reckon we could have given him some coffee some days back."

The way Mathew saw things, he wasn't exactly lying to the law. Just not saying everything, and he had his reasons. For one, had he told the sheriff that Teveler had stopped in camp near San Angelo, maybe even if he said he knew Jess Teveler, the sheriff would have wired telegraphs across the state. And then Mathew would be getting visits from every lawman from here to the Red River—just in case that Teveler, for some reason that only a lawman or bounty hunter could fathom, might drop in for more biscuits, beans, and coffee.

"All right."

"You want some coffee, Sheriff?" Mathew asked.

"What I want is to see my wife and brand-spankin'-new grandbaby. Get out of these wet duds. We done missed poor Jace's buryin' and all. Lost Teveler's trail round Sowells Creek. No luck pickin' it up agin." He shifted in the saddle. "You sure them men with your cows ain't Teveler."

"He said they wasn't," the black man said. "I trust'm."

"We got plenty of food and grub, Sheriff," Mathew said. "You're welcome to some."

"No thanks." He sighed. "I sure hate tellin' Dorothy Karnes that we didn't get that dog that killed her husband. Let's ride, boys."

Mathew cleared his throat. "Go easy around the longhorns, gents. You don't want to get caught in a stampede."

The rains stopped. The skies cleared. The sun baked the land. The drive continued north and east, but the Red River seemed to be a million miles away.

On they went, across the Leon River with little difficulty. They dodged around barbed-wire fences—once unheard of in the state of Texas—where sodbusters had fenced off their fields. Mathew could not blame the farmers, and he wanted no run-ins with any homesteading family, or the law.

They paralleled rivers, creeks, branches, maybe even ditches. They crossed them when they could, sometimes two or three times. Some had names—the Bosque . . . Hannibal Creek . . . Palo Pinto . . . Cane Branch . . . Honey Creek . . . Eagle Creek . . . Mill Branch. Most did not.

"In case you haven't noticed, Mathew," Laredo Downs called out as he walked his horse up a knoll, generously named Warters Mountain, where Mathew sat on the dun, watching the dust. "Fort Griffin's just over yonder way. Still ain't too late to change your mind and pick up the Western Trail." He smiled good-naturedly and offered Mathew the cigarette he had just rolled.

Mathew took the smoke, but pointed it in another direction before he stuck it between his lips. "I like . . . that way."

Laredo laughed. He nudged his horse closer, and this time lost the smile as his voice lowered.

"You know we're bein' followed."

"For some time now," Mathew said. He did not look over his shoulder where Laredo stared.

The old foreman rubbed his neck. "I'd thought we was bein' followed . . . pret' much since Comanche. Then I laughed at my silly notion. I mean . . . it wasn't like it was back when . . ." He stopped quickly.

"When we all knew Dunson was behind us," Mathew said.

"Well." Laredo tried another smile, but it didn't last long. "Well, it ain't Dunson."

"It ain't Jess Teveler, either." Mathew struck the match he had fished out from his vest pocket, cupped his hands, and lighted the cigarette.

"How can you tell?"

"He's showing himself. Been off there for the past three days."

"Three days!" Laredo took off his hat to wipe his brow. "Three? Damn, I must be gettin' old."

"You're paid to move the herd. Not look behind you. And he's no threat."

"Well, he's white. At least." The hat returned to the foreman's head.

"You sure?" Mathew blew out smoke.

"He ain't no Comanch', I mean."

"Probably not."

"What do we do?"

Mathew shrugged. "Free country. Let him ride. He'll probably stop in for a visit sometime."

He kicked the horse and rode down the rise, with Laredo at his side.

They reached the Brazos River. Roughly four hundred miles from the ranch along the Rio Grande. Four hundred miles, forty-four days. One man dead. Maybe twenty head of longhorns lost along the way. A few had drowned. Others just dropped dead along the trail, worn out. Maybe a couple had drifted off unnoticed to be butchered by some grateful sod-buster or road-branded by another drover or rancher who figured that a lost steer was just the same as the spoils of war.

They did not cross the Brazos immediately, however. Instead, they followed it, more or less, on its eastward course, avoiding some of the bends to save time and take advantage of an easier ford near what remained of Fort Belknap.

There, they crossed the river with relative ease and bedded down the herd and remuda near the fort. It had been established back around 1851, abandoned by the bluebellies with the war broke out, then reoccupied a few years after the war. When Fort Griffin had been established just a few short months later, though, Fort Belknap had been abandoned. Nearby settlers had stripped the buildings of just about anything they could use, but the well remained, and the water from it tasted sweet, not brackish.

They rested one day, to let the cattle and horses graze and regain some strength. Soon, they would pick up the main branch of the Great Texas Cattle

Trail—the Chisholm Trail—and head north to the Red River, into Indian Territory, and then cut west for Kansas, Dodge City, and, with luck, a waiting cattle buyer with a satchel full of greenbacks.

Four hundred miles behind them. Another four hundred—a much harsher four hundred—to go.

CHAPTER TWENTY-EIGHT

"Don't like the look of that, no, sir," Groot said, snorted, and spit.

Lightning, still half-asleep despite his third cup of coffee, looked off to the east.

"Red sky at night, shepherd's delight," John Meeker said. "Red sky in the morning, shepherd's warning." The drunk shook his head and gave a little, wan smile. "My pa used to say that all the time."

"From the Gospel of Matthew," Bradley Rush said.

"What's it mean?" Lightning heard himself ask.

"Rotten weather," Groot said. "For sure."

Lightning snorted. "Who cares what a sheepherder says about weather."

"It ain't just the sky this morn'," Groot began. "Last night, I seen some ants scurryin' 'bout, pickin' up the good grub you boys spilt, y'all was so hungry. Ants. Late at night. And my ma always told me that if you saw ants workin' late, then snow or rain was a-comin', sure as shootin'."

"I don't think you have to worry about snow, Groot," Joe Nambel said.

"Boys, I tell you what it means," Groot went on. "It means . . ."

"It means," Lightning's father interjected, "we're burning daylight."

Lightning never quite grasped that concept. Groot would start ringing that triangle bell at the chuck wagon, screaming the same thing: "We're burning daylight."

By thunder, when that loud bell started clanging, jerking Lightning awake when he felt as if he had just closed his eyes after seventeen or eighteen hours in the saddle, the sun hadn't even peeked above the horizon. A body would be hard put to detect even a hint of gray in the sky. Yet every morning—if you'd call it morning—the cowboys would drag themselves out of their soogans, stumble in the dark to the fire and the coffee and biscuits. There they would eat and drink and hardly even talk—till it was light enough for Joey Corinth to rope horses from the remuda, and the cowboys could see enough to saddle their mounts.

"What the Sam Hill are you doing?" Lightning asked.

The red of the morning had faded by then, and Lightning saw no hint of the bad weather that Groot and his glowing morning sky were predicting. What Lightning saw was one of the Mexican cowhands doing the damnedest thing.

Alvaro Cuevas looked up. He had been moving his bedroll from the cantle and lashing it instead to just in front of the horn. The vaquero grinned and replied in rapid Spanish, making a few gestures toward the blue roan Joey Corinth had brought out from the remuda, to his own head, and finally at his groin.

Lightning just blinked. "Huh?"

A couple of rods away, saddling his bay gelding, Yago Noguerra tossed a stirrup over the seat of his swell-forked saddle, and answered: "Alvaro says the horse Joey has cut out for him this morning is . . . eh . . . *grosero*? *Verde*. Bucks *mucho*. A . . . a . . . *hijo de la puta*?"

"I know what that means," Lightning says. "But I still don't get . . ."

"Alvaro wants to have children someday."

Lightning turned to see his father, busy saddling his own horse, the black he usually rode.

"I . . . ohhhhh."

The cowboys chuckled as they continued saddling and bridling their horses for the day's drive.

"Much time as you spend at Gloria's Palace," Joe Nambel said, "I figured you'd know 'bout things like that."

Teeler Lacey had an even more obscene comment that made Lightning's face flush, yet he quickly found himself chuckling with everybody else nearby. He felt relieved, however, knowing that his mother was not in earshot.

"Watch your manners, gents," Mathew said, and the joking ceased—but not for long—for even Lightning's father could not hide his own grin.

For the life of him, Lightning Garth could not understand why everyone felt happy. Certainly, no one could blame the change in mood on whiskey. His father, damn it, had not broken down and allowed each hand a few jiggers of whiskey. The only bottle in camp was the one Groot kept in a drawer in the chuck wagon, and he said it would be used only for medicinal purposes. Cuts, bruised, and raw backsides did not count. Nobody had broken a bone, been bitten by a rattlesnake, or shot in the shoulder.

"Let's get moving," his father said as he swung into the saddle. "We're burning daylight."

For more than five weeks, they had been wet, and they had been dry. Baking underneath a broiling sun or freezing in their soaking clothes after a cold rain. Mostly, they had been bone tired, aching, miserable. Awake before sunrise, then in a saddle till noon, a quick bite of food washed down with coffee, a fresh horse, and back in the saddle. Till dark. Eat what Groot called food. Maybe sleep. More than likely spend at least two or three more hours circling the herd of longhorns.

As they followed along the western banks of Salt Creek, the air turned thick, heavy, humid, and the skies darkened.

"Reckon Groot might've been right 'bout 'em skies," John Meeker Jr. said.

Too exhausted, too miserable to respond, neither Tom Garth nor his brother commented.

"Damn this heat," Meeker said maybe two miles later.

You hated the heat. Then you complained about the rain. You dreaded the night. You despised the day. Especially this day.

It stretched on like all of eternity in hell.

Nothing changed. Clouds of dust, and beyond that, darkening skies. Once, when Lightning dismounted to answer nature's call, he looked west, then east, then south. Blue skies everywhere. Everywhere, that is, except north, the direction the cattle were going. Tom's father appeared to be leading them straight into a black void that spit out brief flashes of white. Too far away to hear thunder, though.

"We're riding straight into a twister," Tom said to himself as he buttoned his britches. "The newspapers in Dallas and Fort Worth will say, 'Those fools deserved to die!'" He laughed and then looked around for a rock or a stump or some slight incline to make it easier to mount his horse.

A lifetime ago—well, forty or fifty days earlier— he would have chastised any honest cowboy who needed to find some way to cheat to climb into the saddle. But no more. He groaned, tried to soothe his aching muscles, and gently eased himself into the saddle before spurring his horse into a trot and catching up with Lightning, John Meeker Jr., and all that dust and misery.

The black void far to the north did not move. Maybe because those three thousand and more longhorns covered little ground. The country seemed endless, flat, maybe some timbers in the hills or along the creeks, but nothing to stop the wind. Although, on this day, the wind was nonexistent.

Yet the grass was good. Maybe that's why Mathew Garth and Laredo Downs kept the herd moving so god-awful slow. Or maybe no one wanted to get too close to that ominous black cauldron that lay ahead.

They stopped at noon, if only briefly. The three drag riders eased their weary mounts to the remuda, picked out the horses they wanted for the rest of the day, and limped and dragged their legs through the thick grass to the chuck wagon. Sowbelly and beans. Warm, filling. Coffee. Hot, nourishing. Stale corn bread left over from last night's supper and this morning's breakfast.

Janeen Yankowski had never served up anything that tasted so good.

Well, Tom Garth couldn't say that he actually tasted the food.

If anyone had asked him, he would have sworn he had ridden fifty miles since dawn. Yet looking back at the country to the south, he wondered if they had made more than three.

A horse pounded the already trampled grass and hard earth, and Tom watched his father ride straight to the chuck wagon. The horse, the liver chestnut named Dollar, looked pretty fresh, and Tom realized that his father had already swapped out his mount from that morning. Yet he did not dismount, just kicked his feet free of the stirrups and stretched his legs out in front of him.

Groot filled a tin cup with black brew and handed it to him.

Mathew Garth drank greedily. If the liquid was hot, he did not appear to notice. He turned his head off to the northeast.

"There's a herd—A. C. Thompson's outfit—about two miles north." Mathew Garth stopped for another swallow of black coffee.

Tom had met A. C. Thompson once. In Fort Worth, if his memory had not failed him. In fact, Thompson lived in Fort Worth but worked from the southern edges of Texas to the cattle towns in Kansas. A professional drover, Thompson would buy cattle from ranchers, hire his own crew, horses, and wagons, and

take a herd north. He had been doing that since
'67—after Thomas Dunson proved that things were
possible—to Abilene and Dodge City and every cow
town between. Some people compared Thompson to
the great cattlemen like Shanghai Pierce and Charles
Goodnight. A few said Thompson was richer than
both of them, richer than God, but he dressed like a
thirty-a-month cowhand, and his house in Fort Worth
was just a shanty next door to the wild district known
as Hell's Half Acre. Not that it mattered. Most of the
time, A. C. Thompson was sleeping in a bedroll
underneath the stars, not in the one-room shack that
collected spiders, roaches, snakes, and his mail.

"Thompson's stopping for the night," Mathew
said.

"Plenty of daylight left," Groot said.

Mathew nodded. "Yeah. But Thompson doesn't
like the black clouds. I don't, either."

"Then . . ." Groot took the cup that Mathew held
out. "You reckon we should bed down, too."

"No." The worn boots returned to the stirrups,
and Mathew gathered the reins. "I don't want Thompson and his eighteen hundred beeves ahead of us."

"Well . . ." Groot considered this.

"If it's raining north, then the Red will be swollen.
I want to be across the river before Thompson or
anyone else. River gets too high, we wait. If we're in
line, that's an even longer wait."

"That makes sense," Groot said, but added, "I
reckon."

"Go wide around Thompson's cattle. They're half-
wild, even compared to our three thousand. I mean
a wide berth." Mathew wiped his face. "We'll move

around them, get back on the trail, bed down three, four miles north. Let's get those beeves moving."

Neck-reining the sorrel, Mathew Garth trotted out of camp and back toward the grazing sea of Texas beef.

Groot dropped the empty cup into the basin, shook his head, spit out tobacco juice, and told Joey Corinth, "You heard the boss, sonny. Best get out of here so we can have the boys somethin' to et when they's done for the day." He spun around to study the sky. "If we ain't loadin' two of each type of critter onto some boat by nightfall."

Tom glanced at Lightning, who swore. John Meeker Jr. joined the melody of curses, too.

Groot sang out, "You heard the boss, gents. Back to work, you malcontents. We's burnin' daylight."

CHAPTER TWENTY-NINE

Tess had expected to be soaked by the time she had helped Groot set up camp and get the fire going, but she caught not even a scent of rain in the wind that had picked up, blowing in from the north. Even the clouds, still black, did not appear to have moved much.

"Maybe that storm'll miss us."

Turning, she saw Groot holding a cup of coffee for her, which she took with a smile.

"You think so?"

"Hope so." Groot pulled a plug of tobacco from his pants pocket. He did not use a pocketknife to cut off his chaw, merely bit into it and pulled off a sizable portion with the teeth he had left. As he worked the cud into a comfortable spot, he tilted his head off to the north. "Big storm, though. Dumpin' buckets. River'll be high."

She looked back. "How far are we to the Red River?"

"Two days," Groot answered. "If the weather holds. Three, maybe, if she don't. There's a little burg where we can load up on any extry supplies we might need. Cross the river the next day."

He began poking the burning wood, spreading out the coals. Tess set her cup on the ground without taking a sip and helped the old cook set a Dutch oven onto some coals he had shoveled out of the fire. He then shoveled out another load of coals and dumped them onto the oven's lid, spreading them out evenly with the shovel.

As Groot straightened, his knee joints popping, he spit tobacco juice into the edge of the fire.

"You might want to ride into Spanish Fort, I reckon, and get yourself another bath." Groot wiped the juice from his lips with his dirty shirtsleeve.

Tess found her cup, took a sip, and smiled.

"Why bother till Dodge City?"

He shrugged. "I just figured . . ." But did not finish.

"Oh."

Tess had not really done much contemplating since she had joined the herd at Dunson's Corner. You did not do much thinking on a trail drive. Up before light, eating what passed for breakfast, hitching the team, then following Groot's chuck wagon to the noon camp. More work. Some food. Back into the wagon and rolling across this flat patch of earth till the night camp. She was close to Mathew. Maybe that's why she had decided to drive the hoodlum wagon. To be close to her husband and close to her sons. She was close, but they were all distant. Especially Mathew.

And now she wondered. This close to the Red River. This close to . . .

"How many years has it been?" she heard herself ask.

Groot studied her a bit. "Since . . . Dunson?"

Tess shook her head. "Since his last drive with you?"

He shrugged. "Five, six years. Thereabouts. Somethin' like that."

Tess smiled. "Six. That's right. I remember. Caldwell."

"Sounds right."

"Did he . . . did Mathew . . . did he . . . ?"

The old cook understood. "Ever' time." He spit again. "We'd come to Spanish Fort. Usually, he'd ride out then. Send the boys to town for a whiskey or somethin', and he'd go yonder way." He motioned toward the east. "Or we'd have to wait on account the Red was floodin', or there'd be another herd or two ahead of us, so we'd have to wait to cross the river. He'd just ride out that way alone. Never said nothin'. But me and Laredo and Joe . . . we always knowed. Never been there myself. But . . . well . . ."

He busied himself with the cookware for a moment, then straightened and looked at Tess.

"He ever talk to you 'bout it?"

"No," she said.

"You reckon he talks to Dunson?"

Her head shook, and she shrugged. "I don't know."

He checked the Dutch oven, but did not open the lid nor add more coals. "Never saw much reasonin' to it my ownself. Visitin' a grave's one thing, I reckon, but talkin' to the dead, tellin' some person long gone what you been doin', askin' 'em how they's doin', just don't see no sense to that at all. The dead don't care what you been a-doin' with yourselves. You reckon?"

She drew in a deep breath and slowly let it out. "I don't see Mathew telling Thomas Dunson how he has been spending the past year, Groot. Do you?"

"No, ma'am. What you reckon he goes there for?"

She sighed. "To remember."

Groot grunted, continued with his work.

Another sip, and she started to ask Groot Nadine a question, but the sound of a horse's snort and the squeaking of leather turned their attention to Mathew Garth as he rode the bay into the camp. He swore underneath his breath as he dismounted, wrapped the reins around a rope that had been strung up between the two wagons.

"Want some coffee, Mathew?" Groot asked.

"Where's supper?" Mathew demanded.

"Criminy, Mathew, we just set up camp. It'll be ready directly."

"You two get to it." He helped himself to a cup from the back of Groot's wagon and walked to the fire, where the big pot rested on a tripod.

"I got 'em peaches," Groot said as he tipped the pot to fill Mathew's cup.

"Thought I'd fix the boys a cobbler. For Tom, mostly. Figured it was right about his birthday an' all. Might've missed it, though. And the boys. And you . . . well . . . you think they'd like that, Mathew? I know—"

"I don't give a damn, Groot. Just get some food in their bellies in a hurry."

He swallowed some coffee, swore, dumped the rest of the liquid onto the dirt, pitched the cup into the dirt, and stormed back to his horse as Laredo Downs rode in.

"Four men night-herding," Mathew told Laredo as he tightened the cinch on his saddle. "Four-hour shifts." Staring, Laredo did not dismount until Mathew had mounted his horse and trotted off toward the herd.

Tess frowned. She could see the hurt in the old cook's face.

"Coffee ain't had time to cook hardly, so that's why it ain't so strong. But . . . I swan . . . Mathew . . . he was always partial to peaches. And Tom . . . I figured . . . You reckon . . . must be nigh abouts Tom's birthday. Don't you reckon?"

"I don't know what day it is, Groot," she said. That much was true, but she had to think Tom's birthday had come and gone weeks ago, back down the trail. She hadn't even thought about it.

"I swan . . ." Groot sighed.

She wanted to reach over and pat his hand, but knew better. Groot had his pride. So did Tess's husband. So did Tess.

"He's changed," Laredo said as he found a cup.

"No . . ." Groot picked up the cup Mathew had dropped and put it in the basin. "It's just . . . well, there's just a lot of pressure . . . to get this herd in . . . to . . ."

"Hell, Groot." Laredo walked to the coffeepot. "Wasn't there pressure the year after that first drive, when he had to do it himself? Or in '72, after that bad winter? Or the year later, when the banks and railroads and practically everybody was goin' bust? Or durin' the bad drought that time a few years back? Wasn't it you and him himself who now thinks he's God A'mighty . . . wasn't it both of you who said that any cattle drive's a gamble? He's changed, I tell you."

Groot Nadine had no answer.

"Come on, Groot." Tess forced a smile. "Let's get supper started."

* * *

She made a point of telling Groot that the peach cobbler was delicious. It was no lie, either. She kept waiting for Mathew to ride back into camp, but he had stayed out, taking the first shift riding around the herd. She overheard Joe Nambel tell John Meeker Jr. that, knowing Mathew Garth, and as crazy as he was getting, the boss man might stay out all night.

"Be fine with me," Lightning said. "He's crazier than a loon."

Tess gave Lightning a hard look. He saw it, but ignored it.

Tom, drinking his third cup of Groot's coffee, rose quickly.

"Why don't you just shut that big mouth of yours, brother?"

"Why don't you make me?"

Now Tess stood. "Stop it. Stop it, both of you. All of you. Your father . . ." She glanced at the others eating. "Your boss. He's not mad. But you're all about to drive me . . . to Bedlam!"

Darkness came. She helped Groot and Joey Corinth with the dishes, got the coffee ready for tomorrow's breakfast, and looked at the cup and plate Groot had fixed for Mathew—for whenever, if ever, he rode back to eat and sleep. Tess pulled the scarf from around her neck and used it to cover the food. Night had not cooled the air, and flies still buzzed around camp.

The wind moaned through the canvas tarp covering the chuck wagon. Still, she smelled nothing like rain. She had seen no clouds before the sun set, except far north toward the river, but the night seemed darker than usual. Yet when she brushed her hair, she felt a static shock. Despite the wind, the night felt crushing, heavy with electricity. Then she saw the flash, way off in the distance. She waited to hear the rumble of thunder, but no noise came. Another flash, but to the south, away from the black clouds along the Red River. And yet still . . . no thunder.

Groot saw it, too.

"That's a bad omen," he said.

Which caused Joe Nambel to mutter a blasphemy. "Ever'thing's a bad omen for you, Groot."

"Go to hell, Joe Nambel."

"All it is, you damned ol' belly-cheater, is heat lightnin'."

Groot opened his mouth and clenched his fists, but before he spoke, or charged Joe Nambel like a raging bull, Mathew Garth rode into camp.

Tess could feel everything change. Her feelings. The mood in camp. Even the air seemed filled with more of that electrical charge, while silent lightning shot across the sky to the south.

"Lightning, Joe," Mathew said as he handed the reins to his lathered horse to Joey Corinth. "Saddle up. I want you two with the herd."

"It ain't my time," Lightning said.

Mathew turned and stared. He did not speak. He didn't have to. Slowly, muttering under his breath, Lightning pulled his hat down tighter and began to unbuckle his gun belt.

"You might want to keep that iron," Mathew said.

Lightning whirled. "After what you preached to me last time? With it lightning like it is?" He started to point south, but spotted something and swung his arm to the north. "There. Seen another flash. It's ahead of us and behind us. You want me to get melted, Pa?"

"You might have need of that six-shooter, son, tonight. Get mounted. Both of you." While they were leaving, he called out to the others, "Sleep with boots on, boys. And your horses close. Joey!"

He strode across the camp toward the remuda.

When he returned a few minutes later, most of the cowhands were heading toward the remuda themselves. Alvaro Cuevas, Bradley Rush, and even Tom Garth drew revolvers from their holsters, opened the loading gates, rotated the cylinders, fished out shells from their cartridge belts, and filled the last chambers—usually kept empty for safety purposes.

Tess withdrew the bandanna—Mathew's bandanna—and held the plate out for her husband. Mathew, however, shook his head and grabbed the cup of coffee.

"Fast breakfast tomorrow, Groot," he said. "Coffee. Biscuits. Fix them some sandwiches—slap some bacon in a biscuit—and tell the boys to stick a couple in their saddlebags or war bags. That'll be their noon dinner."

"They'll need to swap their horses," Groot said.

"They will. While we're riding."

"You ain't gonna make Spanish Fort tomorrow."

"No." Mathew gulped down coffee. "But we'll put some distance between our herd and A. C. Thompson."

The cup, still half-full, fell into the wreck pan. Mathew glanced at Tess and started past her. Suddenly, he stopped.

Tess heard it, too. Distant rumbling. To the south. *Thunder?* she thought. Groot straightened and looked back, too.

"God . . . have mercy." The words came, just loud enough for Tess to hear, from Mathew.

Her right hand covered her mouth. Stampede, she thought, but . . . her head shook.

No . . . their cattle were camped north of camp. It couldn't be . . .

A voice sang out in the night. Joe Nambel's.

"Stam-pede!"

CHAPTER THIRTY

The earth shook.

Sparks catapulted from the fire toward the stars. Horses reared, whinnied. Men cursed. Mathew started for the remuda. Confused, Tess whirled around, looking, and began moving toward the hoodlum wagon. Groot had disappeared. Tess had no idea what she was supposed to do. Hitch the mules? No, the mules were picketed near the remuda. She stopped, turned, made her way in that direction. Lost her balance. Fell onto her buttocks.

Sitting there, she could feel the ground move.

An earthquake? No, that wasn't right. She was pulled up, jerked to her feet, swept into Mathew's arms.

His mouth moved. He screamed something. But whatever he said, the words did not reach her ears. He carried her toward the driver's box of the chuck wagon, lifted her up. She grabbed hold, let her right foot find the wheel, pulled herself into the Studebaker.

"What is it?" Tess yelled. She knew, of course. Joe

Nambel's cry finally registered in her fogged mind. But she could not believe that. Unless she had gone mad, the three thousand longhorn steers they had been driving from the Rio Grande could not be heading—

She gasped. *Heading . . . straight . . . for . . . our . . . camp.*

Mathew had disappeared. From the light from the campfire, she could make out men trying to keep their horses calm, throwing on saddles, quickly, desperately. Mathew would be one of them. And Tom. And Lightning. The wagon shook. She looked back toward the hoodlum wagon. Then she saw Groot, coming from the back of the big Abingdon. He carried the double-barreled shotgun, a twelve-gauge with thirty-inch barrels, in one hand and a canvas sack—filled with shells—in the other. He moved like a drunkard, weaving this way and that. Or maybe it was Tess doing the weaving. Or the wagon, which felt as if it bounced along the old cattle trail.

Groot stumbled to the ground.

That's when Tess heard the hooves, the bawling of panicking longhorns, a gunshot, another. Echoes. More curses. She understood then, and moved.

She dropped down from the wagon, lifted the hems of her skirt, ran to Groot. Found his arm. Pulled him to his feet. Shoved him toward his Studebaker.

"Go!" she roared.

"The . . . shot—"

"Go!"

She could not tell if he heard her, or maybe he just saw the wall moving out of the darkness. Groot moved. So did Tess. She picked up the shotgun as she followed the limping cook. Made a grab for the gunnysack filled with extra shells, but missed. There was no time for a second swipe. Her heart stopped. She forgot how to breathe. But she remembered how to run.

Groot was in the Studebaker, turning, lowering both hands. One snagged the shotgun and quickly dropped it into the wagon. The other latched on to Tess's left wrist. He pulled—almost jerked her arm out of the shoulder socket—and then they collapsed onto the rocking seat of the wagon. Groot almost fell over the other side, but Tess latched on to the back of his suspenders, pulled. He gripped the bottom of the wooden seat with both hands.

Tess screamed.

Bedlam. All around them. Cattle—dull, rangy longhorn steers turned into demons of the night— thundered past them. Groot recovered now, found the shotgun. He aimed. Tess saw the muzzle flash, but she heard no report from the twelve-gauge. All she could hear . . . was hell.

But she felt something else. Behind her. Turning, her mouth opened, and she reached, grabbing for Mathew's right arm, just as the wagon lurched, and he was falling. Somehow, she managed to latch on to his right arm. Her feet braced against the side of the wagon, while pain shot through her back. She had him. The wagon righted itself. Choking dust enveloped her, and she screamed.

"Groot! Help! Groot!"

If he heard, it would have been a miracle. She had not even heard her cries herself. Mathew must have found footing against the wagon wheel, because his other hand grabbed the siding, and suddenly he was in the driver's box himself. Tess turned, and her eyes burned from the flash of Groot's second shotgun blast. The cook opened the twelve-gauge's breech.

His mouth moved. She didn't hear the words, but she knew what he was asking.

She motioned futilely toward the hoodlum wagon. "I couldn't get the sack," she said.

Most likely, he did not hear her, either, not with the crashing, the wrecking, the catastrophe all around them. He pitched the shotgun inside the wagon and sat down heavily on the rocking seat. Only then did he notice Mathew.

Mathew pulled his Colt from the holster, but dropped it onto the floorboard. Tess saw his right hand, barely making it out from the glimmer of fire. A wicked gash swept across the palm of his hand. She could only guess that his horse had shied away in pure panic, and the reins had carved a furrow across his hand. Quickly, she picked up the revolver, thumbed back the hammer, and fired into the charging mass of Texas longhorns.

The powder flash burned her eyes. But she cocked the pistol, pulled the trigger. Again. And again. Till she felt no resistance and understood that she had emptied the Colt. Her eyes had been closed the whole time, and when she opened them, after the orange and red and yellow flashes faded, she saw only darkness. The fire had been put out by the stampeding darkness. She tried to breathe, but dust filled her lungs. Slowly, she sank into the rocking chuck wagon, covered her mouth and nose with her hands, and inhaled. An arm wrapped around her shoulder, and Mathew, her husband, pulled her close.

They did not speak. They waited . . . for death.

Tom Garth spurred harder than he had ever spurred a horse in all his years. He leaned as low as he could in the saddle and gave the roan all the rein the gelding needed. He couldn't see a thing, and prayed that Laredo Downs hadn't been lying to him all those years, saying that a horse has a lot better eyesight than any cowboy.

He felt, more than saw, that he was clear. A roar went past him, and he had to turn hard on the reins to stop the frightened horse. Even then, the gelding pitched a few times, followed by a series of stutter steps. Tom backed the roan up a few more rods. He could sense the stampeding herd of cattle, hear the horrific sound the animals made. He wet his lips and tried to look across the herd. Tried to find what had been their camp.

Nothing.

Not even the light of the campfire.

His head swung northward. Gunshots. Now Tom understood why his father had told the boys to keep their short guns. His heart leaped toward his throat.

"Ma!" His own voice sounded as if it were deep in some cavern. "Pa! Lightning!"

A rider reined in beside him, its own horse pitching in the excitement, which caused Tom's gelding to resume its bucks. Finally, both men managed to get their horses in control, but only by riding behind the herd of stampeding beef, eating dust. Tom glanced to his left at the newcomer, trying to recognize him.

The man had a bandanna pulled up over his nose and mouth. He held a revolver. Tom strained. Unless his eyes played tricks on him, this man wore no boots. In fact, his outfit consisted of filthy socks, well-ventilated summer long drawers, and a light-colored boiled shirt, along with the bandanna and a high-crowned hat.

"Who the hell are you?" Tom asked.

The rider didn't answer. Just kicked his horse into a lope and let the dust swallow him. More riders came, but none slowed down as they galloped past Tom.

"Thompson . . ." his voice mouthed. His brain registered.

A. C. Thompson's herd. That's what had stampeded through their camp. That heat lightning must have spooked Thompson's longhorns . . . How many beeves was A. C. Thompson running? What had his father said? Eighteen hundred.

He understood what had happened now. Thompson's herd had bolted north. Had ransacked the Garth camp. And had crashed right smack-dab into three thousand longhorns bound for Dodge City. Now, both herds were stampeding north in a wild panic. Close to five thousand head of beef. Destroying anything and everything in their path.

"Oh . . . my . . . God!" Tom spurred the roan and hurried after the cattle.

He had no idea if his mother, his father, his brother, his friends were even still alive. He was alive. That's all he knew. And his father, especially over these last couple of months, had taught him one lesson. On a cattle drive, especially this drive, the herd was all that mattered. Save the herd.

Save the herd.

* * *

A steer rammed into the side of the Studebaker, so hard the animal dropped dead with a broken neck. The chuck wagon rocked, tried to settle back, but just then one or maybe two or—hell, who knew, five, ten, more—beeves hit the wagon's underside.

Tess reached for something to hold. She heard Mathew crying out, "We're going over."

The wagon pitched. Tess felt herself flying out into the darkness. She heard the wagon crash, then felt air rush out of her lungs. She lay still, tried to suck in oxygen, but could not manage even a breath. Her eyes would not close, but she could see nothing. Just darkness. She wondered: *Am I dead?*

Suddenly, she was moving, but not of her own accord.

Two hands gripped her blouse and pulled, pulled. Her lungs started to work again. She blinked. And saw the silhouette of her husband as he brought her to the shaking wagon.

"Help me!" She could just make out Mathew's choking voice in the din of chaos.

"Are you . . . all right?"

She couldn't tell if he had heard.

"It's Groot."

He turned. She moved beside him.

Groot lay on the ground, half-seated, gripping his right leg, the end of which disappeared.

Tess gasped. They reached for the underside of the Studebaker, still resting on its side. Tess came onto her knees. Her fingers found a hold. Already Mathew was lifting, and she joined, straining. The wagon budged, just barely enough for Groot to free his leg.

Groot wailed even louder. And just like that, the noise, that jarring, unnerving sound of hooves and hell, passed them, leaving behind only thick dust and echoes. Lightning flashed to the north, to the south. A horse and rider loped past them, but did not stop.

She seemed to understand it then. That she was alive. That they had survived. At least, she still lived. Mathew lifted Groot like a baby, carried him from the Studebaker, and gently laid him on a bed of trampled grass.

"Damn it all to hell!" Groot yelled. "My wagon's ruint. Cattle's spread out all to hell and gone. I didn't get no peach cobbler. And now my gol-durned ankle's practically busted in half."

CHAPTER THIRTY-ONE

Rain came with the dawn, soaking Tom Garth as he rode around the milling herd. His rain slicker remained in the hoodlum wagon back at camp, some miles down the trail. How many miles had those longhorns covered during the stampede? It felt like forever. The cattle were exhausted. So were men and horses. Yet he managed to smile, and a wave of relief washed over him when he spotted a familiar figure moving three longhorns out of a gully and toward the herd.

"Lightning!" Tom yelled.

"Don't spook them, Tom," Lightning called back. But he, too, grinned happily. The longhorns continued to join the others even after Lightning reined his horse to a stop.

"You start another stampede and Pa'll raise holy hell."

Lightning pulled his Russian from the holster. "I'm empty, by the way. Reckon Pa was right about carrying this .44."

Tom could only nod. He had heard the shots as men tried to turn the stampeding mass of beef so that the cattle would slow, mill, and, eventually, come to a stop. Yet Tom had not even drawn his .38. He wondered if he had been too frightened, hanging on to the reins tightly, fearing falling beneath those churning hooves. Maybe not. Not terror, anyway. He had been too busy to be afraid.

"You seen Pa?" Tom asked.

"No." He pointed to the northwest. "Spotted No Sabe and Joey Corinth back yonder way. Roping a steer that got stuck in a bog. How about you? Seen anybody we know?"

"Think I got a glimpse of Bradley Rush during the night. Only other folks I saw were strangers."

"Yeah." He pointed to a brindle steer. "That ain't ours. Ain't Pa's road brand."

"No." He explained his theory, that the heat lightning down south had spooked A. C. Thompson's herd into a stampede. That caused their own herd to run.

"We oughta go check on Ma," Lightning said.

"Yeah."

As they turned their horses, however, two men loped toward them. Tom recognized only one.

Laredo Downs and a man in gray-striped britches, muslin undershirt, soaking socks, and a soggy bowler hat reined in. Laredo grinned. The man with the gunmetal gray mustache did not.

"You boys is a sight for sore eyes," Laredo said. He gestured at the man on the buckskin mare. "You two know A. C. Thompson."

Tom nodded, recognizing the trail boss at last.

"Boys." Thompson's voice came out like a frog's croak.

Laredo asked, "Where's your pa?"

Tom's head shook, but it was Lightning who answered. "We ain't seen him since this whole thing started. Ma, neither." His eyes glared at Thompson, who dropped his gaze and studied his pale hands, which gripped the horn of his saddle.

"Sorry," A. C. Thompson croaked again.

"Ain't your fault, A.C.," Laredo said before looking back at Tom and Lightning. "We got beeves scattered across North Texas. Rain ain't helpin' matters, and we'll need to start sortin' out our steers from A.C.'s." He pointed across the milling sea of beef. "Joe Nambel, Noguerra, and Meeker's over yonder way. I ain't seen hardly nobody from our crew since this ruction started."

Lightning pointed. "That Mex rustler Pa hired and that Rush fellow were over yonder a half hour or so ago."

"All right. I want you two to ride back to camp. See how things are there." Laredo wet his lips, tried to swallow, and wiped the rain off his face. "Maybe . . . you want me to ride along with you?"

Tom shook his head.

"Maybe . . ." Thompson tried again. "Maybe I should ride back to your camp with you boys. Explain to Mathew what happened . . . if . . . if . . ."

Tom's face hardened. Again, Lightning found the words.

"*If my ma and pa are still alive?* That what you mean?"

Laredo interrupted. "I wouldn't advise that, A.C., but we appreciate your offer."

Lightning spit. Turning to Laredo, Tom almost said something, but held his tongue, again. Pa would be inclined to thrash A. C. Thompson for that stampede. And the thought, those words Lightning had just spoken, echoed in his head:

"If my ma and pa are still alive."

"All right, Laredo," Tom said, and turned his horse. "Boys."

Both Tom and Lightning looked back at Laredo. The frog kept his head down now, did not, could not, look the two brothers in the eye.

"We ain't got everyone accounted for," Laredo said. "Not yet. I mean our crew and A.C.'s. Don't worry about the dead beeves you'll find. We'll do a count later. But . . . you come across somebody, someone you know or not . . . if . . . if you . . . if you can tell . . . just fire us a warning shot. Two shots, spaced out, if he's alive. If he's dead, three shots."

Tom could not speak. He merely nodded, sending rain sailing off his hat's brim, and put his horse to a walk.

Dead cattle lay strewn across the churned-up prairie, which now darkened and thickened as the rain kept falling. Tom and Lightning kept their horses in a walk for two reasons. One, the geldings were worn out. Two, a dread kept them from hurrying back to camp. Fear knotted their insides.

After a mile, the rain slackened. Another mile, it picked up again. Tom shivered and realized he was riding alone. Reining up, he looked back where

Lightning had stopped. Tom turned in the saddle and saw what had caught his brother's attention.

The trail resembled some sodbuster's wheat field after plowing. Yet amid all the dark clay, a bush stood, its leaves dripping rain, blowing in the wind that was picking up. The sight struck Tom with wonder. Figure this. In all this hell, in a land thick with dead cattle and crushed earth, a bush grew as if nothing had ever happened.

Looking at the bush, Tom almost smiled, until something else caught his attention. His stomach began roiling. He had not thrown up . . . not yet . . . but now thought he might. A piece of cloth clung to the bush, and, although heavy with rainwater, it moved with the breeze.

Something lay in a little depression in front of the bush. Tom could just make it out now.

"We best . . ." Lightning said.

Tom nudged his horse toward the bush; Lightning did the same. They soon merged and rode easily until both horses began shying away from the bush and what lay beyond the bush. Tom kicked and spurred, but the horse refused to go any farther.

He hoped his brother would dismount, but Lightning remained glued to the saddle. After dismounting, Tom handed the reins to Lightning.

"My gun's empty," Lightning said, finding an excuse. "Let me know if . . . if . . ."

Tom walked, his boots sinking in the mud. He stopped breathing when he realized for certain what he had feared. Moments ago, he thought the crumpled mass of brown near the bush was another dead longhorn, but now he could make out the remnants of a saddle, a bridle, the sorrel's mane, its head. He could smell the excrement, the blood, and he saw . . .

He exhaled and tried to spit, but his mouth had turned to sand. Slowly, he looked back at his brother. His mouth opened, but nothing rose from his throat—except gall.

"Is it . . . ?" Lightning shouted.

Blinking, Tom shook his head.

Tears welled in his eyes, though, and dumbly, he realized that he had drawn his Colt from the holster. He held it awkwardly, pointed at an angle. He did not realize he had squeezed the trigger until the .38 bucked in his hand, and he smelled the sulfuric scent of gun smoke.

He squeezed the trigger again.

Then . . . once more.

"One . . . two . . . three!"

Muscles straining, boots slipping in the mud, Mathew tried again, pushing, lifting, trying to get the Studebaker up just enough. Beside him, Tess groaned, cursed, and then her boots slipped in the mud. She fell, and the chuck wagon dropped back to its side.

"Let me come over yonder and help you," Groot called out.

"You're not moving one inch, Groot Nadine!" Tess yelled as she pushed herself to her feet. "Not after Mathew and I just set your busted ankle."

"But . . ."

"Shut up and stay still." Tess wiped thick mud off her dress, looked at her boots, and spit out water as she ran her fingers across her face. That produced another curse as she left a streak of mud on her cheek and forehead. Rain quickly washed away the grime. She looked at Mathew.

"Try again."

"No use." He removed his hat, wiped his face with his sleeve, and returned the wet hat. Tess was strong, and game. She always had been both, but the chuck wagon was too heavy. He would have to wait until some of the crew returned. He glanced at the leather-burned gash in his palm.

"Come here," Tess ordered, and he followed her.

They had managed to start a fire, protected from a makeshift lean-to they had erected with spokes from the hoodlum wagon and shreds of cloth that had been bedrolls and slickers. Coffee percolated in a pot, and bacon remained in a skillet.

Mathew followed her, and they joined Groot under another makeshift tent.

He sat in the mud, pushed back his hat, and looked at what had once been a peaceful camp. It reminded him of Brice's Crossroads when General Forrest had led the boys against the Yankees north of Tupelo. The bluebellies had them outnumbered close to two to one, but they had routed the Yanks, sent them scurrying every which way but loose. The Yanks fled in a panic, leaving behind the dead and practically anything they could shed so they could run faster.

The hoodlum wagon resembled a pile of sticks. Flour mixed with mud. Bits of cloth littered the ground, along with six or eight dead longhorns. They had salvaged what they could, but it wasn't much. Oh, he had Groot's shotgun, and had found six shells among the threads in the mud that had been a gunnysack. Six shotgun loads of buckshot that would . . . probably . . . still fire, after he had cleaned them of mud, water, and grime. The chuck wagon would be all right, with some grease and a few minor repairs—once they got it righted onto all four wheels. And even a few cattle and horses wandered about, lost in a daze. Mathew could have tried to catch one of the geldings, but he wasn't sure he could rope a thing with his hand gashed from that rein. Besides, riding bareback never appealed to him, and his horse could be all the way to Spanish Fort by now.

He knew to stay put. Let the crew find you. They—whoever remained alive—would return to camp, sometime.

Tess had wadded up a handkerchief and dipped it in the skillet. She took Mathew's right hand and dabbed the gash with bacon grease, then wrapped the piece of silk around his hand.

"Best I can do," she said.

"It'll do." The rain kept falling. "Thanks."

"I got some whiskey in the top drawer back of the wagon," Groot said. "I could use a snort."

"It's busted, Groot," Tess told him. "I checked already."

"Hell." Groot found his plug of tobacco and bit off a healthy chunk.

Something echoed to the north, and Mathew ducked and stepped out of the shelter and into the rain. It wasn't thunder.

Another. Mathew held his breath. Then he heard the third report.

"What's that?" Tess asked.

"Signal." Groot stopped working on his quid. "Three shots, Mathew . . . That means . . ." He stopped, turned to Tess, and swallowed, not the entire quid, and probably not enough juice to make him sick. Groot always had a cast-iron stomach. "It's . . . just . . . a signal."

CHAPTER THIRTY-TWO

"I know what it means, Groot." Standing in the rain at Mathew's side, Tess reached over, took his left hand in her own, and squeezed it, hopefully. Mathew, though, pulled away without returning the gesture and walked through the mud, staring north.

He wondered. When was the last time he had ever felt this helpless? Not during the war, not even at Shiloh. He knew the answer. Forty-plus years back, just after his parents had been massacred along with most of the people on that train bound for Oregon. He had kept following that damned old cow until he ran into that bear of a man with a bull and a dream.

What would Thomas Dunson have done? Well, for one thing, he likely would not have made such a boneheaded mistake as to camp where another herd could stampede straight through your camp, scatter your own beef and horses to hell and gone. Dunson would not have let a horse shy away from him, leave him with a wicked reminder of what wet leather could do to human flesh. No, Thomas Dunson would never have found himself afoot.

Yet here stood Mathew. No horse. He walked around the campsite, kicking up debris with his boots, went to the nearest dead steer and read the brand, then the road brand. Thirty, maybe forty bucks of beef reduced to nothing but a waterlogged slab to feed ravens, coyotes, and buzzards.

Only a chuck wagon left. The hoodlum wagon wouldn't make fit kindling. Most of the supplies had been drowned or dismembered, spread across the campsite by bits and pieces, or blown south toward Nacogdoches.

"You ain't puttin' me out to pasture, Mathew," Groot said.

Mathew looked up, realizing that he had walked back to the lean-to.

"I wouldn't think of it." He tried to smile.

"You're not thinking about sending me home, either," Tess said.

His head shook. "Groot'll need help."

The old cook spit tobacco juice into the mud. "You mean . . . you mean . . . I's still a-comin' along."

"We'll get your ankle checked out in Spanish Fort." Mathew faked another smile. "You can't cook worth a hoot, but you can handle a team of mules."

"Horse apples," Groot said. "You just don't want to pay for no stagecoach ticket all the way down to Dunson City."

"Come in out of the rain," Tess said.

He nodded, but did not move immediately. First, he looked to the north, where the faint reports of three evenly spaced pistol shots had come from. The warning shot. That someone—dead—had been discovered. Then he spotted something off to the south and east, and he looked hard. At first he thought it was a steer, maybe a horse, but then he sucked in a breath, held it, and frowned.

Horse, yes. But with a man sitting in a saddle. The same man, Mathew guessed, who had been following them since Comanche.

"I meant to tell him something." Lightning Garth swept his hat off his head and kicked the mound of mud at his feet. He stared at the soaked ground and what had once been a man.

"What's that, Lightning?" Teeler Lacey asked.

They had gathered on the prairie, not the whole crew, just a few of those who had heard Tom's pistol shots. Meeker, Lacey, Laredo, A. C. Thompson, and two of Thompson's cowhands. The Thompson rider with the brown leather patch over his right eye had brought the spade. A. C. Thompson had pulled a little Bible from the pocket of his coat. It was a small Bible, though, not even half the size of the one Grandpa Dunson had owned, and a tiny thing compared with the one the circuit-riding sky pilot brought out when he came to Dunson City.

"Oh." Lightning looked up. "You know. How he moved his soogans from the cantle to right in front of the horn." He made an idle gesture at his crotch. "For protection. You know? Y'all made some jokes about it." He found himself smiling at the memory, and that, he realized, brought an odd comfort to him. "Well, I was thinking that . . . well . . . last night, during the stampede, my horse bucked a bit, and . . . well . . . I thought I was a goner, certain-sure. Hit the horn, felt as if my *huevos* was heading straight up my windpipe."

Tom's head shook. He could see others smiling and realized a grin crossed his face, too.

"I was gonna tell him . . ." Again, Lightning paused.

"Tell him now," Laredo said.

Anger seized him, replaced that feeling of solace. Lightning slapped the rain off his hat and returned the battered piece of felt to his head. "What for? He can't hear me no more."

"I think he can hear you," Laredo said.

Lightning snorted, then spit into the dirt. Again, he looked at what was left of Alvaro Cuevas. For most of his life, Lightning had heard stories about stampedes, but this had been his first one. He had been told about what eight thousand hooves could do to a man, but there had been . . . what? . . . five thousand longhorns running like mad last night?

The young vaquero had been wearing yellow britches of waterproof yarn. That's the only way Tom had figured out who he had found, from the bits of the twill-weaved cloth. Young Alvaro had said he'd stay pretty dry with those Burberrys he had bought in San Antonio last year. Special britches, imported from Basingstoke, England. Well, that's what the gal at the mercantile had told him.

When the others had arrived, Meeker and the Thompson rider with two good eyes had joined Tom and Lightning searching around for the German silver crucifix Cuevas usually wore, but found nothing but a cleanly severed pinky finger . . . as if cut off by a meat cleaver. No crucifix. The Thompson man had tossed the finger into the pile of remains and mud and blood that had once been a pretty good cowboy.

As Teeler Lacey scooped up mud and began covering Alvaro Cuevas, Laredo Downs said in a solemn voice: "All right, I'll rig up somethin' to mark the grave. Reckon Mathew will want to read over Alvaro's body."

"If Garth's alive . . ." the eye-patched cowhand said.

"You better hope he's alive," Lightning said, staring hard, not at the cowboy, but his boss, A. C. Thompson.

"Let's find out," Laredo said. "A.C., you take your boys off to the east yonder." He pointed with his jaw. "Teeler, when you're done, tie this wild rag to this here bush." He withdrew a bright yellow square of silk, which he placed gently on the bush. "Then you take Meeker, see if you can find Joe, get back to gathering all you can find. I'll get Groot, the boss man, the chuck wagon and . . ."

Lightning did not wait to hear any more orders. He trod through the mud to where he had ground-reined his horse. In a minute, he was in the saddle and trotting south. His brother rode alongside him.

The rain stopped, but Tess saw no break in the clouds, no blue skies, not even a ray of sunlight. Which seemed to represent how she, and all the rest, felt. Relief. Her sons were alive. But that was it. No joy. How could you feel any of that when a poor Mexican vaquero, only in his twenties, had been buried? When probably hundreds of longhorns were dead, and quite a few horses, belonging to A. C. Thompson and Mathew? When Groot Nadine lay soaking in the mud with a busted ankle that had swollen to the size of his thigh and kept turning ugly colors? When Laredo Downs said it would take three days, maybe more, to separate the two herds? When the weather foretold of more rain, meaning the Red would be running wild by the time they could cross and they would have to wait till the waters receded? When Mathew Garth, her husband of twenty years, looked the way he did.

They had righted Groot's chuck wagon, greased the axles, and hitched Lightning's and Tom's horses to pull the Studebaker to the camp a few miles north. They had gone by the grave of Alvaro Cuevas, where Mathew had found the Bible, and read the beatitudes. No Sabe, a vaquero for Thompson's riders, and Yago Noguerra had then sung some hymn in Spanish. The music seemed to linger on long after the final notes. They had made it to camp, relieved—if that were the right word—to find that no one else had been killed, or badly injured, during the stampede.

Groot ordered Joey Corinth and No Sabe about to help with the cooking, and A. C. Thompson had arrived from his camp with his cook, his men, and some supplies.

And now Mathew strode from where he had been sitting, to stand an arm's length from A. C. Thompson.

"A sack of oat flakes?" Mathew said.

A. C. Thompson had been talking. Now he tried to step back, away from Mathew, but Mathew equaled the distance.

"That what you think a man's life is worth?" Mathew said.

"Huh? What? Mathew, what . . . ?"

"You're paying me off for what you did to Alvaro

with a sack of oat flakes?" Mathew rested his hand on his revolver.

A. C. Thompson's mouth fell open, and he paled considerably. No one else spoke. Even Groot had stopped yammering to his helpers. He gawked, stared, mouth agape.

"Mathew . . . no . . . no . . . of course not," Thompson said. "I'm just tryin' to help, son."

"I'm not your son. You've cost me four days, probably more. You've cost me one good man. Whatever you want for absolution, it'll cost you a lot more than feed."

Tess looked around, not surprised to find a wall in the camp. Thompson's men drifted to one side of the fire, resting their hands on the butts of their holstered revolvers, or moving in the general direction toward their horses in the picket line, closer to their carbines. The riders for Mathew spread out around him, even those who—Tess could read it in their faces—thought Mathew was wrong.

She found Tom, on one side of Mathew, thumbs hooked inside his gun belt, his face sick, pale, but the eyes determined. On Mathew's right stood Lightning, and his face frightened Tess even more.

Lightning grinned, and a light shone in his eyes that left Tess nauseated.

She waited. She dared not breathe.

The evening air turned into a tightly wound strand of barbed wire between two cedar posts.

No one would ever call A. C. Thompson a coward, not after all the drives he had made to Missouri and Kansas. Tess saw no fear in him now, just reason, and maybe loss. He seemed to grieve for Alvaro Cuevas.

Maybe Mathew grieved, too, but just did not know how to show it . . . anymore.

Glancing at his men, the old drover must have realized that one move, one wrong step, could lead to more senseless deaths. Exhaling, he slowly pulled his hands away from his own belted Remington.

"The Mex yonder . . ." Thompson thrust his jaw toward Yago Noguerra. "He says the dead boy left a widowed mother and three younger siblings back at Llano Rojo." That was a collection of jacales across the river from Dunson City.

"That's right." It was Laredo Downs who answered. Laredo did not look at Mathew.

"Well, I'll be payin' his wages. Plus any bonus you promised the boys in Dodge. And that family'll never go hungry as long as I'm livin'."

Thompson did not wait for a reply, but turned toward the picket line. His men followed.

CHAPTER THIRTY-THREE

After two days, the weather broke, the sun reappeared, and North Texas began drying out, again. Two more days, and the herds had been separated, the losses totaled, and Mathew Garth pushed his beef toward the river. A. C. Thompson decided—wisely in Tess's opinion—to wait another day or two before moving on toward Red River Station to ford the river, partly to stay clear of Mathew, but also for practical reasons. After all the rains, any trail crew pushing north would have to wait for the water level to fall before they could cross into Indian Territory.

Mathew Garth knew that, too, but he was not about to wait in line for other herds to swim the Red.

They reached the banks first in line, bedded down the herd, and Mathew helped Groot into the chuck wagon, then looked around and ordered Tom to fetch his horse and tag along.

Understanding, Tess smiled, but that did not last long.

"Why can't I go to town?" Lightning asked.

"Shorthanded already," Mathew answered. He said

nothing else. Lightning started to protest, but Tess put her hand on his arm. A warning. For once, Lightning did not argue.

"Should be back before dark," Mathew said as he released the brake. "You got enough grub to cook for the boys?"

"I'm no Janeen," Tess said, "but—"

"You ain't no Groot Nadine, neither," Groot snapped. "Best remember that."

"She's not only a better cook than you, Groot," Teeler Lacey said, "but she looks a damned sight better, too."

"I'll remember you said that, Teeler, lessen that pill-roller in town saws off my leg and I die."

"We'll remember you, too, Groot," Teeler said, "if that happens. Thankin' the good Lord ever' time we eat."

Mathew flicked the lines before Groot could fire back another retort. Instead, the cook wailed as he leaned forward to grip his leg. Turning toward camp as they rode out, Mathew called out to Teeler Lacey.

"Keep a lookout."

Understanding, Lacey nodded. They had not seen the man who had been trailing them for the past couple of days.

By the time Tom caught up with the wagon, they had hit the track that passed for a road and Groot had stopped his screaming and cussing.

"You've never been to Spanish Fort, have you?" Mathew said.

"No, sir," Tom answered. He rode his zebra dun, the one mare in his string. "Two times I went on a drive, we always took the Western Trail . . . Lightning, too."

"Ain't missed nothin'." Groot spit tobacco juice.

* * *

Spanish Fort had changed.

The first signs were the strands of barbed wire that fenced off fields of tall corn or smaller gardens of tomatoes, carrots, potatoes, pumpkins, and turnips. Twice, they passed two farmers who stood behind their fences cradling heavy shotguns, scowling but not speaking as the chuck wagon and rider passed.

"Reckon they don't get so many cattlemen no more," Groot said.

The Cowboy Saloon still stood right on the town square, though, and at least four horses stood tethered at the hitching post. Mathew spotted two other familiar buildings, yet he also found two churches, one Baptist, the other Methodist, and a log building where children played out front on two seesaws and a swing before a petite woman with her hair in a bun began ringing a bell and telling the boys and girls that recess had ended. At least the schoolmarm—unlike the farmers—smiled as they passed.

"Grown some," Mathew said.

"So's that." Groot pointed to the cemetery.

Folks said a giant Indian village had once stood on these grounds. Wichitas or Taovayas, most likely. The Spanish and French had come through here, with Bibles or bullets, but after the Indians had moved on, the town wasn't settled until around the 1850s and didn't begin to boom until a few years after Thomas Dunson's first cattle drive to the railhead. First, the speck on the map had been called Burlington, till citizens tried to get a post office and had been told to come up with another handle, that Burlington had already been taken. So they looked at the old ruins of the old Indian camp and chose Spanish Fort.

Spanish Fort grew as a supply outlet for cattlemen and a watering hole for cowboys—the last stop in Texas. Now that most drovers were using the trail farther west, the town had . . . *evolved?* Was what the right word? Mathew wondered.

Years back, in the late 1870s, the town had been able to support four doctors. In fact, the doctors were so skilled at gunshot wounds—fairly common in a town like Spanish Fort—folks came from as far east as Gainesville and as far west as Henrietta to get patched up, if they didn't bleed out or die of lead poisoning first. But with fewer cowboys getting drunk and angry inside the Cowboy Saloon, most doctors had moved on. Only two remained, and since Doc Allen was out treating a sick family of sodbusters south of town, they left Groot, moaning between curses, in the hands of a rail-thin Missourian named Becker, and stepped onto the warped boardwalk on the square.

"Maybe," Tom said, "we ought to check with the livery, see if they have a wagon for sale."

"Wagon?" Mathew asked.

"Replace the hoodlum wagon," he said.

Mathew smiled. "We don't have anything to put in the hoodlum wagon, Tom. But there's one place you need to go."

His name was Herman Joseph Justin—the sign above his shop said H. J. JUSTIN—yet everyone called him Joe.

A young man not quite thirty, Joe Justin had left his home in Indiana back at age eighteen and went to work repairing shoes in Gainesville. A short while later, not liking working for somebody else, he moved to Spanish Fort, where, with only $5.25 to his name, he went to work emptying spittoons and heating water for a barber. Eventually, the barber grubstaked him thirty-five dollars.

That barber, John P. See, remained in town. He got a new pair of boots every Christmas and wore his pants legs stuck inside those beautiful boots to show them off. He had helped make Joe Justin a rich man, and Joe Justin always paid his debts.

After starting in a one-room frame building that always smelled of leather and wax, Justin had expanded, buying two neighboring buildings and knocking out the walls. Yet his shop still smelled of leather and wax. Boots in various stages of finish sat on just about every inch of space. That surprised Mathew. He had figured that with trail herds off to the west, Justin might be hurting for business.

Inside came the din of men speaking Spanish, English, Italian. A woman said something. Hammers rang out. Sewing machines spun. Mathew found at least three men working on boots.

"Should have known better," he said.

"How's that?" Tom asked.

"Man with his reputation . . ." Mathew didn't finish, for Joe Justin, wearing an apron and holding a hammer, stepped away from one of the cobblers he had been instructing. Dropping the hammer, he strode across the room and stuck out a hand marked with scars.

"Mathew Garth." He did not look at Mathew's face more than a second. His eyes dropped to the floor.

Clucking his tongue and shaking his head, he turned and stared at Tom's boots.

"Those are disgraceful." He looked up and put his hands on his hips.

"That's why we're here." Mathew tilted his head toward Tom and introduced him.

"He had a birthday some time back. His mother thought we should treat him to a pair of the finest boots in Texas."

"In the world."

Pointing to an empty chair, Joe Justin walked to a desk on the other side of the office, where he grabbed pencil and pad and a cloth measuring tape.

"Sit down," Mathew told Tom, "and take off those boots, but keep your socks on."

"You get a pair of boots," Justin said as he placed Tom's right foot on the pad, "from a store. You put them on. You soak them with water. They break to your feet. Wet leather shrinks as it dries. That's not the way I do it. Not the way it should be done. Boot-making is an art. I'm an artist. Boots shouldn't have to be broken in. They ought to fit you like a glove. You got small feet. Most cowboys come through here would kill to have small feet like yours." He looked at Mathew. "Never figured out why in hell a cowboy wants to wear boots that are two sizes too small for him."

Mathew shrugged.

"Your father," Justin said as he took out the measuring tape and began measuring Tom's right foot in various places, "got feet the size of an elephant."

Tom ordered a pair of black boots, eighteen inches high, with white stars inlaid into the uppers, mule-ear pulls, and heels shaped to fit a stirrup.

"Way it works is like this," Justin explained after writing a few notes in the corner of the traces of Tom's feet. "You take your cattle to Kansas. When you come back here, you pick up your boots. Don't you buy no damned boots in Dodge City. I know John Mueller. He'll charge you eighteen bucks for a pair of boots that don't fit worth a damn. You come back here. You pay me that fifteen bucks then. Now . . ." He pointed to a case of five shelves of various boots. "You go over there and pick out a pair. Your feet. Bottom shelf. To the left. You find one that fits, and you walk out with them on. The ones you wore in here, they aren't fit for a trash can. Go on. Your pa'll pay five dollars for those. Shop-made, but they'll last you to Dodge and back. Last you for years. Won't fit like the ones you'll pick up in a couple of months, but a young whippersnapper like you needs two pairs of boots. Those rags you come with, they won't last you across the river. Go on. I'll measure your daddy."

"You've measured me before, Joe," Mathew said.

"You haven't been here in five, six years, Mathew. Feet change. Just like people."

After buying a few supplies and checking the post office for any mail, they made it back too late for supper, which was fine with Groot. He knew what to expect from a trail crew, and the next morning, the cowboys proved him right.

They made fun of the hard cast on Groot's ankle, and Groot, as was his nature, responded by spitting tobacco juice precariously close to their coffee cups or plates of bacon and fried potatoes.

"Yes, sir," Laredo Downs said, "that's about as fine

a boot as Joe Justin's ever made. But how come you didn't get but one boot, Groot?"

"This boot I did get," Groot said, "can stove in your head whilst you's sleepin', Laredo."

"Let me serve, Groot," Tess said.

"No, ma'am. Next thing happens after that, Mathew puts me out to pasture." He lifted his busted leg and shook it feebly. "Damned thing already itches some-thin' fierce."

"I like Tom's new boots better," Joey Corinth said.

"New boots?" Lightning had not even noticed. Now he stood, putting his plate on a stump, and walked over to where Tom squatted by the fire.

"I ride nursemaid on a bunch of smelly beef, and you ride into town to get a new pair of boots?"

All banter ceased.

"Lightning," Tess said, "it was a birthday present. Tom's eighteenth."

"Yeah. Sure."

Tess's eyes turned cold. "You got a pair of boots in Dodge two years ago, Lightning. When you turned eighteen."

"Yeah. After I finished the drive."

Mathew rose from his seat, leaving his plate and cup on the ground. He started to say something, but his lips flattened, and he stared ahead. Within moments, everyone followed his gaze, and everyone wearing a gun rested his hand on the revolver's grip or hooked a thumb in the belt near the holster.

CHAPTER THIRTY-FOUR

"I wondered when you'd find time to pay us a visit." Mathew turned away from the man who had ridden into camp and picked up his coffee—with his left hand. His right remained near the holstered Colt.

"You knowed who I was, eh?"

"Just figured it to be you. What brings you to camp?"

"Saw that grave a few days back. Thought you might be hirin'."

It reminded Mathew of what Jess Teveler had said after Milt Blasingame had been killed, but he dismissed the thought. Although the ex–buffalo soldier wore a battered campaign hat, Mathew could tell that he had shaved his head again, most likely this morning, or last night before he went to bed. Or had he gone to Spanish Fort? Maybe trailed them yesterday? Spanish Fort still had a barber, and the salt-and-pepper mustache and goatee looked neatly trimmed.

The clothes weren't new, and he kept his gun and D ring bowie knife stuck inside the green sash he had been wearing back in Comanche, when he had joined the sheriff's posse that was chasing Teveler.

Mathew said: "Didn't know cowboying was your line of work."

"Man's gotta eat."

Mathew sipped coffee and made a slight head gesture at the coffeepot resting on a tripod over the fire.

"Coffee and grub we have. We can talk about a job later."

That was the invitation. The big black man dismounted with ease, picketed his horse in the grass, and crossed toward the wagon in a bowlegged gait. He extended his right hand. "They call me Reata. But my name's Chet. Chet Chase. I like Reata better."

He had manners. Mathew had to give him that much. He swept his hat off his head and bowed when he saw Tess, and waited in line till all the other hands had gotten their breakfast.

"Late breakfast," he said absently as he sat alone beside the wagon tongue.

"River's too high to cross today," Mathew said.

"Boys ain't in town?"

"I don't like towns. On cattle drives."

Reata smiled, forked a chunk of potato into his mouth, and finished eating in silence. Afterward, he deposited his dishes in the wreck pan, wiped his mouth with a fairly clean yellow handkerchief that he fished out of his back pocket, and said:

"I rode with the 9th Cavalry from '68 to '83. Barbered a spell in Scabtown down by Fort McKavett, then done some liveryin' in Comanche."

"For Paul Ransom?"

His head nodded. "Yes, sir. You know him?"

"I do indeed."

Reata smiled. "He's a man to learn from, that's for sure."

"He teach you how to trail a man?"

The smile widened. "If I was trailin' a man, I wouldn't be followin' you. Because Teveler ain't been around. I know that much."

"But you think he might just show up."

"It strikes me as fairly good odds. You know him. He visited your camp before. I read that much in your eyes." He nodded toward Tom and Lightning. "And theirs. Read worry, too. Which told me that this here Teveler . . . well . . . he might just come visit y'all again sometime."

Mathew sipped coffee. "Paul Ransom teach you that?"

He laughed. "No, sir. I learnt that on my own. Fifteen years of hoss-soldierin', that teaches a man other things."

"Like riding?"

His head bobbed. "I can ride."

"The man we buried, he was a little wiry thing. Vaquero. You get his string. Biggest one isn't nowhere near the size of that monster you rode in on."

"I'll ride what you give me, boss. Gots to be better 'n what the army stuck us on."

"You'll ride drag."

The grin vanished, but he did nod.

"Maybe I'll get promoted up to somewhere that ain't quite so dusty." Eventually, the smile returned. "After all, I was a sergeant when I left the 9th Cavalry."

"I'll let you know. Meanwhile, since your horse is saddled, you might as well ride out to the herd. And keep them company."

"So y'all can talk behind my back?"

"Or you can ride out now. Pay's a dollar a day."

He rose, and shook Mathew's hand. "With . . . maybe a bonus?"

"If the herd brings a top price."

The black man let out a rumbling laugh as he walked to his big horse. "Or . . . maybe . . . a couple of beefy rewards for Jess Teveler."

When Reata had ridden out, Laredo Downs walked to Mathew. "Teveler rides into our camp, there'll be gunplay. You know that."

Mathew shrugged. "Or maybe if Reata's with us . . . Teveler doesn't ride into our camp."

"You didn't hire Jess Teveler," Lightning said, "after Milt got killed. But you hire that saddle tramp?"

"We lost Alvaro," Mathew snapped, "and there was no cowhand to hire in Spanish Fort. I need that man . . . if I'm to get these beeves to Dodge."

He was moving then, dropping his dishes in the basin, telling Joey Corinth to bring out horses from Mathew's, Tom's, and Lightning's string, and saddle a good one for Tess.

"Where we going?" Lightning asked.

"To see a man."

After six years, Mathew wondered if he could find it. The way he remembered, that had proved difficult in 1880. The floods a couple of years back could have washed away everything, including the remains, weeds and saplings could have overgrown the site, or some sodbuster might have filed a claim and tried to farm this country.

He reined up, twisted in his saddle, hooked a leg over the horn, found the makings, and began rolling a cigarette. Eventually, Tess, Tom, and Lightning caught up with him.

"Where we going?" Tom asked.

"You'll see," Tess answered.

It did take longer to find the marker. Weeds had grown higher, and the Red had taken away the elm tree that had always been his landmark. They slugged through mud, up the little knoll, and eventually Mathew dismounted, handing the reins to Tom, and kicked down the high grass until he saw the cairn.

"Watch for snakes," Mathew said, and removed his hat.

The Conestoga arrived at the banks of the Red River in the evening, hours after they should have made camp, when they never should have left Abilene at all. Mathew told Thomas Dunson that they would cross in the morning, but Dunson barked out that they would cross tonight. Now.

His voice had been different. Oh, he had roared like a bear, but Mathew had sucked in his breath when Dunson spoke. Each word had sent pain through the big man's entire body, and Mathew had detected an urgency in Dunson's voice. And something else.

Fear.

He shot Tess a look, but she did not see. She was staring at Dunson, too. So Mathew had left them in the back of the wagon, climbed into the box, flicked the lines, and forced the tired horses into the river.

Horses. They should have used oxen.

He remembered Tess telling him, several days later, how water had filled the back of the wagon as they crossed, how Tess wondered if the wagon might just sink, the horses drown, and the Red take them all to some watery graves.

Briefly, she later conceded, she had feared this was Dunson's way of revenge. Killing them all. Yet Dunson had scooped the water into his pale hands and brought his fingers to his lips. Muddy water. Carrying the earth with it. By then, they were closer to the Texas side, so Dunson felt as if he had been tasting Texas soil. It had given him strength.

When they crossed into Texas, came up the bank, found a good level place, Mathew again had stopped the wagon and came around to the back of the Conestoga. Dunson's voice softened, and he asked Mathew to lift him out of the wagon.

He remembered the moonlight. How bright it had been. As bright as morning sun. He wondered if he looked totally absurd, holding this behemoth in his arms, carrying him like a child until Dunson asked to be lowered to the ground.

Thomas Dunson wanted to stand. Mathew didn't think the old man would be able to, but he did. His feet touched Texas earth, and in the moonlight, the old man seemed alive again.

Dunson's voice, Mathew remembered, sounded so far away. He said that this was Texas, and he had pointed off to the south. He said that he had come home. Mathew had said, his voice choking, that, yes, Thomas Dunson was home. Tess had said nothing. She just stood there in the moonlight. And cried silently.

As Thomas Dunson sank into the grass, touching the land he had loved, the land he had fought for, killed for, and carved . . . even if most of that country, his ranch, his home, lay hundreds of miles to the south. But it was all Texas.

Thomas Dunson was home. Home at last. And he was smiling when he died.

* * *

"There ain't even a tombstone, not even a cross no more," Lightning said.

"There never was," Tess said.

"Why not?" Tom asked.

"He got what he wanted," Tess replied.

"Which was?" Tom asked.

She smiled. "To die in Texas. To be buried in Texas."

"Y'all could've put up a stone," Lightning said. "Or even hauled him to Dunson City. Buried him back home."

"In August?" Tess shook her head.

A blue jay screeched at a mockingbird, and a fish splashed in the river. The wind blew hot. Trees along the riverbank rustled. The horses stamped their hooves and began grazing on the weeds.

"What was he like?" Lightning asked.

"He was just a man," Tess said.

More silence. Finally, Lightning muttered something underneath his breath and returned to his horse. "Never saw no need in talking to no dead person," Lightning said "C'mon, Tom, we're burning daylight."

Tom looked at his mother, then his father, and with a sigh, he, too, returned to the horses. Lightning was about to call out to his parents, but Tom shook his head sharply. "We'll see y'all back at camp," Tom called, and turned his horse back toward the others. With another curse, Lightning followed his brother, leaving Tess and Mathew alone.

"I haven't been here since . . . that day," she said.

His head bobbed. At first, she thought he would say nothing, but two words escaped. "I know."

They looked at the crumbling rocks. Some had been moved. She had to wonder if they had been carried away by wind or rain, or settlers needing a few rocks for a fire ring or maybe even to start a cabin. Or even some kids, or cowboys, who simply tossed rocks into the Red to hear and watch the splashes.

Mathew made no attempt to rebuild the cairn, cut the weeds, and there were no wildflowers to pick here, to place on the grave. Not that Thomas Dunson would have wanted any flowers on his final resting place. He had been buried with his boots on, with his old revolver, and his face had been covered with Texas sod. Enough for a man like him.

A bee buzzed past them. The Red flowed silently.

She had no idea how long they stood there, but at last, Mathew returned his hat to his head. His legs, however, remained stationary, until he turned toward her.

Tess said, "You loved him, didn't you?"

He did not answer directly, but walked back to his horse. As he tightened the cinch, he finally spoke.

"Loved him. Admired him. Feared him. Respected him." He dropped the stirrup, gathered the reins, and swung with ease into the saddle, and waited for Tess to mount her gelding. When she had, and after she pulled her hat down tight, Mathew spoke again.

"He made me what I am today." The horse turned. They rode away, neither of them looking back.

"And sometimes," Mathew told her, "for that, I still hate him."

CHAPTER THIRTY-FIVE

Mathew Garth did not return straight to camp with his sons. Instead, he rode out to the herd. He could hear Reata's rich bass, singing some old song, comforting the longhorns. John Meeker Jr. and Joe Nambel also circled the herd.

Down south, miles down this treeless country where timbers could be found only along the river-banks, such as here near the Red, Mathew could make out the camping places of at least two other herds. And although he could see no dust rising after all the rains, he understood that more herds were coming.

He moved away from the herd, toward Red River Station, the best crossing place for miles. Crossed by so many cattle—millions of them—over the past years, a veritable canyon had been cut into the banks on both sides of the Red.

It had not been just cattle that crossed the river here. Old-timers and Indians could remember when buffalo swam the river here. It was only natural. Salt Creek fed into the river nearby, and the river made a sharp northward turn, which typically pushed the current to the south bank, and thus created a natural place to ford.

Yet it rarely proved easy. It never looked easy.

The river ran fast and high, but not as high as it had been yesterday. Two days more, maybe, three at the most, and they would be across the river and out of Texas. Into Indian Territory.

Mathew let out a heavy sigh. His mind raced back to that first crossing of the Red River with thousands of weary longhorns. At night. When the river ran higher than it was today. When Thomas Dunson demanded that they cross now, with exhausted men, played out horses, and confused longhorns.

Looking across the river, Mathew could see it all. As clear as it had been that night, and that had been like a nightmare.

The massive trunk of a cottonwood, half underwater, then exploding out of the river like some monster, or a torpedo, ramming right into the mass of horses, cattle, and men. Barney Saul and Grant Shallert disappeared, crushed by wood, gored by horns, smashed by hooves, or merely drowned with the force of uncontrollable waters. One minute they had been horseback, trying to keep the cattle from milling. And then . . . they were gone.

But that wasn't all of it. For just minutes after witnessing that tragedy, Mathew had watched Little Slim Reeves, who had always said he feared drowning, get unseated while trying to get some steer out of a sandy spot in the river. Mathew could see Old Leather Monte trying to reach the boy, who was being carried away out of the shallows and into deeper, roiling waters. Old Leather had even tossed a loop toward the struggling drag rider. Slim Reeves had just missed catching hold of the loop. And then Thomas Dunson was screaming something, and Slim Reeves had been pulled under the Red.

Three men. Three good cowmen, one of them no more than a boy, had been killed that time. Dunson had read over their graves, even if there had been no grave for Slim Reeves. No one had been able to find his body, just his hat, but the crew demanded a cross be put up—even if it was just over a soaking, torn hat.

So Dunson had preached another funeral. And fourteen men, including Mathew and Dunson, had stood, hats in hands, and listened. Fourteen. They had left South Texas with thirty.

Mathew looked across the river, at the tree-lined banks and beyond, through the rolling country of Indian Territory. He searched. He fought his memories. He tried to find the place, but he couldn't.

A poet might call this irony, Mathew thought. But poets knew nothing about life, or death. Ironic? Hardly. It was pathetic.

Mathew could find Thomas Dunson's grave. Yet the graves of those three cowboys—Slim Reeves . . . Grant Shallert . . . Barney Saul . . . ? Those were lost forever.

He knew they should wait another day, but Mathew could sense the restlessness of the trail herds waiting a mile or more back. The cattle had rested long enough, the weather already began to heat up, and

Mathew did not like sitting around with notes due.
He could feel Chico Miller breathing down his neck.

"We cross today." His voice rang out in the darkness
as soon as Groot had rung the triangle bell announc-
ing that coffee was hot. His voice stirred more men
that the harsh peals of the cast iron against cast iron.

"What?" Laredo Downs tossed off his soogans.

"You heard me. Eat quickly, boys. I want the lead
steers in the Nations before the sun's barely up."

Again, they wrapped poles to Groot's Studebaker
and held their breath as the old cook and Tess guided
the mule-drawn team across the fast-flowing river.
Mathew rode his best-swimming horse on one side
of the wagon, and Laredo Downs took the downstream spot.

"Don't stop," Mathew yelled as the wagon climbed
up the rise on the northern banks. "I want this herd
halfway to Monument Rocks by nightfall."

The remuda crossed next. Joey Corinth was a
wonder with those horses. And then Joe Nambel and
Laredo Downs led the first steers into the Red.

They balked at first. Even the experienced steers,
not bound for the slaughterhouse, did not like
swirling waters. Shouts and curses rang out behind
them. Horses reared. Cattle bawled. Pushing. Shoving.
Driving the beeves into the river. Until the line
formed, with cowboys swimming their horses from
one bank and back again, whipping hats, nudging the
animals back into line. Up to the next bank, leaving
a watery trail as they climbed the slippery bank and
disappeared over the rise.

A bridge of beef crossed the river, moving. Many

times Mathew had wondered if a man—a younger man than he was by now, of course—with great balance, quick feet, and maybe a special pair of Joe Justin's boots could run across the backs of the longhorns from one bank to the other and not get wet. He remembered back in '79 when Brick Keever, now dead, and a young greenhorn named Shawnee Preston had bet that they would do it the next morning when they crossed the river. Of course, they hadn't even tried.

It was, Mathew thought when the last of the stragglers were climbing up the bank and the winds of the Indian Nations had started to pick up, perhaps the smoothest crossing he had ever experienced.

He spurred his horse up the incline and looked at the long line of beef, weaving across the plains. Although broken to the trail by this time, the cattle had worn down, so Mathew had not promoted anyone to take over Alvaro Cuevas's spot. Instead, he had moved Joe Nambel down to the other flank position opposite Yago Noguerra. No Sabe and Bradley Rush remained at swing, with Reata joining Lightning, Tom, and John Meeker Jr. at drag. Mathew would do any scouting, although he might also spell Teeler Lacey so that the old scout could check out campsites and water holes.

"I wish every river crossin' was like that," Laredo Downs said brightly as he reined in his mount next to Mathew.

Mathew barely nodded. "Best catch up to Teeler," Mathew said. "He'll need you at point."

"All right. Ought to rest 'em. Get an early start tomorrow."

Shaking his head, Mathew turned his horse. "Too

many herds waiting behind us. Probably another will cross today. We keep moving."

Move they did. Quick gulps of coffee near the blackjacks along Blue Grove, where they helped Joey Corinth and Tess gather up kindling and firewood that they tossed inside the strip of canvas that hung underneath the Studebaker. Through the rolling prairie to Beaver Creek for their first camp. They had made fifteen miles that day, practically unheard of. And they were up in the blackness of morning to keep driving north.

Past the mesa and its red sandstone boulders and rocks called Monument Rocks—without stopping to carve names or initials in the sandstone. Even Mathew had unfolded a pocketknife and left his initials on a slab back in '69 on the piles of rocks cowboys had started tossing up as trail markers. Once, those two piles of rocks, roughly three hundred feet apart, had reached twice Mathew's height, with a circumference of ten feet. Now both mounds had collapsed, and wind had left enough tumbleweeds—once unheard of during the early years of the trail—and dirt so that the markers looked like just a couple of natural mounds of earth and weeds.

Past Stage Station, through the oak grove that had been considerably charred and thinned by a prairie fire some years back. On to Rush Creek, and then across the Little Wichita.

By that time, they had forgotten all about the rains, the floods, the bogs, the storms. The sun turned so hot, the wind scalding, that they even began praying for rain.

Prayers went unanswered.

Driving on. Pushing on. Dust and dirt. Saddle sores. Bruises. Sunburns. Tempers turned raw. Groot's cast turned brown. On some days, he could barely stand, so Tess did most of the cooking. She had never been much of a cook, one of the reasons she had hired Janeen Yankowski. Yet no one complained. They merely worked. Fourteen hours in the saddle was a vacation. Eighteen hours, even more, was a typical day. Three horses went lame, and two mules, but they used them when, at last, the delegation of Indians met them before the Washita River and asked for their payment, a tribute, a toll. The lame stock and two beeves that Mathew knew would not make it to the Canadian River satisfied the old chief and his two braves.

"Remember that tussle the Chickasaws give us?" Joe Nambel called out that night during supper. "Chickasaws. Supposed to be peaceable, even civilized . . . one of the Civilized Tribes—but damn if they wasn't after our scalps that time. Remember?"

No one said anything. Not even Groot or Teeler or Laredo, and they had been in that fight. Even Mathew remembered it, for that's when he had first seen Tess after Memphis.

Joe Nambel let it go and focused on the corn bread and beans, one cooked not enough, the other burned. He probably didn't feel like telling the whole story anyway, Mathew guessed. Like everyone else, he was tuckered out.

He knew he would have to slow the pace. They couldn't afford to lose any more horses, and the heat, the wind, the lack of water would kill them if he kept up this relentless drive. Yet when he rode back to check on the drag riders, he stared off to the south. More dust rose into the cloudless blue sky. A. C. Thompson's herd. Plenty of others. All pushing north, then west for Dodge City. And how many herds were ahead of him, bound for the Cut-Off or taking the Western Trail?

Keep moving. Keep driving. Maybe it'll rain.

They swam the Washita that afternoon at Rock Crossing between the red clay banks lined with willows. Well, maybe they didn't exactly swim the river. In some years, the southern bottoms could be tricky, but the northern side was hard rock. On this day, the river was so low the cattle crossed water ankle-deep, then over sandy shoals.

He rode back and forth across the shallow stream that maps labeled a river, forgetting that often it turned crueler than the Red. Keeping the cattle in line, pushing them, slapping his hat, nudging them across.

When the drag riders were bringing the last of the beef across, he let his horse walk, from water to shoal. The sun, he later determined, had baked his brain. He forgot a lesson he had learned about horses and water many years ago.

The horse stopped, began pawing at the sand. The bay gelding confused the sand, gleaming like water, with water. Instead of jerking up the reins, to lift the bay's head, Mathew merely cursed the gelding, calling him a stupid son of a bitch. Actually, it was Mathew who was the stupid son of a bitch.

Thinking the shoals were water, the bay pawed at the sand, then started to sink into the sand, to roll over, to cool off.

A moment later, Mathew Garth found himself partly in water, partly on a shoal, his right leg under eight hundred pounds of horseflesh. He wasn't hurt. Nor angry. And right then, he wasn't even embarrassed.

He kicked free of the stirrup, let go of the reins, and lay back in the shallow water. And broke out in an uproarious cackle.

"Well, I'll be damned."

Mathew opened his eyes and looked up at the voice. The bay rose and trotted off a few paces, lowered its head, and drank. Mathew moved his leg around and slowly pulled himself to his feet.

"Yes, sir," Lightning Garth said, and looked over at Tom while Meeker and Reata kept the cattle moving across the river. "You was wrong, Tom. The old sidewinder ain't forgotten how to laugh after all."

CHAPTER THIRTY-SIX

"Let them graze on the high ground," Mathew called out. "Take advantage of the breeze."

Not that the wind blew cool. But at least it blew.

He had always liked this part of the Indian Territory, this Washita Valley. In most years, the grazing was good. Here, he knew he could fatten up the cattle. Firewood, even wild plums, could be found along the creeks and streams. Cross the Canadian, the North Canadian, and the Cimarron. Gently push the cattle on to Dodge City.

By dawn, they moved again. Water holes became lower, the wind and sun hotter, the horses more skittish. Days ran together. Nights became too short. Across the Canadian, past Fort Reno, moving on, marking the miles with dust.

At the Cimarron River, Mathew rode in to Red Fork Station. In the early 1870s, back when the river had been called the Red Fork of the Arkansas, a trading post had been established and called Red Fork Trader's Ranch. It had kept growing over the

years, and since the Red River War of 1874, it had
resembled a military post. Stuck out in what had once
been the middle of nowhere, it now served as a stop
on a stage line that ran from Arkansas City, Kansas, to
Fort Sill in the southwestern part of Indian Territory.
Thus, it had mail, but, as in Spanish Fort, Mathew
found no letters waiting for him. He hoped that
meant no troubles in Dunson City.

They watered the herd at Bull Foot Station, for a
wolfer at Red Fork Station had told him the water was
good there, despite the lack of rain. Then turned
more west than north, following the Cut-Off to
Dodge City.

Two hundred miles to go. Twenty days, if they were
lucky, maybe even sooner. A lot could happen in two
to three weeks, but Mathew felt pretty good. Even
when the riders came into camp that night.

There were three of them, young men on pinto
horses. One held an old flintlock musket, and another carried a bow and a quiver of arrows. Those two
kept their horses back a little, letting the Indian who
looked the oldest of the three—and he probably had
not seen his thirtieth birthday—nudge his skewbald
closer.

All three Indians dressed in a mix of cultures. The
nearest one, the rider Mathew figured would do the
speaking, wore a green coat, sleeves and collars frayed,
that had gone out of fashion back when Sam Houston
was president of the Republic of Texas. His hat was
straw—the other two donned turbans—decorated
with a deer-hair roach and turkey feather.

"Evening," Mathew said.

"You are crossing Chickasaw land."

Well, Mathew would give the Indian credit for not wasting time, but he could use a geography lesson.

He corrected the Indian. "We *crossed* Chickasaw country . . . weeks back." Caddo Indians. Wichitas. Maybe even Arapahos or Southern Cheyennes. Those he might have expected, but not Chickasaws. And since crossing the Cimarron, they had been pretty much in the Unknown Lands. No one had a right to ask for a tribute, especially not the Chickasaws.

"You took advantage of my addle-brained father."

Mathew looked past the speaker at the two others, both wearing silver armbands, glass beads, and ribbon shirts. The man in the green coat kept speaking, demanding fifty steers and three horses that could actually be ridden.

"The horses your father got will be fine with a bit of rest." Mathew knew that for a fact.

"You lie."

Hearing men rising from their seats, Mathew motioned them to stay put. "Your father had manners."

"Fifty steers and—"

"No." Mathew's hand gripped his holstered Colt. "We paid your father our tribute. This is not your country. It's nobody's. And you'll be leaving our camp now."

This time, he let his men move about.

Green Coat scowled, pulled sharply on the hackamore, and kicked the pinto into a lope. His two companions followed into the night.

"Laredo," Mathew said. "Put two extra men with the remuda. And four more nighthawking the herd."

"Right."

"Maybe you should have bartered with him a bit," Groot said.

"I would have . . . if he had any manners."

Tom Garth hated to do it, but he knew he had to stay awake. Let his father find him asleep in the saddle while circling the herd, and he might get whipped, or buffaloed. So he spit tobacco juice into his hand and rubbed his eyes.

And cursed. Bit his lips. Leaned back in the saddle. Moaned. It burned like blazes, and he thought he might go blind. His head shook. He blinked and blinked, and felt tears, mixed with tobacco juice, flowing down his cheeks. Relief swept through him. He could see. Not that there was anything to see, not at this time of night, but the rising sun made him feel that at least Groot had not blinded him with tobacco juice.

Tom reined up quickly.

Rising sun?

"What the hell is that, Tom?" John Meeker Jr. had eased his night horse away from the lowing steers.

"I don't . . . ." Tom blinked several more times. He leaned forward in the saddle. ". . . know."

"That's west, ain't it?" Meeker asked.

The cattle began stirring, their bawling intensified. Even Tom's horse began acting a little skittish.

"It's not . . . east . . . and . . ."

Meeker finished for him. "Too early for the sun to come up anyhow. Hell, there ain't even no gray skies. Just that . . . glow."

The wind blew harder.

"You smell somethin'?" Meeker asked.

Tom sat ramrod straight in the saddle.

"Oh . . . God."

"Up. Up. Get up."

Mathew jerked the woolen blanket off Tess and tossed it aside, reached down, jerked his wife to her feet. She blinked. He slapped her.

"Up," he said, and shoved her toward the chuck wagon. Groot caught her before she fell, leaned her against the front wheel, and kept walloping the triangle with the cast-iron rod.

Tess blinked, and Mathew started to help Joe Nambel and Teeler Lacey harness the mules to the Studebaker. A shout stopped him. Mathew turned, saw Laredo Downs, already mounted, although wearing only boots, hat, and undergarments.

"Which way should we take them?" Laredo shouted above the chaos.

"They've already started," Mathew said. He had to hurry to catch the reins of Dollar, which had pulled free of its picket. The horse reared. Mathew cursed, pulled hard, ignoring that still-aching leather burn on his palm. When the horse started turning around, Mathew kept up with it and somehow swung into the saddle. He kept pulling the reins hard, keeping the horse turning in a circle.

"Wind's blowing from the northwest," he said. He could barely hear himself. "Groot, damn you, quit that infernal noise."

The clangs stopped. The noise didn't. Cattle bawled. Horses whinnied. Birds screeched.

"Firestorm like this," Laredo was saying, "those winds can shift."

Mathew could smell the smoke. Now he could even see it. The orange wall of flames brightened the northern skies. He watched as Reata and Lightning helped Tess into the chuck wagon. Then they practically threw Groot into the driver's box. Mathew looked at the mules.

Would they be fast enough?

"Get mounted!" Mathew yelled. "Now. We need to catch up to that herd. And outrun that fire."

He kicked the liver chestnut, which had finally stopped turning, and pulled hard on the reins to stop the frightened gelding near the wagon.

"What . . . ?" Tess stopped. She knew. She had seen prairie fires before.

"Tom?" she called out.

"He's with the herd. Warned us. Went back."

"Lightning?" Tess asked.

Mathew had trouble keeping the gelding from breaking into an uncontrollable gallop. "He's . . ."

"No!" Tess's head shook. "Did lightning start the fire?"

The wagon lurched forward, kept moving. Groot lashed out with the blacksnake whip, cursing, screaming, the noise popping as the whip popped over the ears of the mules.

"No," Mathew answered. "Chickasaws."

His horse turned around again, and then he gave Dollar its head. Let the panicked gelding carry him into the night.

The air felt thick with smoke. The ground shook from the hooves of the frightened cattle. Mathew glanced back at the camp. He could see the fire,

Groot's breakfast fire, still burning. They had not had time to put it out. Not that it mattered. Not with the hell dashing toward them.

He rode.

Mathew had ridden this country many times, but rarely this fast, this time of night. One wrong step, and he'd be killed. He knew that. The horse could snap its leg in a prairie dog hole, send him sailing into the grass and rocks. If he was lucky, the fall would break his neck. Otherwise . . .

Fire? That . . . that put the fear of God into anyone.

He could see. Flames illuminated the night, and the dust from the stampeding cattle, the galloping horses, blown by the wind, resembled the sparks that shot across the sky, landing ahead of the blaze, starting new fires.

Mathew closed in on the herd. The earth shook. He yelled. Yet all he could hear was the roar of the fire. Like fifteen thousand furnaces in locomotives. He rode. Hell closed in on him.

Smoke circled all around him, choked him. He could almost feel the soot as it caked his face. Sweat poured down his face, burned his eyes, soaked his shirt. Sweat . . . from the heat . . . or his own fear? No longer could he look at the inferno, for it would blind him. Lower in the saddle, forward, he leaned. He tasted the smoke, the bile. Dollar plunged ahead.

The horse leaped, almost unseated Mathew, and landed on its forefeet, gathered itself, kept running. Mathew looked back, and thought he saw a downed steer. The horse had jumped over it, likely saving Mathew's life, for he had not even seen the downed longhorn blocking his path.

His sweat dried. His skin burned. The wall shot right toward him, carried by a wind that kept changing directions because of intense heat. Glancing back, he saw the fire racing across the rolling prairie. Yet flames licked closer to him, and the roaring reached his ears.

Swirling, roaring towers of flames, like hundreds of tornadoes all on fire, raining sparks and embers, producing winds like the breaths of dragons.

The chuck wagon? It must have made it. Groot could handle a team. Lightning? Tom? Laredo? Teeler? He had no way of knowing.

The wall of flames almost touched him, swallowing him whole, when suddenly he felt warm water splashing underneath him, cooling his legs, his feet, and he understood. He was crossing a stream.

A respite, though. That's all it was. The fire could easily leap across this mere trickle of water. He had to ride, push the gelding harder. Catch up . . .

That's when he understood something. He had not seen any rider or steer since Dollar had leaped over the dead or dying one. He had no idea where he was. But he knew he had to keep riding. Ride . . . or perish.

Then he felt Dollar going down, taking him to the hot earth as the gelding's heart burst.

CHAPTER THIRTY-SEVEN

Smoke wafted in the stillness of morning like fog over a black world. Mathew sat, leaning against the dead gelding. He had removed bridle and saddle, which rested nearby, drying in the sun. On this side of the creek, bluestem—except for the crushed path left in the wake of longhorns, horses, mules, and a chuck wagon—waved in the breeze. Yet across the creek, a black, scorched earth stretched as far as he could see.

Mathew Garth had no idea how far the prairie fire had spread, or how many cattle he had lost. Or men. He had considered taking saddle and bridle and following the trail of crushed grass and trampled earth, but decided to wait. Someone from his crew would come looking, and here he had water and a good view in case anyone came through the ash and soot.

Around midmorning, Mathew heard hooves clopping behind him as he lay on his stomach, drinking water from the creek and washing his face. He came

to his knees, turned, and recognized both riders. He
pushed himself up and let out a sigh of relief.

"Pa!"

Both riders sent their horses into lopes and covered the remaining sixty yards.

The horses turned skittish, though, at the smell of
burned grass, the black world beyond the creek, and
the gelding Mathew had run to death. After dismounting the roan, Lightning handed the reins to
Reata, and walked to Mathew.

"You all right?"

"Now," Mathew said. "The herd?"

Lightning jerked his thumb over his back. "Five
miles I reckon. Maybe six. Got them turned and
milling. Ain't done no head count. Well, we hadn't,
before we took off to see about you and . . ."

Mathew's heart skipped. His stomach knotted.

"And?" he asked.

"Joe Nambel's missing, too," Lightning said.

Mathew turned and stepped into the shallow creek.
The smoke had begun to dissipate, and he crossed
the water and knelt on the banks, pushing his hands
a few inches above the smelly soot and ash. "Anybody
see Joe?" he asked. "During the commotion?"

"Not since camp." The ex–buffalo soldier, Reata,
answered.

Mathew rose and crossed the water again. Nambel
had helped hitch the mules to Groot's chuck wagon.
He had swung into the saddle, galloped off to the
herd. What color of horse had he been riding? Dark.
Mathew couldn't see it well, or recall it.

"Damn," Lightning sang out. "Look at that . . . the
grass . . . it's all . . . gone."

"Big fire." Reata whistled. "We was lucky."

And Joe Nambel? Mathew sighed again. Old Joe. He had been on that first drive with Thomas Dunson, had worked for Dunson, on and off, since before the war. And after the war, after that first drive to Abilene, Joe Nambel had worked, on and off, for Mathew. Always restless, Nambel would drift into Mexico or maybe find some other ranch in Texas. Once, he had even married a widow and tried clerking in El Paso— Franklin, the town had been called back then—but she had kicked him out because of his drinking, swearing, and spurs.

"Reata," Mathew said. "I want you to take Lightning back to camp."

"I'm riding with you, Pa," Lightning said.

"On what? You have two horses. I'm borrowing yours."

"No."

"Yes." He moved past Lightning and held out his right hand. Reata let him take the reins to Lightning's roan gelding. "You get back to camp, get another horse from your string, and come back with two or three more of the boys."

Reata cleared his throat and pointed across the creek. "You gonna ride 'cross that?"

"As far as I can," he said. "Ground's cooling off a mite." He had exaggerated. Mathew honestly didn't know if he could coax the roan across that burned earth. "I need y'all to hurry." He wanted Lightning and Reata gone before he attempted to cross the blackened prairie.

* * *

The stench of burned beef turned his stomach.

Mathew swore he would never eat another steak.

He had pulled two spare shirts and underwear from Lightning's saddlebags, ripped them in quarters, soaked them in water, and tied them over the hooves and fetlocks of the roan, securing them with strips of rawhide around the cannon of each leg.

It helped a little, not completely. Often, when the gelding started crow-hopping, Mathew would get the roan under control, dismount, and lead the horse for several rods. The first two or three times he had felt the heat rising through the soles of his boots and through his socks. Knowing the horse must've felt the burning sensation, too, he had watered down the cloth padding on the gelding's feet. He had to keep a firm grip on the reins as he guided the frightened horse across hot earth and around the grisly remnants of dead cattle and other animals.

A deer. Or something resembling a deer. Rabbits. Rats. Unrecognizable remains. Once he held his breath as he came to what at first he thought was a horse. No, one of the spare mules. No saddle. No body nearby.

He looked back. He could still see where the creek flowed, though far in the distance, and the contrast between green and tan grasslands and the charred remnants of prairie proved startling.

Buzzards and ravens began circling.

A few times he came to spots where coals and embers glowed with a fire that did not want to die. He cut wide berths around those. By then, no water remained in his canteen—which he had removed from his saddle—and Lightning's container had maybe a quarter left.

Oddly enough, he came to patches of grass, untouched by flames, some no wider than a square yard, but others big enough for him to rest his burning feet and let the roan cool down and graze on grass not reduced to charcoal. He could not explain how a fire had bypassed these spots, but it gave him hope. Maybe, just maybe, he would find Joe Nambel in such an oasis, smiling, sipping whiskey from a flask, and joking, "What took you so long to get here, Mathew?"

A forlorn hope.

He found Joe Nambel a half hour later.

Well, he could only assume it was Joe.

The size fit. The blackened spurs and rowels looked like those Joe had always been partial to. The gruesome remains of the horse near him in a pile with four dead steers could have been from Nambel's string. The saddle and bridle had been burned completely, except for the silver and metal buckles and the snaffle bit.

What was the story? Mathew wondered. The one Joe Nambel had brought up at camp . . . days ago. A lifetime. It had been . . . when? Hell, before they had even crossed the Washita. He pressed his fingers to his temples, as if that would bring back that distant memory, make it clearer.

"Remember . . ." Joe Nambel had started. Something about the Chickasaws . . . one of the Five Civilized Tribes . . . The last part came to Mathew instantly, as if Joe were sitting around the fire, coffee cup in hand, beaming a tired smile.

". . . damn if they wasn't after our scalps that time. Remember?"

"I remember," Mathew said, and looked at what once had been a damned good cowhand.

"They had been following the wagon train and our herd for days. Kind of cut short that visit we had planned. Real coffee. Pretty girls. The Donegal and his faro layouts in the backs of Conestogas. Not that we would have stayed long. Not with Dunson somewhere behind us. So we stampeded the cattle. That was a gamble. That they'd keep running north. That it would bring the braves out into the open. That Tess and her friends and The Donegal would be able to follow us in their wagons. Crazy. Just plumb crazy."

He leaned his head back, took off his hat, and cut loose with that wild yell of one of Nathan Bedford Forrest's boys. A rebel yell. Well, he hadn't eaten since supper, felt tuckered out, and scared. So, to Mathew's ears, that rebel yell sounded just like it had back at Brice's Crossroads . . . at Shiloh . . . at skirmishes that had never been named and never remembered.

"We started at night, Joe," Mathew said. "Finished at dawn. 'Glorious as all get-out.' Remember, Joe. That's what you said. After it was all over. 'Glorious as all get-out.' Yes, sir. Hell of a story. You always could tell some great stories. It certainly was, Joe. It most certainly was."

He returned his hat to cover the wet mop that was his hair. Glorious? Far from it. It had been ugly, brutal, vicious. They had given no quarter.

And he, Mathew Garth, had ordered it. Screaming to ride all of those Indians down, that dead Indians wouldn't spread the word, wouldn't sneak up on them and swipe a beef or two. He remembered Buster McGee and the lance that had gone through his sides, and how the bloody point and feathered ends held up both of the dead man's arms. No one had been able to pull the lance out of the poor cowboy, forcing Cherry Valance and Groot Nadine to break off the ends and bury Buster with wood and likely some feathers and maybe a few brass tacks in his lungs.

Mathew wondered if that fight had been what had truly hardened him. Maybe that's when he saw how close he truly was to Thomas Dunson, how much alike they were.

A coyote yipped. A bit early, for it was midday by then, and the sun, the wind, and the remnants of the fire turned this part of Indian Territory into a blast furnace. He looked south, wondering about A. C. Thompson, and the cattle herds behind Thompson. Had the fire reached them, sent their beeves running? They would have to skirt around the fire's path, for longhorns and horses needed to graze, and there would be nothing to eat here till next spring.

He wondered if this fire would mark an end to the Chisholm Trail's Cut-Off to Dodge City.

Again, he looked at Joe Nambel's remains.

He had not told Reata or Lightning to bring a shovel. Or Thomas Dunson's Bible.

CHAPTER THIRTY-EIGHT

They killed Bradley Rush while he was pouring coffee. The bullet caught him in the throat and sent him flying backward, where he crashed against the rear wheel of Groot's Studebaker, the back of his head smashing against the boxing with a sickening thud.

Yago Noguerra had been pulling on his boots after replacing his filthy socks. They shot him twice. The first bullet caught him in the stomach, and he fell backward, rolled over onto his side, and pushed himself on hands and knees, coughing, praying in Spanish, and spitting out blood before the second bullet slammed into the top of his head.

Groot was reaching for his shotgun, but tripped, yelling in pain and grasping at the plaster cast that had been blackened with dirt and soot and grime. Laredo Downs reached for his pistol, only to realize that he still wore his long johns. Some cowhands slept in their clothes, but Laredo never could sleep like that. And he had left his spare clothes back in his war bag back at camp the previous night. The fire had come up on them too quickly, and all his clothes had been, everyone assumed, burned by now. He stopped, froze, spread his arms away from his sides as he yelled, "No, Tom. Don't!"

Tess echoed Laredo's warning.

Yet Tom Garth was diving for the Winchester in the scabbard of his saddle, lying on the ground, drying out along with the saddle blanket. A bullet caught him in the shoulder. Another carved a ditch across the inside of his left thigh. He crashed to the ground, came up, kept crawling, pain masking his face, reaching out with his good arm for the carbine.

That's when Tess dived and knocked him down. She rolled on top of him as he cried and cursed, and she looked up at the men walking into their camp.

"Don't," she pleaded. "Please." She almost hated herself for begging.

The white man laughed.

"Don't you fret yourself to death, Tess of the River. I might have need of young Garth directly." He turned his revolver, already cocked, and aimed it at Groot.

"Cookie. If you don't stop that racket, you won't be feelin' that bum leg of yours no more."

Groot bit back the agony. Joey Corinth, keeping his hands above his head, carefully moved toward the cook and knelt beside him.

"That's good," Jess Teveler said. "That's real good." He pulled a silk bandanna from his back pocket and tossed it to Tess. "There. Plug one of the boy's holes with that. Then I reckon you best rip off part of that dress of yourn to patch up the other hole in your boy. And after that, fry us up some bacon. With biscuits.

You, ma'am. I don't want that belly-cheater nowheres near no knife or hot grease or nothin'."

They herded those out with the herd into camp. No Sabe, John Meeker Jr., and Teeler Lacey looked surprised, worried, but none were bleeding. And none wore any weapons.

"Where's Lightning?" Jess Teveler directed the question at Tom, who leaned against his bedroll.

"Looking for Mathew," Tess fired back from the fire.

"I asked him." Teveler sipped coffee.

"Pa'll . . . be . . . He'll kill . . ." Tom lay against the bedroll. Tess swore.

"Easy. I don't take bein' cussed by men or tramps from Memphis."

"Shut your filthy trap, Teveler."

The gun came out of the holster, the hammer cocked, and the barrel trained on Groot Nadine. "Cookie," Teveler said, "I don't need you at all. Remember that before you speak to me again."

Tess turned the bacon. Teveler had left the three Chickasaws riding around the herd and remuda. Now she understood why the Indians were so far from Chickasaw country. They had no intention of bartering for a toll for the cattle. Jess Teveler had probably guessed that Mathew would not pay a tribute, and even if he had, they still would have set the prairie ablaze.

In addition to the three Indians, four men rode with him. Two were cowboys, from their looks, who had been riding the grub line for months. Two were gunmen. They reminded her of the men who had ridden with Dunson all those years ago when they had arrived at Tess's camp. Only worse. She glanced at the body of Bradley Rush. He had been one of Dunson's hired guns. He had changed his ways. Had been a good hand on the drive. And he had died, with a bullet that had broken his neck. He had died, probably not knowing why, or how.

At least the cowboys had dragged Rush and the poor young vaquero under the wagon, covered the bodies with blankets. One of the killers had even made the sign of the cross over the two men.

"You say Garth was lookin' for somebody," Teveler asked.

"I didn't say," Tess replied.

"All right." Teveler's head went up and down, and he grinned. "Be a shame if he got cooked like that bacon you're burnin'." He laughed. "That was one hot fire. Huge. Didn't think it would burn that much. But that sure helps our cause."

"Your cause?" Tess pulled the skillet off the fire.

"My cause. Your cattle."

She knew that. She just wanted to hear him say it.

Two horses whinnied, and Tess rose. So did Jess Teveler. They watched as Lightning and Reata rode into camp. On one horse. Riding double. She knew what it meant and breathed easier.

They had found Mathew, who had taken one of the horses and gone after Joe Nambel. Mathew was still alive.

She frowned. Or . . . had they found Joe Nambel alive, and Nambel had borrowed the horse to look . . . ?

It didn't matter. All that mattered now was staying alive. Keeping Tom alive.

Tess pressed her lips tightly. She looked around,

but the only weapon she had was the skillet and a
fork. One of the saddle tramps stood behind her. She
heard the metallic click as he cocked his revolver.

"Nice and easy, folks," Teveler said. "Just let 'em
ride in easy. We's just visitin'. Let 'em think that. I
don't want no more bloodshed." He chuckled. "On
account that I ain't sure those longhorns won't
run again. Figured they was too tired when we come
a-callin'. But now . . . shut the hell up."

Reata loped the horse into camp, and Lightning
swung down. Then, Tom yelled, "Reata. It's Teveler!
Kill him."

Tess held her breath. She knew the black man had
been chasing Jess Teveler. She knew . . . or thought
she knew . . .

Reata swung from his horse, pushed back his hat,
and laughed.

"I know that, boy." The burly ex–buffalo soldier
nodded at Teveler, who returned the smile. "How's
things, Jess?"

Standing in the center of camp, noticing Tom and
his bandages for the first time, Lightning Garth
looked completely baffled.

It made sense, now. Reata had been with that
posse in Comanche that was chasing Teveler, but
he had actually been working with, or maybe for, the
outlaw. Make sure the posse didn't get too close, or
put himself in a position to warn Teveler. Then he
trailed the herd and when the time became right,
rode in to camp and got himself a job. All the while
planning this . . . this . . . this . . .

Tess spit.

"Where's your pa, Lightning?" Teveler asked.

He started to answer, then put his hand on the butt of his revolver.

"You don't want to do that, Lightnin'." Reata pressed the barrel of the revolver he had drawn into Lightning's spine. "You got a friend in Jess Teveler, Lightnin'. A real good friend." With his free hand, the old soldier reached over and lifted Lightning's .44 from the holster. He pitched the Smith & Wesson behind him and answered the question Teveler had thrown at Lightning.

"Garth's back yonder, six miles. A creek stopped the fire on the northwest side. You didn't tell me you planned on burning the whole damned country, Jess. I didn't want to get baked."

"You didn't." Teveler chuckled.

"Well, Garth borrowed the kid's horse," Reata said. "Went into the charred-over country lookin' for a saddle tramp named Nambel."

"That right, boy?" Teveler asked.

"I don't know," Lightning answered.

Teveler laughed harder. "That's right, Lightnin'. You don't know. You don't know at all. But I do. Mathew Garth—"

"No!" Tess screamed. "Don't."

"Shut up. Your own ma didn't even—"

"Lightning," Tess cried out. "You have to listen to—"

"Shut that gal up, Creede."

The cowhand put a gauntleted hand over Tess's mouth and wrapped a strong arm over her midsection, lifting her off her feet, pulling her back. Lightning started for him, but Reata again stopped him with the gun in his back.

"Just listen to Jess Teveler, kid," the black man whispered.

"That ain't your ma, boy," Teveler said. "And Mathew Garth ain't your pa."

And Teveler told Lightning Garth everything. That his mother had been some hussy named Edna. Poor Edna's husband had died a hero wearing the gray and fighting alongside General Patrick Cleburne, but the old rebel hadn't been Lightning's father, either. Because in Memphis, well, some women didn't have much of a choice.

Tears streamed down Tess Millay's face.

"Nobody knows who your pa was," Teveler said. "Hell, for all we know, it could've been Reata there. Or Creede."

"No, boss," the saddle tramp said. "Never been to Memphis."

Teveler told other stories, about Memphis and The Donegal. About the Boar's Head and the *River Palace*. He said that Mathew Garth was nothing but a cattle thief who had stolen a herd from his own foster father and had, in more ways than one, been responsible for Thomas Dunson's death. Most of the blame, though, Teveler put right on the woman crying, struggling against Creede's iron grip.

"She nudged Cherry Valance's gun hand," Teveler said. "Right when he was drawin' on Dunson. Valance had been aimin' to wing the big cattleman, but instead, the bullet hit him in the middle. So Dunson killed Valance. Well . . . it was actually Tess there who killed Valance with that little nudge. And that nudge also killed Dunson. That's the woman who lied to you, who told you she was your ma. She done it so she could get Dunson's ranch."

That was a lie. Oh, she had hit Cherry Valance as he drew his revolver, but that had been for Dunson. No, she had done that for Mathew Garth, even though he was nowhere near the wagon train by that time. Cherry Valance had no equal when it came to pistol-fighting. He could have killed Mathew Garth, and he would have killed Dunson. Instead, Dunson was only wounded, and Cherry Valance was dead. Dunson could have lived, too, had he shown any sense, not insisted on traveling in the back of a Conestoga from Abilene and across the Red River.

Lightning no longer looked like the cowboy he had become. He stood there, face pale, a frightened kid. Confused. Not sure of anything.

"Now . . ." Teveler lowered his voice. "Here's what I want to ask you, Lightning. You think a mother like that, a cattle thief like your dad. You think they care one whit for a bastard child like you? You ain't even their blood. They'd toss you away like the core of an apple." He pointed to Tom, lying unconscious, tossing and turning, sweating, maybe bleeding to death, dying. "That's their blood, boy. That's who'd get the ranch with Tess and Garth lying six feet under."

Teveler nodded at Creede, who released his grip on Tess.

She fell to her knees and looked up, reaching out for Lightning, trying to say something. But all she could do was just cry.

"My God," Lightning said. "It's . . . it's . . . it's . . . Oh, hell, it's true. Ain't it? Ain't it, Ma? *Ain't it?*"

"I . . ." It was all Tess could choke out.

"Remember," Reata whispered, "who got the new boots in Spanish Fort."

Lightning straightened, stared at Reata, then at Tom, and briefly at Jess Teveler before his eyes locked on his mother's . . . or who he once thought was his mother.

"What is it," he said after a long moment, "that you want from me?

CHAPTER THIRTY-NINE

"So," Jess Teveler said, "here's the deal: You can come with me and Lightnin', and after we sell these cattle in Caldwell, you'll make a whole lot more money than you ever dreamed you could. Won't be no thirty a month, that's for certain."

Lightning looked around, wondering. He felt numb from it all. All his life had been a lie. He couldn't even look at his . . . no . . . she wasn't his mother.

"Caldwell?" Laredo Downs snorted. "They ain't shippin' herds out of Caldwell no more. It got civilized last year."

"They is for me. Man I know worked it all out. Him and me got it all figured, you see. But you ain't goin' with us, old man. I wouldn't be caught dead ridin' with a man wearin' nothin' but his unmentionables."

Even the Chickasaws laughed at that.

"Well," Teveler said. "What about it?"

To Lightning's surprise, and even more to Jess

Teveler's, the cattle-stealing Mexican named No Sabe merely shook his head.

"Damned fool greaser," Reata said.

Teveler shook his head. "Guess there ain't much point in askin' you, is there?"

Teeler Lacey spit tobacco juice.

"What I figured," Teveler said, and turned to John Meeker Jr.

"How much money?" Meeker asked nervously.

"Way I figure, if the steers bring thirty a head, we'll pay all of you two thousand each. And if the prices are higher . . . ? Well, ride with me and you'll be wealthy men."

Meeker licked his lips. At length, he nodded.

"Boy?" Teveler asked.

"Go on, kid," Groot told Joey Corinth. "They'll kill you if you stay."

"But . . ."

"Go on."

And Joey Corinth stepped away from Groot's Studebaker.

"Well," Teveler said. "That 'bout does it, don't it?" He moved to Tess. "Except for you, lady. You'll be comin' with us. You and your *real* son." He turned toward Lacey and Laredo. "Case you boys think about tryin' somethin' foolish."

Lightning didn't like that at all. His stomach twisted. He wanted to be shut of the green-eyed liar and the self-righteous Tom Garth, whom he had always looked upon as his kid brother. He didn't need any reminders that he was a low-down nobody. But he said nothing.

"Reata."

Lightning turned as Jess Teveler walked to the big black man. "Fetch Mr. Garth back to camp, boy. Then catch up with us." The old buffalo soldier nodded, mounted his horse, and loped off toward the southeast.

"You gonna kill these men?" Lightning heard himself ask.

Grinning, Teveler strode across the camp and put his right arm around Lightning, pulling him close. "No need, Lightning. I ain't cold-blooded or a liar. Not like some you've knowed." He shot a glance at Tess Millay and laughed. "No, you see, the fire we set. That burned better than even I predicted. Any herds won't be comin' this way. They'll have to cut around, pick up the trail farther west. So ain't nobody gonna come across these folks for a spell. And afoot, they ain't goin' far. By the time someone finds 'em and if they gets foolish enough to try to catch up with us, we'll be rich and havin' us a high ol' time down in Mexico, spendin' money like we's a Carnegie or a banker . . . or . . . a Mathew Garth."

As Teveler moved away, Lightning watched the Indians lift Tom and load him into the chuck wagon through the opening in the front. Tess Millay climbed into the Studebaker to be with her son—her *only* son—and Teveler ordered Meeker to drive the Studebaker. They had strapped all the weapons onto one of the mules, and the cowhand named Creede led it out of camp.

Joey Corinth pushed the remuda north. The Studebaker rolled. The Indians went to the rear of the herd as they began getting the longhorns up, bawling, moving slowly.

Lightning swung into the saddle and started off toward the drag.

"Lightnin'."

He turned in the saddle and saw Jess Teveler waving him over. "Drag's for tenderfeet, sonny. Come on up with me. At the point."

Lightning turned his horse. He did not look back at No Sabe, Groot, Teeler Lacey, Laredo Downs . . . or the two dead cowboys covered with blankets.

A flour sack was not a fitting bandage, but it was the best, cleanest, closest thing to one in Groot's lumbering Studebaker. Tess changed the dressing on Tom's shoulder. That was the troublesome wound. The ditch in his leg had been clean enough, a grazing wound, deep, painful, but easy enough to treat. But the bullet remained in her son's shoulder, and if he lived to see Caldwell—Tess didn't know exactly how far they were from the Kansas border town— lead poisoning would likely have already set in.

They were cramped inside the wagon, but that kept Tom from moving around too much. She had a canteen and constantly wet the rag she had placed over his forehead. He sweated feverishly. She bit her bottom lip.

A rider loped up beside the wagon, and she heard Jess Teveler's voice. The next thing she knew, Teveler had climbed into the driver's box, muttered something to John Meeker Jr., and slipped through the canvas opening. He knelt, and grinned.

"Just wanted to check on you, Tess."

"This bullet needs to come out," she told him.

"Tonight."

"Now."

His head shook. "Want to get a little farther from your ol' camp, Tess. You don't mind if I call you Tess, do you?" His grin widened.

"You worried Laredo and Teeler will catch you?"

"Nah." He waved his hand in a dismissive gesture.

"So . . . you want to get farther away so Lightning and I won't hear the gunshots. When Reata rides back to kill them all."

He gave her a respectful nod.

"After he kills your husband, Tess." His voice had turned cold, deadly, and the eyes told Tess that he could easily kill Tom and her, too. He had all he needed, with Lightning riding with him, of his own volition.

Tess refused to bend or buckle. "Which is why you wanted Lightning," she said. Let him kill her. She wouldn't show weakness to a man like him.

Pulling himself through the opening, Teveler shrugged. "My pard's fixed some things in Caldwell for us, but I figured it might be easier sellin' Mathew Garth's cattle with an heir with us. I think things through, Tess."

"Do you?"

He shook his head, but relented. "We'll doctor your boy tonight. Might need him in Caldwell."

Teveler told Meeker to keep glancing back inside the wagon, make sure Tess Millay didn't find a knife to plunge into his back. Then . . . he was gone.

Fanning himself with his hat, wondering what would take Reata and Lightning this long, Mathew

Garth heard the whinny of a horse and pushed himself to his feet. The sun was fairly low by this time of day, and since the rider rode in from the west, Mathew had to shield his eyes. He rested his right hand on the butt of his gun until recognizing both horse and man. Often, you could tell a rider by how he sat in the saddle, how he rode a horse.

Reata.

Mathew looked beyond, trying to find the outline of more riders. Or even dust.

Nothing. Reata came at a slow pace.

Something had happened. Panic briefly shot through his body. Lightning? No. No, he didn't think that was it. The rider neared. No shovel. Not that Mathew could spot. And he didn't think Reata would be bringing Dunson's old Bible, either.

The man road casually, confidently.

He remembered during the war while riding with Forrest's cavalry. Sometimes, a soldier came down with this paralyzing bit of premonition. He knew he would die in the next battle. Seven times out of ten, those forewarnings proved true. In all his years with the Confederacy, Mathew, himself, had never felt such a hunch. Yet now, something came over him. A feeling . . . but not of his own death.

"Howdy," Reata called out, waving a gauntleted left hand. Left hand. The old soldier was right-handed, and that horse wasn't the bucking type.

"Where are the others?" Mathew called out. He left his right hand on his Colt.

"Comin'." Reata reined his horse to a stop and tilted his head west. "Back yonder a ways."

"I see." He did not take his eyes off the old horse trooper.

Now Reata nodded at the blackened bodies on the scorched prairie. "Reckon that's Joe, eh?"

"Yeah."

"Well, too bad. I can start diggin' a grave." He turned his horse around and began a slow dismount.

It was the turning of the horse that raised Mathew's awareness. Easiest thing in the world to do would have been to simply climb out of the saddle, but Reata had turned around and then started to dismount. The big horse would serve as a shield, hide his movements, so that Mathew would not see him pulling his revolver.

He did not think how he would explain this to Reata if he was wrong. Mathew drew his revolver.

Yet he reacted too slow. Reata brought the revolver up over the horse's neck. The gun roared. The horse, well trained, stayed put. Mathew felt the bullet punch into his body and fell back, squeezing the trigger before he landed on the charred earth. He heard the horse scream, hooves pounding, Reata's curse. Mathew's bullet had grazed Reata's horse. Another shot blasted, kicking up ash and dirt where Mathew had been.

He rolled more, stopped, went backward, and loosed another shot. The horse, eyes wide with fright, galloped past him.

"Damn!"

Reata's oath was the only word spoken.

Lying on his back, Mathew raised his Colt, thumbing back the trigger. Reata leveled his own revolver. Their shots rang out as one, just before Reata's horse loped right back, between both men. The big horse must have been running toward the pile of bodies that had been horse, cattle, and man. The scent, the sight, the fear turned the horse back. It galloped away from this black, violent world. Or tried to. The horse screamed, reared, and fell on its side.

Mathew had pushed himself up. Sitting, he leveled the Colt, steadied it with both hands. When the horse collapsed, he was ready. If he missed, or even if he hit Reata but didn't kill him, he figured he was dead.

Dust and ash erupted from the ground as the horse hit. Reata screamed in rage, or maybe shock.

Mathew squeezed the trigger.

CHAPTER FORTY

He didn't know how he even made it this far.

Thirty feet. It felt like three thousand miles. Mathew looked at Reata, spread-eagled on the ground, eyes open, his mouth locked in surprise, and death. Mathew fell against the horse, dead, already beginning to draw flies. Flies in a charcoal world. He leaned against the horse's body, set his smoking Colt at his side.

Reata's heavy slug had torn into the fleshy part of his stomach, right side, maybe halfway between the bottom of his rib cage and his waist. It hadn't hit any vitals, as far as Mathew could tell, but it had blown a hole in his back at almost a straight line. Blood already soaked both front and back of his shirt. If he didn't get that bleeding stopped, he would soon be deader than the black man lying near him.

First, he pulled out the makings and rolled a smoke, sticking the cigarette in his mouth, the paper bloody from his fingers. He didn't light the smoke, though. Not yet. Instead, he pushed out one cartridge from his shell belt. Another. Two more. Next, he loosened his bandanna and laid it on the ground, unrolled, unfolded, a napkin on the dirt. With a groan, he shifted his weight so that he could draw the barlow knife from his pants pocket. That exhausted him, and he leaned back against the horse, lungs working like the pistons in a steamboat's engine room. He dared not close his eyes. Fall asleep, and he would never wake up.

Taking in a deep breath, he pushed himself up. The exertion made him turn his head, and he threw up. Wiping his mouth, he opened the blade of the knife and went to work on one of the bullets. Sweat poured out of him, burning the bullet wounds, stinging his eyes. He could taste salt on his lips and tongue. Eventually, he pried the lead bullet away from the brass cartridge and dumped the black powder onto the bandanna.

Gunsmiths always made this look so easy.

It practically killed him to get the powder out of four bullets.

Again, he leaned back against the dead horse while finding the box of lucifers in his vest pocket. Now he struck the match and brought it with his bloody right hand to his cigarette. He drew in smoke, held it, let it out. That revived him more that a cup of Groot's coffee or a shot of rye whiskey. Leaving the cigarette in his mouth, he brought his right hand down and carefully picked up the bandanna that held the gunpowder.

He sat up. Thought he might vomit again, but the nausea passed. His bloody hand brought the piece of silk to his back, for that wound bled the most. His left hand removed the cigarette from his mouth after another long pull.

Think, and he'd lose his resolve. He leaned over, bringing the bandanna to his back, moving the cigarette across his body. At practically the same time, he packed the hole in his back with black powder, which the glowing end of the cigarette touched off.

Mathew Garth screamed.

He fought to stay conscious. Sleep meant death. The smell of burned flesh sickened him, and he retched again, but there was nothing in his stomach to come up. After the dry heaves passed, he found the cigarette and returned it to his mouth. The smoldering bandanna had a giant hole in it, so he knew it wouldn't hold any gunpowder, and he tossed it aside, red embers devouring the threads. His skin burned, but the bleeding stopped . . . in his back. He still needed to plug the entrance wound.

He lacked strength to separate bullet from cartridge and collect more black powder. He looked at his stomach. Now that wound became the spigot. Again, he leaned against the horse. Turning his head, he spotted Reata's canteen. Throat parched, mouth aching, he groaned as he reached for it, had to push himself up, but at last his left hand grabbed the canvas strap, and he dragged it over the horse's withers. He set it between his legs, pushed out the cork, and brought it to his mouth.

It gagged him. Burned his lips, tongue, throat. Exploded with a concussion in his gut that he thought he might throw up again.

Whiskey. The damned fool had ridden out with nothing but a canteen filled with the vilest rotgut that could be found in Spanish Fort. His eyes burned. Again, he fell against the horse and returned the cigarette to his mouth, hoping the smoke would ease the rawness.

Which gave him another idea.

Straightening, he looked at the canteen. He wasted no more time. Puffing on the smoke, he lifted the container and dumped the foul liquor onto the bullet wound, screaming at the fire in his belly, and bringing the cigarette to the wound.

This time . . . he passed out.

The moon was rising by the time he reached the creek. He never thought he would have made it.

Falling onto his knees, he reached into the water, brought it to his face, savoring the coolness, the freshness, the moisture. He knew better than to drink fast, but cupped his hands again and brought them to his cracked lips. The water cooled him. He knocked off his hat and ran water through his hair, and then drank again.

Mathew Garth had never felt so alive. Instead of ash, he smelled the fresh grass on the other side of the creek. Those scents revived him more than the water.

He refilled two of the three canteens he carried, then bathed the gunshot wounds with water before pouring a dab of forty-rod whiskey from Reata's canteen onto the cauterized bullet wounds. He probed the wounds with his fingers, gently, feeling the coarseness of the skin, the tightness of the flesh around the scarred holes. His fingers came away without the tackiness of blood. The whiskey, raw as it was, might stave off any infection.

Maybe he'd live . . . after all.

For ten minutes, he rested, soaking his boots and those aching, swollen feet in the water.

Get up, the voice told him.

Mathew opened his eyes. He had not slept. Only seconds had passed.

Get up. Move, boy. Keep walking, you gutless wonder.

He recognized the voice. That voice had driven him across the fire-scorched earth for miles and miles. It had told him that he couldn't bury Reata or Joe Nambel, not if he wanted to live. That Joe Nambel would understand, that he was in a better place now, and that Reata didn't deserve a hole in the ground. The voice had reminded him that he had said words, good words, maybe more fitting words than something from Proverbs or Corinthians, to poor Joe Nambel. That Reata deserved no words, either. Let him rot.

"Funny," Mathew had told the voice. "Coming from you."

Get up, the voice had said. *Start walking. Or lie down and die.*

So he had walked. And now, again, the voice told him to walk.

He came to his feet, collected the canteens, and crossed the creek.

Keep moving, the voice told him.

The voice. Thomas Dunson's voice.

He walked.

Feverish still. He had lost a lot of blood. Had crossed miles of blackened earth with only a few swallows of water. Sure, he knew the voice was nothing more than his own hallucinations, but the voice—Thomas Dunson—kept Mathew moving.

He wondered: *What voice drove you all that time? After*

we left you alone with a horse and took your herd? What voice drove you after us?

He did not see Dunson, just heard the voice, though he did picture the iron-willed man: Dunson, blood spilling down his shoulder from a bullet Cherry Valance had put there. Cherry, wounding the big man instead of killing him, drawing his Colt because he had known Mathew would not, could not, have pulled on Thomas Dunson. Dunson had refused to let anyone look at the bullet wound, and Mathew had sent him on his way with a sack full of flour, salt, beans, salt pork, coffee, some whiskey to treat the wound, and fifty paper cartridges for his revolver.

Walk, boy, the voice said. *Walk, Mathew.*

He walked.

Mathew did not ask the voice anything, though. He did not want to go mad. Just wanted to reach . . .

Reach what? What would he find? A missing herd. He knew that much. And Reata made him think that maybe Jess Teveler was behind this all. Maybe he had been wrong, blaming those three Chickasaws for burning the prairie. Maybe that had been Teveler's handiwork. He'd find out when he reached camp. If he could reach camp. Find camp. Four, five, six miles. Something like that. That's what Lightning and Reata had told him. Maybe the herd would be there. Maybe . . .

He walked.

You damned fool, the voice told him. *You know better than that, Mathew. Don't get your hopes up, boy. I taught you better. Walk. Walk. There's no herd waiting for you. No cup of that crap Groot Nadine calls coffee. Walk. Walk. Don't think. You'll find nothing but dead bodies there.*

He walked.

The whirling of a rattle stopped him. Nothing like a rattlesnake to wake you up, make a delusion disappear. He located the direction of the rattling and gave the snake a wide berth, pressing on—although he had no idea if he were moving in the right direction.

A coyote called out in the night, and others answered, until their yips and howls turned into a nightmarish opera.

He walked.

Until . . . he stopped.

The voice had not spoken to him in a while. It hadn't needed to. No longer had Mathew needed any encouragement. He had moved, maybe not in a straight line, but he had moved. Walking. Stumbling. Moving forward. He had no idea how long it had been since he had left the creek. Or how many minutes had passed since he had heard the voice.

Five or six miles. That was the distance from the creek to the campsite. Even in boots, a man could walk a mile in twenty minutes, a half hour. Well, maybe, unless he had two plugged holes in his body, one the size of a four-year-old's fist.

Mathew panted, and lifted the canteen toward his mouth. Quickly, he realized it was the whiskey, and he let it slide back into place, and brought up another, Lightning's canteen. He drank. Leaned forward. Stared.

Another delusion. An apparition. Ghost? It looked like one. The grayish figure of a man. Two other figures, darker ones, he seemed to detect in the night. All three had stopped. Staring. The gray arm pointed. The figures spread out. Began approaching.

Mathew drew the Colt from its holster and cocked the hammer back as silently as he could.

The gray figure stopped. So did the others. Maybe twenty yards from Mathew.

"Mathew? Is that you?"

"Shut up!" Mathew heard himself answer, and he knew his sanity rested on some precipice. "You're dead! You're . . ."

"Mathew!"

No. It wasn't the voice. The gray figure ran toward him. So did the darker ones at the ghost's side.

But it was no ghost. Mathew dropped the Colt to the ground. He stepped toward the gray man and found himself falling to the ground.

The gray man caught him, held him up briefly, and lowered him onto that sweet, tall, lush grass.

"Mathew. By grab, it is you."

Mathew's eyes fluttered. He wet his lips with his tongue. His heart raced, his lungs labored for breath, but he smiled.

"Laredo, where's . . . ?" But he was asleep before he could finish the question.

CHAPTER FORTY-ONE

"I need some help getting my son out of this wagon," Tess called out.

Around the campfire, none of the bushwhackers—not even Lightning Garth—looked toward the Studebaker.

"Then," Tess shouted, "I'll do it myself." She climbed through the opening in the canvas onto the driver's box, moved over, and leaped to the ground. She didn't even fall, but kept her balance, pushed back to her feet, and walked to the back of the wagon and grub box. Quickly, she found two knives and moved to the fire.

That's when the Chickasaws and the man named Creede reached for their weapons.

That's when Jess Teveler chuckled.

"She ain't comin' for your scalps, boys." He nudged Lightning, who did not respond.

Tess moved between two of the white men Teveler had hired, and they slid away as she knelt and placed the blades of the knives in the fire. "That bullet has to come out," she said.

Her eyes locked on Lightning. He tried to match her gaze, but just couldn't do it.

Jess Teveler laughed. "I reckon a chuck wagon's clean as a hospital, ma'am."

"You weasel."

"Such salty language . . . Well, that's what I'd expect from a riverboat wench." He recrossed his legs at the ankles and turned to Lightning. "Fine mother you got raised by, boy."

"She's not my mother."

Tess came up, leaving the knives in the fire. "No, Lightning Garth. I'm not your mother. I'm just the woman who risked my life, made myself your mother's midwife, helped deliver you. I was your mother's best friend. Her only friend. Your mother died in Abilene. So, no, I'm not your mother. I'm just the riverboat wench who sat up with you after you had a nightmare. Who changed your diapers. Wiped your nose. Bottle-fed you from Abilene to the Rio Grande. Who kept you out of an orphanage in the state of Kansas. Who gave you a name. I was the woman who taught you to read, because there was no school. Who took you to San Antonio to be christened, because there was no church or preacher in Dunson City then because there was no Dunson City. I stayed with you and prayed—yes, Tess Millay prayed—when you were sick with the measles . . . and again during the diphtheria and cholera outbreaks . . . and even when you had the colic. I read stories to you. I sang to you. I cut your hair, bandaged your cuts, kissed your hurts, and set your arm when you broke it when you were nine years old. I baked your birthday cakes before we hired Janeen, because God knows Groot Nadine couldn't make a cake if his life depended on it." She sank back to the fire.

Her last words came out as a whisper. "No, Lightning Garth, I'm not your mother. But I brought you into this world. And, so help me God, I can take you out of it."

Groot held the steaming cup to Mathew, who took it and stared.

"It ain't nothin' but broth made from beef jerky. Them rapscallions didn't leave us with nothin'."

"Yeah," Laredo said. "Horses gone. Only reason we got that cup is it was in Teeler's saddlebags."

"They did leave us our saddles," Teeler said. "Just nothin' to put 'em on."

"And matches." No Sabe smiled. "In case we wished to start another inferno."

As Groot tore away Mathew's shirt to examine the wounds, Mathew sipped the broth. Weak, but even that little bit of liquid gave him some strength.

"You done a passable job with your doctorin', Mathew," Groot said. "Give you that much."

Mathew set the cup, now empty, on the ground. Gray started appearing in the eastern horizon. He had slept through the rest of the night, meaning Laredo, Teeler, and No Sabe had carried him the final two hundred yards to camp. He had been lucky. Or maybe Thomas Dunson had been a pretty fair guide.

"Let me see," Mathew said, wetting his lips, "if I can wrap my brain around what all happened. Go over it again."

Groot and Laredo did. Jess Teveler had stolen the

herd, wounded Tom, murdered Yago Noguerra and Bradley Rush, taken Tom and Tess hostage, and lit out for Caldwell.

"Caldwell," Mathew said flatly.

"Laredo told him that burg was done as a cow town," Teeler Lacey said, "but Teveler, he said somethin' 'bout how somebody had worked out a special deal for'm."

Mathew scratched his nose, rubbed the beard stubble on his face. Maybe. Maybe it made sense. Two hundred miles to Dodge City, or seventy, maybe even less, to Caldwell. Rustlers generally didn't like to do too much work, and if Teveler had some inside man to help out with selling stolen beef and getting it loaded and shipped out east quickly, Caldwell would be the best spot. Hell, the law and Caldwell hardly had ever been synonymous.

"That sumbitch Meeker went with 'em," Teeler Lacey said. "Yellow bastard. So did that kid wrangler."

"Hey," Groot interjected. "I told Joey to go with him. You let up on that boy. He's a fair hand." Groot looked down at Mathew. "See, I figured they'd murder us all. Didn't see no reason Joey ought to get kilt."

"They wasn't gonna—"

But Mathew cut off Lacey. "Yeah. They were. I figure Reata was coming back this way after he killed me."

He sighed. John Meeker Jr. The wrangler, Joey Corinth. And . . . Lightning. Mathew spit into the sand.

"We looked around a spell," Laredo said. "Me and Teeler. After they took off with the herd and Reata was gone. Made it to the creek. Filled up the one canteen they left us—and only on account that Tess must've knocked it out of the wagon when they pulled out. Wanted to keep lookin' for you, but . . . well . . . thought it best to come back here. Had no idea where to start looking in that burned-out countryside. And didn't . . ."

"You don't have to explain, Laredo," Mathew said. "Or apologize. Sitting here. Waiting. That was the right thing to do." He hooked a thumb at the old cook. "Groot wasn't going to be walking much."

"But I reckons I'll have to," he said. "Nothin' to eat here except a few bits of jerky. Ain't got no guns. No hosses. Nothin'. Reckon we can try to make it back to Red Fork Station."

"Or Caldwell." Mathew was looking north.

Well, Tess had to give Lightning that much. He had helped get Tom out of the wagon, had even insisted that the Chickasaw with the green coat and the man called Creede help. They had found a level place, near the fire, and everyone had moved away—except Jess Teveler—to let Tess go to work with knives, hot water, and whiskey that Green Coat had fetched.

And Lightning. He had stayed. He said nothing and barely looked at Tess. But he had held Tom down as she probed the hole in his shoulder with the knife. He had sweated and paled, but Lightning had been steady, and strong when she needed him. He had poured whiskey over the knife blades. He had picked up the flatted lead slug that she had pried out of Tom's body, examined it, and then slipped it into Tom's shirt pocket. He had even cleaned out the wound with whiskey and water, and he had been the one to cauterize the hole with the red-hot blade from his own knife.

And when it was all over, he had wiped the blade of his knife on his chaps, picked up what had passed for surgical instruments, and walked away from Tess as she bandaged Tom's shoulder with the strips of cloth. Oh, yeah. Lightning had ripped up one of Tom's shirts to use as a bandage.

But during it all, he had said not one word. And now, he stood by the chuck wagon, sharing from a bottle with the man named Creede and another man in green-striped britches and a red and blue plaid shirt.

"Ma . . ." Tom's eyes fluttered open.

"Tom." She pressed a finger over his lips to keep him from talking. "Just be quiet, son," she said. "You're my son . . . you know that . . . don't you?" She felt tears welling, but not for long, because she had decided she was done with crying. It didn't accomplish a damn thing but make you look weak and pathetic.

Tom swallowed. She gave him water and ran her fingers through his hair, humming some song—one she remembered singing to Lightning when he was just a baby. Tom was alive. Conscious for now, though he would soon be back asleep. And Tess would sleep at his bedside. Just like she had done when Tom had been young, and sick, and fragile. Just as she had done with Lightning, too.

Dawn.

They ate the last of the jerky and drank water. Mathew sent No Sabe back to the creek to refill the canteens. They had emptied two last night, including Reata's of his rotgut. And most of that had been poured out onto the ground or used again to clean Mathew's bullet wounds.

No Sabe hadn't returned, but he had been gone only an hour. Now the men—Mathew, Groot, Laredo, Teeler—stood staring off to the south, at a line of dust. Too much for a dust devil. And not blowing like a dust storm.

"Damnation," Laredo said. "That's . . . it's gotta be . . ."

"Cattle herd," Mathew answered.

"You reckon . . ." Groot said.

Mathew did not reckon. He knew. Twenty years in this business? Damned right, he knew.

"But . . ." Teeler Lacey started, but stopped.

Mathew nodded. "Makes sense. Somebody went around the fire's path. Probably lower downstream that creek. Cut up this way to reach the Cut-Out. Pure luck we just happen to be in their path."

"Iffen they don't turn afore they get here," Groot said.

Mathew started, but stopped. Pain raced up and down his side. He had to catch his breath.

"Teeler . . . ?" he said weakly.

"I'll walk," the old scout said. "Goes agin my stripes. Walkin'. But I'll do it. Catch up with 'em. Bring 'em up back this way if they wasn't comin' here already."

"Thanks." Mathew started to sit, but now he stared off to the north.

"You ought to wait till No Sabe gets back," Groot said. "Take a canteen with you."

Lacey said: "Nah. They'll have water in the chuck wagon. I'll drink then. Is that . . . ?" He, too, stopped, staring at Mathew and then at what Mathew Garth had seen.

"Dust," Lacey said. "More dust."

"Yeah," Mathew said. "But that's no trail herd."

It was moving too fast, and not big enough.

"Teveler?" Laredo asked.

CHAPTER FORTY-TWO

Some son of a bitch kept screaming. Lightning Garth rolled over in his bedroll, brought an arm over his right ear, tried to block out that infernal racket. He knew he had drunk too much whiskey last night—compliments of the Chickasaws, known as great whiskey runners throughout the Nations—and wanted to sleep. But somebody kept yelling, and now others were joining in, and, despite the pounding in his head, he heard Jess Teveler's voice.

"The hell do you mean, Creede?"

"They's gone! All of 'em."

"Who the hell was on watch?"

"That runt. What's his name? Meeker?"

Lightning's eyes opened. He brought his arm, gently, off his head.

"The darky's gone, too." That came from one of Teveler's gunmen, a gent with a blond mustache who called himself Addison.

Someone kicked Lightning's boot, cussed, and kicked again.

"I'm awake," Lightning moaned, and pushed

himself up. His mouth felt awful. Whatever the Chickasaws were smuggling, it had to be the worst Lightning had ever drunk.

"Get up." It was Teveler.

Lightning rubbed his eyes, looked around for something close that would help reduce his swollen tongue.

"What's wrong?" he finally managed to choke out.

"Everything, damn it. That punk Meeker found some spine after all. And that damned puny little wrangler. They made off with the horses—all the damned horses, even the mules—sometime last night!"

His head no longer ached. At least, Lightning didn't feel the throbs anymore. He swayed, caught himself, and pulled himself up, somehow managed to stand.

"What?"

"You heard me." Teveler slapped his hat against his thigh. "How come nobody heard all that racket? A whole damned remuda? Horses and mules don't tiptoe and—"

"All of us was pretty liquored up," Creede said.

Yeah, Lightning thought, and since they had pushed the herd, already weary after running during the firestorm the previous night, Jess Teveler himself had said that they had no cause to worry. The cattle certainly wouldn't stampede again, especially not after being driven ten more miles, and no one would be coming after them. It was, Teveler had bragged, reason for celebration. They'd tie one on again once they reached Caldwell in five days or so.

"Shut up." Teveler spun around, spit, cursed again, ran a hand through his hair. "Where the hell is Reata?"

"He never come back, boss," Addison said.

"Son of a bitch!"

Lightning shook his head, trying to comprehend everything he heard, or thought he had heard. His brain still seemed befuddled by all the rotgut. And all that he had learned since yesterday.

Suddenly, someone started laughing. A musical laugh. Far away, then closer, and familiar. Lightning knew that laugh. Turning, he saw his mother, sitting next to Tom, who lay asleep in his bedroll near the smoldering embers of last night's fire.

"How does it feel, Teveler," she said, "to be afoot in this country?"

Jess Teveler stepped toward her, his hand on his revolver. Lightning's stomach seesawed. He bit his lip.

"I promise you this, wench," Teveler said. "If they catch up with us—which they won't—you won't be the first to die. No, lady. You'll see your boy barkin' in hell before I put a bullet between your eyes."

Teveler's finger pointed at the sleeping Tom Garth.

A sea of longhorns, mostly dark but with many other colors, covered the hills, taking advantage of the breeze. Mounted cowboys circled the herd. Coffee boiled in a pot over a fire. Bacon fried in skillets. Dutch ovens cooked bread. Beans simmered in a big pot.

Mathew Garth pushed extra shells into the belt. Beside him, Laredo Downs, wearing borrowed clothes, buckled a rig over his waist, then lifted the Schofield from the holster and checked the cylinder.

"I appreciate this, A.C." Mathew dropped the remaining slugs into his vest pocket. He, too, wore a clean shirt, compliments of a cowboy named Easy Reno, a fair to middling cowhand Mathew had fired two years back.

A. C. Thompson handed Mathew a cup of coffee.

"We Texians stick together, Garth." The old cattle drover grinned.

Mathew sipped coffee. He wanted to smile, but couldn't. "I was born in . . ." He had to think. "Iowa."

Thompson chuckled. "Don't worry, son. I won't let the boys back home know."

The drover accepted a cup one of his cowhands brought over and shifted his hips, leaning forward as he spoke again to Mathew. "But, son, we'll be ridin' with you."

Joey Corinth was bringing Mathew's blood bay from the remuda. The wrangler had put Bradley Rush's saddle and bridle on the gelding.

"Thanks, A.C.," Mathew said. "But this is our fight."

"Which is why we'll be ridin' with you. Our fight. We stick together." He held up the hand that didn't hold coffee to stop Mathew's protest before it could begin. "I'll leave my greenhorns, my younger boys, with the herd. But you'll need some help gettin' your cattle back this way. And you might need some help with those rustlers. Bunch of my boys ain't no strangers to gunplay, during the War for Southern Independence, and in tussles agin rustlers ourselves, Comanch', bandits from the other side of the Rio, and guys they just didn't like. Like I said. Texians like us stick together . . . no matter where one of us happened to be born."

The look on the drover's face told Mathew that he had lost. A hollowness enveloped him. He stared at his cup of coffee for the longest while, and finally looked A. C. Thompson into his piercing blue eyes.

"A.C. . . . about that stampede . . . about what I . . ."

"Don't do no apologizin', kid," Thompson said as he turned away. "From what I hear tell, that wasn't you talkin', but some man named Tom Dunson. Just know this: Glad to have you back, Garth. And proud to ride alongside you."

When Mathew turned, with Laredo Downs at his side, he saw other men waiting for him, holding the reins to their horses, with borrowed six-shooters and carbines. No Sabe . . . John Meeker Jr. . . . Teeler Lacey . . . even Joey Corinth. Groot Nadine, using a Winchester as a crutch, even stood there, waiting.

"Groot," Mathew said, "you can't ride . . ."

"Just watch me," the old cook said.

Dust rose toward the south. Lightning Garth swallowed down the bile and tried to stop sweating. At the edge of camp, Jess Teveler used a spyglass to see who was coming. Teveler needed that telescope, but Lightning didn't.

"Damn." The gunman collapsed the brass scope and handed it to Addison. "How'd they get them horses?"

Addison had opened the telescope and brought it to his eye. "How'd they get that many men?" Addison asked.

"Shut up." Spinning on a boot heel, Teveler called out to Creede, "Any sign of those Indians?"

When Creede's head shook, Tess Millay laughed.

"Did you really think those Chickasaws would come back?"

Earlier that morning, Teveler had sent the three Indians, afoot, to find the remuda or steal some other horses. They hadn't returned, and Lightning had to think his mother was right. If they found any horses, those Indians would be hightailing it back to the Chickasaw Nation. They knew when to fold a hand.

The two other white men, Benson and Kennedy, hurried in from the herd. Afoot, they had been trying to keep an eye on the longhorns. Now they checked their weapons.

"They've stopped," Addison said.

All eyes went to the dust cloud that drifted with the wind. Now Lightning moved toward Addison and Teveler. He counted a dozen riders . . . before he stopped counting.

"Maybe it's . . . just . . . some . . . strangers passin' through," Kennedy said.

"Only one of 'em's coming in." Now Addison collapsed the telescope and pitched it onto a bedroll.

"Just one?" Creede strained his eyes.

Lightning Garth shot a quick glance at his mother. He knew who it was.

Mathew Garth cringed as he slid from the saddle. Pain racked his body, and he wondered if he would have the strength, let alone the gumption, to finish the job. Reaching up, he drew the Winchester from the scabbard, deciding it would be easier to work a .44-40 carbine than to try drawing the Colt from the holster. He patted the blood bay's rump, and the gelding walked off.

"Come to make us some deal, Garth?" Teveler called out.

"We buried three of our men today," Mathew said. "Joe Nambel, Yago Noguerra, Bradley Rush. There are no deals. Just a rope. Or lead."

"What about the darky, Reata?"

"Didn't bury him," Mathew said. "Coyot's have to eat."

"So you come here . . . to die?" Teveler asked.

Mathew's head shook. He studied the camp. Teveler and one man stood just behind Tess, who sat next to Tom, lying on a bedroll near what had been a fire. Mathew couldn't tell if the boy remained conscious, but at least he was breathing.

Another man, cradling a sawed-off shotgun, stood near the chuck wagon. Mathew spotted the barrel of a rifle between the canvas tarp and the wooden side of the chuck wagon, giving him the location of the fourth man. The fifth man, a lean, blond gent, so thin he had to be a lunger, stood at the far edge of camp. And the three Indians? Mathew didn't see them and that troubled him. Finally, there was Lightning Garth, standing over slightly behind Tess and Tom.

"I came here to kill you, Jess Teveler." He never took his eyes off Teveler, even when he addressed the others. "This is between you and me. You others have no part in this. But if you take a hand"—his head tilted back to the south—"and my men and A. C. Thompson's ride in to kill you all."

Teveler laughed. "You're a damned fool, Garth. You seem to forget that I got a winnin' hand right here. Your son. Your real son. And your wife. So here's what you'll be doin'. You fetch us horses. And we ride out of here. Because if you don't, I kill your only son. And Creede here . . . he makes you a widower. You was a fool, Garth, to come here alone."

Now Mathew did look away from the killer. His eyes locked on Lightning's. "I didn't come alone," Mathew said.

"Kill them!" Teveler screamed in panic, or rage, or both.

"No!"

Lightning didn't remember screaming. He didn't even remember whipping the Russian from his holster. Yet it bucked in his hand, and Creede was staggering back, tripping over his spurs, and toppling over . . . dead from the bullet Lightning had put in his back.

"Lightning!" Tess jumped as Teveler palmed his revolver. She stretched out, trying to cover Tom's body.

Lightning turned the barrel of his smoking .44 toward Teveler, and then the breath whooshed out of his lungs as something hard tore through his back. Addison . . . standing behind him . . .

He dropped to his knees, but paid no attention to Addison or Kennedy or Benson. He aimed the revolver at Jess Teveler, squeezing the trigger as a second hammer slammed into Lightning's back.

Tess found the pistol Creede had dropped. Covering Tom's body as much as she could, she brought the pistol up, cocked it, fired at the man called Addison. In the corner of her eye, she saw Lightning, on his knees, then pitching forward. She screamed, cocked and fired the pistol again, and waited for Jess Teveler to put a bullet in her brain.

Mathew levered the Winchester, aiming from his hip. He saw Tess diving over Tom, finding the pistol dropped by the man Lightning had killed. He saw Lightning falling. Saw Jess Teveler shifting his Colt to kill Tess. Then Teveler was buckling from a bullet fired by Lightning.

The Winchester roared, and Mathew knew he had to spin. Dropping to a knee, he shot the man with the scattergun, then riddled the canvas covering of Groot's Studebaker, splintering the wooden frame. After jacking another round into the carbine, he turned back and put two more bullets into Teveler's falling body. Again, he aimed at the wagon.

His ears rang. Cattle bawled, but the worn-out longhorns had not stampeded. He could vaguely make out the sounds of galloping horses, and knew Thompson, Laredo, and even old Groot were charging to join the fight.

But the fight was over. Mathew looked at the wagon, but no movement came from inside the chuck wagon, and he decided that the gunman hiding in the Studebaker was dead. He spun around, wondering about the Chickasaws, decided they had skedaddled. The outlaws lay dead . . . and . . . maybe . . .

Dropping the empty carbine in the dirt, Mathew ran.

Tess reached him first, rolled him over as she sank onto her buttocks and gently lifted Lightning's head, which she cradled in her lap. A shadow crossed Lightning's paling face, and then Mathew knelt beside them, took Lightning's hand in his own.

"Mama . . ." Lightning's eyes, filled with tears, opened. She saw him as she had seen him years ago, the time he had broken his arm jumping out of the barn. Scared. Just a scared boy. "I don't want . . . a new pair of boots, Mama," he wailed. "I just want . . . you."

"I'm all right, Lightning." Tess could barely see now herself. Tears blinded her. "It's all right, son. Everything is fine. Everything will be fine."

"Mama . . ." Lightning coughed. "I love you."

She smiled. "I know that, Lightning. I've always known that. And I've always loved you."

CHAPTER FORTY-THREE

Men, women, kids lined both sides of the boardwalks of Caldwell, Kansas, as three thousand longhorns rode down the street—just like in those olden times, that long-ago past that had ended last year. Or so the farmers that had taken over the once-lawless town had thought.

The cowboys seemed behaved, exhausted, and the steers, practically played out, looked gentle as milch cows as they moved slowly down the street to the railroad tracks and the shipping pens that had been empty all year.

One of the railroad men opened the chutes, and the cattle began moving into the pens.

At the point, Mathew Garth swung from his horse and wrapped the reins around a hitching rail. Laredo, Teeler, and one of A. C. Thompson's men began moving the cattle. A man in a white shirt with a paper collar climbed up and began counting the steers as they moved into the pens.

They had debated that back in the Unknown Lands, but Mathew said since Teveler had a buyer waiting in Caldwell, they might as well give him the business. At least see what kind of price the buyer had in mind. Besides, Mathew wanted to meet Jess Teveler's partner, although by now he had a good idea who it was. So A. C. Thompson had sent some of his boys to help Mathew's crew get the beeves those last sixty miles. A.C. was even riding flank.

"Your name Teveler?" a bald man with a sack suit called out.

Mathew stared at the man. "Garth," he corrected. "Mathew Garth."

The man stepped back. "Oh, I'm sorry, Mr. Garth. We were told you wouldn't be making this drive."

Mathew looked beyond him. "I'm here," he said.

"And Caldwell's glad to have you, sir. Welcome. You'll likely be the last herd ever shipped out of this town. And one of the last Texas herds, everyone's been saying, to ship out of the state of Kansas. Even Dodge City, folks say, might be seeing the end—"

Mathew stopped him. "Who's the buyer?"

"Armour packing house," the man answered with suspicion. "Out of Kansas City. I'll send for him. Didn't you . . ."

"And the price?"

"That's up to the Armour representative."

Mathew hitched up his gun belt.

"And where is my pard, mister?" he asked.

"Blaine House," the man answered. "It's over on . . ."

"I know where it is." Mathew turned. "Nice dogs you got there."

When Chico Miller opened the door in his second-story room at the hotel, Mathew busted his jaw. The banker fell backward, knocking over a chair, landing on his bed, and falling onto the chamber pot the maid hadn't gotten around to emptying this morning. A Remington derringer fell out of the banker's coat pocket and onto the urine-soaked rug.

Mathew was inside the room, shutting the door, as Chico rolled over.

"Your dogs are at the shipping pens, Chico," Mathew said. "What brings you to Caldwell?"

The banker couldn't answer.

"Surprised to see me, Chico? Like I'm a bit shocked to see you here . . . this far from Dunson City and all."

It made sense, Mathew decided. Now. He even thought back to when the Mexican rustlers had set up that ambush. Remembered one of the bandits had dog crap on his sandals. Chico Miller took those pretentious, but cowardly, hounds everywhere . . . even to Caldwell, Kansas. And he remembered the cigar Teveler had been smoking, and the ones they had found in his bloody vest pocket. Havanas.

Chico Miller's mouth opened. His sweaty right hand fell on the .41, but did not move . . . yet.

"You give me a loan," Mathew said, "but you figure I'll never make it to market. You did everything you could to keep me from completing the drive. The way I see it, even though it went against your grain, you even sawed through the axles that killed Milt Blasingame. I underestimated you. You figured you'd have yourself a nice ranch property on the Rio Grande. And you figured to split the profits from a stolen herd with a murderer named Jess Teveler. Maybe—since a lot of folks still think of me as the man who stole Dunson's herd—I can appreciate that.

But then you have the gall to try to turn our son against Tess and me. Well, sir, I'm giving you the same chance I gave Jess Teveler. Bullet or a rope, Mr. Banker. You call the tune."

Folks later said civilization came to Caldwell on that August afternoon in 1886. The last Texas cattle herd was sold and shipped out of Caldwell, at $33.25 a head.

And the last gunshot was fired in the city limits.

CHAPTER FORTY-FOUR

Grass grew high along the Red River, and the air smelled of rain.

Typically, Texas cowboys would not do any work that they could not do on horseback, but that evening, no one complained. They cleared the patch of earth of weeds, nailed whitewashed wood together, and fenced in the top of the knoll overlooking the river to the north, and Texas to the south, east, and west. They placed the granite marker on the grave.

Mathew Garth took off his hat and studied the tombstone. No birth date, not even a year, for Mathew just didn't know. He knew the year Dunson died, of course, but as for a date, that he could have only guessed. Besides, Dunson would have thought this better than just some R.I.P. with a name and some years.

"I should've put this up twenty years ago," he said. "A man should be remembered."

"He'll never be forgotten," Tess said.

HERE LIES
THOMAS DUNSON

Who Lived and Died
For Texas

"You want to read over him?" Groot asked.

Mathew's head shook. "That I did . . . twenty years ago." He replaced his hat and looked at the men surrounding him. Usually, after a trail drive, most of the hands would stay in town until they had spent all their money in the saloons and cribs and bathhouses. But this time, everyone had left Caldwell together. Since Caldwell was civilized now and didn't really want to deal with a bunch of drunken cowboys. A. C. Thompson and his men had returned to Indian Territory to finish their own drive, one of the last, folks were saying, that Dodge City would be shipping out.

No Sabe stood next to Laredo Downs, who stood slightly in front of Teeler Lacey, who stood to the right of Joey Corinth. Groot Nadine leaned against the fence, and parked near Groot's Studebaker, Tom Garth, with one arm still in a sling, sat in the buckboard, scratching the ears of one of the Olde English Bulldogges.

Birthday presents, Tess had decided, for her two sons. Mathew didn't know what good dogs like that would be on a ranch, but he had not argued.

In the back of the wagon, Lightning Garth leaned against a pillow. The other bulldog licked his face, and their son laughed.

Tess came over to Mathew, pulled his hand into hers, and squeezed.

"This is nice," she whispered. "You think you'll be coming up here again sometime?"

His head shook. "No. Things are changing. They were saying even in Caldwell that the days of the long drives are over. We'll be shipping from Denison. Or Fort Worth." He chuckled. "Maybe even Dunson City."

"What are you gonna do with yourself then?" Laredo Downs asked.

Mathew put his left hand on his back and strained. The wounds from Reata's pistol still ached. "I'm getting long in the tooth for this," he told the foreman. "I might turn the ranch operation over to our two sons."

Groot spit tobacco juice into the grass. "How in hell would you spend your time if you wasn't workin' cattle?"

Mathew grinned. "Well, I'm on the board of directors for the bank. Which needs a new president."

Somewhere on the other side of the Red River, a coyote yipped. The two dogs began whimpering.

"Let's go home, Ma," Lightning said.

"Yeah, Pa," Tom said. "Let's go home."

Mathew looked at the grave one more time, then gazed into Tess's eyes of jade.

"Yeah," he said. "Let's."

AUTHOR'S NOTE

I don't remember when I first saw *Red River*—probably in high school—but I did take a date to watch when it played as a student union feature my freshman year at the University of South Carolina. I probably came across a copy of Bantam Books' mass-market paperback 1948 release of Borden Chase's novel *Red River*, originally titled *Blazing Guns on the Chisholm Trail* and serialized in the *Saturday Evening Post*, when I was in my twenties.

Anyway, I've watched *Red River* countless times, reread Chase's novel probably three or four times, but never imagined writing a sequel until Gary Goldstein, about as knowledgeable a film buff and western editor as they come, approached me with the idea.

Which became *Return to Red River*.

Director Howard Hawks's film version of *Red River* and Chase's novel have differences—especially in the outcomes of some major characters. I frequently turned to Chase's book but avoided the movie while writing this. Even so, when a friend asked whom I imagined as Mathew Garth while writing the book, I had to concede: "Well, an older Montgomery Clift." And the voice I heard in my head whenever Dunson showed up in flashbacks was always John Wayne's. Groot, however, wasn't Walter Brennan, but Wally Roberts, a cook who has fed me on a few trail rides— the last of which left me with two fractured ribs. Thanks, Wally. But you are a much better cook than Groot Nadine, and you're not bald.

I'd also like to acknowledge:

Nonfiction writers Frank Clifford (*Deep Trails in the Old West*), David Dary (*Cowboy Culture*), Harry Sinclair Drago (*Great American Cattle Trails*), Wayne Gard (*The Chisholm Trail*), J. Marvin Hunter (*The Trail Drivers of Texas*), Sam P. Ridings (*The Chisholm Trail*), and Don Worcester (*The Chisholm Trail*), for their source material.

Kim and Patricia Chesser of Burnt Well Guest Ranch in Roswell, New Mexico; and Roxanne and Galyn Knight and their sons of the K5 Ranch near Springerville, Arizona, for letting me experience cattle drives firsthand. It's not a job, by the way, that I'd care to do full-time.

The New Mexico Children's Foundation asked me to use a person's name in my next novel as an item in its annual fund-raising auction. Janeen Yankowski won. I've never met Janeen, but appreciate her generosity, and the foundation's, for funding nonprofit children's organizations throughout the state.

When I mentioned this project to Ol' Max Evans, author of *The Rounders* and *Goin' Crazy with Sam Peckinpah and All Our Friends,* he told me about when he met Borden Chase while trying to find a screenwriter for *The Rounders* (Burt Kennedy eventually got that job). As a tribute to Max, a true cowboy, friend, and mentor, and Borden Chase, I recast Max's remembrances of

Chase and his "pretentious" dogs that kept getting bushwhacked by coyotes.

Finally, the scene where the horse mistakes shoals for water and lies on Mathew Garth came from Jay Wolpert. The screenwriter of *The Count of Monte Cristo* (2002) shared that memory in a tribute to our mutual friend, Cotton Smith. Jay witnessed something like that happen to Cotton, about as good a horseman as you'd find, on a trail ride near Wickenburg, Arizona. Like Mathew in my novel, Cotton laughed when it happened to him. I'd witnessed a similar incident on a trail ride in Texas. And it almost happened to me once in New Mexico. I wasn't laughing.

Cotton Smith, author of *Ride Away* and many other westerns, was a great friend. He died unexpectedly while I was working on this novel, which I dedicated to him. After all, Cotton and I talked about *Red River* countless times. He'd say, "John Wayne should have won the Academy Award for that performance," but I'd counter, "He was great, but if anyone was robbed that year, it was Humphrey Bogart for *The Treasure of the Sierra Madre*." And we'd laugh.

When he asked me what I was working on, I told him: "You'll probably never speak to me again, but it's a sequel to the novel that became *Red River*."

"That's great," Cotton said. "You'll do a fantastic job. Can't wait to read it."

I don't know if I did a good enough job, but I'm sorry Cotton didn't get to read this. He was, as cowboys used to say, a man to ride the river with.

Santa Fe, New Mexico

GREAT BOOKS, GREAT SAVINGS!

When You Visit Our Website:
www.kensingtonbooks.com
You Can Save Money Off The Retail Price
Of Any Book You Purchase!

- **All Your Favorite Kensington Authors**
- **New Releases & Timeless Classics**
- **Overnight Shipping Available**
- **eBooks Available For Many Titles**
- **All Major Credit Cards Accepted**

Visit Us Today To Start Saving!
www.kensingtonbooks.com

All Orders Are Subject To Availability.
Shipping and Handling Charges Apply.
Offers and Prices Subject To Change Without Notice.